STRONG MYSTERY

STEAMPUNK MAGICA SERIES
BOOKS 1-3

RAVEN BOND

IMPISH PRESS
SHORELINE, WASHINGTON, USA

Raven Bond/Impish Press
PO Box 65198
Shoreline, WA/98155
www.impishpress.com

Publisher's Note: This is a work of fiction. Names, characters, places, and incidents are a product of the author's imagination. Locales and public names are sometimes used for atmospheric purposes. Any resemblance to actual people, living or dead, or to businesses, companies, events, institutions, or locales is completely coincidental.

Cover Design–Ria Loader

Strong Mystery/ Raven Bond.—1st ed.

Mystery, Murder, Magic, Who Done It, Science Fiction, Fantasy, International Crime, Alternate History, Steampunk / Raven Bond, Author

ISBN 978-0-6924688-2-1

CONTENTS

Dedicated to the amazing Steampunk community

ACKNOWLEDGEMENTS

What you have in this book is a collection of my early adventures with the Sorcerer Owen Strong and his mysterious companion, Jinhao. While it has become almost cliche to say that writing is a solitary art, after the writing phase, revising and publishing a book requires the work of many. I wish to recognize some of the many contributions that have made the current volume possible.

To my beta readers, thank you for your time and honest feedback. I would especially like to thank Josh for his insights, and for making of himself a sounding board for my strange ideas. To my editor and publisher, thank you for believing in the world of Owen and Jinhao, and for polishing my words. This work is truly beyond my dreams. To everyone who has bought the stories, written to me, shared reviews and expressed your enthusiasm—thank you. You have kept the creative energy going, and continue to do so.

Finally, and most importantly, I would like to thank my beautiful alpha reader and red-haired muse, Ria—not only for her insights and patience, but also for her love—love is the wind beneath my wings. Thank you.

The Resting Lion Inn, Lou Hu, China,
1884 A.M. (After Mithras)
Chapter 1

The Trader has decided that we shall stay the night here and go on in the morning," Lee Shen said to Jinhao. "You can take first place in the stable loft. I shall lodge in the main house."

Jinhao nodded wearily at the old trail boss. He was looking particularly tired this evening. It had been a long day of travel that started at dawn in their last camp. Everyone was ready for the ease and relative safety of an established rest stop.

She had examined the ancient inn with approval in the flickering light of the oil lanterns. It had seen better days but was still respectable, with a strong wall around it and plenty of oil lanterns to banish the darkness from the main areas. Shadows still lingered in the corners of the warren of buildings. She dismounted, handing her reins to the stable boy who stood attentive in the courtyard.

She turned, giving the dismount order to the other caravan guards, together with their individual special tasks for the evening. The more routine tasks would take be taken care of without her supervision. The pack attendants began unloading the Trader's boxes under the watchful eyes of the guards who would see the goods placed safely in the stables.

She doubted, however, that anyone would be interested in the Trader Chen Lu's dyed silks, which made up the bulk of their cargo. To her eye the tightly packed bales looked much the same as must a hundred other such parcels. However, she set a careful watch over the travel cases in the same way as she had on the long road journey, more in an attempt to assuage the nerves of the old Trader than out of necessity.

Chen Lu, Master Trader from the Imperial City, had assured her during a long night watch that the dye patterns were exceptional enough to command very high prices among the foreigners, and should be guarded with particular care. As those were anonymously rolled up and out of casual view, she took precautions but was not particularly concerned. The guards knew their job and she could leave them to it. The few pieces of silver and fine amber jewelry the Trader carried were in a small strong box that rarely left his side.

The merchant caravan had traveled many miles over the last five days, traveling down the Imperial Road from the capital to the border town of Lou Hu, stopping at camp sites along the way. The town of Lou Hu was regarded as the gateway from the Middle Kingdom of Han to the outlying province of Hong Kong.

Hong Kong was its own special city. It was the demesne of the Great Dragon, Lohan, who in his wisdom, and for his amusement, allowed a mixture of government. The Government comprised both Chinese lords and the foreign British, all advising, and definitely answering to the Dragon, rather than the Imperial Court. It was said that many years ago the Dragon had greeted and allowed the British Traders to enter the covered bay because of their Magia and their sorcery, both of which made for shiny things to intrigue him. The Dragon had then, it was said, ordered the Imperial Emperor to open the area to the British. Whatever the truth of it, Hong Kong province was the only Imperially sanctioned trading port for foreigners in all of China. It was also true that Hong Kong was ostensibly administered by a joint Government of the Han and the British Empires and had been so for many years. Jinhao knew of the Dragon.

In the distance Jinhao heard the whistle of an approaching steam train. The train would travel all the way to the city of Hong Kong. The Trader Chen Lu, not being wealthy enough to make use of the steam railroad, still led a trade caravan down to the province of Hong Kong every spring, as did many others. This meant pack horses, attendants, and, in these uncertain times, more guards than was usual to protect against bandits. The increased requirement for experienced guards afforded Jinhao the perfect disguise for her to flee the Imperial City. After all, she reasoned, who would remark on one more swordwoman caravan guard?

She had quickly displayed the acumen and discipline that had caused Lee Shen to appoint her guard leader. Unknown to Jinhao, the canny old trail boss had recognized in her the training of an Imperial Adept. Despite her best attempts, Jinhao stood out like a wolf among the sheepdogs. The Trader intended to have a smooth trip with no dominance issues among the guards, and he had readily appointed her to ensure that none occurred. Jinhao had picked up the reins of authority without any difficulties. Given that Imperial Adepts were usually held close to the Throne as bodyguards, he wisely said nothing of his suspicions. He was simply glad that she was along. If she was pursuing her own clandestine interests at the same time, he could respect that. Should bandits attack the caravan, he was sure that Jinhao would deal with them in short order.

Adepts channeled a mystic force into martial prowess beyond the capabilities of ordinary folk. Surely everyone knew that. Aside from that, he did not care if he inconvenienced the Dowager Empress by borrowing her Adept. His disregard for the feelings of the Dowager Empress was a sentiment that, if Jinhao had known it, would have caused her less worry on the journey. Although he had accorded her the loft sleeping space, as befitted her rank as guard boss, rather than accept it, she would keep her usual practice and take her sleep in a place where making a quick response to danger was assured.

Like most public rest houses, this one had a common room where travelers gathered and were entertained. As the hour was late, there were only two locals in the inn, to judge by their simple gray tunics and loose trousers. Most travelers wore either colorful travel robes, such as the Trader wore, or a mix of brown and black linens and leathers, such as those worn by Jinhao and the other guards of the caravan.

Jinhao ate by herself in the common-room as was her habit. Her traveling companions had learned that she was scrupulous about both her duties and her privacy, they gave her space to herself. She watched the pack attendants and off-duty guards at their dice game in one corner while Lee Shen coaxed the portly old Trader to take some more wine. She was glad that Lee Shen looked after the nervous old Trader; she doubted that she would have had his patience. She dug into the spicy fish stew that was common to the province, her mouth reveling in the burn of the spices, then took another mouthful of rice to cool the burn down. After the bland dishes of the northern court, the meal almost tasted like home. Home, as a child, had been here in the south.

After dinner, she checked that the Trader's strong box was secured to her satisfaction in his rooms. There was only the one way in or out of the suite. She had placed her most attentive guard, a dour Tamil named Wong, on the Trader's room, while he and Lee Shen ate in the common room. To carry a strong box in public was tantamount to screaming "I have something you want to steal!" Luckily for Lee Shen and for Jinhao, the portly Trader was a veteran of the road, understanding the need for discretion.

As she headed downstairs a most raucous din alerted her. Drawing twin swords from over her back, she quickly hurried down to the common room, fully expecting to find brigands forcing their way into the inn.

There, instead of invading bandits, she saw a single Westerner surrounded by a whirlwind of the inn's house servants; they were bustling around and away from him with cries of distress. The man was somewhere in his thirties, clean shaven and wearing a black travel cloak with red trim. He held in one hand a walking cane made of some kind of red metal, a Sorcerer's cane if Jinhao ever saw one. Doubtless this was what had the servants in a turmoil. Western Sorcerers were not much seen outside of Hong Kong itself, and had a reputation of being capricious.

The man was pleading with them to wait and listen to him, speaking in passable Mandarin. Jinhao was impressed. Most Westerners never bothered to learn any language but their own. What the poor man did not realize was that Mandarin was as foreign to the servants as Russian or English. Lou Hu was situated in Shenzhen Province, which was largely settled by Tamil and Hakka ethnicities, rather than Imperial Han. The fact that the Middle Kingdom was composed of different peoples was largely lost on Westerners. She sheathed the swords across her back as she strode into the room.

"What is the difficulty here?" she asked the man in English. Most foreign travelers spoke English, and he looked as if he might be British himself. He startled, then looked relieved at her appearance.

"At last. Someone who speaks the Queen's tongue," he replied in the same language. "All I want is a room and a bath for the night. They," he pointed at the fleeing servants, "took off as if I were a bandit."

The innkeeper chose that moment to come striding out from the back of the inn, a heavy cudgel in his hands. Jinhao quickly stepped between them.

"What is this, what is this?" the innkeeper shouted. "Foreign devils threatening my staff?" He brandished the club in the Westerner's direction. Jinhao spoke to the innkeeper in his native tongue, Hakka.

"There has been a misunderstanding. This eminent person," Jinhao said, pointing to the stranger, "simply wishes a room for the night and a bath. Do you have such available?"

This brought the innkeeper up short. His face took on a canny look.

"Well," he said hesitantly, "I might. But it will cost him extra. No one will want to come near his room after he leaves. I will have to pay someone to come in from the outside to clean it."

Jinhao had no patience for this sort of haggling.

"Do you or do you not?" she asked the innkeeper shortly. The man's face took on a stubborn look.

"He will have to pay in advance!"

She nodded sharply and turned to the Westerner.

"Do you have money to pay for the room?" She asked in English.

"Well, of course," the stranger replied. "Incidentally, what language is it that you are speaking? I am not familiar with it."

"Hakka," Jinhao replied. "Most of the locals are not Han. While your Mandarin is very good, likely only he," she nodded at the landlord, "will really understand you."

"Payment," the innkeeper demanded.

"Give the man money," Jinhao instructed the Westerner.

He held up an Imperial gold talent.

"Will this be enough?" he asked. The innkeeper snatched it out of his hands, while bowing deeply.

"Welcome," the innkeeper said in broken, badly accented English. He bowed again. "You come this way." The Westerner looked at Jinhao.

"Follow him. You should have no more trouble." She forbore from telling him that he had just likely paid enough to buy half the inn. The Westerner executed an intricate bow towards her, one worthy of the Imperial Court itself.

"My thanks," he said in perfect court Mandarin. "My name is Owen Strong. I am a Peer of the Realm of Her Imperial Highness, Elizabeth the Third of Britain. Whom do I have the pleasure of addressing, that I might make offering to the Gods?" Jinhao had to struggle not to respond in kind which would not be in keeping with her disguise of old linen and leathers. Instead, she managed a sketchy bow of the kind that an untutored guard might make.

"Jinhao," she said shortly. The innkeeper bobbed impatiently in the background.

"You should go with him," she repeated. The Westerner turned towards the innkeeper.

"Well, lead on." The Westerner made a hurrying motion with his hands, then picked up the single bag at his feet.

"My thanks again," he said with a shorter bow in her direction. Jinhao gave him a nod, watching him climb the stairs after the innkeeper.

"You seemed comfortable with the foreign Devil," Lee Shen remarked, appearing at her elbow.

"I could not stand the commotion," she replied. "Besides, he was simply a man like any other."

Lee Shen grunted.

"Perhaps," he said. "Although I am not accustomed to having men nearby who can call fire like a sword. It may be different for you."

Jinhao thought he could have little idea just how accustomed to it she was.

Lee Shen continued.

"Still, it was well done," he said. "Dealing with him calmed old Chen Lu right down. He was almost hopping with anxiety at the unlucky appearance of the Westerner."

Jinhao imagined the portly old Trader hopping from foot to foot, wringing his hands. She suppressed an impulse to giggle. It would not do to make fun of their employer, no matter how comedic his displays of worry had been on the road. Lee Shen nodded, as if guessing her thoughts.

"He was ready to pull up and go back on the road," he added. Jinhao whirled her head to look at him.

"Surely not," she said in surprise.

Shen cocked his head to one side.

"I convinced him that it was too late," Lee Shen said. "Too dangerous to move around in the dark. Still, a *Quizi* is an uncanny thing."

"You do not know that he is *Quizi*," she said sharply. *Quizi* was Mandarin slang for "Tricky Foreign Demon", a term that had become very popular here in the south over the centuries.

"I do not know that he is not," Lee Shen returned. "Such a meeting is uncanny in itself, I feel it in my bones."

Jinhao failed to reply, suddenly feeling the crawling tingle up her neck that she felt before a premonition. Lee Shen looked at her, noticing her shiver.

"You feel it too," he observed.

"Perhaps," Jinhao said diffidently. She had no desire to explain to him her birthright. Lee Shen nodded emphatically.

"Damn right," he said forcefully. "Mark my words, uncanny. Anyway, the Trader wishes to be off in the morning, as do I. Best get some sleep."

"Shall I post a guard at his door?" she asked.

"No need," Lee Shen rolled his eyes. "I shall sleep in his room on the floor. So much for a real bed tonight."

Jinhao allowed herself a small smile.

"Better you than I," she turned towards the door. "I had best see to the others in the stable." Lee Shen grunted in agreement.

~ ~ ~

Jinhao was just unrolling her sleeping blankets on the rooftop when she spotted trouble. While the trail boss had given her the preferred spot in the stable loft, she had learned that it caused much less resentment if she was generous in such small matters with the other guards. Besides, she preferred to sleep in a place that was hard for an opponent to reach, yet gave her a quick escape should she need it.

Her Adept trained eyes saw the shadowy figures steal across the main house's rooftop. She paused thoughtfully, watching them. She should give the alarm. Stealthy figures sneaking across rooftops were up to no good. Once again though, she felt the tingly fingers of her intuition across her neck.

Picking up her sword tack with a sigh, she gathered her Qi and leaped across the distance from the stable rooftop to the main house, landing feather-light on the slates. Keeping to the shadows herself, she spied the dark figures creep forward and silently enter a window. She counted three of them and frowned. That was too many for common thievery or killing, as one was usually enough if they were at all competent. These figures moved as if they were indeed very competent.

She was certain from her earlier reckoning that the window did not belong to her employer. That should have been the end of her obligation in the matter. She should raise the house to deal with them by shouting the alarm. Instead she followed her intuition, drew her short swords and padded forward. A muffled cry and the flare of light from the window in question caused her to speed up, diving through the window like a dart towards its target.

Jinhao came up in a roll inside the room, blinking at the sudden illumination. A ball of light floated in the middle of the room throwing strange shadows against the walls. She slashed out by instinct as she came to her feet. One of the shadowy figures from outside crumpled, eerily silent as it fell.

One of the others, covered head to foot in close black coverings, turned towards her, drawing dual swords as they crept towards her. Jinhao spared a quick glance to see the Westerner she had helped out before struggling with the third assassin. Then she had no more time. Their fellow closed in on her.

They exchanged a testing pass with their blades. Jinhao was surprised. Whoever they were they had Adept training. No one else could match her speed and precision without it. Her surprise came from not being able to sense his Qi. From his movements, she was almost certain it was a man. She should have been able to do sense his Qi or energy. They circled each other, still in the same eerie silence as before. Not even the meeting of their blades produced any sound. It must be some form of *Quizi* sorcery she decided.

She could tell her opponent was also surprised at her abilities. She wondered who they were, and if she knew them. It was impossible for her to tell with the head covering, but whoever it was should recognize her. There were not that many adepts in the hall. If they did recognize her, they gave no indication of it. Instead Jinhao almost lost her head to a quick combination move from the monkey form. One blade sliced the air where her neck had been the moment before.

Her opponent's miss served like a shock of cold water might, clearing her mind of idle chatter. Gathering her Qi, Jinhao moved, blades a blur in the closing moves of the crane form. Her strike landed solidly. Her opponent's head rolled free, severed cleanly by the sharp adept-forged blades. She turned from the kill towards the remaining assassin, snapping her swords down to clear them of blood. She paused as she saw the Westerner thrust out with his cane towards the assassin's chest. A gout of flame sprouted from the assassin's back where the cane touched.

As the Assassin fell, Jinhao could hear the twin blades fall to the wooden floor. Whatever the strange sorcery that had kept the deadly fight silent, it seemed to have died with him. The Westerner looked up at her with the glowing cane tip pointed towards her. He stood, she recognized, in some kind of prepared guard pose, similar to a stance she would take before engaging a foe.

Jinhao, to her chagrin, giggled. She supposed that given the circumstances she should be impressed by the figure he cut. After all, with the sorcerous light overhead, together with the smell of human death that began to fill the room, it made for impressive surroundings. However, the Westerner was wearing some absurd white robe that flapped around his knees and made him look quite ridiculous. He cocked an eyebrow at her.

"Well," he said, lowering his cane, "either you are brave enough to laugh when death looks you in the face or you are no part of whoever they were." He gestured at the dead bodies. "In any event, I like a brave person. So, are you friend or foe?"

Owen Strong, she remembered his name, and such a strange name it was too. She forbore from giggling again. Really, her tendency to giggle at inappropriate moments was her bane. It was simply that others didn't see the humor that she did in life. Instead she sheathed her swords across her back, looking at him squarely.

"I am not a foe," Jinhao said clearly in English. "I am not certain I am a friend, but I am not a foe." She knelt and pulled the face coverings free of the one she had beheaded. She let out a sigh. She did not recognize him, although that might mean nothing. There were whispers of disaffected recruits who had failed to complete their training. She supposed this was one such. The Westerner, Owen Strong she reminded herself, came to kneel beside her.

"You reacted then as if you expected to know him," he remarked. Jinhao stood abruptly.

"You do not know anything about me," she said shortly.

"True," he said rising more slowly. "In fact, I do not even remember your name from earlier. And do you?" Jinhao frowned in confusion. Was he asking her if she remembered her own name?

"What do you mean?" she asked.

"Do you know him?" he asked patiently, leaning on his cane. "And also, what is your name?"

The frown lifted from her face as she nodded in understanding.

"No, I do not know him," she said. She tossed her head. "You may call me Jinhao."

He bowed.

"Well, Jinhao," he said, "it seems I owe you again for help." She waved his comment away.

"I needed the exercise," she said. "And what made the silence around them?"

"Ah," he raised a finger. "That I may have an answer for." He knelt again by the man he had been fighting and felt around the corpse's chest. He gave an exclamation, gingerly holding out a piece of chain. At the end of it was a melted bit that might have been a medal at one point before his fire had struck the man.

"I suspect that this was the culprit." He frowned as he examined it. "It was made by a powerful Sorcerer too. It is too damaged to discover who it was though by its resonance alone." Jinhao nodded.

"So this is a Western magic thing that is in the possession of expensive Han Assassins," she said darkly. "Do you have such persons come after you often?"

He grinned at her ruefully as he stood up.

"Not really," he said. "In fact, this is the first time." He looked down at the dead man contemplatively. "If I did not know better, I would think this Uncle Stephen's handiwork."

He shook his head at her questioning regard. "Oh, he isn't really an uncle, that's just what we called him." He stopped whatever he was about to say and looked attentively at the wall as if seeing something there invisible to anyone but himself.

"Hmm..." he said sharply. "Did you bring a guest?" Jinhao frowned, trying to see what he meant. All she could see was the wall and the open window she had come through.

"I do not know what you mean," she replied. Owen Strong cocked his head to one side as if listening to something. He made an arcane pass with his cane. A line of red light no thicker than a thread came from out of the window to touch her on the head.

"Yes..." he said absently. "Definitely a sending, definitely not European, and just as definitely aimed at you." He looked at her quizzically. "Have you run afoul of a Sorcerer? I do not even know if the Han have Sorcerers? Do you?"

Jinhao's eyes narrowed in thought. It must be the slimy court Sorcerer, Xu, who was a pet of the Empress. She had no idea that her rejection of his amorous advances would lead to his sending some evil magic after her though. If he had sent a Court Demon, it was most serious.

"Come, come," Strong said impatiently. "You clearly know something. Out with it. I cannot help you if you will not share what you know!"

"Yes, Han do," she said hesitantly, "Very rare. The Imperial Court employs one such. His name is Xu. He will have command of the Imperial Demons. They are very dangerous." The man, Owen Strong, rubbed his hands together smiling. Surely he could not understand the danger they were in!

"Demon, eh?" he nodded briskly towards the window. "Well, my wards should keep it out." As if to underscore his statement, a very brief flash of light came from the window. "Well, at least for a while," he amended.

Jinhao thought that she could faintly hear the snarling of some beast like thing. She shivered despite herself.

No steel or Adept powers could stand against the claws of a Court Demon. The power to summon such things was reserved for use only by the Throne alone. Or, she thought hotly, the corrupt Sorcerer of a corrupt Empress bent on a shameless revenge for an imagined slight of the heart. The Westerner, Strong, looked at her again.

"See here," he said earnestly. "Do you care about this Xu at all?"

"No!" she replied fiercely. "I loathe him! It is because I do not care for him that he has sent such a thing I am sure!"

Strong nodded briskly.

"Right then." He looked around the room in the glow of light cast by the globe of mage light overhead. He rummaged in a pack beside the bed. With a cry of triumph, he waved a pair of writing brushes over his head. He thrust one of them into Jinhao's hand.

"Here is what we do," Strong said to her. The flash of light and almost subliminal growl came again. Strong looked in the direction of the window.

"Hungry little bastard. Where was I?" He held up a brush, gesturing emphatically.

"Ah yes! Here is what we do. Take your brush and dip it into some of that blood oozing everywhere. Draw a circle with it that is about so big." He vaguely gestured at the floor of the room. Jinhao looked at the brush with some distaste.

"That seems disrespectful," she said. Strong had already begun drawing the circle on the floor. He looked up at her with an arched eyebrow.

"Is a Demon sent by this Xu likely to be respectful?" he asked mildly.

"No." she agreed reluctantly. She knelt to begin the macabre task. Bright flashes and a louder audible growling from the window saw her finish her task, with her half of the circle meeting the half drawn by Strong. Owen hopped around her to draw strange symbols against the edge of the circle.

"There," he said with a satisfied air. "Now stand here," he pointed with his cane at a spot farthest from the window. She promptly moved to stand where he directed. Strong moved to stand near the window, brush in one hand, and cane in the other.

"Should we not be within the circle?" she asked. All the pictures she had seen of Western Sorcerers showed them standing within a circle like the one they had drawn on the floor. Owen spared her a glance over his shoulder.

"No, we are exactly where we are supposed to be," he said. He rolled his shoulders as if preparing to lift a heavy weight. "This is a different type of circle. I intend to lower my wards and invite it in. No matter what you may see or hear, stay where you are, and do not cross the circle no matter what."

Jinhao opened her mouth to protest, then closed it again. What was she to do? This was a type of fighting that she was unfamiliar with. Despite his strange British ways, he seemed to know what he was doing. She drew her swords, despite knowing they would do little except to provide her with something to clasp with her hands. She had seen the aftermath of a

Demon attack before. Still, if this Owen Strong was wrong, she would at least go down fighting.

The ending appeared, at first, to be almost anti-climactic. Strong, still in his ridiculous nightgown, raised his arms, chanting in a strange language Jinhao did not recognize. The flashes of light and the growling stopped suddenly. Strong hopped to one side and with a quick swoosh of his brush closed the last arc of the circle. He then came around the circle to stand near her.

"Now watch," he said breathlessly. "And remember what I said, do not cross the circle."

Jinhao watched the empty space enclosed by the blood circle. A tall shape gradually formed in it, scaled and crocodile-snouted, with sharp horns and far too many teeth. A wave of sulfur-tinged stink accompanied its appearance. To her horror, the thing had no eyes, only blank flesh where they should reside above the snout. The thing seemed to snuffle around blindly until it reached the edge of the circle where it was met by another flash of light. The monster shrank back as if wounded. Owen straightened beside her, his voice booming at the towering thing.

"You are the servant of Xu the Court Sorcerer!" The thing turned with surprising speed to regard Owen with its sightless eyes. The crocodile snout opened and words flowed from within, in a melodious tone of voice.

"Xu has commanded me to rend the flesh of one that I have scented in this place," it said. "I am the servant of no human!"

"Be that as it may," Strong replied. "Still you do his bidding." The mountain of scaled fangs snapped its snout at this.

"I must do as Xu asked," it said in that same beautiful voice. "If I do not succeed in the task, Xu will cause me more torment."

"You cannot succeed at the task, for I have imprisoned you," Strong pointed out. "I could simply leave you here until the sun comes up. The rays of the sun will cause you much torment."

"This is so," it acknowledged. "Know that should I escape this prison I shall rend you for the pleasure of it alone."

"I do not doubt that you may try," Strong said pointedly. "However, I have another proposal." The thing seemed to sink back on unseen haunches.

"What is your proposal, human?" the Demon asked. A forked tongue lolled from the reptilian snout.

"I will allow you to return from whence you came, provided that you give oath never to seek harm to myself, the one Xu sent you to rend, or any other being of this existence."

"I cannot swear such an oath as you propose, human. Xu will summon me again from my abode to rend more of your kind."

"What if I give you the means to rend Xu and then you must return to your realm with peace between us evermore?" Owen asked. The thing regarded Owen for what seemed to Jinhao like a long time.

"You would do such a thing?" it asked. "Why?" Owen shrugged.

"Xu is no friend of mine, and clearly an enemy" he said. The Demon nodded its snout vigorously.

"I will do as you propose, human," it said. Jinhao thought she detected a note of bloodthirsty glee in the beautiful voice.

"And your oath that you will neither harm me or any other, except Xu, on this plane of existence, nor cause any to come to harm."

"Very well," the thing seemed to dip its snout in resignation. "I do so vow." The Western Sorcerer regarded the Demon as if testing the truth of its words. Finally, he nodded as if to himself, raising his cane.

"Then I shall send you back to the one who has summoned you," he announced. "Remember your oath!"

He pointed the cane at the monstrous Demon, directing Magia while speaking in that strange throat-tearing language that he had used earlier. The mountainous form of scales and fangs faded slowly from sight. When it was gone, Strong staggered slightly. Jinhao made to catch him only to have him throw up a palm to stop her.

"No, I am fine," he croaked. "Doing a Demon-turning like that takes it out of you is all."

"I thought that you would kill it," Jinhao said.

Strong laughed at her.

"What on earth for? That Demon had never done anything to either of us. This way, it destroys your lovesick, demented Sorcerer and goes home. And without ever being able to hurt another human. I would call that a victory. I do hope you meant it about not liking this Xu, as he's likely Demon-bait at this point."

Jinhao thought of the slimy Court Sorcerer and all the transgressions that he was known to have committed. She shook her head solemnly.

"No," she said. "Nor do I suspect that any other shall mourn his passing."

Strong nodded and slapped his hands together.

"Well then, all's well that ends well," he looked around the room, taking in the dead corpses and the circle of blood. "I suppose that I shall have to speak to the landlord about another room to sleep in, as well as pay a cleaning fee on this one, despite the enormous amount I've already given him."

Jinhao looked at him with surprise.

"You knew that you paid him too much..." she asked.

"Of course," Strong replied. "Sometimes it is simply easier to appear as the stupid Westerner. Horned One knows I can afford it!"

Jinhao looked at him with something akin to respect.

"If you wish," she said, "I shall speak to him for you." Owen smiled at her.

"That would be most helpful," he said cheerily. He gestured to the blood-soaked white robe that he wore. "I don't suppose that he would have a spare nightgown as well."

Jinhao gazed at the offending garment with bemusement.

"Is that what it's called? Why do you wear it?"

"Well, it is what one wears to bed," Owen said. "At least if one does not have companionship to keep one warm."

Jinhao shrugged. Different peoples had different customs. Why bother to sleep in clothing at all? Surely the British were no stranger than the northern hill men who covered their bodies in the fat of yaks.

"I shall ask him," she promised. She waved her hand in front of her face. "I suspect that the stink shall cause him trouble enough though."

Owen shrugged his shoulders, obviously not concerned.

"Can't be helped," he said shortly. "It's what the air is like in their world. When you invite one to come to our world you have to expect that to happen." She looked at him quizzically.

"Have you often visited the Demon world then?" she asked incredulously. Again the shrug of shoulders.

"I like to be well traveled," Owen replied blandly.

She blinked at his calm acceptance of such strange things.

"I see. I shall go then and talk to the landlord." She gazed again at the curious white garment. "I shall also see if he has any 'night gowns', although I feel that you should be prepared for disappointment."

Owen cocked an eyebrow at this statement.

"Do you mean that he will not have any night gowns or that I will not have any company in bed?"

"Yes," Jinhao replied, smiling sweetly. "Best be prepared to do without."

It took Jinhao some time to arrange things to her liking and required Owen Strong to open his purse again to soothe the aggrieved landlord. Finally, though, Jinhao got to clean up and return to her sleeping place on the roof of the stable.

She knew that the dawn could not be far off. Deciding that sleep would not be hers this night, she settled to gaze at the stars from her lofty resting place.

As she absently looked at the starry pageant above her, she saw a falling star streak across the sky. The brilliant streak of light morphed in her sight into a line of light across a dark velvet cloth. Jinhao knew that she must be seeing a vision. She knew these occasionally occurred in her family.

In her vision, the line was connected to the Britisher, Owen Strong. As was the way of such visions, the cloth had vanished. Strong stood against the skyline of Hong Kong, holding one end of the brilliant line. The other end was held by a mass of people, some Han, and some European. Together they held the line against a swirling mass of dark clouds that threatened Hong Kong. The clouds broke against the bright line as they advanced, Strong and the others standing firm against the storm.

The vision was shattered by one of the caravan guards poking his head through the trapdoor of the roof and calling her name. Jinhao came to herself and absently answered him.

"Ay, Jinhao," the man replied. "It is as well that you are dressed already! That old woman of a Trader wants us to go quick like. Seems there is some rumor about the *Quizi* that has him scared to stay a moment longer."

The *Quizi*, the foreign Demon, she thought. No, his name was Owen Strong, and he had proved last night that he was no evil Demon. She remembered his stand against the true Demon.

Perhaps, she thought, the plan that Grandfather had sent her north to carry out simply needed a remake. Yes, she thought, eyes still spinning with the aftermath of vision. Perhaps he could be the one they were waiting for. It seemed unlikely, given that he was not only foreign, but a Sorcerer as well, but there was no arguing with vision. One either followed vision when it came, as Grandfather had always said, or let it go by. Jinhao shook herself and hurried to the ladder that led to the main house of the inn.

Lee Shen met her as she was descending from the loft. He turned from directing the loading of the pack horses and raised a hand to call her to him. He appeared to be more worried than usual.

"Ho Jinhao," he said, a look of concern on his face. "There are wild rumors going around among the inn staff about your behavior with the *Quizi* last night." Jinhao blinked at the outrageousness of this remark.

"My behavior?" she asked incredulously. "What in the nine hells does that mean?" Lee Shen's face became crestfallen at her tone.

"Then it is true," he said almost sadly. "You were with the foreigner last night."

Jinhao placed her hands on her hips.

"What if I were?" she challenged. "I did nothing to endanger either the caravan or any member of it. My off-duty time is my own, as we agreed."

She forbore from mentioning the Court Demon as that would lead to all kinds of questions that she would prefer not to answer. If the Demon had caught her out in the wilds, as would have happened the night before last, likely every member of the caravan would be dead, and she would be dead along with them. The old trail boss looked even more uncomfortable.

"Do not misunderstand me," he said almost pleadingly. "I have any number of friends who are British or, hells, worse in Hong Kong. It is that he is a Sorcerer too!" He looked at the ground, unwilling to meet her eyes.

"What are you trying to say?" Jinhao pressed.

"Chen Lu asked that I release you from your employ with us," Lee Shen said miserably. He produced a small coin bag, holding it out to her. "Here are your wages."

Jinhao almost sighed in relief. Now she was completely free to follow the path of the vision. She took the small bag from his hands.

"May you have a safe journey to the city," she said to him gently. The poor man looked as if he had been asked to kill his dog.

"It is unjust," he insisted to her. "I almost quit in protest, but I have a wife ..." Jinhao held up her hand, stopping him from making more apologies.

"It is as it is supposed to be," she said. "I hold you blameless in this." The old man bowed to her.

"Should you wish it, I shall be at the Electric Eel wine house. I shall be hiring for a caravan going north, and I would like to hire you to go along with it." Jinhao smiled at the old man.

"Perhaps," she said easily. "I shall certainly come and raise a cup of wine with you."

With that they parted, expressing many further sentiments of respect and admiration between them.

Jinhao walked out the door of the stable into the mild morning sunlight, her slight tension easing as she allowed the responsibility for the trade caravan to fall from her shoulders.

~ ~ ~

Owen Strong was just entering the courtyard wearing his red-trimmed black travel cloak again. Jinhao noticed that he openly carried the cane made of red metal. She may not be as well-versed in esoteric matters as others in her family, but even she knew that the red metal was the mark of someone powerful, or at least someone quite wealthy. Jinhao also noticed that his eyes were constantly moving, analyzing and judging. All the while he affected the air of the dissolute young nobleman. She nodded to herself, recognizing the pattern. He was no dandy, whatever he might play at. This insight gave her renewed resolve. She strode up to him purposefully. He gave her a wan smile in return. He was clearly not a person who enjoyed mornings, or at least not a morning after the magical exertions of the previous evening.

"Good morning, Jinhao," he said in High Court Mandarin. "I hope that you are none the worse for our little adventure last night?"

She bowed to him right hand over left fist, as one would to a comrade in arms. She was not surprised when he returned the gesture.

"I am well, Owen Strong," she replied. "It seems that I owe you a life debt for saving me from the Demon last night."

Strong raised an eyebrow at this.

"I would think that the debt goes both ways," he replied, "as your intervention with the assassins was most fortuitous."

Jinhao bowed her head at this statement.

"Perhaps," she replied looking directly at him. "None the less, as is our custom, I must accompany you under the terms of the life-debt."

"What?"

"Do not be alarmed," she produced the coin purse that Lee Shen had given her. "I come with my own source of funds."

"It is not that," Strong protested. "It is simply that I travel alone." Jinhao nodded at this.

"Under the life debt, I must accompany you or forfeit my life in shame," she said sadly, shaking her head.

"Well, we cannot have that," Strong replied. "Damn Mandarin," he muttered in English. "I thought that you just said that you would have to kill yourself if you couldn't come along with me."

"But I will have to," Jinhao protested in the same language. "If I do not, and it becomes known, then anyone may end my life who finds out!" She looked at him with wide-eyed innocence. "May one ask where you are bound this day?"

The Britisher shrugged in his cloak.

"I have a fancy to see Hong Kong and perhaps settle there," he said brightly. "I have been traveling around a fair bit, and heard that the city is an interesting place for the unconventional. Do you know it?"

Jinhao smiled at him.

"Then we are both in luck," she replied. "For I know the city well, and I, too, am—how did you say? Unconventional, also."

Strong regarded her for a handful of heartbeats.

"You are an Imperial Adept," he stated baldly. Adepts only came in two types; those who were under Imperial authority, and those who were rebelling against the Throne. To not be of the first was to be an outlaw.

"No longer," Jinhao replied. "You have seen the trouble I am in at Court." She regarded him levelly. "You are followed by expensive assassins that seek your death. You are no common British nobleman."

Strong looked nonplussed at this statement.

"Well, yes," he admitted, "but I am retired from all that."

"Yes," she replied calmly. "Much as I am retired from being an Adept I think."

He laughed at that.

"Very well," he said gaily. "Let us both keep our secrets, and stop this talk of life debts and the like. Together we shall see what diversions this Hong Kong has for us, shall we?" He stuck out a hand. "Deal?" Jinhao looked at his outstretched hand. She took it firmly in hers.

"Deal," she said, trying not to smile. Owen Strong released her hand. He pulled a watch on a chain from within his cloak.

"I was contemplating taking the morning airship south to the city," he explained. "We still have time to make it. I trust you are not afraid of flying?" This time Jinhao allowed herself a smile.

"I enjoy it immensely," she said with a secret smile. "Although it has been some time since I flew."

"Very well," Strong replied. "Let us be about it then!"

Jinhao smiled even more broadly. There was no need for him to know that there was no life debt custom among the Han. He was British, after all. And there was her vision to follow.

BOOK 2
STRONG MAGIC

Hong Kong, 1885 A.M. (After Mithras)
Chapter 1

Owen Strong leapt down from the carriage, his nostrils flaring as if he were hunting. The scent of the yellowish night fog almost reminded him of London, a bit less sulfuric perhaps, but coal was expensive here in Hong Kong. The air carried wisps of incense and strange musk, scents that Owen found oddly exhilarating.

Behind him stepped Jinhao, hooded and enigmatic in her dark night cloak. The evening was merely cool to Owen, being used to colder climates. However, he'd been told that it was actually considered cold by local standards, the weather having become unpredictable almost everywhere these days.

Owen noted Jinhao edging up behind him, but kept his focus on the gray building that loomed before them, with its single, dark door.

Delicately, he spun out his awareness, honed as much by his time in the Crimean War as it was by his tutors in sorcery. Briefly, he touched a powerful focus of man-made energies, withdrawing as quickly as he could to avoid the other Magian detecting him. He felt a surge of excitement. Their information had been correct. The old warehouse did conceal their quarry. Now, if only they were still in time to save the Duke's niece

Owen heard the nearby carriage springs creak, as it released the burden of Inspector Yu-An Gregg and the chief Magian of the constabulary, Sir Charles Foster. Gregg came to stand beside him, looking at the warehouse building with distaste.

"You sure that's it, Milord?"

Owen was only the second son of the late Duke Harold Strong—may his memory endure. The title counted for little here. British younger sons had been coming to this bewildering city, a city that was neither British Colony, nor Chinese fief, for nearly a hundred years seeking their fortunes. Owen's purse, which his older brother filled regularly, commanded more respect than the title.

Gregg however, was a class snob, one who would never let Owen forget his place in society, not even for a moment. Gregg hawked, and spat onto the sideway, then looked at the building again.

"I don't like it," he said in his thick English. "I don't like it at all."

"He's there, Gregg, never doubt it! And if we're lucky, so should be the Duchess," Owen said to the detective. He squared his shoulders as if readying for a battle. "Can you not feel the evil radiating from it?"

Gregg hawked again.

"I leave that to you Magian types," he said shortly. "What do you say, Sir Charles?"

The mutton-chopped Official Sorcerer waddled forward and peered through his thick eye glasses at the building. He sniffed dismissively.

"I suppose it's possible. This is the Pangyaun District, however," he pronounced with disgust, looking around at the dilapidated buildings that flanked their target, "and the miasma could have any number of causes." He clicked his tongue.

"It is a rather large building, Inspector. We should wait for the reinforcements. Even if Strong is correct," his voice left little doubt about what he thought of that possibility. "I doubt that running around in there will profit us more than bruises."

Owen had found the little man's arrogance and, he now suspected, his cowardice, insufferable even before this pronouncement. He checked a retort, and turned back to Gregg, speaking in as reasoned a tone as he could manage.

35

"I tell you, Inspector," Owen pressed, "I sense the same aura in that building as I did before. Our villain is in there, and, almost as certainly, so is the Duke of Chu's niece. We must hurry. As I said before, given the astrological timing, there may be only moments to save her."

Gregg squinted at Owen, saying nothing. Finally, he sighed.

"You've been right so far, Milord." His hand reached under his coat and emerged with a long barreled pistol, the short charge tube at the butt end glowing balefully.

"Foster," he ordered wearily, "we're going in."

Owen raised an eyebrow in surprise when he saw the weapon in Gregg's hand.

"An aether gun, Inspector?" Owen had seen few of those since leaving the army. He knew that such weapons were severely restricted in civilian use by the Crown. The glow of the aetheric fluid in the handle told his practiced eye that it was probably charged with lightning.

Alchemical artificers had learned to fashion devices that could manipulate the elemental powers in much the same way as the power Owen could wield with his mind and body as a trained Sorcerer. Magian was the term in polite society these days for one who could use Magia. Some insisted on the term to denote modern scientific methods as opposed to the hedge witchery of olden times. Owen personally didn't care what they called him. He'd learned that power spoke more loudly than a dictionary, and he doubted that Sorcerers would be replaced by machines anytime soon.

Gregg gave a half-embarrassed shrug.

"Special issue. If this madman is as powerful as you say, it seemed warranted." He fixed Owen with a stony look. "Mind you, Milord, you best be right. I have to answer to the superintendent himself just for drawing this from the armory."

Owen gave the Inspector a short nod of respect. Gregg was a good sort for a policeman, he'd found, for all his avowed cynicism. He seemed as honest as the police ever were here, and he truly seemed to care.

Being the only half Chinese Chief Inspector in the city's department couldn't be easy for him. Their doings tonight could easily see Gregg's career broken, just for following the word of a civilian such as Owen.

Rather than acknowledging any of that, Owen simply replied.

"Let us be about it then." He hefted the electrum walking stick that was far more deadly in his hands than Gregg's gun.

"You're not going," Gregg said bluntly. "I'll not be responsible for a civilian, let alone a noble one. Wait here for the reinforcements. Sir Charles," he hefted the gun, addressing the older man, "let's go."

Foster pulled an electrum wand from his sleeve.

"Very well," he harrumphed, "but this is foolishness." The clear crystal on one end of the wand began to softly glow, while the black crystal on the other end seemed to swallow the light around it. The two began walking towards the door without another word to Owen.

Rather than protest, Owen passed a meaningful look to Jinhao over his shoulder. She nodded silently. Her cloak flowed from shoulders to the ground, revealing a loose black tunic and pants with a close-fitting hood of the same color that left only her eyes visible. Over her shoulders, Owen could glimpse the hilts of twin blades. The woman moved in a silent blur, vanishing around the corner of the building

Owen silently wished her well, and then ghosted up behind the two men who were now standing before the door. Sir Charles Foster's wand glowed against the shadowed doorframe; Owen sensed the working. He swore softly, hefting his cane.

"What the devils do you think you're doing?" Owen hissed at Foster.

The squat man startled, then snapped at Owen without turning his head.

"Checking for wards, Strong. This isn't my first tea party, you know," the contempt was now clear in his voice.

"You'll trigger any wards he's set you, fool, let alone alert him that we're here," Owen snapped back.

"That will be enough," Gregg hissed. "Milord, I thought I told you..." his rebuke was cut off in astonishment as a circle of angry, pulsing, red energy appeared under their feet, alive with crawling lines within it.

Quickly, Owen activated one of his tattoos, feeling it burn against his skin as he focused its energy through his cane. The three men flew backwards through the air carried by Owen's air spell, just as the circle exploded in a fiery cloud that roiled upwards.

Landing in a tangled heap, Owen scrambled to get his feet under him.

"That's torn it," he exclaimed. "He knows we're here!" He ran for the door, slamming his shoulder against it to no effect. Gregg, shaking himself off, ran up behind him.

"It seems to be metal beneath the wood," Owen exclaimed. He stood back and started raising his cane.

Gregg tried the door with his shoulder and then roared in Mandarin.

"Mother's sweaty arm-pits! A steel door in the Pangyaun? A steel door I don't know about?" He moved back, raising his gun.

"Save your power, Milord," he continued more calmly in now un-accented English. "No one sets up a steel door here without official sanction—my sanction. The bastard has made me mad now."

Owen averted his eyes as a flash-crack erupted from the gun's muzzle, and then another. Owen blinked away the after-spots swimming before his eyes as there came a sound of tearing metal. Gregg's foot had kicked in the door.

It fell with a resounding crash, and both men looked into the dark cavern of the warehouse beyond.

"Where's Foster?" Gregg turned to look about him. "Foster!" He called over his shoulder, "Get in here!"

"I, I think I'm injured," came a weak voice from where they had fallen after Owen's air spell. Gregg sighed loudly, the thick accent back in his voice.

"What was that at the door, Milord? I'm thinking that we definitely need more Magian help before going in after that."

"Fire ward," Owen replied shortly. "Sorry for the rough ride; I felt it best to get us out of the field as quickly as possible."

A woman's scream came from within the gloom of the building.

"There's no more time, Gregg. We have to go now!" Owen shouted, sprinting forward. One by one Owen activated his tattoos of power as he ran. That fire ward had not been set by a dabbler, no matter how deranged. Owen feared he'd need all the power he had before all was done.

Looking about in the dim light that came through the doorway, he was confronted by tall walls of stacked crates.

The scream came again, followed by a voice pleading in Mandarin. Cursing under his breath, Owen lit the gem set in the handle of his walking stick, giving him a low light to see by. Choosing a path between the stacks, he moved on as quickly as he could.

As he threaded his way among the stacks, he felt the thrill of impending battle course through his body like an old lover. He didn't realize he'd missed it quite so much.

Was this really why he'd gotten involved in this affair despite his own high-sounding ideals, for the hope of fighting again? Was he really that crass? He pushed aside the thoughts when he saw a stronger light around a corner of stacks. Dousing the light of his gemstone, he peered around the corner and froze before a scene from some version of a Christian hell.

In a circle of light cast by a mage lantern hung above them was a metal table with two men standing next to it. One was an older man, clad only in a rubber apron and boots, goggles with an array of lenses sprouting from his head. The other, in threadbare clothes holding a tray was clearly an Animated.

Animated were made by Necromancers from the body parts of living persons, then given a kind of false life by their creator. If Owen had any doubts about his theories concerning the disappearances, they were laid to rest by what he now saw.

A young woman lay on the table, struggling with her steel bonds. As the older man took up a thin blade from the tray and turned to lean over her, she screamed again. Time to put a stop to this, Owen vowed. Readying himself, he stepped around the corner.

"Stop!" He shouted out. "Archibald Renton, you are called to challenge!" If his theories were correct, Renton's ego would not allow him to refuse a Sorcerer's challenge. While they battled it out, Jinhao should be able to get the girl to safety. He had no doubts that Jinhao was even now hiding in the shadows waiting to strike. At least, that had been the plan.

The old man looked up, the light reflecting off of his lenses, making him look like some grotesque insect. Instead of showing distress at Owen's appearance, he cackled.

"Are you the pansy-assed lording who has been dogging my steps? I'm not surprised that you showed up after that knock on the door."

Owen stepped closer, his walking stick pointed at Renton like a gun.

"My name is Owen Strong, Renton, and I call you to challenge."

"Challenge?" The old man wheezed, then cackled again. "You have no concept of the power I wield!" He pointed towards the shadows in a sweeping gesture first to the left, then the right with the thin blade. "Rend him, my pretties!" He waved a hand dismissively, "That for your challenge, lordling!"

Owen heard the sudden shamble of many feet. Out of the shadows emerged horrid shapes. Some were freakishly tall, while others were as small as children. Their patchwork of limbs and heads were attached to the wrong bodies, and all of them were reaching out towards him in eerie silence. There were a lot of them, closing around him in a half-circle.

Owen pulled energy from his fire bond-mark until it felt like a coal on his chest. A thread of white hot fire lanced out from his cane towards Renton. It splashed harmlessly against an invisible barrier feet from its target and was snuffed out. Owen ground his teeth in frustration.

Renton cackled again. "Oh my," he exclaimed. "Did I forget to mention the permanent blood wards around this table?" He waved his knife hand contemptuously.

"Run away, lordling, or die; I care not. I am running out of time here." Renton turned back to the woman strapped on the table. "Now my pretty, don't squirm so," he crooned, "I shall make you a beautiful part of my creations. You'll be immortal. But you must stop squirming so!"

A black streak fell from the ceiling, twin cleaver-like blades flashing. The head rolled off one of the taller animated, while Jinhao landed feet-first on a smaller one, crushing it under her. She rolled under the swinging arm of the one she had just decapitated and came up in a whirling vortex of destruction.

"Aim for the legs," Owen shouted. "You can't kill what isn't alive!"

There were at least a dozen or more Animated boiling up out of the darkness. Jinhao had apparently heard him and was focusing on cutting the silently shambling horde off at the knees, literally.

Gregg swore, readjusting his aim. Lightning boom-cracked from his gun and another of the Animated fell, legs missing. Owen bit back his disgust as animated began to crawl towards them, undeterred.

He focused on his aether mark, and one of those enigmatic marks he had been gifted with by those who had no name, trying to combine their energies. To his knowledge, no one had ever attempted this blending before. If it didn't kill him, it should be rather spectacular.

He collapsed to his knees with the effort of channeling the energies, his very blood feeling as if it were boiling, and then with a great cry, slammed his walking stick upright into the floor. A sheet of purple-tinged energy flew from the jewel in the handle. Half of the Animated it touched dropped like puppets with their strings cut. Owen had the satisfaction of hearing Renton scream as his "pretties" fell. At least the madman's attention was on them now, the girl on the table forgotten. Renton was pointing frantically at him, screaming for his creatures to kill him.

Owen panted, leaning on his stick. Well, at least he wasn't dead yet, although he wasn't sure that was an improvement. He struggled to rise, every inch of his body crying out in protest. Two of the creatures were shambling towards him. He could see Jinhao fighting for her life against half a dozen of the creatures across the room.

The flash-crack of lightning over his head heralded the arrival of the redoubtable Inspector Gregg. One of the giant Animated approaching Owen crashed over on its side, with one leg missing. It was followed by the other one as the Inspector's aether gun spoke again.

"Good advice, that, to aim for the legs," the Inspector commented, coming up beside Owen. "How do we kill them for good?" He fired again, stopping one of the ones he'd just shot from crawling forward by shooting at its arm.

"Renton," Owen gasped. "We have to kill Renton—only way to stop his Animated." Gregg shifted the gun, firing at the screaming Necromancer only to have his bolt succumb to the same fate as Owen's fire spear.

"No," Owen said, struggling to his feet. "Shoot the other Animated first! We can only get through the wards with a physical attack. "

Gregg promptly shifted aim again, and the Animated around Jinhao began falling and writhing around her. With a backflip through the air, she threw a stream of iron darts at Renton as she landed. The Necromancer jerked, dropping his long thin blade, as the darts struck home. Suddenly, the tall animated that had been Renton's attendant reached forward, pulling Renton off the ground by his hair.

Renton screamed as the Animated held him there. The scream was cut off as the creature sliced through his neck with one blow of a sickle-shaped instrument. The mage lantern went out, plunging the room into partial darkness.

Owen watched the tall Animated's actions towards its master in some confusion. He was sure that Jinhao's darts had been Renton's death blow. Perhaps the creature had broken free of the evil Magian's command at the last.

Owen shook himself. No time for speculation now. The Duchess had still to be rescued. He raised his cane, pulling on the energy in one of his tattoos. A wisp of light danced on the tip of the red-metaled stick, providing a wan illumination. Out of the corner of his eye he thought he saw the shadow that was Jinhao flit off in pursuit of the Animated and its grizzly trophy.

"Here, Gregg," he said, striding into the now-dead Magian Circle. Together they unbound the weeping girl, Gregg speaking soft words of reassurance in Mandarin.

Chapter 2

Owen leaned on his walking stick as the Duke of Chu's van rattled away, pulled by the giant Golem. It was fascinating to Owen that something that big could run so fast.

His Grace could afford to hire one of the Cabbalist Sorcerers that kept the construction of the artificial beings a tribal secret. It was a mark of cachet to be able to hire a Cabbalist and, despite their traveling ways, the Hebrew tribes were very particular who they did business with. No one would dream of crossing them either; the lessons of Prague three hundred years earlier were still remembered.

Inspector Gregg stood beside him watching the van wind its way up the street.

"Duke was grateful," he finally said in his thick English.

"It was a touching reunion," Owen agreed. He looked at the Inspector sideways. "Now what do we do?"

Gregg hacked and spat into the street and turned to look at the swarm of constables coming in and out of the building behind them.

"Do?" He repeated the word sourly. "I get to spend the rest of the night riding herd on this lot." He looked at Owen "You? Maybe you should go home. The superintendent should arrive at any minute."

Owen smiled thinly.

"And we wouldn't want to have to answer too many awkward questions."

Gregg nodded jerkily.

"Glad you understand." He paused, "I have a question. Who was the person in the building who killed Renton?"

"I thought that one of Renton's Animated went berserk and killed its creator," Owen said blandly. "After the death of its creator, all the remaining Animated stopped. Doubtless, the berserk one ran off with the head, before the motive energy of the Necromancer fled its body."

That was the story that Owen had come up with after the fact. It might even be true in part. The suspicion that Gregg was humoring him proved true with the Inspector's next words.

"That's right." Gregg nodded. His craggy face watched the milling officers without expression. "Moves like that, could almost think it was an Adept. But Adepts are only Chinese, and they do Magia with their bodies, like what you sort do with your rods." He sighed. "Very few Adepts. They are all either Imperial, or they follow rebels against the Empress." He turned towards Owen. "I would hate to learn that there is an Adept in my city to make trouble with the Imperial Court, Milord."

"I'm sure that need not be a concern, Inspector," Owen said smoothly.

Gregg held his eye for a moment, then nodded again. He held out a bag.

"Memento of the evening. Seems someone left a handful of bloody iron darts lying around."

Owen took the bag from Gregg's hand.

"Why, Inspector, how very considerate of you," he said in a delighted voice. "I shall treasure it always as a remembrance." A fine rain began falling from the skies.

"I will remember, too," the policeman said solemnly. Gregg hesitated. "What you did tonight, you should get the credit for it, Milord. It was you who discovered it was a Necromancer, and who it was."

Owen turned his face up to let the rain wash over him.

"No bother, Inspector," he said. "I didn't do it for any credit."

"Then why did you get involved?" the inspector demanded. "I know it wasn't for money, and you had no personal interest that I can find."

Owen shrugged.

"It seemed Renton needed stopping." He shook his head like a dog, and then lowered his chin, hair a-tumble, to smile at Gregg. "To be perfectly honest," he said brightly, "I have no idea why I did it. But it feels good, doesn't it?"

Gregg gave a snort of disbelief. "The saying is true: you English are all mad."

Owen spread his arms wide, smiling happily.

"Madness does keep boredom at bay, so they say." Suddenly serious, he brought his stick up to his forehead in a salute. "Good night, Chief Inspector. And thank you."

Gregg nodded back.

"Thank you, Milord." He looked up at the rain. "I could arrange transport if you wish."

"No," Owen said cheerfully, "I believe I shall walk for a bit." With that he turned and strolled up the street, swinging his cane, while whistling a bawdy dance hall tune.

Chapter 3

Owen had gone just around the corner when he was joined by Jinhao, who was wearing her cloak again.

"Ah." Owen said, not stopping his saunter. "There you are." He held out the bag. "This is yours, I believe."

The bag vanished beneath the cloak. Owen held out his arm and Jinhao placed an arm within his as the pair kept walking.

"You could have taken the carriage," she said to him. "I would have made my way back just fine."

"Nonsense," he said. "Rain is invigorating. Besides, I wished to see how you'd gotten on. I assume that you heard everything between Gregg and myself."

"Yes, he is much more intelligent than he shows, that one. I tried to follow that—thing, to end its misery," Jinhao admitted, "but I lost it somehow." Her shoulders moved beneath the cloak. "I am sorry. My Qi was sorely depleted by then."

"No worries," Owen said breezily. "As I said to Gregg, the thing was probably maddened with pain by Renton's death wound. There is a bond between a Necromancer and its creations, you know. It either tried to end Renton's suffering, or," he shrugged his shoulders, "the mind within broke free of Renton's control at that moment and sought revenge. Either way, good show on ending Renton."

"It was necessary," Jinhao said calmly. They walked on in companionable silence for a space. Finally, Jinhao spoke again.

"You did not answer Gregg honestly, Owen. I know why you got involved in this affair. It is because you are noble, noble like a hero in a tale."

Owen shook his head, and laughed, "Well, I do have a patent of nobility, it says so right there on the paper."

Jinhao smiled from under her hood.

"Always the light touch with you, is it not my friend? Laugh if you wish, but I know better."

Owen stopped swinging his cane, gripping it like a vise.

"Honestly, Jinhao, I truly do not know why I got involved. The noble-sounding words are just that, noble sounds. I can say, though, that I felt...alive, I suppose you could say." He twirled the cane absently as they walked. "Perhaps I'm simply bored. Deuced if I know. I do know that I am eternally grateful to you for agreeing to accompany me on this mad hunt."

"There can be no talk of debt between us Owen Strong, as you well know," she replied calmly. They came upon a brightly lit intersection where a single horse cab waited forlornly in the rain for a fare. Owen raised his cane in a hail, and hooves made a loud clatter as the cab man moved towards them.

"We've talked about that, Jinhao." Owen said shortly. He lowered the cane and turned towards her, smiling again. "But see here. We are in deadly peril of becoming serious, when we should be celebrating a great victory over the slimy Necromancer."

"What do you say that we pop around to Mrs. Schmidt's, and see if we may engage some company for the evening? I'm sure that there's food and a bottle back at the house to go with it." Mrs. Schmidt's was the most renowned pleasure house in Hong Kong. They had each been delighted to discover the other's appetites in such things. They had not, for various reasons, consummated such desires with each other.

Jinhao laughed, touching his arm.

"Again with the light touch! Alright," she said, smiling back, "fighting does leave one...hungry, I admit. Yes, certainly!"

Owen gave the cab man directions. They were both grateful to be getting out of the rain for a while. As they settled themselves, and the cab clattered along the streets, Owen suddenly sat bolt upright.

"Damn me," he gasped.

Jinhao pulled back her hood with a look of concern.

"What is it? Are you injured?"

"No, no," Owen reached into his vest pocket, pulling out a flask. "I completely forgot I had this with me. We could have had a drink way before now."

Holding it up, he pronounced, "To victory!" He nodded towards her, speaking in Mandarin, "And to beloved comrades in arms!" He took a large drink.

She took the flask from him, and held it up with a soft smile.

"As you British say: hear, hear!" She knocked the fierce spirits back and looked at him.

"Why do you say that, by the way? What sort of agreement is it to say, 'listen, listen'? Listen to what?"

"Well," he replied taking the flask, "It all goes back to the old days, when they would start royal proclamations with it."

"Yes, yes," she said crossly, "I know what a proclamation is. But I am not proclaiming. You are."

"Well—it doesn't really mean listen," Owen started.

"You don't know, do you?" she interrupted him in triumph. "You English always start a sentence where you don't know what you are talking about with 'well'."

"Well..." Owen caught himself. "Now see here, that's hardly fair!"

The cab rolled on through the puddles and rivulets of water-soaked streets. The rain continued to drum down on the roof of the cab, adding to the noise of the carriage wheels and creaky springs.

Chapter 4

The woman turned onto the dilapidated street at a brisk walk. Her disguise as a freelance courier allowed her to blend in perfectly. No one noticed a courier with a message bag. The fact had served her as well in her previous exploits as it had tonight. She climbed the rickety stairs of the building at the end of the street and knocked on the door.

It was opened by an old man with a shock of white hair.

"So," he said with a deep accent, "you have returned again. I trust that the gun worked well?"

She barged her way past him. "Not on the streets, you fool." She pulled off her short-waisted jacket to reveal a tube strapped to her arm, with wires leading to a box on her belt.

"Yes, everything went according to the plan. As of tonight, Sir Stanley of the Trading Board is no more, and as efficiently as the others." She thought back to how, disguised as a courier, she had come up to her targets and simply appeared to hold out her hand. The silent magnetic gun had fired the poison bullet so fast that there was no time for them to cry out.

She held up the arm with the tube.

"I need the gun reloaded for another shot."

"Another..." the old man said absently. He unstrapped the tube from her forearm. He reached inside a small box covered in frost with a thin pair of pliers. Gingerly taking something from within, he placed it down the tube and handed it back to her.

"You know," he said proudly, "no one has ever made a thing such as that which you hold. Death undetectable given by magnetic gun and frozen darts of poison is a new thing. Even General Hoffstein should be pleased."

Funny that you should mention the General," she said, as she finished strapping the tube on her forearm. "He gave me the next target himself." She raised her arm as if inviting the old man to shake hands. His eyes widened in fear. There was a barely audible hiss and the old man clutched his chest before falling over. She looked down at the corpse.

"Sorry, Hans, old boy," she said. "The General and I both agree that you talk too freely. Besides, Alchemists are a penny a dozen in Austria, I hear." She raised her arm. "They'll re-create this."

She looked around the makeshift laboratory. She would have to take the remaining frozen bullets, but otherwise there was nothing for her here. She glanced at the clock on the mantle place. She would just have time to return home and change for the funeral.

Chapter 5

Owen's house lay in what was called the Yiban Fanshui District. Yiban Fanshui meant literally "halfway" in Mandarin.

Owen was never sure if it referred to the fact that it was halfway up the side of Government Hill, or that those who lived there were either halfway up to riches or halfway falling down into the poverty of the lower city. He suspected that all the meanings were true. The Chinese were never ones to waste a good metaphor, especially one so apt.

As the day was cloudless but cool, he had advised Barton that he would take breakfast on the terrace. Lounging in only a sky blue silk robe, he sipped the strong tea blend he preferred, and lit the first and best cigarette of the day.

He could see out over the lower city. It was a bewildering swarm of buildings, from the neat manor houses nearby, down to the dung fire haze of the crumbling slums that ringed the warehouses and establishments that served the

Port off in the distance. Hong Kong was a deep-water port, through which flowed vast sums of goods and money, some of them even legal.

In the mid-day sun, the teeming city that had drawn fortune seekers from every corner of the globe for over three centuries, and continued to thrive with the bustle of modern seekers, looked so small from his vantage point above the city.

Far from giving him delusions of grandeur, the view always reminded him of the knife-edge dances of power and honor that were the city's true lifeblood. He knew that from farther up the hill, his own modest dwelling would appear as little more than a dot to be covered by a thumb, and perhaps as easily crushed, should those who lived up the hill so wish it.

He wondered idly how it must all look to the Dragon, Lohan, who ruled the city as his own private territory, from the top of the hill.

Owen took another pull of the cigarette and lay back, lifting his tea cup. He would refuse his more somber meditations today. Last night had seen the victorious ending of a monster too obscene to live, not to mention the reunion of one of the most powerful men in Imperial China with his niece.

On a more personal note, Lily, from Mrs. Schmidt's, had been both enthusiastic and skilled,. His pleasure of the evening was followed by a marvelous breakfast from his housekeeper, Mrs. Han.

Judging from the sounds he'd heard upstairs, Jinhao was still enjoying her diverting company of the evening, though what she saw in those muscle-bound Norsemen, he would never know.

Yes, he thought, life was too good not to savor. He looked down at a small carved stone box on the table. Should he indulge? The Black Lotus gave opium-like dreams to Magians for hours. Perhaps later; he still wanted to talk to Jinhao whenever she emerged.

Barton, his majordomo and butler, wheeled out onto the terrace. Owen had kept the clank man since his childhood. Though the alchemical construct might be limited in its abilities, Barton was one of the few things he had held onto from home.

"There is someone here with an urgent message from home, Sir." Barton's voice sounded like a wheezing pipe organ as he made the announcement. Before Owen could respond, a dapper, finely dressed man with white hair and a trimmed beard breezed onto the terrace behind the mechanical. Owen froze. Sir Stephen Partridge was the last living man Owen wanted to see.

"Well, Owen, aren't you going to invite an old man to sit with you?" Sir Stephen asked briskly. "Really, your manners have not improved." The man looked at Owen while leaning on a wooden cane with an electrum handle. "Though as it's nearly noon, I doubt that's lunch you've just finished. Still keeping to your disgraceful ways, I see."

Recovering himself, Owen waved at a chair across the low side table.

"I'd invite you to sit, but I doubt you'll be here that long. As for my disgraceful ways, I thought it the height of rudeness to force your way into someone's house uninvited." Owen raised his eyebrow.

"Nonsense," Sir Stephen retorted. "Barton here invited me in."

"Barton," Owen asked, his eyes never leaving Sir Stephen, "who is the person you just admitted?"

The clank man's body shuddered as its internal gears turned. "He is a messenger with an urgent message from home," Barton piped.

"I see," Owen pursed his lips. "And did the messenger first announce himself?"

"He announced himself as Sir Stephen Partridge," Barton finally said.

"And what are the standing rules about Sir Stephen Partridge?" Owen asked.

"Master is never at home to Sir Stephen Partridge," the clank man replied with great firmness. The two men could hear the cogs turning at a furious pace. "A messenger with news from home is always to be admitted at once." The gears ground so loudly, that for a moment it seemed as if the mechanical man would burst apart. "Master," Barton finally asked, "is there a problem with my service?"

"Not at all, Barton," Owen reassured the old tinplate. "Would you kindly get another cup for our guest?"

"Of course, Sir," Barton replied. He turned his torso around on one wheel and rolled off.

"I would have been very perturbed if you had hurt him, you know," Owen said as Sir Stephen sat in the chair.

"Really, Owen," Sir Stephen protested. "I would never wish to do so. He's much like the old family retainer, isn't he? What do you take me for?"

"A liar, a thief, and a mass murderer," Owen replied crisply.

Sir Stephen's eyes flashed at that.

"Are your hands so clean, Strong?"

"You know they aren't," Owen said in a dead voice. "You made sure of that."

Sir Stephen snorted, his eyes raking Owen up and down contemptuously.

"And look at you now, gone native, and wallowing in decadent waste and self-pity. You used to be one of the best. You took the markings of all five elements at a younger age than anyone in the history of the Order! And now, I doubt that you even know where you set your Focus down, gaudy thing that it is. I taught you better than this, I would have thought!"

A small aether gun appeared in Owen's hand, its fluid tube glowing balefully in the sunlight.

"I happen to know exactly where my Focus is, Partridge. But, as you may remember, I am no longer a member of the Obsidian Order, and I do not follow your rules."

Sir Stephen's eyebrows shot up as he looked at Owen with disdain.

"An aether gun, Owen?" His lip curled slightly. "How positively plebian. Do you really think I have anything to be afraid of from that pop gun?"

Owen nodded towards the short-barreled gun in his hand, and fixed Partridge with a steely-eyed glare.

"This little beauty is called the Ferocious Ferret. If you knew how much it cost, I believe that even you would agree it is anything but plebian." Owen's eyes held those of his former mentor.

"I suspect it gets its name because its teeth are quite big for such a small thing." Owen frowned at his unwelcome guest. "If you could correctly divine the elemental mix it's charged with, you might deflect the blast before it blows a large hole in you. But as you are currently less than four feet from me, it would be an interesting challenge for your reflexes, don't you think?" Owen's smile was as chill as a frigid northern wind.

The two men stared at each other, unmoving. Then Sir Stephen chuckled, and slowly raised both hands in surrender. He tilted his head towards his cane, which was still in his right hand. At Owen's silent nod, the old man carefully lowered his elemental focus to the floor, where it rested.

"My boy, I see you haven't lost a thing," he said, holding up his hands to show that they were empty. Owen kept the Ferret centered on his former mentor's chest.

"You know," Owen said casually, "I have often dreamed of a time like this, when I might end your life with a flick of the finger." He was no longer smiling. "And do be careful, Sir Stephen. I am no longer 'your boy' or your anything else for that matter."

"Do you still blame me for Balaclava?" Sir Stephen asked quietly. "I admitted to you then that it was a mistake."

"I find your use of the term mistake interesting when referring to the slaughter of four thousand true Englishmen and Herne alone knows how many Russians and Persians," Owen rasped.

"It ended the war," Stephen insisted. "And not only did we obtain the super-weapon the Austrians had developed, but the carnage encouraged its inventor to defect to Britain."

"Where he promptly built a weapon for you as the price of your friendship," Owen shot back.

Sir Stephen lowered his hands, placing them flat on his thighs. "Of course he did," he said irritably. "You know how the Game is played. The Lords of the Planes assured us that it would put the Austrians in check, as well as curtail any Persian expansion, which it has."

"You know," Owen said mildly, "you might not place so much faith in your spirit friends as you do."

Stephen's face colored red at this.

"The Lords have had guided the interests of Britain since the days of Elizabeth the First! When, I might remind you, the great Dee himself founded our Order. Are you now wiser than him?" he challenged.

"Oh, I make no such claim," Owen said carelessly. "I simply point out to you that the Lords are, by their own admission, neither human nor Gods. You might consider that their goals are not Britain's goals."

"Nonsense," Sir Stephen snapped. The old man peered at Owen. "What happened to you on that mission, Owen? After the dust settled, so to speak, you appeared with that gaudy electrum cane, and you simply left us." Stephen wet his lips. "Where did you get that cane?"

"I received it from a chance acquaintance," Owen replied.

Stephen's brow furled. "And where did you meet this 'acquaintance'?"

"Why, on the mission, as you so cleverly deduced," Owen's smile did not touch his eyes.

"Well, where is this 'chance acquaintance' now?" Stephen asked.

"I gathered that he's something of a vagabond," Owen shrugged, the gun rock-steady in his hand.

Stephen's eyebrows rose again in disbelief. "Are you saying that some tattered vagabond just gave you an expensively crafted elemental focus?"

Owen shrugged again, "I didn't say he was a poor vagabond."

Stephen scowled. "Kill me then, rather than insult my intelligence."

The gun vanished from Owen's hand.

"Oh, I'm afraid that you do not go to the barrows that easily. Curiosity has rather gotten the better of me. You knew what reception you'd get from me, so now I want to know why you wanted to talk to me so badly." He turned his head. "Besides, here comes Barton with your cup, and hopefully more tea."

After the clank man was dismissed, Sir Stephen curtly refused Owen's offer to pour. Sitting back, the younger Sorcerer looked at him over his tea cup.

"Well," Owen said pointedly, "you can either tell me what you want to talk to me about, or I can kill you, I suppose."

"After you left," Sir Stephen began briskly, "we kept track of your whereabouts and your doings. There were those that wanted you removed permanently, you know. I argued against it, and it was agreed that you should simply be kept under watch. When I discovered that you had settled here in Hong Kong, and even taken a Chinese woman as a leman..."

"Yes, yes," Owen interrupted, "I grant that the Order pays very efficient spies, and I am not ungrateful that you called off the dogs, as you probably need them alive. As for the 'Chinese woman' being my leman..." Owen, in turn, was interrupted by a voice from the entryway.

"Leman is one of your words for lover, is it not?" Jinhao flowed into the room, her long black hair loose to her waist. She was barefoot, and flashing plenty of thigh, as her patterned, silk robe was only fastened by a single tab at the waist. Owen had no doubt that she was armed in some way, though he couldn't spot the weapons at first glance. She perched on the lounge next to Owen, reaching for the empty tea cup. "It is a most unusual word. Why do you not simply say lover?"

Owen shot her a glance that he hoped she would take as a warning to be careful what she said. The waters around Sir Stephen Partridge were always deep.

"In the old days," Owen said mildly, "the Wise recognized ten kinds of formal relationship. As time passed, the forms evolved and changed. Leman indicates an ongoing intimate relationship, where the partner has no possibility of inheritance of title."

Jinhao finished making her tea. "Ah, I see." She flashed Owen a dazzling smile. "Thank you. And is the word used only for women, or is it used for both sexes?"

"The word for a male would be limen," Owen replied weakly. He wondered what she playing at.

Jinhao looked at Sir Stephen and straightened her back like a spear.

"I am Jinhao." She sipped, regarding the man impassively.

Sir Stephen smoothed his face and inclined his head. "Sir Stephen Partridge. Your servant, madam."

Jinhao smiled at this.

"A pretty sentiment. Please to continue your conversation." Sir Stephen shot Owen a pained expression. Watching him, Jinhao merely smiled, waiting for him to continue.

"You may either speak now," she said, "or Owen will speak of it later." She moved her shoulders in a manner that was half ironic shrug, and half challenge.

Owen kept his face carefully blank, and after a moment Sir Stephen began speaking again.

"Yes, well," the old man recovered himself and turned his regard to Owen, giving him a thoughtful look.

"I am only here on a brief stopover, while on other business. My airship leaves tonight. While here, a situation has come to my attention that could be quite dire. Frankly, I am here asking for your help."

"I no longer work for the Double-O," Owen said crisply. "I believe that we are done here."

Sir Stephen's eyes flashed.

"Damnation, man, you've made who you don't work for all too clear! I said help." His hands clenched as they rested on his thighs.

"You claim that you find the Disintegrator so abhorrent," he said with some heat. "How would you like to see it used on this city of yours?" He jerked his head at the view. "What happened on the field at Balaclava would be nothing compared to what would happen here. The weapon has been improved since then. All of this would be gone in the blink of an eye. I doubt even the Dragon could withstand it. If something isn't done, that possibility is all too real, I can promise you."

Owen sat back, keeping his face impassive.

"Go on." He gestured to his old mentor to continue.

Sir Stephen paused to gather his thoughts, and leaned forward with his face much more composed.

"It is little advertised, but next week there is going to be a new series of trade talks here between the dual administrations of the city, both British and Imperial, and with the other Great Powers. The subject of the talks is about trade access to Hong Kong. The diplomatic and economic stakes are exceedingly high." He waited until Owen nodded, understanding the situation.

"Last week, the head of the Austrian Embassy trade department, a chap named Kruger, was found dead. Three days ago, the head of one of the most prominent British trading houses, Lord Hastings, died in his front foyer."

"I seem to recall hearing about that," Owen said. "I was somewhat preoccupied, however." He waved a hand in dismissal. "Still, coincidences do happen."

"I know about your activities," Sir Stephen said dryly. His eyes glittered in the sun. "Last night, the head of the British Trade Board, Sir Stanley, was also found dead."

Owen sat upright. "That is too much, even for coincidence." He sat down his tea cup. "How did they die?"

Sir Stephen spread his hands, "No one is really sure. There are no reported signs of either violence or any of the forms of Magica at the scenes, not that the Austrians would be forthcoming about that. The 'official' cause of death in each case seems to be heart failure." He held up a finger to forestall the comment Owen clearly wanted to make.

"Mind you, all three men were hale and hearty, with no known prior illness. The oldest was Sir John Hastings of Hastings Shipping and Trading, and he was fifty-one."

Owen rubbed his chin, and then looked at Sir Stephen, frowning at what he was hearing. "Who do you suspect?"

Partridge slapped his thighs in frustration, going so far as to gesture broadly with his hands, in a rather continental fashion. "Rather say, who don't I suspect, and that would only be the Aztecs." He shook his head, in dismissal of his own conjecture.

"Not their style. Besides the fact that they do little trading outside the Western Hemisphere," Partridge continued. "They are finding it too fruitful to poke at us across the borders of the American colonies, to find appeal in something like this situation." He marked them off with his fingers.

"The Egyptians?" he asked. "They have no expansionist ambitions that we are aware of." He bent another finger in his macabre count.

"The Persians are well known to want a port such as Hong Kong, but their new boy-King seems reluctant to advance." Partridge closed another finger into his palm.

"That leaves us to consider the Austrians." Partridge raised an eyebrow at Owen, and received a nod in return.

"We have good intelligence that the Austrians are massing a war fleet in some little cluster of islands near Hong Kong." Partridge leaned forward. "We are almost certain they will have a Disintegrator, and if they do, that they will use it. It will be Balaclava all over again."

"By the merciful gods," Owen breathed for a moment as it all came back to him. Owen remembered battle of Balaclava too well. His nightmares would never let him forget it.

It happened during the Crimean War, with the Alliance of Russia, England, and Austria, fighting against Persians. As a covert operative at the time, Owen had crossed the battle lines to warn the Allied garrison at Sebastopol of a surprise Persian attack.

He remembered the tense faces of the commanders as he reported, and his own shortness of breath from the mad dash. He even remembered the smell of his own fear, and the sudden greyness on the faces of the commanders as he delivered the news. Thirty thousand Persians, composed of regulars, animated, Necromancers, plus a thousand of the elite Magia-wielding warriors called "Immortals", were even then advancing on their position.

He remembered the laugh of the general of the Austrians as he boasted, too soon, that it meant even more "demon sinners for them to send to hell."

The Holy Austrian Empire disavowed any use of Magia, claiming that their goddess decreed it so. Having no Sorcerers, animated or Constructs to add to their battle line, they were likened to weak children on the modern battle-field. Owen wasn't sure what the Austrian commander was referring to; however, it had seemed vainglorious to him at the time. He had shrugged it off, knowing only that the Austrians were fanatics. They were a people who covered their faces from the world, lest their Sun-Goddess see their visages and find one of them 'unworthy.'

He remembered, uneasily, that the next morning had dawned as clear as could be. Owen had taken his place amongst the spell-casters of the British Regiment. They were literally outnumbered three to one, but their morale was high, and they were ready and willing to fight to the last. Owen felt proud to be among such brave soldiers, and such courageous warriors as these men and women.

He had tensed as he saw the moving line that was the Persian animated. The animated moved in a fast shuffle, with brutal cleavers and great swords in their undead hands.

"Steady on," called the Magi's Colonel. She walked up and down the rows, inspecting the enlisted and the Magia, confirming to herself that they were ready. She met the eyes of many in the ranks as she passed, giving them encouragement, and her confidence.

"Watch out for their Necromancers," she warned. "Sing out when you spot one, everyone, and then concentrate your casting. Ignore the Animated. Every filthy Necro we bring down kills a hundred of them. Steady on."

Owen had noted a strange thing out of the corner of his eye. The Austrian section of the line had opened to allow a peculiar vehicle to come forth from between their ranks. Behind its smoke stack rose a box-shaped device of some kind. Owen watched as tiny men made adjustments to it.

The vehicle stopped and seemed to emit a strange vibration, one that Owen could feel through the ground— even at a distance. As the vibration grew stronger, he noticed that the Persian line began to falter. Suddenly, an animated exploded in the first rank, quickly followed by more. But it wasn't just the animated who were flying apart in a crimson carnage. The Persian Immortals on griffin–back soon began dying with just as much violence.

The vibrations began to climb in repetition and intensity. Owen saw the Austrians run away, only to succumb to the hideous device themselves, destroyed by the vibrations before they had gone a dozen paces.

Everyone the vibrations touched clutched their heads in agony. Around Owen the Magi also began to scream in anguish before falling down dead, blood running form their ears and eyes.

Swearing, Owen raised the double shield that the Order had taught him, only just in time to avoid the same fate. As soon as he was shielded, he began preparing a fire bolt to defend against the machine.

Crying as his comrades fell around him, he launched the bolt. When it struck the evil device, there was a huge explosion, followed by the absence of everything.

When Owen awoke from that cataclysm, he was in shock. That moment was when his new life had begun. In horror and agony. But it would not do to continue to think of that time now, and best to avoid thinking of that time at all in the presence of Sir Stephen Partridge.

He shook himself mentally, pushing aside the memories, and reached for his tea cup. In that moment he wished the tea was something much stronger, but he would show no possible weakness before Partridge.

"Surely even the Austrians aren't that mad," Owen protested.

Sir Stephen gave an elegant shrug.

"Our intelligence tells us that if they succeed in assassinating the British Head of Trade, The Duke of Claremore, when he arrives for these talks, they will declare Hong Kong an ungoverned city, and march in to restore order." Sir Stephen harrumphed at this.

"Order for the Austrians would look like total devastation. I doubt even the Dragon could survive contact with a Disintegrator."

"The help..." the old man emphasized the word, "I would ask of you, is to find this assassin before they can kill the Duke of Claremore and start a war. I fear such a war, a world war, would be the end of us all." His face looked to Owen for a moment to be grey and haggard, before he composed himself and restored his glamour again. After a few breaths, he appeared once more, the hale, yet elder gentleman.

"Will you help us all, Owen?"

Owen took his time lighting another cigarette. As the smoke blew out his nose he finally spoke.

"Why me?" He turned his head to look out at the city that now appeared to have come under threat from the same horror that haunted him from the past.

"You have only yourself to blame for that," Partridge said dryly. "We did have a reasonably competent, permanent, field agent here. However, that was before you killed him last night."

Owen's head whipped around, "Renton? Renton was a member of the Order?"

"Don't go all righteous on me," he demanded. Partridge's voice sharpened. "Yes, we knew what his hobby was. If we had any idea that he had fallen so far..." Again, the elegant shrug, "That's what we get for not having enough senior agents." That Owen had been one of those senior agents went unspoken.

Owen looked out at the city below him. The thought of it ravaged by the unholy arts of the Austrians was not to be borne.

"Alright, I'll look into it."

Partridge smiled at him. "Good show." He reached into his coat pocket, pulling out a hand-sized piece of white, polished stone. "You may find this useful."

Owen carefully took it from him. The writing on one side caught his breath: "Be it know that the bearer of this does the work of the Crown. All aid and assistance shall be given unto them. Regina Elizabeth, the Third of that Name." He stared at it, willing his eyes to focus, but the words didn't change.

"*Carte blanche*, my boy," Partridge said. "For the Wooded One's sake, use it well." He stood up. "Now if you don't mind, I have a sky ship to take." He held up his empty hand. "May I pick up my cane?"

"Provided you tuck it under your arm," Owen ordered. The old man did as he was asked, making a show of it.

"Barton will show you out," Owen stated blandly.

Partridge looked at Owen in surprise. Courtesy demanded that Owen show Partridge out, if they were allies.

"If that's how you want it," Partridge said gruffly, "So be it."

"Do not make the mistake of thinking that this changes anything, Partridge," Owen replied coldly.

Barton shortly appeared at Sir Stephen's side to escort him out.

"Just don't fail at this," he snapped at Owen. He followed Barton out without another word.

Owen poured himself a fresh cup of tea, wrapping his silk robe more firmly about him. Suddenly he felt chilled, despite the warmth of the day. He gazed off into the distance at the mountains and the bay, and then moved his gaze over the city. Finally, he spoke to Jinhao, his gaze still on the view before him.

"Well, I apologize for having my past make such an unpleasant intrusion on a beautiful day."

"Owen, who was that man?" She asked the question carefully, with unaccustomed hesitance.

Owen sighed, and turned to face her directly.

"Yes, I used to belong to a secret service of the British Crown called the Obsidian Order," he confirmed. "I really can't tell you much more than that without risking your life, which I will not do."

Jinhao nodded, and decided to approach the matter from a different angle.

"Is what he was saying about the city and the Austrians true? I thought they disavowed your Magia."

Owen lit yet another cigarette, giving his tense hands something to do.

"Oh yes, they disavow it. Their Goddess tells them it is wrong. Except that somehow Alchemy, and what they call 'Physicks,' is very much allowed and is assiduously cultivated." He exhaled a cloud of obscuring smoke before continuing.

"As for the Disintegrator, it does exist. I have seen it at work." He turned towards Jinhao. "I do not doubt for a moment that the Austrians would use it."

"What shall we do then?"

Owen gave her his wry grin.

"We, is it? I shall value your presence on this. Mind you, it will hardly be the romp that finding the Duke's daughter was."

"Where do we begin," she asked.

Owen closed his eyes until they were a mere slit in his face, as he sometimes did when thinking hard. Then he tilted his head at her, a subtle smile quirking his thin lips.

"How do you feel about playing a widow?"

Chapter 6

The British Embassy, Main Street

This way, My Lord, and eh, Madam." Phineas Horton, Third Secretary of the British Embassy, ducked his head as he entered the low door to the morgue at the bottom of an unremarkable set of stairs.

The morgue existed for British citizens who had asked that their remains be returned to the homeland. Given the general uneasiness death caused the living, its presence in the building was signaled only by a discreet plaque on a plain door at the top of the stairs.

In the center of the chilled room, which smelled of carbolic, formaldehyde and alcohol, stood a single table with a sheet draped over it.

An older man, with out-sized muttonchops that were as gray as the rest of his clothing, came striding towards them, wiping his hands on a towel.

"Here now," he said sharply, "What is all this, Horton?"

Secretary Horton wrung his hands, clearly uncomfortable with the situation, his role in it, and the place in which he found himself.

"Please forgive the intrusion, Doctor," he murmured, "but we have a bit of a delicate situation." He waved a hand towards Owen and Jinhao.

"This is Lord Ivers, second cousin of the niece of Sir Brandon. He just arrived by sky ship this morning. And this..." the Secretary gestured vaguely in Jinhao's cloaked direction, but did not look at her directly. He directed his embarrassed gaze at the floor, and coughed discreetly.

"This is Mi-Ling, a distant relative of Sir Brandon." He coughed again, and looked at the doctor. "A close, but em, eh, a distant relationship," he said rather awkwardly. "They wish to pay their respects."

The doctor's eyebrows briefly rose, as he caught the implication that Jinhao, or rather Mi-Ling, was the deceased Sir Brandon's undeclared mistress. He stepped forward, extending a hand to Owen.

"Doctor Marston, Embassy physician," he declared. "My sympathies, Milord. A shocking thing that he should be taken from us so young." Releasing Owen's hand, the old doctor gave a formal bow to Jinhao.

"You have my deepest condolences on your loss, Madam."

"Thank you," Jinhao said in a voice that held just the right amount of quaver, Owen thought with admiration. He was surprised as he had no idea she could be such an accomplished actor. She stared at the table, her delicate hand obviously trembling.

"Is that Brandon?" she whispered.

"It is," Doctor Marston said to her gravely. He continued to address Mi-Ling, while he looked a question at Owen.

"Are you certain that you wish to do this? I have cared for the body as I may, but still it is not for the delicate of constitution."

"I was just off ship when I heard the terrible news," Owen said mournfully. "I gathered Mi-Ling and came here directly. I wonder if you can tell us how Uncle Brandon passed on."

"Heart attack," the doctor said with conviction. "The poor soul was found collapsed in the front foyer of the Embassy. I assure you, Milord, that we did all that we could." He sniffed dismissively, "We even called in the Embassy Sorcerer, but there was nothing to be done." Marston glanced at Owen's electrum cane and his face stiffened as he thought better of his last words. Some Sorcerers were very touchy about their powers, and only too happy to prove them.

Owen gave his most charming smile to the man. It was clear that the Doctor was one of those who distrusted Sorcerers, despite their having been part of British culture for centuries. Some people naturally distrusted what they could not have themselves. Owen didn't blame the man. He distrusted Sorcerers as well, only for very different reasons.

"Yes, well," Owen drawled. "I'm sure you did everything you could. Whole thing would have been a bit above me, being only an apprentice Fire caller." He hefted the cane carelessly. "Still, it's a bit of tradition on our side of the family, you see; must keep up appearances."

Owen watched the Doctor's face relax. Fire callers were a penny a dozen, as most could barely light a lamp, and thus were unlikely to either take offense, or be a serious threat.

"The Secretary here tells me that the body is to be shipped home tonight," Owen continued, "so this may be Mi-Ling's only chance to say good-bye." Owen managed to look both sincere and bothered at the same time. Clearly he was only attempting to do the family duty, and wanted to be done with it as soon as possible.

"Please," Jinhao stood by the table, her eyes fixed on the sheet. "Please, may I see him?"

The Doctor stirred himself, coming over to the table, and then took a firm grasp of the sheet covering the body.

"Of course," he said quietly. "Please be brave." He pulled back the sheet, and Jinhao gave a great keening cry, collapsing on the dead man's chest with intense bouts of sobbing.

Owen had to marvel again at her acting ability. He wondered, not for the first time, what Jinhao had been before that fateful meeting of theirs on the border with China proper. The other two men in the room looked away, embarrassed at her display.

"Please, gentlemen," Owen asked gently, gently patting Jinhao's shoulder as if in comfort. "Might we have a moment of privacy?"

The doctor and the Secretary were only too glad to leave the room to the wailing lover and the younger relative. As the door clicked shut, Jinhao stopped crying.

"Good job," Owen said, squeezing her shoulder. "You almost had me believing you there for a moment. Help me get this sheet off, I need to see the whole body."

Jinhao smiled at him.

"Western men are so hopelessly romantic about a woman's tears," she said happily. They wrestled the heavy sheet to the floor.

Owen's original plan had been to present himself at the Embassy as a distant relative on a Grand Tour. That was not unreasonable, as many younger nobles made a journey around the world, pestering their relatives as they went.

He only needed a few minutes alone to examine the body. While he could simply have presented his carte blanche and demanded to see the body, gossip about a highly-credentialed Sorcerer snooping about would have spread through the colony like the plague, alerting the assassin, if there was one.

To that end, he had dressed in a rather modern suit in the Connolly house colors of emerald green and gold. He had been pleasantly surprised when Jinhao presented herself in an almost-matching Western afternoon dress, fashionably knee length, complete with the appropriate hat, gloves and shoes.

Arriving at the Embassy, they had been given over to the officious care of Phineas Horton, Third Secretary. Secretary Horton had droned on and on, showing no signs of ever letting them out of his office.

That was when Jinhao had broken down in tears and, with Owen following her cues, they had 'confessed all' about the secret romance between Sir Brandon and Mi-Ling. Horton had moved surprisingly quickly after that, finally leaving them alone with the body. It had been a very satisfying ruse.

Owen quickly passed his cane over the remains, the blue stone in the handle glowing softly, while the body shimmered different colors as if in response. One by one, he silently called on the marks of the five elements bound on his body, seeking to learn the cause of death. Finally, he lowered the cane, leaning on it with a frown.

"Well, Partridge was right," he mused, "there is no sign of Magia, no residue of poisons, and nothing else amiss, except his death. There is also no sign of heart congestion, or trauma, though the heart has, of course, stopped beating. In fact, I will be damned if I can find any reason for him to be dead at all."

"Then we must examine the body itself," Jinhao stated. She began at the feet, running her hands over the skin as she peered closely at it. "There are many ways a man might die, or be caused to die."

Owen glanced at the door. "Yes, well, you'd best be quick about it. I doubt that our stalwart gentlemen's 'romanticism' will extend to them finding you fondling his naked corpse."

Moving swiftly and neatly, Jinhao examined the limbs, the torso, and finally reached the head. There, she rolled back the eyelids, then opened the mouth and sniffed.

"Ah," she looked up at Owen. "Smell this." She held the mouth open.

Owen gingerly leaned over and sniffed.

"He smells rather like musty almonds," he remarked. "Surely not something he ate?"

Jinhao shook her head.

"There is a poison that leaves only the faint odor of almonds, and then only for a short while." Her brow creased. "But it would take too much of the poison to be eaten and not to be noticed. Usually, it is only found on blades or needles. There must be a wound."

Now Owen began searching the body as well. After examining the hands and arms, he started at the neck and moved down. He pointed at a tiny red spot on the chest.

"Hallo, what's this?"

Jinhao bent close enough her nose almost touched the body.

"I do not know. If it is a wound, it is very small." She looked at Owen. "If it is a weapon, I cannot think what would leave such a tiny mark."

"Clothes," Owen said quickly. He glanced around to see a neatly folded stack sitting on a cabinet shelf. "Come on," he said. "Let's get him covered."

They poured over the clothing, holding up each piece to the Magia light in the ceiling, "Got it!" Owen exclaimed. He held up the shirt for Jinhao to see a very small hole, barely a parting of the thread.

"Yes," she hissed, holding up the brocaded vest next to the shirt. A small point of light shone through both items of clothing. At that moment, the door opened, and they turned to find a frowning Secretary Horton and Doctor Marston regarding them.

"Ah, yes," Owen said glibly. "Dear old Uncle Brandon did wear only the best, did he not? He folded the shirt and placed it back on the pile. "You can't find quality like this anymore, I dare say." He patted the pile of clothing while smiling.

"I think that you should both go now," said a reproachful Doctor Marston. They were accompanied to the front gates by a silent Horton, who was doubtless happy to see them go.

Owen paused once Horton had returned to the building.

"Well, we can now say with some certainty that Sir Brandon Connelly was likely murdered." He said dryly and raised an eyebrow at Jinhao. "How rare is this poison you suspect?"

Jinhao glared at a drunken Persian sea man in a purple tunic, who careened too close to them. The man promptly careened the other way, knocking over the chicken cages on an old Chinese man's back. She turned back to Owen, both of them ignoring the furor of loose chickens and shouting, the chaos quickly carried away on the tide of humanity moving along Main Street.

"Not rare, but not common," she replied. "It is made from the roots of a plant. Most Alchemists will have the means to make it." She frowned. "There are better poisons; usually it is used on a blade to cause the target's muscles to slow for a short time, which makes it a favorite of dishonorable fighters. Its main advantage is that it leaves no trace, other than the smell. The liquid has a most bitter taste. It would take a very noticeable dose to kill by food or drink." Her frown deepened. "This is not right, somehow."

Owen nodded resignedly.

"Right then. Well, there is nothing for it. We will have to examine the other bodies." He pointed forward. "We'll need to go down to Fei Street to catch a cab."

As they walked through the crowd Owen said casually, "You know, I don't believe that you have ever mentioned what you did before we met."

Jinhao turned her body to avoid a clank man as he rolled by her.

"That is correct, I have not," she remarked. "It has not seemed relevant. No more than your Order has, yes?"

Owen winced inside. She had him there. After avoiding a rather large North man dragging a wheeled cart that was loaded down with lumpy sacks, he spoke again.

"Right. Well, allowing as how we both have things in the past we would prefer not to speak of, I must observe that you were as good as any confidential agent back there."

A group of priests in red and orange passed Jinhao, chanting and waving censers from which came clouds of fragrant incense.

"Thank you," she acknowledged. "The skills of dissembling have proved useful."

"As is your knowledge of poisons," Owen said off-handedly.

Jinhao shrugged her shoulders, "Those skills have also proved useful."

They reached the corner of Fei Street through which ran another river of humanity. This one was composed of conveyances of all types, everything from rickshaws drawn by weary runners, to hansom cabs and carriages drawn by every beast known to man. There was even a steam car, moving slowly through the flood, a dark skinned padjum seated majestically above the crowd on the back of the contraption.

After considering the options, Owen hailed a horse-drawn coach.

"I do wonder sometimes why you continue to stay with me," he remarked, as the coach began to pull over to the curb.

Seeing the rich dress of his fare, the coach man simply opened the carriage door and pulled down the attached step. Owen held out his hand for Jinhao who took it to climb within.

"Really, Owen, we discussed this," she said serenely. "After you saved my life at Xiopling, I owe you a life debt, and must honor my duty. Where are we bound?"

"Hastings Trading and Shipping," Owen called up to the driver, before swinging into the seat beside her. He placed his cane upright between his legs, hands restless on the handle.

"We will see if we can find a way to examine the body of Sir John Hastings, although Gods alone know what they have done to it after a week. If they follow the Old Ways, it's likely already burned, but we should at least try." He turned in the cab to look at her seriously.

"As for this 'life debt' business, need I remind you that I have already said you don't need to follow it? I release you and all that."

"Yes, I do," Jinhao said in the same unruffled voice, "And no, you cannot."

Owen looked out the window, watching the crowd pass by, while images plagued his mind of what a Disintegrator would do to the busy crowd he was seeing.

"This may become an ugly business before it's over," he muttered. "Still, I am glad of your presence, Jinhao."

Jinhao allowed herself a small smile.

"I know," she said simply.

Chapter 7

Hastings Trading and Shipping

As luck would have it, they arrived at the offices of Hastings Trading and Shipping to find that a ceremony honoring Sir John Hastings was just finishing.

Owen glanced at the white bunting that hung from every possible surface of the huge interior, as he took a flute of mead from a white-clad server. The ceremony seemed to be a peculiarly Hong Kong mix of British and Chinese. Both cultures shared white as the color of death. However, the musicians who were playing drums and flutes in the background were definitely Chinese, while the drinking and the singing Bard moving among the many guests was decidedly British. There were billowing clouds of incense everywhere.

The guests were likewise a mix. While there were many dressed in white British suits and dresses or Chinese robes of the same color, there was also more than a sprinkling of rich jewel-toned clothing of varying extravagance. Owen's stomach clenched as he spied a small cluster of Austrians standing by themselves, their black face-scarves matching their uniforms. The Austrians were a small black cloud in a sea of white and color.

"Well," he murmured to Jinhao as he sipped. "At least we don't have to worry about Sir John's body being burned up." He inclined his head towards the far end of the room, where a golden bier lay on a raised pedestal. A cluster of priests and priestesses of various Deities stood around it.

"Yes," Jinhao replied. As was her want, she had refused the proffered mead. "However, I doubt that we can simply walk up and start examining the body."

Owen smiled at her, then he drained the flute, placing the empty on a passing tray.

"We should pay our respects at least," he said. "You never know what opportunity may present itself."

Jinhao rolled her eyes slightly. She knew that smile.

"We should," she agreed, "Although if you get us arrested or worse, our 'opportunities' will be somewhat restricted."

Owen clutched his chest dramatically.

"You wound me," he said as they moved towards the bier. "When have I ever led you astray?"

"That night at the Boar's Head," she replied mercilessly.

Owen waved her comment aside. "They were sore losers. You can hardly blame me for that," he protested. "Besides, I thought in this case that we would try the honesty tactic."

"Honesty," Jinhao looked at him and raised an elegant eyebrow. "This will be interesting."

Suddenly, a large, swarthy man was standing in front of them with a drink in his hand, blocking their path. His stark white tunic and trousers were relieved by a deep purple sash covered in badges and colored ribbons. On his right hip rode a black-hilted knife.

"Owen Strong," he smiled expansively. Oiled ringlets framed a dark face in which white teeth gleamed. "I had heard that you had retired here in this interesting city, but did not credit such a thing."

"Susa," Owen nodded warily in greeting. "It is true. I am retired, and living here now. What brings you to our lovely city?"

The large man spread his hands, careful not to spill his drink.

"Bah. I am stationed here to be a consultant to our glorious embassy, for my sins." He turned to Jinhao with a bow worthy of a royal court.

"But Owen, it is most unfair that you have already found the most beautiful jewel in the country! Do you know, O Fair One, what a dangerous reprobate you have taken up with? You should come with me, and I will shower you with precious stones that, although they will pale beside your beauty, shall assist you to outshine the stars themselves."

Jinhao smiled at him.

"And if I should run off with one whose name I do not even know, what would you think of me?"

"Jinhao," Owen said dryly, "This giant who fancies himself a poet is Susa Sassanid. Susa, this is Jinhao. Susa is one of the Ten Thousand Immortals of the Persian Empire, as well as one of the best agents the All-Seeing Eye has ever had."

The whole world knew of the Immortals, the famed Sorcerer-warriors of the Persian Empire. Some even hinted that it was the Immortals, rather than the Dynasty, who ruled the Empire.

"Please, Owen," Susa said with wry grace, "Modesty requires that I correct you, the best agent of His Divine Majesty, Cyrus, may Zoroaster light his name." He smiled at Jinhao.

Jinhao inclined her head, clasping her hands together in front of her.

"I am honored. I have never met a member of the Persian Immortals before, let alone the best secret agent of the Empire." The slight inflection she gave to the word best hinted that she doubted the truth of it.

Susa's eyes widened and he let out a great hoot.

"I like her, Owen! She is much better than your usual fluff." His eyes narrowed slightly, "But, Lady Jinhao—it is Jinhao, yes? There is no second name?"

"Jinhao is sufficient," she responded indifferently.

Susa smiled again, teeth agleam. "You see, Lady Jinhao, I am only a humble consultant for our embassy these days, despite what our mutual friend may say. Much as our friend here is retired, yes?"

"Susa," Owen pressed. "I truly am retired." Susa's eyebrows shot up at this assertion.

"Truly?" Susa's arms waved around, gesturing to encompass the room.

"And I suppose that you are a friend of Sir John Hastings come to pay your respects?" Susa nodded as if answering his own question. "There is no retiring for such as us, my friend." He drained his glass and set it on the tray of a passing servant, snatching up a full one to take its place in the large paw of his hand. He quaffed a good portion of the glass and sighed.

"There is so much tragic death lately," Susa rumbled. "First the Austrian official. May Ahriman eat their hearts. Then Sir John died." He looked meaningfully at Owen. "And now I hear that the British head of the Trading Board has also passed beyond the veil." He drank again. "It is seeming not so good to be a trader these days. It is fortunate that my family is forbidden the filthy occupation."

"And what is Persia's interest in all these tragedies, Susa?" Owen asked quietly.

The giant spread his hands again.

"As I say, Owen, I am only a humble hanger-on at the embassy." He placed one finger along his nose. "But if I were to guess, I would say that even in the glorious Empire of my king there are those who do worry about such filthy things as trading and gold. Such a number of tragedies would not, cannot, go unmarked. Mind you, I believe my king is satisfied with what he has, but there are always others, yes?"

Owen nodded.

"Especially with the new trade talks starting in a couple of days," he ventured.

Susa returned the nod, taking another quaff of his drink.

"As you say, my friend." The big man looked up and smiled again. "But I see that my lord is signaling for his faithful hound again." His ringlets quivered as he inclined his head towards a group of Persian diplomats. "My work is never done."

"I hope that you enjoy your retirement, my friend," Susa's voice dropped to a low basso. "While the waters are lovely here about, be careful. I fear that they may be unaccustomedly deep for one swimming alone." He bowed to Jinhao. "When you are ready to leave this northern bandit, come to me and I will treat you like a queen!"

"But what would your other wives say?" Jinhao asked innocently. "After all, I am sure that a man of your many accomplishments must have seven or eight already?"

Susa hooted again. "Actually it is six, pretty lady!" He looked at Owen again. "I do like her!" With that, the giant moved through the crowd with a grace that belied his size.

"That was interesting," Owen remarked thoughtfully, watching the man go.

"I take it that you are old acquaintances?" Jinhao asked.

"Oh, yes," Owen said absently. "The last time we saw each other was Tunis I think. We tried to kill each other, while hanging from a sky ship."

Jinhao turned to look at him. "And what happened?"

Owen shrugged.

"We're both still here. More importantly I wonder why Susa is here in Hong Kong."

"Doubtless, he is wondering the same thing about you," Jinhao remarked dryly. "I am wondering why he felt it important to tell you that his government has nothing to do with the deaths, and that they also think someone committed murder."

Owen grunted and frowned thoughtfully.

"Caught that, did you? I am wondering the same thing." He tapped his cane on the floor. "Well, we should still pay our respects."

To the right of the steps leading up to the bier stood a richly dressed entourage, centered on a strikingly pretty young woman. Her upright bearing and shoulder crest marked her as the new Head of House Hastings.

If anyone personified the British Empire, it was its trading families. For centuries, the brave had ventured away from the home Isle and, by skill, wits, and sometimes outright piracy, returned home with wealth and honor to found their own dynasties.

Some, like the Hastings, had chosen to settle in the countries where they made their wealth. Still, they sent their children to schools back "Home," they toasted the Monarch every Birthday, and had planted the British flag from the windswept plains of America to the southern bays of Australia. They were the Empire's lifeblood, its modern nobility, and they knew it.

Owen approached the group, and stopping the correct distance away, bowed with his right hand over his heart towards the upright woman. "Lady Hastings," he said, "Please allow me to convey my sorrow at your loss."

The young woman acknowledged him with a regal nod. The only signs of distress were the dark rings under her eyes that even cosmetics could not hide.

"My thanks to you, Sir, on behalf of my House and myself," she said in a clear voice. "I must confess that you have me at a disadvantage. I see what I believe are the colors of House Connolly, as well as your Rod of Art, but I know of no Sorcerers of that House currently in the city."

Owen straightened up from his bow.

"Ah, yes, well I can see where the confusion may arise; forgive me, Milady." He bowed again, "My name is Strong, Owen Strong of House Strong, at your service and at the service of your family." He flourished a hand towards Jinhao.

"This is my noble companion, Jinhao." Jinhao affected a short bow of equals before returning to stand silently behind him. The news of this announcement was electric in the group before them. Those that didn't straighten up in surprise took their cue from their mistress and reluctantly bowed in response.

"My Lord," Lady Hastings said without a trace of surprise in her voice. "It is I and my family that stand at your service! Truly you do honor to both my father, and to his House." There were advantages to having a famous name, Owen reflected. It was not the first time he had taken advantage of his Father's shining glory.

"I only wish it could be under kinder circumstances, Lady Hastings," Owen said soberly. "I must plea for private speech with you concerning your father's untimely fate."

Before Lady Hastings could respond, a dignified, but younger and male version of Lady Hastings stepped forward.

"Now, see here, My Lord," he began stormily, "If indeed you are who you say you are, this is hardly the time or place for such words, let alone a plea for a private audience!"

He was stopped by Lady Hastings' hand on his arm.

"You forget what I am, John," Owen heard her say to him. "I would speak to this man. You stand in my place to the guests until I return." Raising her voice she spoke to Owen.

"Please forgive him, My Lord. I plead the circumstance of grief."

"Of course, Lady Hastings," Owen said with another bow. "As a guest, there is nothing to forgive."

She nodded her thanks, and turned away from the entourage.

"This way, My Lord," she said, moving towards a doorway along one wall. An older woman with a rod sheath at her waist followed determinedly behind her, glaring distrustfully at Owen. He judged she must be the House Sorcerer. He would be distrustful as well in her place.

He was frankly amazed that the Lady Hastings had agreed so readily. While the Strong family name carried a certain honor, he doubted that his word alone would grant them such an audience. With a nod at Jinhao to come along as well, he followed the two women towards the door.

The doorway led them onto a long covered veranda that held a breathtaking view of the harbor. Lights of different colors began winking and glimmering on the waters as the sun sank in the sky. Overhead, a sky ship silently floated by, the tips of its spines faintly gleaming in the gathering dusk. Lady Hastings rounded on Owen, the pinch-faced Sorcerer at her right shoulder.

"Now, My Lord, what word have you to say about my father's death?" she rapped out in a voice like steel. She crossed her arms over her stiff white dress and awaited Owen's reply, a determined fire in her face.

Owen straightened his shoulders, noting that the noblewoman before him was a far cry from the demure lady in mourning she had appeared inside.

"I am investigating the deaths of Sir John and some others, My Lady. I believe that your father may have been the victim of malice."

The older woman behind Lady Hastings stirred as if to speak. Lady Hastings held up a hand to stop her.

"A moment if you please, Melinda," she ordered the Sorcerer, never taking her eyes off Owen. "Are you a member of the police?"

"No, My Lady, I am a private agent," Owen replied, matching her matter of fact tone.

"I see," said the Head of House Hastings. "Do you know how my father was killed?"

Owen shook his head. "We have some theories, My Lady. That is why I am speaking to you."

"I see," the young woman repeated. Her face and voice could have been carved from granite. "What do you require of me?"

Owen attempted to look apologetic. "I'm sorry for this, My Lady, but we need to examine his body—that is to physically examine it."

"This is outrageous, My Lady!" the Sorcerer burst out from behind Lady Hastings. "Both Doctor Syn and myself did all that we could to save your father. As we have both stated, it was a heart attack that killed him! There was nothing anyone could have done! That you should even listen to this—this stranger and his ravings, is an insult to your father's memory, especially on this day of all days! I shall call the guards."

"You will do no such thing, Melinda," Lady Hastings ordered, turning to the older woman. "You forget both who and what I am. I am the Head of House Hastings now, and I know he is speaking the truth. I shall avenge my father as is my right as Head of House. You may leave us, Melinda."

"My Lady," the Sorcerer rocked back as if slapped. "He is a Sorcerer," she protested.

"I am aware of that," Lady Hastings said. "My Lord Strong," she asked raising her voice. "Do either you or your companion intend me either harm or compulsion of any kind?"

"No, My Lady," Owen replied calmly. It appeared that Lady Hastings was establishing herself as no one's figurehead. Owen was too familiar with the power plays that bedeviled great families, and said nothing more.

"Leave us," Lady Hastings repeated. The House Sorcerer moved past her mistress, her gaze shooting figurative daggers from her eyes at Owen as she left.

Lady Hastings turned back to Owen, speaking as if nothing had occurred.

"And if you are wondering if this is simply a young woman's fancy, My Lord, you should know that I am True Born. Naturally, that is not commonly known, and I trust to your discretion. If, however, your beliefs are borne out, I shall see my father avenged, I so swear it."

Owen nodded. If one person out of a hundred had some talent for using Magica, perhaps one in a hundred thousand was born with the gift of divining the Truth of a person's words when they heard them. Owen had some sympathy for her. If anyone was looked at more warily than Sorcerers, it was the True Born. Normally the bearers of such a gift were dedicated to some priesthood at an early age. That someone with the ability was Head of a Great Trading House would make them very formidable indeed.

Owen bowed his head at her declaration.

"As is your right, of course, My Lady. It is those beliefs we intend to test, in the hopes that they will lead us to those who are responsible."

"And how do you propose to test them?" she demanded. "My father shall be consigned to the flames by nightfall." She glanced out at the fading light, "Which is not far off. Even I cannot stop the ceremony now, and he lies in full view until the torches are lit."

Owen gave her the smile that had caused Jinhao to roll her eyes earlier.

"I have a thought on that, if My Lady is willing?"

The Priestess of the Goddess of the Cauldron gave a start as the new Lady Hastings climbed the steps to the bier with two strangers, and then resumed her chanting. If the Lady Hastings wanted to say her farewells personally, it was none of her concern.

The trio stood before the cloth-of-gold covered body. Owen arranged both Lady Hastings and himself to screen Jinhao from the view of the surrounding priests.

"It has to be now, Jinhao," he muttered under the chanting. Quickly Jinhao pulled back the cloth to reveal the face and upper body of Sir John Hastings. Wordlessly, she pointed to a tiny fading red mark on the dead man's chest.

Chapter 8

Lady Hastings stood with them outside the building that was Hastings Shipping and Trading while a footman ran to flag down a cab for Owen and Jinhao.

"I still fail to see what a tiny mark on father's chest proves," she demanded. "It is smaller than a flea bite. In fact at this time of year, it probably is a flea bite."

Owen looked to Jinhao, who had stayed curiously silent through the whole affair, then turned back to the young heir.

After the discovery on Sir John's chest, Owen had attempted to extradite himself and Jinhao from the ceremonies, only to find that Lady Hastings had attached herself to them like a burr to their sides. Weaving in and out of the well-wishers that stopped them every few feet, Owen had hoped that Lady Hastings would finally leave them at the door. Instead she doggedly followed them outside. In leaving the ceremonies Lady Hastings was, in all likelihood, causing a scene, or at least some consternation within.

"We believe that the assassin somehow introduced a poison through that wound, My Lady," Owen explained briefly.

"Wound?" Lady Hastings face showed her surprise. "That tiny mark? But how?"

"When we know that My Lady, we will be one step closer to finding the killer," Owen replied. He decided to take advantage of their relative isolation to question her further. "Forgive me, but were you present when your father collapsed?"

"No," she answered. "I was in the building of course, as it was a business day, but I was upstairs. I came as soon as I was called down with Lady Ap Rhys and the House Sorcerer."

"So you and the House Sorcerer arrived at the scene at the same time? What did you see?"

Lady Hastings nodded, clearly thinking back to that day.

"Yes. One of the clerks came to get Lady Ap Rhys, the House Healer, to see if she could help my father." Her face briefly twisted. "When we reached him, he was lying on the floor. Dr. Syn was bent over him. Lady Ap Rhys began the laying-on of hands immediately, but it was already too late, he was just...gone. Mistress MacAllister, the House Sorceress, arrived just as we were closing his eyes. She tried to help also, but it was to no avail." The heiress dabbed at her eyes for a moment, then looked at Owen dry-eyed.

"I am sorry to have you recall this Lady Hastings," Owen said sympathetically. "You are doing splendidly. Was there anything, or anyone that seemed out of the ordinary? Think carefully."

She frowned in concentration.

"No, nothing. There was just father on the floor, with the courier tube lying beside him. Everyone was running about, it was a scene of madness, as you may imagine."

"Courier tube," Owen pounced on the anomaly. "What courier tube was this? Was your father expecting a courier? Is that not normally something that someone else would handle?"

Lady Hastings shook her head. "He was not expecting a courier that I know of. It was his habit to 'stretch his legs' as he put it about that time of day. He would step outside the front door for a time." She smiled. "I believe that he often indulged in a drink of brandy while he was outside. He kept a flask on him. I am sure that he thought no one knew. It would not have been the first time that he had intercepted a courier while he stood outside. He usually simply took the tube from them."

"I see," Owen said. "And what happened to this courier tube?"

She startled at that question.

"Why I have no idea, now that you mention it. I simply assumed it was some routine thing. People are always sending contracts and such through the couriers. It must happen a dozen times a day." She looked at him. "Do you think this is important?"

"It could be," Owen temporized, "Or it might be nothing. Would you, of your kindness, enquire about it and let me know the answer?" He produced a card with his address on it.

Lady Hastings clutched the card.

"Of course," she said, "Anything that might be helpful. But I shall have to give the task to another. I am coming with you."

Owen struggled not to allow his dismay show at her pronouncement. He looked to Jinhao for support, and saw the same silent, inscrutable face.

"I am sorry Lady Hastings," he said as gently as he may, "but that simply isn't possible. We work best on our own, and we know not where this inquiry may take us. Besides," he continued, "you have a duty to your guests and your father still."

She clenched her hands into fists at this.

"But this is my duty! You cannot simply leave me here after such pronouncements as you have made. I may be useful in your inquiry with my truth talent!" Owen was saved from further awkwardness by the arrival of both the coach, and the younger male version of Lady Hastings, who was running up to them.

"Sister." he panted, out of breath. "We are almost at the raising of the cup speeches! You are needed! Mr. Richards told me to come and find you!"

Lady Hastings swiveled from Owen to what was clearly her brother then back to Owen again.

"My Lord Strong," she said desperately, "I plead with you!"

The footman opened the coach door, and Jinhao climbed inside without another word. Owen sketched Lady Hastings a bow.

"I promise that I shall inform you of our results, Lady Hastings. Rest assured that you have already been of enormous aid. Please," he said climbing up into the coach, "see to your guests."

Owen watched Lady Hastings reluctantly enter the building as they drove away.

"Well..." he declared as he sat back in the padded seat. "That was decidedly awkward at the end there." He turned towards Jinhao. "You might have been of more help you know. What's come over you?"

"You were doing fine," she replied absently. "I saw no need to interfere. I am now thinking of couriers."

"Yes..." Owen breathed. "Courier would be a perfect disguise for our killer. They are everywhere in this correspondence happy age we live in, or so it seems. And the disguise would only take a messenger bag, really."

Couriers were ever present in modern cities, carrying everything from messages across the street to state documents for officials. Most couriers worked for established companies that were trusted and bonded, but in Hong Kong there was nothing like unions or guilds to prevent anyone from picking up a bag to earn a few bob.

After a moment's thought, Owen shook his head. "It is not enough," he declared. "The delegates arrive tomorrow for the reception at Government House, before the talks start. There must be what, a dozen, legitimate courier companies in the city? And that does not count the independents and more questionable actors. We do not have time to chase down every courier in the city."

"Perhaps we could approach it from the other side, so to speak?" Jinhao stirred in her seat. "The poison would require an Alchemist, to make it in the strength we are thinking of. I know of one that may have heard of something. What time is it?"

Owen took out his pocket watch. He peered at it in the gloom of the cab.

"Just on seven of the clock."

"Excellent." Jinhao nodded. "He should just be opening for the night."

Owen snapped shut the watch,

"An Alchemist who keeps night hours? Very good, let's go pay her a visit."

"Him," Jinhao corrected. "We should stop at home first, and change into clothing that is a bit less...respectable. His shop is in Joy Luck Street."

Owen pursed his lips.

"In that case, much less respectable, I should think."

The Street of Joy and Luck was only a short distance away from where they had started their day at the embassy on Main Street, but the contrast could not have been greater. Just as the dignified stone buildings along Main Street were turning off their lamps and emptying out, the less grand wooden facades on the Street of Joy and Luck were opening.

By the time Owen and Jinhao disembarked from their cab, anonymous in hooded night cloaks, the street was bustling with people seeking various vices and pleasures, as well as the swindlers, pickpockets, and toughs who preyed on them.

The crowd was from a dozen nations and empires. As Owen followed in Jinhao's wake, a group of uniformed Russian sailors staggered past, roaring out a song which they marked time to by waving bottles in their hands, splashing the unwary with spirits. A pair of Azteca nobles stalked the street, resplendent in bright colored feather capes and tall headdresses; those passing by gave them plenty of space.

Another group of high-fashion British ladies flounced by in daring costumes, laughing, all of them wearing little more than body paint, together with the many-tiered skirts inspired by the recent excavations on Minos. Owen thought he even spied a live snake on one lady's arm.

From overhead, the paper lanterns shone in the open fronts of buildings, spilling light in an array of different glowing colors across the pedestrians, while barkers vied with street musicians for the attention of passers-by.

Some of the more expensive establishments had hired freelance Sorcerers, who filled the air in front of their doors with moving illusions that beckoned people to come within.

A rich fog of incense, hemp and tobacco mixed with alcohol and perfumes hung over the street like a fragrant cloud.

Jinhao turned abruptly down an alley way. They passed various colorful people, conducting the kinds of business usually conducted in such places. When the inhabitants saw they were neither constables nor interested, they calmly went back to their transactions.

Jinhao turned into a narrower alley way which broadened into a trash-filled area with a door lit by a single lantern. Jinhao turned to Owen.

"Roberet is a Frankman," she said in a low voice. "He is suspicious of all the British. It may be best if you allow me to do most of the talking." Owen shrugged.

"He's your contact, I follow your lead. Although if he's like most Franks I've met, for the Gods' sake try to come to the point in under an hour, and remember that we are not made of money."

The ghost of a smile touched her lips.

"He does go on, it is true. I doubt, however, that coin will be an issue."

With Jinhao still in the lead, they entered the Alchemist's shop. Owen looked around. It looked like most Alchemist shops, with tall shelves lined with bottles that were filled with mysterious ingredients. The shelves lined the walls, and an unpronounceable smell filled the close air. At the far end of the narrow shop, a bas relief of the five Chinese elements dominated the wall, with the usual stained wooden counter below it. What was unusual was the dark-haired Chinese man, in street wear, behind it. No Alchemist's robes, or amulets on this one. He looked to Owen as if he'd be more at home in the alley they had just passed through than in the shop. He also didn't look as if he was happy to see customers at all.

The man watched them unspeaking until Jinhao stopped a few feet away from him.

"We are looking for Roberet," she said in lower dialect Mandarin, "Tell him it is an old friend from Barley."

The man's eyes shifted from Jinhao to Owen and back again.

"Roberet isn't here now. You should come back tomorrow."

This clearly wasn't what Jinhao was expecting. She frowned at the man and tried again, with more force.

"Tell him it is an old friend from Barley." She followed this with a hand gesture that was so atypical that Owen was certain it was a recognition sign of some kind.

When they had met, Owen had asked if she had any current Imperial entanglements that he should be concerned about. When she had said no, perhaps he should have asked if there were other entanglements as well.

He knew that she was an Adept, and that Chinese Adepts were under the will of the Chinese Imperial Court, on pain of death. There were no freelancers. That meant that she was a runaway, or something similar, at least.

Jinhao had hinted only that she was fleeing romantic troubles in the North. The few comments that she had given indicated she had no love for the current Imperial Court, ruled over by the Dowager Empress. At the same time, she had been scathing about the various rebel movements stirring the pot, both here and in the kingdom.

She was good company for an embittered Sorcerer, and he instinctively trusted her. He was good with his instincts. He suspected that she would say much the same about him, even though both of them clearly had secrets. Owen could be comfortable with secrets.

The man again shifted his eyes from her to Owen, and back again. This time he gave an insincere smile and wiped his hand across his forehead in a clumsy counter-sign.

"Oh," the man said, still in gutter Mandarin, "The old friend from Barley." Owen restrained himself from rolling his eyes.

Surly Man, as Owen had decided to call him, opened the wooden gate that guarded the back of the store and pointed through a curtain.

"He is downstairs," Surly Man said, holding the gate open. As soon as Jinhao was through the gate, Surly Man slammed it shut in front of Owen.

"Not you," he said in English. He gave Owen a stony stare that Owen was sure was supposed to be intimidating. "That a problem?"

Owen twitched aside his cape, revealing his cane. He adopted an attitude of casual waiting as he leaned on it. Owen watched Surly Man's eyes flicker down to the cane, and saw his body stiffen. Owen smiled at him. Surly Man recognized the cane for what it was.

"No problem at all," he reassured Surly Man cheerily, also in English. He looked past Surly Man to Jinhao. "Have a nice time dear. One hour please, and remember what else I said."

Jinhao rounded on Surly Man in hissed Mandarin, "I vouch for this man! He is to come as well!"

Surly Man hissed right back,

"Things are different now! You want to see Roberet, this is how it is!"

Owen pretended not to understand a word of what they were saying. Sometimes it was a good thing to be under-estimated. Jinhao looked to Owen,

"I am sorry for his rudeness," she said in English. "I will be back shortly for you."

Owen waved a hand, and settled himself for the wait.

"Really, it is alright. I shall wait here. Mind what I said though!"

With a nod she went through the curtain while Surly Man held it open. Another man, big with muscle just going to fat, squeezed through from the other side, passing her by. He looked belligerently at Owen. Owen decided he would call him Burly Man. Surly Man spoke with Burly Man for a moment then Surly Man also vanished behind the curtain.

Yes, it was a good thing to be under-estimated some-times, Owen reflected. He was certain that if Surly Man knew Owen spoke Mandarin, he would have been much quieter when ordering Burly Man to wait a count of one thousand before killing him.

Chapter 9

Jinhao had known that there was something wrong from the moment that the stranger behind the counter had tried to send her away.

Perhaps she should have left then, but she held that Roberet was a friend, and if he was in trouble, she would help. Cautiously she stepped down the wooden stairs towards what appeared to be a storage cellar, a single hanging mage light trying, in vain, to banish the murky shadows. The clerk from upstairs was behind her.

Focusing her will, she heard the breathing of six, no, seven men hiding among the crates. One of them apparently knew how to watch his breathing. Even if they all possessed guns, she judged that an encounter would be within her capabilities. She then heard the clerk draw an edged weapon, probably a knife, from inside his tunic. Instead of turning, she continued to play along as expected, pausing on the bottom step to turn back in apparent confusion.

"Where is Roberet?"

The clerk brandished his knife in her face.

"Keep walking," he snarled. "Right out into the middle of the room." If she took the knife away from him, broke his arm and then smashed in his ugly face, she might never learn the fate of Roberet. Instead, she remembered to look startled, and then, turning quickly, scampered to the center of the room.

Once she was under the mage light, shapes appeared from out of the shadows that resolved into hard-faced men holding weapons of different kinds, swords, knives, and clubs. One of the men in a black tunic and pants, holding a saber, stepped fully into the light, regarding her with dead eyes.

"What is this," he asked the clerk with a jerk of his head towards her.

"She came in with a *Quizi* Sorcerer, and asked for Roberet shameless as could be," the clerk replied. "I figure them both for spies." The other men stirred at his words, muttering. "We should leave here now; they may have the place already surrounded."

Saber wielder silenced the others with a single gesture. His saber flowed up from his side until the edge was on line with Jinhao's neck while he edged forward.

"Is this true," he demanded. "Have you brought the *Quizi* here?"

Jinhao regarded the man. Not only the leader, but he had instilled a measure of discipline in the others. She approved. From his movements, she would judge that he had some training in one of the northern sword schools, but not training in the military, and certainly not from an Adept school. She decided to stop playing the game.

"Not all foreigners are *Quizi*," she replied levelly. "He is a friend. I have already given your man here the recognition signs, which should be enough. Where is Roberet?"

The leader must have seen something in her eyes. His stance shifted from a careless 'let's threaten the girl' pose to a ready fight stance. Neither his eyes, nor the sword, moved away from her. Calmly, he turned to the clerk.

"Is this so? Did she give you the recognition signs?"

"She did give me the signs for the thieves," the clerk sputtered, "But not our signs. Why are we wasting time talking? Let us kill the spying bitch, and get out of here!"

"Wait," the voice came from the shadows. Jinhao figured that it must belong to the one who knew how to regulate his breathing. She was surprised when a swarthy foreigner stepped into the light. He was gaudily dressed in red and green striped pants, with high boots and a black vest. A sky jack then, one who crewed a sky ship.

Around his hips were strapped two aether guns in cross-draw holsters. Jinhao took in the expensive weapons, including a bandolier of the faintly glowing reloads and revised her estimate. Not merely crew, she surmised, but most likely a captain, and a successful one at that.

"If she has the signs, then she might be one of ours," the man said. He stopped at the edge of the circle of light, hands resting easily on his gun belt.

"Do you recognize her," asked the leader.

"No," the sky jack replied easily. "But that means nothing. I will call for Madame, and we should also gather in her companion. There may be a misunderstanding here."

"Too late for the *Quizi*, I told Fat to kill him." The clerk snapped while hopping from foot to foot. "I tell you—Ahuggh!"

Whatever else the clerk might have told them was cut off by Jinhao's right sword spearing into his throat. She pivoted in a blur of speed, the blade ripping free in a spray of blood, while her left blade severed the weapon hand of the man next to him. The leader was still struggling to free himself from the folds of Jinhao's night cloak, with which she had entangled him.

The sky jack was uncommonly fast, she noticed. He had already drawn his aether-guns, though he had not yet brought them to bear. She gathered herself to execute a forward roll that would bring her upright inside his aim and within reach of her blades. Killing the surly clerk first had been an indulgence she hoped not to regret.

She was a muscle twitch from starting the roll, when the sky jack shouted in surprise and dropped his guns as if they had become suddenly too hot to hold. Around her, cries of shock were accompanied by the clatter of weapons hitting the floor.

Owen had arrived.

She spared a glance at the stairs. Owen stood on the steps, illuminated by a blue glow from his cane jewel on the one hand, and a bright, flickering of flames between the fingers of his other hand.

"No one moves unless you wish to taste the flames," he shouted in Mandarin, fingers weaving bright patterns in menace.

No one moved.

He spared Jinhao a smile and a greeting in English.

"There you are Jinhao! It seems that your friends play somewhat rough." He nodded towards the men still gripping their hands in pain.

Jinhao spent a heartbeat in marvel at the control he exhibited. She knew Western Sorcerers could call up elements such as fire. To direct that fearsome force such that it heated the weapons alone required discipline that was seldom seen.

Straightening up in a centering move, she flicked her blades clean of blood, allowing herself to show a smile back at him. He did indeed look like a foreign demon, standing on the shadowed stairs, with fire light flickering over his face.

Though she knew what effort it took him to work such Magia, he appeared completely relaxed.

"They are hardly my friends," she replied also in English. "In fact, I have not been properly introduced to any of them." She gestured with a sword at the defeated enemies. "Stand over there, where we can see you all," she ordered. The cowed men shuffled obediently into a line.

The leader, who had finally freed himself from her cloak, snarled at her, spittle running down his chin as he held onto his burned hand.

"Traitorous sow," he spat in Mandarin. "It matters not whether you are paid by that foul harridan who calls herself Empress, or by the foreign demons themselves! Your day will come! The people will be free!" He vowed.

Jinhao looked at him coolly. "I should have known that only someone as stupid as a revolutionary would seek to kill based on association alone. We care nothing for your politics, nor are we with the Pinchers." She raised her swords slightly. "Although should you ever again imply that I am a minion of the monster that warms the throne, you shall be a head shorter, I promise you." The man went silent, glaring hatred. "Now," she demanded briskly, "Where is Roberet?"

"Jinhao," Owen interrupted. "There are others entering the room from the back."

"He is safely with me," came a voice from the darkness. Jinhao knew that voice, though she did not expect to hear it here. A Chin woman stood at the edge of the light, a pair of sabers in her hands. She looked at Jinhao with no more recognition than Jinhao hoped she reflected back.

"It is all right Owen," Jinhao cried out. "These are my friends."

"I have many armed fighters at my back," the woman said. Jinhao could hear them as they attempted to pad silently into the room, while keeping to the deeper shadows. "They will shoot you all down where you stand." The woman looked up at Owen. "Put down your cane, Sorcerer."

Owen grinned at her, his face shadowed like a skull. The woman was bold, he'd give her that. No Sorcerer would willingly be parted from their Focus. It didn't matter how many elemental marks were bound into the skin, without a Focus a Sorcerer was helpless to call on them.

"Oh, I rather think not," he returned. "You could tell your people to put down their guns. Even air rifles can be made to explode, you know."

The woman's head swiveled to the foreign skyjack. "I hope you can explain this Rodrigo."

"Madame," the sky jack began, "I was just having a discussion with Senor Liu here."

127

"You were attempting to rob us in our hour of glory!" The leader of the rebels shouted.

"Be silent." The woman had command in her voice. "You show a remarkable lack of awareness for your position. I will come to you." She turned back to the sky jack. "Continue."

The sky jack bowed his head to her.

"As you wish, Madame," he acknowledged. "As I was saying, I was discussing things with Senor Liu when one of his men brought in the young woman with the swords. He said that she was a spy, even though she knew our recognition signs, and he intended to kill both her and her Sorcerer companion there." He gestured at Owen.

"I was attempting to stop this folly when the young woman took matters into her own hands, so to speak. That is Liu's man over there without his head." He indicated the bloody body on the floor.

"At that point, the Sorcerer entered the discussion with the trick of making all our weapons too hot to hold." The sky jack made a shrugging motion with his hands. "That was how things stood when Madame entered." He looked up at Owen, "That was an impressive trick."

"Thank you," Owen returned with a slight bow. "I have plenty more I can show you if need be," flames still flickering between his fingers.

"That should not be necessary," 'Madame' replied. She turned towards Liu. "Is what he says true, Liu? Are you really that stupid?"

"It is true that Yang brought her down here," Liu protested in Mandarin. "But I was still making sure of things. This was my meeting and my responsibility. We cannot be too careful when we are so close."

"Oh shut up," Madame snapped. "You are close to nothing. And you can speak English, it won't sully your mouth." She held up her free hand. "Wait, I have reconsidered that. Do not speak at all, just leave. Our association is at an end."

Liu opened his mouth, appeared to reconsider, and then opened it again, looking like a fish.

"Let us take our weapons at least. And there is one dead man, and one maimed one to be accounted for."

Madame raised her sabers.

"Count yourself lucky I let you leave with your heads. As for your men, as you say, your meeting, your responsibility. Now go, before I lose all patience and forget how inconvenient killing you would be!" Madame looked up at Owen, still poised on the stairs.

"Master Sorcerer, would you, of your kindness, please come down from the stairs so that these men may leave?"

At a slight nod from Jinhao, Owen snuffed the flames between his fingers.

"Of course," he replied. He sauntered down the steps and stood near Jinhao as the woeful group of revolutionaries marched up the stairs, Madame's men prodding them along with the barrels of their military-grade rifles.

Soon, only Jinhao and Owen faced the sky jack and the woman he had called Madame. Jinhao was very aware that at least two of her men had faded back into the shadows. It was likely that even now, Owen and she were targeted by hidden weapons.

"I understand that you are seeking Roberet," the woman said. It was not a question, though Jinhao chose to answer it as if it were.

"Yes," Jinhao replied. "I am called Jinhao. My friend and I need to speak with him on a matter totally unrelated to what just happened."

The skyjack bent to retrieve his aether-guns in one fluid motion, with both guns holstered by the time he came erect. He looked at Owen.

"That was a very impressive trick. I am Rodrigo de Vega, Captain of the *Windfahr*. Who do I have the honor of addressing?"

Owen bowed, and stood easily, facing Rodrigo.

"I am Owen Strong. I apologize if my 'trick' as you call it, caused you any discomfort, Captain. In my defense, I was rather hurried. I would never seek to make an enemy of so renowned a pirate as yourself."

Rodrigo stroked his moustaches at this, nodding.

"I prefer to call myself a free trader. Likely you are confusing me with my famous cousin, Rafael." He shrugged his shoulders. "It is a common mistake. But I assure you, no apologies are needed. There is no shame in being tricked by the renowned Lord Strong of the Britannic Empire."

"You are generous Captain," Owen replied. "But I fear that you may be confusing me with my brother, who is Lord Strong of Strong. I have little renown compared to either my brother, or my late father."

De Vega smiled at him.

"Ah, it can be so confusing who is who in these strange lands, yes? Still, I am honored to make your acquaintance, Lord Strong."

"The honor is mine, Captain de Vega," Owen returned with a similar smile.

"If you two peacocks are quite finished shaking your tail feathers, perhaps you, Rodrigo, could show Lord Strong to Roberet," the regal woman ordered. "I wish to have discussion with this Jinhao for a moment."

"Forgive me," Owen said to her before the Captain could respond. "But I wish to thank you for your intervention. I believe you know who I am, but I have not had the pleasure..."

The woman's face broke into what may have been a smile.

"Have you not? Well, know that I am called Ching Shih. Perhaps you have heard of my renown?"

Owen bowed to her deeply.

"Everyone has heard of the renown of Ching Shih, even in distant London. The Captain of a Thousand Ships is the most renowned, ah, free trader in the world."

Ching Shih laughed out loud at this.

"I am called pirate from Vladivostok to Siam, Lord Strong. I have no fear of the word, or little else. Still, I thank you for your manners. Now, please Lord Strong, go with Rodrigo. We shall follow presently." Jinhao nodded at him.

"It is all right, Owen," Jinaoi said.

The Sorcerer raised an eyebrow at her, but simply nodded. Jinhao knew by the light in his eyes that there would be questions later.

As the two men went off, escorted by the men hidden in the shadows, Ching Shih cradled her swords in her arms and regarded Jinhao.

"You are supposed to be at the Emperor's Court, last I heard. Now I find you here with a foreign Sorcerer. Grandfather must be beside himself."

Jinhao sheathed her own swords in the scabbards across her back. She bent to retrieve her night cloak. She examined it, finding it still wearable.

"Listen to you," Jinhao retorted. "As if you ever cared what Grandfather thinks, O Pirate Queen." She fastened the cloak around her shoulders, adjusting it so that she could draw the blades easily.

"The Emperor is a boy in a man's body. The Dowager has seen to that," Jinaao stated. "I doubt that there is much I could do there, as a mere bodyguard and concubine. I have had another idea. Grandfather will have to come up with something else if he does not agree. He always does."

"True," Ching Shih sighed. "That is why he is Grandfather. Still, it is good to see you, it has been too long..." The older woman shifted her sabers to the crook of one arm, holding out her other towards Jinhao. "Come, I will take you to Roberet. He has been working on something for me."

Jinhao smiled back, taking her sister's arm.

"It is good to see you as well, my sister. But seriously, working with political revolutionaries?"

Ching Shih sighed again as they walked arm in arm.

"It seemed a good idea. But I fear there will only come trouble from those fools. I will tell you more about it." The two women leaned their heads together as they walked towards the hidden entrance. "But first, tell me more about this foreign Sorcerer," Ching Shih said.

"Ah, I believe our meeting was guided by Heaven's Fortune, and the seed of my idea," Jinhao replied. "He is most impressive and agreeable. I have convinced Owen that

I must repay a life debt for his saving me by killing a Demon. I believe it was sent by someone in the Dowager's Court."

"He killed a court Demon? That is impressive," Ching Shih agreed. She frowned. "But there is no life debt custom among us, and certainly not with foreigners."

"He doesn't know that," Jinhao replied blandly. "He is a foreigner."

The older sister looked at her for a moment in surprise, and then they both burst out laughing.

Chapter 10

The Frank Alchemist Roberet droned on and on in his terrible Anglic about what prominent Alchemists his family had been in Paris, how the tragedy of the Austrian invasion had forced him to flee to this forsaken place, and how impossible it was to find a decent wine, let alone a good cup of coffee.

Owen pretended to listen to this monologue while nervously watching the little man bustle from one glowing glass vial to another.

The sky ship captain, de Vega, had left in a great hurry after depositing Owen in a chair at the Alchemist's laboratory. Owen wished he could have gone with him. The little Alchemist, Roberet, was clearly in the midst of a working, moving from one task to another. Occasionally he would interrupt his own monologue to lift a beaker of swirling colors, sniff it, and then dump it into a larger container floating over a blue flame. Owen tugged at his collar nervously.

Magica was generally divided in the West into Sorcery and Alchemy. Both required an inborn Talent, but otherwise they were governed by different principles. While Sorcery required that the Talented create a blood-bond with an elemental power, and use an external Focus such as his cane to manifest those powers, Alchemists could use their Talent in combination with various ingredients to create manifestations that were more or less permanent. The manifestations created by Alchemists could then be used by anyone, whether or not they were Talented themselves. Alchemical elixirs, for example were in high demand both to cure diseases and improve health.

Others in the Alchemical discipline had begun branching out, creating new materials, such as the super strong and light materials that the bigger sky ships were made of. They even created the aetheric fluids that enabled a weapon to shoot an elemental force, rather than depend on compressed air to fire a projectile.

Alchemists kept their processes a closely guarded secret, and shared those secrets only with each other.

Owen knew that Alchemical Workings required as much, if not more, concentration as spell work did. He also knew that disrupting the Will of an Alchemist during a working courted catastrophe. The few times Owen had seen Alchemists at work, they had all been very silent, intensely concentrated and precise. Roberet was not at all like that.

Roberet splashed another vial into his floating container, sending glowing globules everywhere. The ugly little man looked more like a mad baker mixing a cake, than like someone altering the physical structures of the material world. He could only hope the Frank wouldn't combine the wrong things, while talking incessantly, and blow them sky high or worse. It had been known to happen.

When the door opened again, Ching Shih, the Pirate Queen as she was called in the broadsheets, entered side by side with Jinhao. Owen noticed that the two seemed very comfortable together, as if this was not their first meeting. He filed that information away for the moment, but he vowed that he and his companion would have words later.

Roberet looked up at the intrusion, and slammed a beaker down on his worktable, approaching Jinhao with a wide grin on his ugly face.

"My little flower," he exclaimed, throwing his arms wide. "Don't touch the apron dear. The mess on it might turn your skin green," he warned. Jinhao returned his smile and the two carefully exchanged kisses on both cheeks.

"Roberet," Jinhao said lightly, "It has been too long."

"It has indeed," the Frank replied. "Oh," he said holding up a gauntleted finger, "Give me a moment to take this off the boil." He shuffled back to the work table and glanced into the floating container.

"Yes," he muttered to it, "We'll just let you cool now for a time." Picking up a pair of tongs he moved it off the flame, where it continued to float in the air over the table.

"Your Aetheric fluid should be ready in a day or so now, Mistress Ching," he said. "I have created a new method that will allow me to mix the base into a larger matrix, which should be enough for that big cannon of yours."

"Pardon me," Owen said through a tightened throat. "Did you just say that you were creating enough Aetheric fluid to power cannon?" So far as Owen knew aetheric weapons were limited in size by the amount of Fluid they required. While he'd seen pistols and rifles, common wisdom held that anything bigger was simply too costly and unstable to fuel. Not even the British Navy had Aether cannons; Battle Sorcerers had compressed air cannon, clockwork ballistae and catapults, but not Aetheric cannons. The implications were as unsettling as the monstrous weapons of the Austrians.

"Oh yes, Mistress Ching Shih had been most generous in funding the experiment," Roberet said, peeling off his heavy gauntlets. "It is only a Fire manifestation you know, and that is only the concentrate there," he nodded towards the container. "You could simply load it into a big gun and get nothing more than a burp at the moment." He paused, as if realizing the growing silence in the room. "Oh, perhaps I should not have said anything?"

"It is alright Roberet," the Pirate Queen, Ching Shih said, "Although we can talk more of this later." She fixed her gaze on Owen. "Jinhao and her friend are not here about that. I am certain Lord Strong here is aware that one little experiment with one little gun is not worth mentioning."

Owen nodded slowly. The British military would dearly love to know about such a capability he was sure.

"Perhaps, perhaps not. If you can answer my condition I can perhaps be a gentleman about it."

Ching Shih's lips tightened at his words.

"You are bold for one whose life is in my hands."

Owen smiled at her from where he sat.

"I've been told that before. Yet, here I am. While I don't work for Her Majesty's government, that does not mean I am not still a loyal subject."

Ching looked at Jinhao with a grim smile.

"I may like him, if I do not kill him first." Turning back to Owen she frowned at him. "Very well, state your condition."

"I want your word that you do not plan to use this thing either to aid the rebels in disrupting Hong Kong, nor that you plan to use it against Her Majesty's armed forces."

"That is two conditions," the Pirate Queen corrected. "As to the first, I have no plans to aid those bumbling fools you met earlier today. That was a miscalculation I will not repeat. As to the second," she shrugged. "I do not plan to ever attack anyone's Navy. If they are stupid enough to get in my way, I will fight them however I must. Does that word of a yellow-skinned woman meet your conditions, Lord Strong?"

Owen bowed in agreement at her words.

"Then I think I will be a gentleman about it. That is, if you can trust the word of a pale skinned foreigner," he replied archly.

The Pirate Queen threw back her head and laughed. "I think I will like you and not kill you!" She turned back to Jinhao, "I leave you to your business." With that, the woman swept from the room, leaving the three of them alone.

Roberet motioned Jinhao to take the other chair in the room.

"Well, that was uncomfortable," he remarked with concern. "I hope it does not lose me Mistress Ching as a client. She pays so well." He looked at Owen with suspicion. "Are you really here with this Britisher, little flower?"

"Yes," Jinhao replied as she settled into the chair. "We are looking into a number of deaths that we believe were caused by application of Tesarine oil. I thought you would know which Alchemist in the city could make something strong enough to do this." Jinhao described the nature of the wounds they had found, together with their suspicions.

Roberet stared into space for a moment, then shook his head.

"No, that makes no sense. Tesarine is too weak on its own to do what you describe. Mostly it is the by-product of refining the curie plant from Southern Azteca, which is then sold to duelists seeking an advantage." He smiled at them both.

"Alchemists like to squeeze every drop, so to speak, from everything. The curare plant is both difficult to obtain and very expensive." He frowned. "The main product of the plant is deadly enough when rendered, although it has a short life, and must be entered into the blood stream to work." He frowned again, "But, if you have the plant itself why not simply use that, or pick something else entirely?"

"How would one use this plant rendering?" Owen asked curiously. Using poisons was forbidden among the various operatives in the Great Game of Nations including his old Order. It was one of the unspoken agreements that Owen had never really understood; dead was dead as far as he was concerned. You could kill a target any number of ways, from Sorcery to a knife, to tricking someone into falling off a cliff. However, using a poison would call down such retaliation on the agent and their colleagues that it wasn't worth it. Owen had not realized that the custom left such a gap in his knowledge of dealing death.

"The usual means is to dip a dart or other projectile in the rendered liquid, and then use the implement to pierce the skin. Poison will not work unless it enters the blood," Roberet mused. "The little people of the Azteca rain forests use it this way with their blow guns. You can put it on a blade, but it does not last long when exposed to air or water."

Now it was Owens turn to frown, "There were no darts or projectiles found either in or near the bodies."

"Perhaps a needle of some kind," Roberet suggested. "Something attached to a ring perhaps?"

"No," Owen objected forcefully. "Think about it. Our killer has a very thin needle in his hand which is awkward enough. They must then either thrust it into the chest," Owen gestured. "Or if it is on a ring, they have to do either this," he made a slapping motion, "or this," he punched with a fist. "All the while in public, with no one remarking on such extraordinary actions. In the case of Sir Hastings, they would not only have to strike him, but then Sir Hastings carries a courier tube into the foyer, without raising an alarm, before collapsing. No," Owen shook his head, "there is something we are missing here, something clever and diabolical."

Roberet made a very Frankish gesture with his hands. "I can tell you that very few private Alchemists could afford such a substance, and my—sources—would have advised me if they were bringing any curie plant into the country, if only to see if I would out bid their original order maker. There is little honor among such people."

"I presume by sources you are referring to smugglers," Owen said.

"Think of them rather as free traders," Roberet suggested. "While the trading companies do some 'extra cargo' they do not carry such things, as a rule."

"Then we are back to the beginning," Jinhao remarked.

"Perhaps not," Owen said. "Roberet, is there anything that makes this Tesarine oil different from the more powerful rendering, whatever you call it?"

"In the Frank lands, we call it curare," the Alchemist replied. His frown turned his ugly features even more demonic. "Unlike curare, Tesarine can be made into a salt form, as it does not lose efficiency if you either boil or freeze it, but no one has found a use for the salts yet." He shook his head. "That is the only difference I can think of, besides it being much less potent than curare." He turned to Jinhao, "I am sorry I cannot be of more help to you and your friend, little flower."

Jinhao rose, and Owen followed her lead, also standing.

"You have helped greatly, old friend," she said to him. "I shall come again when I may."

The answering grin cracked the ugly mask into something that seemed more humane.

"You are always welcome here, little flower, even if you bring the stinking Britisher." He swiveled towards Owen. "You think what I do in my experiments with Mistress Ching is evil, Britisher?"

"I think that we have enough ways to kill each other in job lots as it is, yes. If you wish to call that evil then you may do so," Owen replied.

"You will have cause to thank Roberet, before long, Britisher," the Alchemist grimaced. "You think what I do is evil? You did not see the black Austrians destroy my beautiful Paris. Their weapons lit the sky day and night, causing such great explosions that whole blocks were wiped from the ground in the blink of an eye."

Owen had been in Hong Kong when the Austrian armies had marched into the Frank lands, supposedly to spread their Marian faith. Unfortunately for the Franks, that meant you either accepted their religion, or you died. He'd heard little about it, save what the regular news sheets reported, which he largely ignored as unreliable.

"Then you are saying that the Austrians already have these aether cannon you are creating," Owen ventured.

Roberet laughed, if such a tragic sound could be called that.

"Oh no. What the demons have is much worse. They have the means to shoot projectiles at you with great speeds over far distances. You can see the shells distort the very air in passing, they travel so fast. Our Sorcerers could not stop them. It is not elemental, no. Perhaps if you Sorcerers could meld your powers all together, instead of one by one, maybe you stop them, but I think that big Fire cannons are a real start to fighting the black Marian scum. Soon, not even your mighty White Isle is safe from them. You watch, the Austrian will change everything!"

Owen regarded him gravely. He already knew the Austrian evil, even if his former superiors had not listened to his warnings. "I fear you already may be right," he said sadly.

Chapter 11

They did not see either the Pirate Queen or Captain de Vega again.

Instead a much closed-mouthed member of a sky ship crew, judging by her gaudy dress, showed them out the front door. As they stood outside the door, Owen peered at his vest watch by the lantern's light. They had been in there barely two hours. The din from the Street of Joy and Luck had swelled in volume since they had entered the store. Well, time flew when you were busy, or so his father had always said.

Jinhao edged closer to him.

"There is something that I must tell you," she spoke low as if feared that they might be over-heard even over the near-by street noise.

Owen smiled at her, her face highlighted by the single lantern's glow in their little cul-de-sac.

"Only one thing," he remarked with a raised eyebrow. "I believe that there are a few more than that. For instance, I never knew you had such *interesting* acquaintances."

Was Jinhao actually ducking her head in embarrassment? Owen couldn't be sure, perhaps it was merely a trick of the uncertain light.

"Yes, that is another matter to discuss," she admitted. "This is much more important. Ching Shih told me that the revolutionaries we met tonight plan to kill everyone at the trade reception tomorrow night. They plan to start some kind of rebellion against the Chinese Imperium, using the city as a rallying point."

"Damn them all to the Black Wood," Owen said tiredly. "Did our gracious hostess also tell you how they plan to do this? While we are on the subject, why should we believe anything the Pirate Queen says to us?"

"You may believe her always. I do." Jinhao proceeded to relay the plans Ching Shih had shared with her. The rebels had placed themselves as extra servants hired for the reception, intending to smuggle in weapons. At a certain time in the evening they intended to strike, killing everyone.

"Simple, and bloody effective," Owen muttered. The reception would have all the officials of the joint-city government present, as well as all the diplomats, influential families, and junior bureaucrats, not to mention the trade delegates themselves.

What the stupid idiots failed to see, is that far from starting some romantic revolution against the Dowager Empress, such a thing would call down the wrath of every powerful nation in the world. The nations would have to retaliate to such an atrocity, likely sparking the very world war that Partridge feared. Owen felt the weight of it settle on his shoulders.

"Come on," he said in a morose tone, "Let us go home."

"But what shall we do?" Jinhao fell into step beside him. Together they turned out of the cul-de-sac and began threading their way past the denizens of the alley conducting their business. They joined the stream of the bustling profane crowds on the Street of Joy and Luck, moving slowly towards the cross street where cabs and other conveyances waited to ferry the revelers.

Owen gave a great sigh.

"To answer your question, Jinhao," he said at last, 'I really do not have a clue." He gripped his cane in anger by the haft, pushing his way through the crowd, Jinhao kept to his side by the clever use of her elbows. Others began getting out of the way of the grim-faced Sorcerer, recognizing the red metal cane and what it meant. Sorcerers were almost a law onto themselves in Hong Kong. While the city police would make a Sorcerer answer for any mayhem they might do, it would be of little comfort to the victims of that mayhem afterwards.

The threads of a simple tune pierced Owen's brown study. He stopped abruptly, head coming up like a hound looking for the source of the music. Ignoring Jinhao's question, he started pushing through a knot of people that had clustered around one of the vagabond musicians that littered the street. When he reached the front he stopped and stared at what he saw.

A young Chin dancer dressed in the popular idea of what passed for a Persian harem outfit stood stock still. Another countryman played a British pennywhistle behind her. The tune he played was one that Owen hadn't heard since he was a child, only then it was played by an old, red-haired Bard in the family great hall, when his father was still alive. The song was called Bridett's Answer, and as the tune wove its sweet melancholy air, the woman began to dance the story that went with it. So beautiful and precise were her movements that no words were needed. Owen would have followed the story even if he did not know it.

Bridett's heart's delight, the Lord Owen, was missing. Bridett searched high and low for him to no avail. No one, not King, nor Bard, nor Sorcerer could answer her as to where he might be. Unknown to mortal ken, Lord Owen had been secretly taken by the undead servants of the jealous Necromancer Mathin, spiriting him away to their shadowy realm, with only the birds to witness the deed. In desperation, Bridett asked the birds if they had seen her love.

The birds were so frightened of Mathin that they would not tell her what they had seen, all except for one brave wren, who told Bridett to follow him if she wished to know the truth of her lover. The wren led Bridett to the Dark Wood's edge, where she was met by one of the Shining

Folk, whose beauty is both awesome and terrible to those of mortal blood. The Shining One whispered to Bridett the fate of her love, sharing with her the secret knowledge by which he could be reclaimed, and placing in her hands a hammer.

Armed with her love, Bridett then went to where three streams danced in union and built there a forge, the flame of which she blew alight by the secret art of the Fair Folk. The birds gladly brought her the materials she asked for, being shamed by their earlier cowardice. The hammer belled in the forge both day and night, until the moon mother was full again. Then, with a tall thing like a staff wrapped in dark cloth she asked the wren to take her to the hidden place of Mathin.

Bridett was challenged by the evil Necromancer Mathin himself, at the doors of the Undead dwelling place. She unwrapped the coverings of the staff, to reveal that it was a shining spear made of red metal. Denouncing Mathin, she thrust the spear through him. The doorways of the undead broke open at Mathin's death, and Bridett pulled forth Lord Owen. The lovers embraced.

The Chinese dancer stopped as still as a statute once again, and the crowd sighed as one. The pennywhistle player began a jaunty sea chantey and the dancer deftly made a motion towards the basket set out for coin.

Owen reached for his coin purse as if in a dream and bent to place it in the basket. He knew now what he had to do, even though he had vowed to himself that he would never do it. He had to go to the edge of the Dark Wood and take counsel of the Shining Folk, or of a certain one of them at any rate.

The dancer's eyes caught Owen's as he stood up from the basket. For a moment, Owen would have sworn the girl's eyes were as blue as Bridett's were supposed to be in the tale. The dancer bowed in his direction.

"You are most generous, Lord." When she looked up again, Owen saw that her eyes were the dark brown he expected to see.

He shook himself and mumbled something about the greatness of her dancing. A British demi-goddess couldn't really look out of the eyes of a Chinese street girl, could she? Could she? He turned to find Jinhao looking at him. Something on his face must have drawn her concern for her forehead creased.

"Owen," she asked urgently, "what is it?"

Schooling his features, Owen gave her his best cocky smile.

"It is nothing, Jinhao," he assured her. "I now know what I must do next." He began pushing through the crowd. "Come on, let us go hire the means to be home."

There was none of their usual banter as the horse-drawn cab carried them across town. Owen stared out the window while Jinhao watched Owen in silence. Finally, as they were getting close to Owen's house, he stirred and looked at her.

"It would seem that our unspoken agreement regarding our separate past lives has become an obstacle."

"You wish to know about my relationship to Ching Shih," Jinhao said quietly. "Very well, she is my older sister."

Owen leaned forward, searching her face in the changing shadows of the cab. He was surprised by the answer. He'd expected Jinhao's usual dance of deflection.

"Do you mean she is your blood relative, or that you are both warrior women of action kind of sisters?"

"Yes," she replied. Now it was Jinhao's turn to look out the window.

After a moment Owen leaned back with a sigh, "Well," he remarked, "that must make family gatherings interesting."

Still looking out the window, she replied with a wry tone in her voice, "We have not had such a gathering in a long time."

Owen thought of his own family past. What was that saying about throwing stones while living in glass houses? Growing up the younger son in the house of the famous Lord Robert Strong, Protector of the Realm, also had its challenges; challenges that his older brother Richard had always been quick to point out that he, Owen, had failed at, a point of view which Owen could only agree with.

"Still," he said to her, "and I apologize for being so blunt, but now I must know. Are you involved in either her operations or the schemes of these rebels?"

"I have not seen my sister for some time," she answered directly. "I am sure seeing me today was as much a surprise for her as it was for me. She has chosen a different path from mine. As to those fools we encountered," Owen could almost hear her lip curl in the shadows, "while I feel the pain that has driven them to such a place, they are not—professional—enough for my taste."

A burst of light from the cab window illuminated her face, Owen had rarely seen it so impassioned.

"If you are asking me if the Empress should be thrown down, then yes, may boils devour her, she should! She is a vain monster whose touch corrupts all about it, and the throne has made her touch very long indeed." She leaned back in her seat, composing herself. "It is not really so different from the days of your King Richard. I have read some of your histories."

"Yes, well," Owen drawled. "Richard was an obsessive warlord and we were well rid of him. Amuiel should never have joined with his grandfather William when he came begging across the channel. The only good things ever to come out of Normandy are the wines and the cooking. Still, it took Elizabeth the First most of her reign to straighten it out. I hope we are past such foolishness now."

"Just so," Jinhao agreed. "We have also had our bad rulers. However, now we must also deal with the foreigners who support her. I doubt that we may simply send you all packing as you did the Normans."

"Do you wish we were gone, Jinhao?" He asked her softly.

"Why not ask me if I wish the sun to rise in the west, or water to flow uphill" she asked.

"You are here, and I doubt that your country folk will go away even should Lohan allow it. What is the point of such useless questions," she asked, exasperation clear in her voice.

Taken aback by the strength of her answer, Owen could only continue to seek clarity.

"I am seeking to know where your allegiances lie, Jinhao. In what I do next, it may matter."

"The answer to that, Owen Strong, is very simple. My allegiance lies with you," she said simply. "Where does yours lie Owen? Do you even know? And what is it that you will do now?"

The cab chose that moment to stop in front of the house. Owen smiled at her weakly.

"That last I may not tell you. Poor return for your trust I know, but know also that I mean to not have this city the center of a war if I can help it. As to the rest," he shrugged. "I would have answered that I am a subject of the Queen, but now, I honestly don't know." He peered out the window.

"And unless I am much mistaken we now have Lady Hastings awaiting our arrival home. How delightful."

Chapter 12

It turned out not only to be a night cloaked Lady Hastings, but her House Sorcerer as well.

Barton, in true clank man butler mode, had offered them hospitality, but MacAllister, the Sorcerer, had been reluctant to pass the threshold of another Sorcerer without Owen present, which was understandable. Not only was there ancient custom involved, but the Sorcerer might expect there to be traps set for the uninvited blood-bound who entered within.

Once past the awkwardness of Owen extending an invitation to Mistress MacAllister, which she flatly refused with a dour face, Owen escorted Lady Hastings to the parlor, leaving the Sorcerer outside.

Jinhao excused herself as soon as possible, leaving only Owen and the young heiress to be served tea by a whirling Barton.

After taking the obligatory sip from her cup, Lady Hastings spoke.

"I must apologize for Mistress MacAllister's behavior, Lord Strong. She has hardly been herself since Father's death. It is almost as if she blames herself for it, even though she did all she could."

"Thank you, Lady Hastings," Owen nodded, "but I assure you, no offense is taken. It is a trying time for you all."

"Thank you, My Lord," the young woman replied. She sat her cup down. "Now to the purpose of my visit. As father has been properly sent on, I wish to aid your inquiry into his murder."

"My Lady," Owen said carefully, "while I can appreciate your position, you must understand that there is more at stake here than avenging your father's death; more than that I cannot say."

"Such as thinking that more murders will be committed, possibly with the aim of disrupting the forthcoming trade negotiations" she asked archly, "or that you have already formed a plan to forestall them from occurring?" She gave a dark laugh for one who seemed so young, as she regarded Owen's blank face.

"Come now sir! I would be a poor Truthsayer if I could not discern the truth of what you do not say as well as what you do."

Owen pulled a cigarette from his case to hide his consternation. It was only after he had it alight that he spoke again.

"Your Gift is truly impressive, My Lady. Given that, I beg you to use it now when I tell you that involving yourself with my investigations would only place you in the gravest danger."

Lady Hastings cocked her head to one side.

"I wonder how you do that," she remarked, looking at Owen. "It is as if a veil has been drawn over you. I can sense only that you believe the Truth of your spoken words, but nothing else at the moment. How very interesting. Everyone lies you know," she stated matter-of-factly. "Even when they believe what they are saying is the Truth, there is always the tiniest voices inside them that whispers other things. But suddenly your voices are gone."

She shook herself as if to clean away something uncomfortable.

"But as for your assertion, I am well aware that it might be dangerous, yet I will not be denied my Funath!" Owen regarded her while silently running the disciplines the Obsidian order had trained him in against a Truthsayer. That she had used the word Funath, the old term for a House War against a wrong done to its honor, was, he knew, deliberate. She was appealing to his station and upbringing, a formidable argument in other circumstances. A pretty face alone she was not.

"Forgive me for asking, My Lady," he finally said, "but you are some seventeen or eighteen years of age?"

She straightened solemnly.

"I shall attain twenty summers this year if the gods are kind." Her cheeks colored. "I know that I should already be hand-fasted, but besides the considerations of the House, there are not many young men who appeal to me."

Owen finished his cigarette, stabbing it out on his tea saucer. Formidable indeed, he thought to himself. Owen could only imagine what she would be like at fifty, in the prime of her power.

"No, I imagine not. Very well, My Lady, I cannot stand in the way of Funath." He took a breath and considered her. "Tomorrow evening, there will be a reception for the trade delegates. I assume that you have an invitation already?" At her nod, he continued. "What I want you to do is listen to every person that is present. Note anything that may seem duplicitous, and signal me so." He raised two fingers of his right hand to his brow. "I will come as soon as I may."

Lady Hastings frowned. "This is hardly what I had in mind. If it is as every other reception I have ever attended, everyone present will be duplicitous, that is practically a given."

Owen raised an eyebrow at this.

"I did not say it would be easy Lady Hastings. What did you imagine, uncovering an overlooked clue, or skulking down dim alleyways, exchanging bullets and spells as if in some cheap novel?" The squaring of her shoulders told him that was exactly what she imagined.

"No, My Lady," he pressed on. "As you pointed out, this is something that only someone with your unique talents can supply. I can think of few tasks more dangerous, or more useful than bringing to me Truth at such a gathering." He stood up and Lady Hastings stood with him. "Can I count on your aid, My Lady?"

Lady Hastings squared her jaw, looking up at him. "You may, My Lord. I would plead with you only one boon, that I be present when the killer is denounced."

"I cannot grant you that," Owen answered truthfully. "There is still much to be worked out. But I may promise you that they will be denounced, and that you will be among the first to know."

The woman nodded her head sharply.

"Very well, My Lord. I will accept that for now. I also have another oddity for you. When you asked about the courier tube I inquired of the staff about it. "

Owen schooled his face at the news.

"And was there such a tube," he asked.

The young heiress frowned.

"Not that anyone has found." She reached into her evening bag, and held out her hand. "They did find this when they were cleaning up the area though. No one is sure what it is."

Owen took from her a small curved piece of metal. He also frowned at the strange thing.

"Do you believe it is important?"

Owen smiled at her.

"I am not sure, Lady Hastings, but it is precisely the sort of thing I had in mind for you to do. Can you keep the news of this quiet?"

"Why yes, if you think it best."

"That is all I can ask, My Lady," he replied. "As the hour is late, may I escort you out?"

As Owen escorted her out to her coach, the House Sorcerer grabbed his arm, holding him back. "Have you dissuaded her from this romantic foolishness of Funath?"

Owen looked at the older woman coldly.

"I suggest you ask your liege that, Mistress," he snapped shortly.

"Don't think I don't know what you're doing," she hissed at him as Lady Hastings called out to the coach men. "I will challenge you before I let you take my station in House Hastings, you nothing of a younger son!"

Owen raised his eyebrows in surprise. Was the woman mad, he thought to himself? There was no stretch of the imagination that would get him to consider such an idea.

"While I am sure your station is very fine, Mistress, I assure you I have no interest in it." Whatever answer the Sorcerer would have made to this was forestalled by Lady Hastings calling for her. Mistress MacAllister climbed into the coach without another word. Lady Hastings looked a question at Owen.

"I trust there is no difficulty?" she asked.

"Not at all, My Lady," Owen replied affably. Lady Hastings smiled at his response.

"I believe that is the first lie you have told me," she said cheerily, "Until tomorrow My Lord!" She bounded into the coach while Owen was still bowing. He watched as it clattered off downhill, then turned to go back inside, where he found Jinhao picking over the remains of the tea service.

"You did very well with her," she said as he entered the room. "That should keep her out from underfoot."

"Didn't anyone ever tell you that listening in on conversations uninvited can lead to you hearing something you don't want to hear? Here now, that's the last scone! I demand half." His hand swooped in and gathered up half of the scone she had just parted with a knife, wolfing it down.

"Yes they have," the Adept replied as she spread jam on her half scone. "And it has been my experience that the saying is often true." She paused to take a bite.

"That has saved my life more than once." She looked at Owen critically. "Has no one told you that eating too fast will cause you to choke to death?"

Owen was unabashed as he finished the crumbs of the very fine scone.

"Yes they have, and it hasn't yet," he quipped. He held up a finger. "Wait here a moment." He returned with a thick scroll, that Jinhao recognized as the type that told Barton, the clank man, what to do.

"Barton," Owen said walking up to the tall mechanical man, "Open for instructions please." The metal man shuddered in place, and a doorway unfolded in his chest. Owen threaded the scroll through a series of rollers and pins, then nodded. "Roll instructions and close, please." Barton shook again as the scroll began moving and the door closed.

Barton moved his head back and forth, as he processed the instruction set.

"Instructions for Beth-Lous-Non rolling Master Owen," he crackled, "Order of particulars please."

"The study, from one half hour from now, until I emerge," Owen said crisply. "All contingents are to be applied."

"Very good, Master Owen," Barton responded. "Shall I clear the service now?"

Owen smiled at him fondly.

"Yes Barton, thank you."

The cog man began to load the plates and cups onto the tray. Jinhao moved her legs as he did so, looking at Owen suspiciously.

"What are you doing?"

Owen hefted his cane, looking decidedly determined.

"Stopping a war, or at least trying to. I will retire to the study now. No matter what you may hear or see, do not under any circumstances try to enter it. Should Barton tell you to evacuate the house, do so at once, and do not try to stop him no matter how strange what he does may seem. Can you do this?"

"You are going to do some sort of spell working," she guessed, brushing the crumbs from her gown. "But it sounds very dangerous. Should I not also accompany you? I have for other workings of yours."

Owen regarded her seriously and shook his head in regret.

"I'm sorry, really, but no, not this time. I need to know that you will do as I ask. It will not only be dangerous for you to do anything else, but may also be dangerous for me. Can you do this?"

Jinhao nodded reluctantly.

"Yes, I can do as you ask, but I feel my swords should be there at your back."

"Believe me," Owen said earnestly, "There is nothing I would like more. But it simply isn't to be done. Do not be concerned. Most likely all this is mere precaution, and nothing will come of it."

"Perhaps," she returned, "But I do not think that you think so." Owen bent over her hand as gallantly as if they were at court. She felt his lips, cool and dry, against her skin.

"Oh", he said, straightening, "would you mind taking this to your Alchemist friend to see what he makes of it?" Owen held up the strange piece of metal that Lady Hastings had given him, passing it to her.

She regarded it in her palm.

"I think you are trying to get me away from whatever it is you're doing."

"Nonsense," Owen denied, "It might be important. Fare you well, Jinhao, and good night," he said softly and turned towards the study door. Her eyes followed his back until the door closed with a finality that seemed oddly disturbing. She was startled from her thoughts by the voice of Barton.

"Would Mistress Jinhao like more tea? Given the hour, I would suggest the green." The cog man stood inhumanly still, the filled tray poised in one metal hand.

Well, if Owen was going to do whatever it was he was doing, the least she could do would be to wait up for him.

"Do you know what he is doing?" she asked the metal man.

"I am sorry, Mistress," Barton buzzed, "but I do not understand the question."

No, of course you don't," she muttered darkly. She looked again at the metal shard. "I shall be going out Barton," she said, "however, tea when I return would be lovely. Thank you."

Chapter 13

Owen closed the study door, the ward sealing on its own, just as he had designed it to do, against such a day as today.

His eyes took in the shelves lined with books against the walls, the comfortable chair with the mage light on the end table. To be honest, he was simply stalling. He knew what he had to do. He removed his coat and tossing it on the chair, followed it with his cravat, in a splash of purple against black, and began unbuttoning his shirt.

The theories on the need to be naked to perform a Greater Working had always struck Owen as specious at best. If Magia was not inhibited by stone walls, he didn't see how mere cloth could stand in the way of his Will. In the same way, the notion that it added to the power by forming some connection to every Sorcerer in the past who had also gone bare skinned, did not really make sense to him either.

Owen suspected that the true reason was much the same as it was for Sorcerous dueling. It was impossible to hide mastery of an element if the blood-bond etched into the skin glowed when called upon. Normally invisible, the sigils would light with an inner fire on the Sorcerer's body, showing clearly what elemental forces they were bound to, and could call upon. No matter the truth of it, he wasn't about to ignore any of the forms tonight if he could help it.

Naked, he padded across the rich Persian carpet that covered the floor to the cabinet set into a bookcase. His Air sigil glowed faintly on his chest as he unknotted the spell lock on the door. Reaching within, he removed the electrum brazier, charcoal, and a small box of herbs, locking it again with a gesture and the power of Air.

Looking carefully at the pattern of the rug, he judiciously set the brazier at the rug's exact center and filled it. You could say what you would about the Persians, but they understood Sorcery. The rug had been made for exactly the kind of Working he was going to do tonight. It would save him hours of drawing lines in blood and herbs, in order to prepare to channel the energies he would call upon. When the brazier was filled, he crossed back to the chair, moving it so that was no longer on the rug, and picked up his cane. He faced a full length mirror that stood near the opposite wall from the chair.

In the mirror, he saw a tall man, dark of hair, beardless, and strong like his name, stare back at him. His arms were crisscrossed with faint scars from sword fights, with one along the left side of his chest from a fight he had nearly lost. His eyes looked back at him, shrouded and dark rimmed. He looked older than he remembered looking, and then banished such thoughts as he focused his inner power.

Unlike the slap-dash spell-slinging that made up every day Sorcery, this would require calling on the full extent of his powers, for what he intended was nothing less than the manifestation of a powerful being from another world.

Fire was the easiest to call and the hardest to control. He called to it, feeling the wild power of it fill his veins with heat. Burning suns and stars exploded across his vision, and he felt Fire's exaltation threaten to overwhelm his reason. Wrestling with it, he tamed the wildness to a warm glow ready to flare at his Will. He saw in the mirror the deep red bond glow to life just below his belly button, and breathed out as the glow steadied.

Water was next, to balance the Fire. He called out with his spirit, feeling the blood flow through his body, pulsing in rhythm to the currents of the deeps, mighty and rolling with all that had been and ever would be. He felt the powerful pulling that would drown him in its drum-beat, where he might be lost forever. Using a whisper of Fire, he brought the rhythm into harmony with his heartbeat. Looking into the mirror, he saw the flickering blue glow ignite just below his throat, and exhaled.

Air followed. He called to it, feeling a wind caress his skin in the closed room, the wind lifting his feet off the carpet. The rush of a million voices filled his ears, threatening him with madness. With a touch of Water, the voices dimmed, soothed by the compassion of the endless depths.

The sigil flared into golden light over his right breast and his feet touched the floor again at the winds' retreat.

Next he called upon Earth, feeling his body grow ever heavier. The low slow grumblings of the stone miles below him filled his bones, calling him to lay down with them, to claim the release they offered. A caress of Air buoyed him up with the knowledge that it was not time for him to yield to such a siren song. A deep emerald bond mark appeared over his left nipple as he exhaled.

Balanced between the Elements that made the World, he reached deep within to call upon Spirit, the Power that all the other elements flowed from, that held the very World in its center, as lightly as a grain of sand. His heart was flooded by the infinity of that power, and he longed to dance among swirling stars and endless blackness until he dissolved into the beauty of it all.

He called on all four Elements together and returned to gaze at the body in the mirror, seeing a brilliant design of white fire, lined in blackest black, spring from the center of his torso.

Before he would call on the next bond, he doused the Mage light in the ceiling with a hand, and covered the mirror with the black shroud that was rolled up on top of its frame. Mirrors could be windows to any Demon or Sorcerer that flew on the aether between the worlds. Owen had no desire to be either spied upon, or interrupted.

Turning to the brazier, he pointed at it with his cane, and the charcoal glowed into life, the special herbs sending up wisps of light as they gave up their essences to the heat. It was the smoke that would give the Other a means to anchor in this World.

Owen called upon the raw power of all five bonds and began speaking in the tongue of the Shining Ones, a language that human mouths could only speak with the greatest of difficulty. The sounds twisted the very air, booming off the walls of the study, then fell into whispers, only to surge in volume once again. Owen felt the corresponding bond respond to the Calling, burning like a brand on his forehead in its attempt to rend the walls between the Worlds. The tendrils of radiant smoke swirled together faster and faster as he spoke. With a final word, he thrust his cane to strike with a loud bang on the floor.

The smoke coalesced into a tall figure, more beautiful than any mortal woman, more handsome than any man. Owen felt his body respond to its beauty, even as he fought down the responses. Where eyes would be on a mortal, violet fires shone. The figure turned these glowing orbs on Owen.

"So you have called to me," it said in a voice that soared sweeter than a thousand Bards, screeching like the legs of a million beetles. The figure seemed to nod in satisfaction. "As I have predicted you would."

"Nothing has changed," Owen rasped out. "I am still of the same mind as when you branded me with this Bond, against my will."

The figure wavered in the air.

"Indeed? Do you not recall that it was only by the bond that your life was saved? Let me remind you." The figure made a tossing motion towards him.

Owen stood again on the Crimean battlefield, the infernal weapon of the Austrians sending out its rending vibrations. Owen knew that the next wave would disintegrate him, as it had every fighter on the field. With his heart filled with defiance and fear, he aimed his cane at the machine, channeling every grain of energy that a Master Sorcerer could summon. The wood of the cane exploded into splinters and a tear appeared in the World, a tear that Owen fell into.

"Without the bond to my world," the Shining One said, "you would not have been able to survive there, nor return to your world with your spirit and mind intact." It regarded him curiously, "Why do you still begrudge this?"

"You told me a lot of things," Owen growled. "If I am not to believe in your *country folk*, why should I believe what you say?"

"Why not," the voice soothed. "Have you found any of what I told you to be untrue?"

When Owen came to after falling, it was in a place where even the colors were strangely wrong. His memories of that place were mercifully dim, but he knew that the being who now stood before him had cared for him, had even healed him. The being had told Owen that others of his kind had been dealing with the Obsidian Order since the Order's founder had learned their language, nearly three hundred years earlier. The Great Doctor had made the Shining Ones the Order's allies, helping to shape the British Empire as it spread across the globe, or so the humans had thought.

Owen's rescuer had revealed that, to them, humanity's affairs where merely an amusing diversion, despite the high-minded rhetoric they espoused. They viewed the Order much like favorite pets, as they played their own games with the flesh and blood of mortals.

His rescuer believed that this meddling had created a dangerous imbalance in humanity's evolution, and that the Austrian's alchemical physicks, devoid of any understanding of Spirit or Balance, threatened to tear the very universe apart. After revealing these terrible understandings, she/he had offered Owen a gift of the Electrum cane he now carried, and had sent him back.

Owen had appeared in a small Greek fishing village, with the cane at his side. The revelations of the Shining One has caused him to resign from the Order. He could not bear the thought that all he had done, all the suffering he had caused, and had seen, was merely some grand chess game for bored Spirits. He had wandered the world until he came to this city half-way around the globe, and eventually now to this meeting.

"No," Owen said between gritted teeth. "I have found that what you said about the Order was true, at least. But men were not meant to be pawns in your games."

"Then why have you called upon me?"

"I need your aid," Owen admitted. "There is a scheme to ignite a world war by assassination. You have ways of knowing things, as well as power beyond what we might know, it has always been said. I need your aid in stopping this."

The Shining One flared more brightly for a moment causing Owen to shield his eyes. It took him a moment to realize this was a form of laughter.

"You object to our interfering on one hand, then ask for that interference on the other. How typical of your kind. No, I will not stop what is to be."

"Then at least tell me the identity of the assassin," Owen pleaded.

"The killer is greed and fear, as it so often is for your folk," the Shining One replied wearily. "The seeds of the Shadowed Ones that you call the Austrians begin to bear their terrible fruit."

"I do not understand," Owen said perplexed. "Are you saying that an Austrian is the assassin? Who are they? How can I unmask them?"

"Yes and no, no and yes," the being answered. "You already have seen the mask, but your eyes do not notice, and it is so easy. The one you seek is the one that you should expect to be at the side of dying men first."

Owen frowned. That made no sense to him at all. The beautiful being in front of him began to dissolve back into the incense smoke.

"You bore me," He heard as if from a great distance. "I shall go elsewhere unless you have something more entertaining, or..." the voice picked up just the slightest bit, "you wish to let me out of this smelly circle, into your world."

Strong smiled to himself, pushing more energy into the defense of the circle. He'd awaited this. The thought of an unbound Old One loose in his world was more terrifying than a world war, and he wasn't about to let it happen.

"No, I think not," Strong said clearly, "I close the Door."

The two wrestled back and forth, their Magia almost a physical thing to Owen, like a strong wind he leaned against. He heard a loud sigh, and felt the air pressure slump as the doorway closed.

He remembered to turn on the oil lamps with his fire calling. That took the last bit of his energy, and he slid to the floor, unconscious before he came to rest.

Chapter 14

Owen awoke on his lounge on the outside terrace. He was wrapped in blankets, with Jinhao hovering near him.

"Good, you are awake," she said briskly. "Drink this." This turned out to be strong coffee with a heavy brandy chaser. Owen found that a few sips laced warmth through his body, while also clearing his head.

He wet his lips. "How did you get into the room," he finally managed to ask.

"I convinced Barton that something not covered by his orders must have happened," Jinhao said. "Did you really expect that some alien spirit would possess you or destroy the house?"

"I cannot answer that," Owen croaked. He sipped more of the coffee and brandy. It was quite invigorating. He felt the cobwebs fly from his head as he remembered the events of last night, and his failure to learn anything useful, despite the danger. "It would appear that I've been something of a wishful fool."

Jinhao frowned at this. "And you will not tell me more about what you are talking about?"

"I promise you, Jinhao..." he began.

"It is not safe for me to know," Jinhao finished for him disgustedly. "I will accept that you have secrets, Owen Strong, but if you are inviting powerful Demons into my dwelling, I believe that I have a right to know, and to know what it is."

Owen opened his mouth slowly. "You are absolutely right, and I apologize," he said finally.

Her eyebrows shot up at this.

"Almost this possession I could believe. Did you just apologize and agree with me?" She held up her hand before he could speak. "We can talk of this later. Roberet had something interesting to say about the little metal shard, and Lady Hastings has sent word that she will call on us."

Owen almost groaned.

"Why ever is she calling on us?"

"She claims to have gathered a clue using her Truth Sense." Jinhao cocked her head at Owen. "You look terrible. Did you at least find the answers you were seeking?"

Owen preceded to tell Jinhao what the Spirit had said, without going into the Spirit's origins.

Jinhao frowned. "The one who should already be there." She shook her head. "That makes no sense whatsoever. Are you sure this is not a prank?"

Owen drained the coffee mug, handing it to Barton.

"I am not sure. They do not think like we do, you know. It could have been legitimate, or he could have simply wished to torment me with the hint that he knows more than he does." He shakily sat up.

"What did Roberet have to say?"

Jinhao replied excitedly.

"He examined it and pronounced that it was the casing of a round from a magnetic gun. Not only that, but that there were traces of frozen Tesarine oil as well."

"Magnetic gun..." Owen asked.

Jinhao nodded.

"Yes. It works by using magnets to propel a bullet to un-heard-of speeds. The frozen Tesarine would liquefy as soon as it pierced the skin." She smiled.

"Yes," Owen mused. "Now we know how they were murdered. Did Roberet say how big the weapon had to be? Or who could make such a thing?"

"That he was not sure of, but from the shard, he would guess a tube no wider than a cigar." She shrugged. "As for who, he told me that he could make such a thing in a year now that he knows about it. It would take a very smart Alchemist indeed."

"Which still points to our friends the Austrians," Owen said. "But why kill their own man?" He thought aloud. Suddenly he snapped his fingers. "Tube. Concealed so along the arm. You aim it as if you're going to shake hands with the target."

Jinhao brightened visibly.

"Yes, it would take practice to aim but could work. But if it is the Austrians, how will we find the killer?"

Owen shook his head.

"We shall not if it is. But I am inclined to think that it is someone the Austrians have hired or suborned in some manner. 'The one you expect to be there' is not some name-less assassin." He struggled to stand up straight. "You should be careful," Jinhao said, offering her hand for assis-tance. "I thought you dead not that long ago."

"Nonsense," Owen said heartily, "Nothing that won't pass. Barton, give me an arm will you?" The clank man ex-tended an arm. "That's a good clockwork gear," Owen said approvingly. "Now get me to my room, get a basin of hot water, and see to some food for me immediately, and tea for company." He turned to Jinhao, "When is Lady Hastings expected?"

"Her note said eleven o'clock," Jinhao answered.

Owen glanced through the doorway into the front parlor.

"And it is now just after half ten," he said with satisfaction, "Plenty of time." He looked at her diaphanous night-gown pointedly. "While that may indeed be charming, would you also like to change into something more appropriate for tea with a guest?"

With that, he had Barton assist him up the main stairs. Jinhao frowned again as there was a scratching at the front door, a sound that, fortunately, only she heard. When she opened the door, there stood one of the street urchins that roamed the city freely.

Often times they were mixed children that no one wanted, or orphans thrown on the streets by bad luck. The dirty child's fingers quickly flashed in an intricate pattern. Jinhao gestured for him to come inside, and quickly. "You should not be here," she said to him. His response was to make the finger patterns as before.

She strode over to the writing table. She began to write angrily.

"Alright," she said coldly. "But this is the only time, until I can meet him face to face, you understand me?" She rolled the scrap of paper up into a tube, and held it out to him. He snatched it away from her hand as if she might bite him instead.

"Good," she nodded in approval. "You should fear me. And if that message goes astray, I will give you cause to. Now, go." The urchin flew out the front door. Jinhao looked at the clock, and sighed. She just had time to don a presentable Western dress.

She came back downstairs to find a nattily-dressed Owen seated in the front parlor. He was gulping tea and destroying a series of finger sandwiches. On seeing Jinhao's look, he looked up defensively.

"It takes a lot of energy to do what I did last night. This is the fastest way to replenish it."

Jinhao nodded her understanding.

"It is the same after I have used my abilities. Perhaps the two disciplines are not as foreign to each other as we have been taught." Her lips curled upwards, "Perhaps you should teach me some of your Western tricks."

Owen chuckled around his food.

"And you will teach me how to spring through the air across a room? Wonderful," he said drily. "Then we shall have two governments with a reason to hang us both."

The Front bell rang.

"That would be Lady Hastings, I presume," Owen remarked. "Let Barton get the door. It would not do, to answer it ourselves." He put down his cup and plate. "Now that hunger is abated, let us see what Lady Hastings has to say for herself."

Barton announced the Lady Hastings as she swept into the room. Discreetly behind her, came the House Healer, Lady Ap Rhys, looking for all the world as if she had eaten a sour lemon, as she glanced around at the furnishings.

"Lady Hastings," Owen stood, bowing in an exaggerated court style. "You do my home too much honor."

The young woman dipped a short curtsy in response.

"Ah no, it is you that does me honor in receiving me, Lord Strong!" She raised a fan, opening it with a snap. "I believe I have discovered the murderer of Papa," she announced, all the while fanning herself.

"Truly," Owen responded lazily. "Still, I can see that this has put you all out of sorts, do sit and partake of some tea won't you?" At a nod from Owen, Barton pulled back a chair for Lady Hastings. She looked at the chair for a moment, and then with an audible sigh sank into it. Owen gestured to the House Healer that she take the remaining chair.

"No thank you, Milord," the older woman replied. "It would not be proper."

Owen flopped down at the day table across from Lady Hastings and next to Jinhao.

"Oh, we are anything but proper here, Lady Ap Rhys, but you must suit yourself." Taking up the tea pot, he poured for Lady Hastings, "White, and sugar?" When her tea had been placed in her reach he refilled both Jinhao's cup and his own. He sipped with satisfaction and leaned back in the chair.

"Now, Lady Hastings, please tell me how you've come to such a conclusion. Please omit nothing."

"Well, last night you asked me to keep my Truth Sense open for clues, and I did just that," the young woman said with pride. "Even though it gives me the most horrible headaches and the most depressing view of people." She sighed, "It's easy to forget that everyone lies when you're not confronted with it all the time right in front of your face, so to speak."

The young heiress took another sip of tea.

"I believe that it has paid off however," Lady Hastings said animatedly. "I would casually ask everyone I came into contact with if they were sad that Papa was gone." She looked at Owen sharply over her cup, "Only one person was lying when they said they were, and that would be Terrance McDougal, our chief engineer." She paused for dramatic impact.

"When I questioned Master McDougal as to his latest project, construction down on the docks, he lied again, although I could not say what specifically he was lying about, the sense doesn't work quite that well without more pointed questions that I was sure would arouse his suspicions. Instead, I went to look at the records for the project." She set her now empty teacup on the table. 'I am no engineer Lord Strong, but it seems to me that the project is costing much more than it should."

Owen sat his own cup down, straightening in his chair.

"And so you surmise that Master McDougal killed your father in an attempt to hide his larceny. Who else have you told this to?"

"No one save Ann here," Lady Hastings indicated the House Healer. Her face bore a distinct frown.

"Besides, who would I tell that it would do any good? The constabulary would be no help, nor would the governor. I know what I have found would not be seen as evidence, yet, I am convinced!"

"If I might suggest, Lady Hastings," Owen said sympathetically, "leave the entire matter in my hands. I promise you I shall see the person, or persons, responsible for your father's death are brought to justice."

"Persons," Lady Hastings said sharply. "Then you think it that more than one person is responsible?"

"I think it entirely possible, but by no means certain," Owen replied.

Lady Ap Rhys, the House Healer, stirred from her relaxed guard behind Lady Hastings.

"There is always another alternative, Milady."

Hastings nodded at this.

"Yes, I have not forgotten." Seeing Owen's question, Lady Hastings said, "Ann has reminded me that I may invoke the right as Head of House to try and, if need be, convict Master McDougal myself, a fact that I must confess to you brings me a certain satisfaction to think on." She shrugged.

"Papa, though, always said that taking the law into your own hands was seldom just, and never really removed doubts." She clenched her jaw, "I will have no doubts, Lord Strong."

"I'm glad that your father was such a wise man Lady Hastings," Owen said quickly. "I shall leave you with no doubts, you have my word on it."

The young heiress nodded as if in relief.

"I shall leave it in your hands then, Lord Strong," she said and then leaned forward, "Mind you, if I am not satisfied within the fortnight, then I shall convene that special House Court." Her smile held all the warmth of the frozen plains of the north lands.

Owen bowed his head to her.

"As your Ladyship wishes," he replied. Raising it again, he held up the teapot. "More tea, My Lady?"

Lady Hastings abruptly stood bolt upright.

"No thank you," she answered. "I have already taken up enough of your time, and that of Lady Jinhao, as it is. Besides, I'm sure that you wish to go about spelling or investigating or whatever you do."

Owen and Jinhao rose as well.

"Of course, Lady Hastings. I shall inform you when events warrant giving you news. Let me see you out."

"No thank you," the heiress said again. "I'm sure that we shall be quite well served by your clockwork man here. Wonderful conceit by the way, Papa did away with all of ours some years ago, too much trouble to upkeep."

"His name is Barton," Owen said stiffly. "And he is a valued member of this household."

Lady Hastings face showed her surprise at this.

"Well, of course," she finally said. "My favorite clank man was named Samuel. I cried when Papa sent him away." She turned towards the mechanical butler. "Please show us out, Barton," she requested softly.

Barton whirred, and from his speaker grill came a chirpy voice.

"This way, Lady Hastings."

Owen and Jinhao watched the two Englishwomen leave. Once they had gone Jinhao turned to Owen, whose brow was creased deep in thought.

"Do you believe that her theory is correct?"

Owen started himself from his internal study.

"What"? He waved a hand in dismissal. "No. I doubt it very much. There are too many unanswered questions. How did he manage to come across so sophisticated a means of killing? Why was he not remarked upon by anyone as having been there when Lord Hastings was murdered? And what about the other killings? What possible reward could the Chief Engineer of a House hope to gain by sabotaging the trade talks?"

Jinhao stood up.

"As to your first question, he is an engineer, yes? Among your people does that not mean that he has both Magia and the gear-making knowledge? Perhaps that is how. As to your other questions," she shrugged. "It seems there is only one way to get the answers you seek."

Owen sighed, still befuddled from the events of the previous evening.

"Yes," he said resignedly, "Fancy a trip to the docks?"

She moved around the table, gracefully moving her skirts out of the way.

"I am already going to change clothes for the dockyards. However, perhaps you should stay here? You have had a difficult night."

Owen came to his feet at what he perceived as a challenge.

"No, but give me a tot of brandy, and I'm good to go," he avowed.

Chapter 15

Owen carefully counted out the gold coin that was the agreed-upon payment to the Wizard.

They had wanted to get to the docks as quickly as possible, and were, therefore, obliged to take more expensive transport than usual. The large golem stood impassively under the yoke, while his Master, clad in a long, blue robe, threaded through with Cabbalistic runes, counted the coin with Owen.

The Wizard nodded, beard wagging.

"That will do," he said, satisfied. The old Wizard sniffed the air, looking at Owen. "Sure that you don't want me to wait, Sir? The spirits smell very restless today."

Owen raised his eyebrow in skepticism.

"Spirits," he echoed. "Why it's barely past noon. You shouldn't have to worry about spirits when there are hours of sunlight left."

The Wizard shook his head.

"This is the Hong Kong docks, Sir. Lots of old Magia and death down there." The Wizard made a warding gesture with his left hand. "I wouldn't charge you more than half a royal to wait. You could be assured, then, that your way out of the docks was safe and un-haunted." He nodded towards Owen's electrum cane. "I can see that you have some knowledge yourself, but it never hurts to have an extra at your back."

Owen pursed his lips in thought.

"I thank you Master, but I'm sure we'll be all right." He didn't add that he was curious if this worked on all the tourists, which Owen was sure the old Wizard had taken them for.

The Wizard nodded agreement.

"Well, just remember that I'll be back down this road in an hour or so."

Owen grinned, a little wildly, his curiosity aroused.

"We'll remember and we might even be ready to engage you again, Master Wizard."

"Well you're a good spoken one, I must give you that. Beware the spirits, now!" With that, he took up a staff and directed the Golem forward. The large man-like being huffed, then the cart began slowly moving, picking up speed as it went.

"What was that all about," Jinhao asked, as Owen watched the cab go up the road.

"Oh, I suspect that he was seeking a larger fare from us," Owen replied dryly. "Warned me about spirits on the docks."

"Oh is that all," Jinhao remarked. "But it is still daylight. It is true that there are haunts at night, but I have never heard of one during the day."

"Exactly," Owen agreed. "And you won't either; that is because the sun's rays destroy unbound ectoplasm."

"That," Jinhao pointed disgustedly, "I presume, is the Hastings' new construction." Her finger pointed out a large, tall building, with a crane hauling steel girders up into the sky. All around the base of the building scurried people, who vanished and re-appeared out of the fog of exhaust generated by the building.

"Yes," Owen said. Jinhao could hear the hint of pride in his voice. "It will be the tallest structure on the waterfront. Able to take the cargoes from sky ships coming in from above, and from merchant ships coming in from the water, and storing both cargoes in the warehouses in between. McDougal has taken the principles of blending steam powered engines with Magia to a whole new level." He began walking towards the immense construction, Jinhao gliding along beside him.

"Thus do you English spread your smokes and stinks throughout the city."

Owen smiled at her disapproval.

"Oh come now Jinhao, you can't stop progress. Between the safety wards, levitation spells, and using elemental power, it has made building safer than ever before" he said cheerily.

Whatever else he was going to say was cut off by the sight of the side of the crane buckling, its load of heavy girders falling with shocking speed onto a group of workers below. It all happened with such speed that the only thing the pair could do was throw up their hands up to protect their sight.

As they uncovered their faces in the aftermath, they could see workers rushing towards the crash.

"Come on," Owen cried springing to join them. One of the tall better dressed figures who was clearly pointing and shouting orders saw them coming and turned to run away from the crash.

"McDougal, stop!" Owen cried after him. The man looked over his shoulder and ran faster.

"I have him," Jinhao cried, running even faster. Owen already winded, let her continue the pursuit. Bending over to catch his breath, he straightened to find himself surrounded by surly construction workers. "Can I help you," he gasped out.

One of the leather apron clad ones spoke revealing a gap-toothed mouth.

"We wants to know what you wants with Master McDougal," he growled ominously.

"Shouldn't we be tending to your poor brothers instead," Owen asked. He hefted his cane. "As you can see, I am not without resources that could save lives."

"We sees that fancy spell stick of yours," Toothless says, "And that gets us to wondering, perhaps you caused all this."

"Ridiculous," snapped Owen. "Where's your own Magian? Surely you must have one?"

Toothless nodded towards the tumble of steel.

"He was part of the group wot got it," he said menacingly. "Perhaps you should be getting' it too."

Owen pulled on his Earth rune, standing still.

"I doubt you'll find me as easy as your last bar brawl."

"Oh, talk it now, will you?" Toothless jeered at Owen. The others encircling Owen laughed with him. Toothless suddenly sprang at Owen, swinging a metal bar at his legs.

His face grew astonished when the bar bent, and Owen appearing to be unmoved by the blow. The others screamed, charging in. Rather than take their blows, Owen pulled on his Air rune. A stiff wind fanned out from his center, blowing them all down.

Owen dramatically raised his cane and brought it down into the ground, while calling on his Fire rune. A bolt of lightning sprang out of the clear blue sky to stop inches above his head.

"Enough," he cried. "Are you convinced now that I could have already made life very unpleasant for you all if I wanted?"

From where he lay on the ground, Toothless looked up, dazed, at him.

"I reckon so," he allowed. Owen smiled down at him, and offered his hand.

"Good, he said, "then let's lend a hand to those poor brutes under the girders." Toothless took his hand and Owen effortlessly pulled him to his feet using the Earth rune to brace himself. It jarred Owen right to his bones, but it wouldn't do to show weakness now.

"Right then," Owen said. "Can we get something to lift those steel beams out of the way?"

"We can rig somethin'," Toothless replied, "But it would work better if we had one o' them liftin' spells to aid us."

Owen hefted his cane, "Well, you've come to the right place for lifting spells'." He grinned.

McDougal frantically keyed the lift as Jinhao closed in. She leapt, grabbing onto the lift's cage, only to have to let go again when the lift came to a narrow passage. McDougal grinned down at her with a hoot and a wave.

Jinhao studied the girders and scaffolding that interlaced the inside of the huge building. Setting her course, she centered her energy, then began to spring upwards, leaping from handhold to planking. There was more than one way to beat him to the top.

McDougal pulled open the cage door, just as Jinhao sprang over the side of the building to land on the rooftop in front of him. He snarled, and clawed free a pepper pot pistol from his vest. The gun's barrels flashed in the sunlight as they rotated, a small jut of air accompanied each round as he fired.

Jinhao ducked, weaved, and bent to avoid the deadly bullets, until McDougal's pistol ran empty.

"Why are you doing this," Jinhao asked. "We only wish to talk with you."

"Talk, ye call it?" He spat. "That's not what I been told. Well you won't do to me as you done to his Lordship, not for a few thousand Guineas, you won't."

"A few thousand," Jinhao repeated. "What are you speaking of?"

MacDougal laughed, throwing aside the empty gun and cocking his fists. Jinhao recognized it as that quaint martial form called boxing.

"I admit I took the money, but it would have all been repaid by the time the building was finished. I wouldna have had to take it, if the damned smuggler hadn't asked for more money to haul my dear Sophie and Rowan here, so as we could build a new life." He moved his fists as if pumping them. "Well, come on then," he snarled, "Come on."

Jinhao obliged the tall engineer, moving to put his hand and arm into a lock that still enabled him to stand while bending him half over from the pain. He screeched as she applied pressure.

"Now," she said satisfied at last, "We will get back into the lift and descend where you will tell all this to my partner." The big man tried to pull away and screamed as Jinhao squeezed again.

"And should you keep trying that, I will break your arm before you get free." He stopped struggling.

"That's better," Jinhao purred. "Now right this way" She lead him back to the lift, never letting go of his arm or allowing him to stand up straight.

She was as surprised to see Owen with his suit coat off, covered in grime and blood as he was to see her gently leading her catch.

"Well, I see that you have caught the elusive Mr. McDougal," Owen observed. "I've been lending a hand here."

"So I see," Jinhao replied. She applied pressure to McDougal's arm, causing the man to groan and remain bent over. "Where do you want him?"

Owen glanced around to see that fortunately the workers were still all focused on the relief efforts, and rescuing their injured fellows.

"We need to have a quiet talk with him, but not here." Owen pointed towards an abandoned wreck next to the construction. "Let's go there." Owen looked over his shoulder to make sure they still weren't seen. "And let us go quickly."

Once in the sheltering gloom of the wreck, Owen turned.

"Let him up please." Jinhao allowed the Engineer to stand upright again.

"I tell you, I did not kill Lord Hastings!" cried McDougal.

Owen looked at him through hooded eyes.

"Perhaps. Then you can explain the missing money?"

McDougal pulled at his beard.

"As I told the girl, yes, I took the money, but only so my Sophie and our daughter could make the passage out here as well. The money would have been returned before the job was finished, I swear it!"

Owen raised his cane, flames licked down its length.

"I do not have time to deal with lies, McDougal," Owen said sternly. McDougal paled. He tried to back up only to find that Jinhao's long knives blocking his way.

"No," he said, "I swear that it's all true! All of it!"

Owen nodded. "I believe you." The flames vanished. "But you still have your Mistress to answer to. What she will say, I do not know." Owen turned, clearing the way for McDougal to leave.

"You mean you're letting me go?" McDougal looked at Owen in astonishment.

"I am not your mistress' agent," Owen explained. "Perhaps this will teach you to rely on a smuggler's honesty."

"Gods keep you, Milord, Gods keep you!" With that he ran into the sunlight.

"Why did you let him go?" Jinhao asked.

Owen shrugged.

"As I explained, I am not Lady Hastings' agent. The man is clearly not the killer." He sauntered out to stare at the wreckage. He was pleased to see that McDougal had resumed his place of command, overseeing the rescue efforts. "Besides," Owen said, "I believe that there has been enough grief here today."

"What is it you were just saying about the warding and the power of Western Magia?"

"Well, that should have held up. Clearly the operator lost control of the safety levitation spells at the wrong time. The warding should have alerted..." Strong stopped in his tracks. "Good Goddess of the Forge," he murmured.

"Owen," Jinhao said, "What is it?"

"Shh," Owen hushed her. "Give me a moment." His fingers traced out something that only he could see. "Of course!" He turned to Jinhao. "I know who the assassin is!"

"What!" Jinhao exclaimed. "Who?"

Owen pulled out his watch.

"We still have time to get dressed and meet Gregg for the festivities! Come, I'll explain along the way."

Chapter 16

Liu tugged at the white servant's coat as he climbed down from the delivery van. It was too small and fit like band of iron across his shoulders.

No matter, he smiled to himself. After today, all the people of Hong Kong will be free. He turned to begin supervising the smuggling of guns into the reception for the trade delegates. He was brought up short by the sudden appearance of the *Quizi* Magian from the shop, accompanied by an inspector from the police, both dressed for the reception in fancy clothes.

"Liu Qwan Tze," the inspector rumbled, "You are hereby bound by the authority of the City Law. Surrender."

Liu began to reach for the knife at the small of his back. The Magian raised his cane slightly.

"I really wish you wouldn't."

Liu sneered at Owen.

"I would beat you, Magian, without your tricks."

"Perhaps," Owen agreed easily. "But then you would have to face her." He cocked his head towards the roof of the van, where Jinhao, dressed and masked in her black outfit, appeared. Constables sprang out as if from nowhere, seizing Liu's people and their cache of weapons. Liu's shoulders slumped in defeat.

"Here now," Owen said cheerfully, "let's move over here out of the way shall we?"

Together Inspector Gregg and Owen escorted the defeated revolutionary across the street.

Liu looked at them defiantly.

"No matter, place me in your worst prison. Hang me if you will. We will not be stopped."

"Oh, you misunderstand us completely," Owen replied. "No, no, we are not going to take you into custody. We are letting you go."

Liu paled. "Letting me go," he echoed. "But the others will think..."

"That you betrayed them," Owen beamed at Liu. "It should be interesting to see how understanding your brothers and sisters are, comrade." Liu choked.

"You know what the trouble is with you radicals..." Owen asked fiercely. "It is that to you there is always one simple answer, 'kill off the ruling classes'. You never think about the people who depend on the order the ruling class brings. The kind of peace that allows the farmer to bring his rice to market and not be cheated; the kind that allows a little girl not to go hungry because some bandit stole her dinner. What do you have to replace that with? Nothing but slogans and violence that feed your ego." He snorted in disgust.

"Get out of here before I forget how very elegant it will be to have the rebel leadership turn on each other."

Liu looked franticly from Owen to Gregg. The police inspector shook his head implacably.

"Go," was all he growled. Liu turned and ran down the street.

"You enjoyed that little lecture," Gregg observed, looking at Owen.

"Did I?" Owen wondered aloud. "I suppose it was a bit indulgent of me. Still," he twirled his cane, "Someone needs to speak for the ruling classes, and we usually do such a bad job of it ourselves." He turned back towards Peachtree House, the official residence of the two governors, and site for the trade reception. "At least you can tell them to start the reception now."

Gregg shrugged. "They already did," he said. "Seems the 'ruling class' always knows better." He smiled sourly.

"What?!" Owen exclaimed. "They were to wait!" He began running towards the building. Jinhao leaped down as he passed.

"Get into your reception clothes and find a way in. The assassin is inside!"

Owen's heart was pounding by the time he reached the front of the august building. He slowed down under the watchful eyes of the guards, both Royal Marines and Chinese Imperial guards. It wouldn't do to appear out of the ordinary now. Not knowing where the assassin was, raising an alarm might cause them to act, and in the commotion, the assassin may succeed in their grisly task.

Instead, Owen presented his card to the Seneschal, and entered the gaily dressed crowd that milled around the spacious great hall. He'd just spied the delegates off to a side, and had begun working his way through the crowd towards them, when a very richly dressed Chinese man appeared before him.

"Your pardon, young Sorcerer," the old man's white mustache quivered. He gestured towards Owen's cane. "Is not such an overt display of one's powers considered vulgar?"

Pulled up short, Owen studied the old man. He wore a silk over-robe so expensive that Owen was sure it would buy his neighborhood, let alone his modest house. Other than that he was unadorned. No badges of House or rank, not even a dagger.

"Some would say it is bad manners indeed," Owen replied slowly. There was something about the old man that made you not want to dismiss him as just another rich Courtier. "But I have never found it wise to hide what you are."

The old man smiled.

"Have you not? What a strange thing for the son of Lord Strong to say as he takes his nights among the whorehouses and lotus dens of a backwater colony."

Owen felt his face flush. Who was this old man? He'd passed dueling with insults some time back.

"I am not hiding," he said stiffly. "Anyone who wishes to may find me." He should shut his mouth, but that wasn't his style. "As for Hong Kong being a 'backwater colony' it is anything but. Rather it is a...a blending of the best of both our races, to our mutual benefit." He eyed the other man's rich arraignment. "At least you appear to know that."

The old man smiled at him.

"You are as direct and ill-mannered as reported. I like that. More, I would talk with you on how you see this blending of our two nations." He held up his hand. "Another time perhaps, may be more auspicious. You were going this way I believe?" he waved towards the delegation and began walking that way as well. The crowd seemed to melt before them until Owen and the old man stood near the delegate party. The assassin was just placing themselves in the impromptu receiving line.

"Excuse me," Owen said.

"You must do as you must," the old man said.

Owen sprang forward just as the assassin was reaching the delegates. Owen grabbed the assassin by the forearm and yanked their arm straight up towards the ceiling. There was a tinkle of the spent projectile that could be heard over the sounds of surprise coming from the crowd. Owen pulled back the sleeve of their tunic, revealing the strange tube device.

"Here is your assassin, My Lords and Ladies," Owen cried out like a showman. He grabbed harder as she struggled, and he turned towards the snarling face of Melinda MacAllister, Sorcerer of House Hastings.

Chapter 17

But how did you know it was Mistress MacAllister" Inspector Gregg asked.

Gregg and a couple of constables had come running in while Owen was wrestling with Mistress MacAllister. They had relieved her of her wand as well, and produced a pair of specially-made manacles that made calling upon a sigil extremely painful. Now she stood quietly between the Queen's peacekeepers. A crowd, including the trade delegates, had gathered around Owen, Gregg and the thwarted assassin, taking in every word.

"It was very simple once you really looked at it," Owen said off-handedly. "When Lord Hastings was shot, Lady Hastings reported that she reached her father first, even though her office was on the second floor. Mistress MacAllister arrived sometime after the House physician had been called for, and Lady Hastings and the House

Healer were already there." Owen glanced around at his rapt audience.

"Why should this be? As House Sorceress, Mistress MacAllister should have been aware from the moment our assassin crossed the Wards with hostile intent that something was going on. She certainly should have been aware when the Head of the House was wounded. Her Wards would have told her at the moment he was hurt. Yet, was she about the main house on guard? Was she running towards Lord Hastings as he lay on that floor?" Owen shook his head

"No, she was running away from him. To someplace where she could remove the physical parts of her messenger disguise, and then arrive back." Owen turned to look at the assassin. "I admire your resolve, there. It could not have been easy to return to bend with concern over the man you had just killed."

"But why, Mel," Lady Hastings cried. "He depended on you, trusted you as if you were another daughter!"

"But I wasn't a daughter was I," Mistress MacAllister hissed, "merely the hired help, to be tossed aside, to be ignored while that fool who called himself a Hastings threw away everything in these new Trade Talks. I was close enough to him that I heard it. By the Gods! The MacAllisters knew how to fight for what was theirs! And I'd not spent twenty years beggin' scraps from your table to be turned out when you lost everything due to his lofty ideals."

Owen held up the strange tube that had been strapped to her wrist, hidden by the long sleeve of her tunic.

"But you didn't come to that conclusion entirely on your own, did you Mistress MacAllister?"

He handed the tube to Duke Caldwell.

"This fires a small needle of solidly frozen Tesarine. The Tesarine, once it penetrates the skin, vaporizes, due to the incredible speed at which it is fired. This tube fires the needle not by compressed air, or even chemical combustion, but by magnetism. I submit that its construction could not have been done by Mistress MacAllister, but only by an advanced nation state who prides themselves on making such toys." Owen was looking directly at the Austrian delegation as he spoke this last.

The veiled leader of the Austrians shook their head.

"You have no proof of such an accusation! Even if it were to turn out to be Austrian work, the government cannot be held responsible for every watch-maker that creates something."

Owen looked at the black-clad leader coolly. "Perhaps it's time you did take responsibility, before someone does so for you."

Jinhao eeled her way towards the front of the Chinese arc of the spectators. She placed herself to the left of the old man who was watching the show intently.

"So, granddaughter," he finally said, not turning to look at her. "You were supposed to get close to the boy-emperor and bring him into the fold. Instead, I find you carrying on with an Anglo Magian even more decadent than you or your sister. You bring me disappointment as great as her own."

"Ching Shih sends her love and respect Grandfather, even as I do," Jinhao replied with a bowed head. They were talking in an old way familiar to them both, a way that outsiders could not overhear. "Your plan for the Emperor is too late, I fear. The Dowager Empress has long-since crushed from the Emperor all that remained of any kind of human feeling."

The old man hissed between his teeth at the unwelcome news.

"Then you feel we must replace the line? I dislike having to do that."

"Perhaps," Jinhao allowed. "It was while I was coming to relay such unhappy news that I came across another plan that unifies us with the Anglos." She nodded towards him, "Owen Strong."

"The Magian?" The old man finally looked at her. "I like his spirit, but I fail to see it."

Jinhao's lips made a small moue, as she offered her thoughts to her grandfather.

"He only requires a small bit of guidance, grandfather, and he could be the name that both Han and Anglo would raise up as a shield against any evil."

The old man grunted in reply. There appeared to be some contention from the Europeans below, something about a correct challenge to legal dueling. Even the Austrian leader was shouting. Jinhao found the English tongue confusing when speakers started shouting at once. Quickly Jinhao told the old man about the Austrian threat of war, and their powerful vibration weapon.

He listened to her report impassively, only stopping her when the Imperial Governor whispered in his other ear. She could see him straighten up at the news.

"It would seem that your intelligence is correct," he murmured. He straightened the crease of first one sleeve then the other. "Your sister sends that there is a European fleet sailing towards the city, and it is flying the Austrian flag." He turned, looking at his youngest grandchild, who saw the red glowing in the back of his eyes.

"You understand that I cannot let this go unchallenged," he said sternly.

Jinhao again bowed her head.

"Of course not, Grandfather," she answered. The old man's glance lingered for a moment at her bowed head.

"Do not try to follow me. Your sister shall provide what help I require. That is a command, do you understand?"

"Yes, Grandfather," she replied, head still bowed.

He nodded in some private satisfaction, turned and ghosted from the room. Jinhao raised her head, looked below and frowned. She had missed something. The officials were marking out the boundaries of a Western dueling circle. It appeared that Owen Strong was in trouble.

Chapter 18

Owen Strong was in trouble.

He'd lost the argument for a regular trial once Mistress MacAllister had raised the ancient challenge. As the accuser, Owen would have to fight. Why the Duke was allowing a three hundred year old law to be played out now, Owen couldn't begin to guess. Unless Caldwell had an interest as well? Gregg was still attempting to stop it, all gods bless him.

"My Lord," Gregg bellowed. "The crimes that the woman is accused of occurred under Hong Kong law. She should be tried under the law by the Hong Kong courts."

"We do not see it that way Inspector," the Duke said evenly. "We assert that this is an internal affair of the British Empire, and as such it should be dealt with by British laws. I'm sure our peer, the Imperial Court Ambassador concurs."

The Chinese official spread his hands, unwilling to cause even more of an incident.

"Of course. Inspector you have done good work today, but I perceive you are weary now. Perhaps some rest is in order."

Owen had neither time nor thought to spare for the argument. If he was fighting, as he knew he was five minutes ago when the Duke had entertained Mistress MacAllister's ravings and challenges, then he needed to focus on the fight, not to mention get ready for it.

Formal duels were one of the few times that a Magian was required to be naked. Owen suspected that it was so the Magians could show off their sigils like peacocks, but there were two sigils that Owen had no desire for anyone to see, as they would be if activated. Those were the sigil of the Obsidian Order, and the sigil given to him by the otherworldly being. He began to remove his clothes slowly while some Magians in the ducal party laid out the formal circle.

He had just handed his suit coat and cane to one of the Duke's boys, when a mighty roar shook the very stones of Peachtree House. Everyone crouched down in alarm as a huge hot wind blew over them. Owen looked up, his heart catching in his throat. There was the most magnificent sight he had ever seen. The Dragon rippled through the air, away from him, glowing golden in the azure sky. As he watched, Jinhao's familiar whisper came to his ear. He never could catch her sneaking up on him.

"There is an Austrian fleet in the waters," Jinhao said. "He goes to warn them off, I hope. How can I help you?"

Owen went back to undoing his cufflinks.

"Hold these," he said dryly. Jinhao took them and looked him in the face. "I do not think that you should do this thing," she pronounced.

Owen gave a small laugh. "I don't think so either," he said. "They," he tilted his head towards the delegation, "seem to have a different idea."

"But why," she asked, puzzled.

"Well, I would guess that someone in the government sees this as an ideal way to rid themselves of both a troublesome former agent, and silence whatever deal they may have offered MacAllister there." Mistress MacAllister had already stripped down. She was currently performing a series of postures and breathing patterns that were supposed to increase focus, much to the attentive regard of many of the males present. Owen was grateful her antics would distract from anyone looking too closely at the sigils on his own naked body.

Jinhao raised an eyebrow at his summation.

"I see," she slowly hissed. "The British would kill one of their own?"

Owen shrugged.

"I honestly have no idea, but I would offer her an embarrassing deal as well, to try to turn her against her Austrian handlers, that kind of thing." He slipped off his shirt and stood naked before her, sigils faintly glowing against his torso and arms. He reached out a hand and the boy placed his cane in it. "Well, best be about it then." He smiled at her a madcap grin.

"Shouldn't you be doing those postures and things," Jinhao asked.

"What, those..." Owen replied. "They look pretty don't they?" He raised his cane, and a dome, almost like a heat haze, rose from the places where the Duke's people had energized the circle they had laid out.

MacAllister quickly stopped what she was doing, and grabbed her wand from where one of the Duke's men had tossed it to the ground before he quickly stepped outside the perimeter of the dueling circle.

Owen looked up to where the Duke stood, expectantly. If he was thrown off by Owen's sudden gesture he tried not to show it. What nearly undid him was Strong's younger pup catching his eyes just for a moment. Those cold eyes of his seemed to say, "I'll play your game and then I'll come for you". The Duke had reports that Owen was a reprobate and dissolute, but those eyes could have belonged to his father.

The Duke wet his lips.

"By ancient law and custom, Mistress MacAllister seeks to defend her honor on the field of Magia, against Owen, Lord Strong, on the charge of murder. May the Gods watch and render judgment."

MacAllister began as Owen knew she would. There was nothing subtle about her temperament. A stream of fire blossomed outward from her wand. Owen was ready, his water sigil primed for release. The onlookers were astonished that Lord Strong should employ such a beginner's counter with the corresponding beginner's result; when the fire stream met his waterfall, the resulting steam quickly filled the dome, making it impossible for anyone inside or out, to see anything.

Chapter 19

Do you find the accommodations to your liking, My Queen," asked Captain de Vega.

They were aboard his sky ship, the *Wayfahr*, crammed into a basket de Vega had called the Captain's lookout, on the underside of the craft. As she was sitting in a comfortable chair with silk cushions, together with expensive furs around her legs, Ching Shih could not complain.

In fact, she would not, under any circumstances, let a word of complaint exit her lips. It would never do if it were known that the Terror of the Western Isles, the Dread Pirate Queen, was afraid of heights. She kept her hands firmly clenched beneath the furs and gritted her teeth.

"Yes, de Vega", Ching Shih said crossly, "I am fine, and don't call me that! How long before we sight the Westerners?"

De Vega shrugged. "It seems only appropriate for the Pirate Queen of the Eastern Seas to have that title. We should sight the Westerners at any moment now, provided your informant's information is correct. There is a tea that many find most soothing for those unaccustomed to heights..."

"My sister's information usually turns out to be depressingly accurate," she growled at him. "Nor can I be cloudy-headed when there's a battle afoot."

"True." Di Vega waved a purple-gauntleted hand. "Nor, I submit, can you be frozen in one spot. To direct a sea battle from the air has never been done before. You will need to move about without distraction." His eyes met hers, "I have no doubts about Madame's courage, nor her wisdom."

Ching Shih laughed, a low throaty sound. "I knew there was a reason that I made you my Second," she declared. "Very well, bring me your potion. I only pray that Jinhao's paramour has it wrong about what that vibration bomb can do."

De Vega started to reply when he was interrupted by the cry of one of the lookouts, "Dragon, two points to starboard! Dragon I say! Two starboard!"

"What is that," De Vega said crossly. He strode angrily to the left side of the nest. "I have strict rules on drinking while... Madre Dios! He is right!"

Ching Shih was by his side in a moment. Her heritage made her eyes unusually sharp, so she needed no spyglass in order to see clearly. She hissed at what she saw.

The dragon was moving through the air, body rippling like a serpent, shining like molten gold. It was a common mistake to attribute wings to dragons. Their long serpentine bodies did not require them. Ching Shih's heart skipped a beat. Lohan went to war. That would be the only explanation for him being in dragon form.

"I have never seen such a magnificent thing in my life," de Vega breathed, his eye on the Dragon. He swung his glass forward of the golden form. Look," De Vega pointed, while handing her the spyglass. "There are the Austrians."

Ching Shih took the spyglass, her eyes raking over the Austrian formation.

"They only have one sky ship, a spotter I suppose." They had six themselves, a tribute to de Vega's abilities to make raiding from the sky profitable.

De Vega smiled wolfishly.

"And now we shall teach them how foolish that is, as well as whose skies these really are." He began shouting orders to the crew. The ship slowly turned to take up position behind the dragon.

Ching Shih knew that the spines of the sky ship were really long poles, each tipped with an alchemical solution that repelled the ship from the ground, so that it floated like a cork on the water. She also knew that the ship moved by repositioning the poles so that the ship was pushed along. De Vega calculated the required pole placements in his head, a feat which made Ching Shih admit she was simply an old sea pirate. The future belonged to men like de Vega, air pirates, but for now, he belonged to her.

She quickly stalked around the command nest, all thought of heights irrelevant.

"Signal the other sky ships to follow us in. We'll attack the fleet; keep them engaged until the sea ships can close."

De Vega nodded.

"It shall be so, My Queen!"

"And don't call me that," she snapped at him.

Neither they, nor their lookouts spied the small craft that detached itself from the Austrian flagship, now moving slowly towards them.

Suddenly a great wave of vibration came sweeping over them. The ship shuddered, stopped suddenly in place. Far below, Ching Shih could see the ripples the vibration device made in the water.

The Golden Dragon set forth a mighty roar which seemed somehow to quell the vibrations. He hovered like a humming bird for a moment, studying the small craft. With another roar, he swooped down, lifting the light boat and its deadly box-shaped passenger.

He ended the threat of the vibration device by the simple expedient of crushing it between two claws, the remnants of the device falling harmlessly into the ocean.

De Vega shouted for the ships to attack, and the *Wayfahr* dived towards the Austrian flagship under de Vega's direction.

The flagship was flanked by two destroyer-class ships. All three ships began firing their deck cannon, in an attempt to ward off the aerial attackers. At de Vega's command, the sky ship began firing back with the new aether cannon, concentrating fire at one of the destroyers. The hot bolts of Magia-fueled fire reached some vital magazine and the ship blew up with a blinding flash.

Ching Shih felt a rush of air, and saw the Dragon streak past them. He grabbed the other destroyer by its main mast and lifted it into the air. At an attitude of a few hundred feet, he let it fall back into the ocean, where it became a pile of wreckage when it hit the plane of water.

The *Wayfahr* meanwhile, hovered over the Austrian flagship. De Vega bellowed for boarding, firing his aether pistols as quickly as he could. Ching Shih, grinning like a mad woman, was the first over the side, waving the large broadsword that had made her fearsome reputation.

She landed lightly on her feet, beheading one of the grey uniformed Austrians as she came up off the deck. Muttering curses de Vega shot the two that were coming up behind her, then drawing his own rapier, jumped to land near Ching Shih. For long moments there was only the sound of harsh breathing and the ring of broadsword and rapier against boarding cutlass.

Finally de Vega panted, between engagements.

"You know, you are supposed to wait until the rest of the boarding crew can jump with you."

"Bah," Ching Shih replied, "Where's the fun in that?" With a deft twist of her wrist, she gutted her next opponent, inching ever closer towards the raised area that held the bridge. "I want the damned admiral before he slips away!"

As the rest of the boarders jumped over, gradually the way to the bridge became clear. As de Vega shot the steel lock out of the bridge hatchway, Ching Shih kicked it in. Inside, amid the gleaming instruments of the ship's bridge stood three masked figures. For Ching Shih it was not difficult to pick out the admiral, whose black uniform was covered with gold braid.

She raised her dripping sword to aim it at him.

"I am Ching Shih, called the Pirate Queen of the Seas. I order you to surrender your ship and your fleet before we kill more of you."

The Admiral stared at the bloody apparition before him. He did not lack for personal courage. He had been born into a military family, and had been chosen by the Priestess of the Sun herself to lead this mission. He knew that the Holy One would say that he should keep fighting, but being a military man, Horst von Stuben could not abide the waste of men and ships that would follow his pointless defiance.

"I surrender," he said between gritted teeth. "Tell the fleet to stand down."

"No," one of the other masks exclaimed. "We shall fight on to victory!" He clawed at his holster. A gunpowder shot rang out before Ching Shih could react. The officer slumped to the floor, Admiral von Stuben raised his smoking pistol in a gesture of surrender. He placed it on the deck.

"Now," he said. "Perhaps we can deal with the surrender more quietly."

"Very well," Ching Shih said. "Communicate with your ships and have them raise a white flag of surrender." They all winced as they saw the dragon drop another of the Admiral's ships from a great height, only to have it shatter like scrap iron and kindling as it hit the water.

"I would do so quickly, before the Dragon leaves you no ships to order."

The Admiral gave orders and signal flags were raised and secret messages sent away.

De Vega prodded the Admiral outside, and they all stood in horror at the remains of the once-powerful fleet. Of the twelve ships of the task force, barely half were somewhat intact. They watched as the undamaged ones tried to save their comrades with the help of the boats and sky ships of Ching Shih's fleet.

"*Mein Gott*," the Admiral breathed.

"Aiya," Ching Shih said. "Now you can carry back home the message that Hong Kong, that China, will no longer be any European conquest."

As if for emphasis to her words, the Golden Dragon roared as he passed overhead, making his way back to the city.

Chapter 20

Everyone was startled when the walls, the floor, and even their stomachs began to vibrate. Their attention had been on the duel, even though the only thing visible through the fog-like steam was an occasional flash like lightning.

As quickly as they had started, the vibrations stopped. Everyone was so busy talking about the strange vibration, looking at the walls in askance, that many missed the dome of the dueling circle being released. Their attention was drawn back to it by the cries of the other spectators.

What they saw was the protective circle down, the steam dissipating like morning mist. Owen Strong strode proudly from it. He held out a hand for his clothes. Jinhao wordlessly handed him his pants. Two of the Duke's servants ran to a crumpled form that lay on the ground. They bent to examine the fallen. After arguing among themselves for a time, they both stood up, and one called up to the Duke.

"She's still alive, Your Grace. We are not sure what has been done to her, but she is breathing."

The Duke scowled.

"The Duel was to be to the death! Lord Strong, fulfill your duty!"

Owen had just replaced his evening jacket.

"I believe I have, your Grace. The law simply states 'until one of the two shall no longer be able to raise a defense'. I would offer that Mistress MacAllister has lost as thoroughly as if she had been killed." He reached into his jacket and pulled out a silver cigarette case. Slowly, he tapped the end of the cigarette alight and blew smoke upwards. "Besides, I am more interested in hearing what she has to say concerning her arrangements with certain nobles within the Empire, aren't you, your Grace?"

The Duke's face turned red, and he choked in indignation,

"See here, sir! Do you mean to imply that I had something to do with this—sordid affair? I will call you out myself!"

Owen grinned like a skull.

"Oh, come now, Caldwell, I've said nothing of the kind! Although," he continued musingly, "it would be of interest to see what Mistress MacAllister has to say." He raised an eyebrow at the apoplectic Duke.

"My Lord Governor." Owen turned to the English Governor General of Hong Kong, who was standing next to Duke Caldwell. "Would you be so kind as take not only Mistress MacAllister into your care, but also Duke Caldwell and the Austrian delegation?"

The Governor stepped away from Duke Caldwell, with a look of disgust on his face.

"While I can gladly take the criminal, Mistress MacAllister, I'm not sure I have the authority to detain either a Ducal Ambassador, or a group of accredited delegates of a foreign power," he said with great sadness in his voice.

"May I approach," Owen asked. At the governor's nod, Owen made his way through the throng, climbing the stairs to the stage where the delegates stood.

Owen pulled the *Carte Blanche* from his vest pocket, holding it out wordlessly to the Governor General, who took it. His eyebrows rose inch by inch as his eyes ran over the words.

"My God, man," he breathed, "do you know what this is?"

Owen grimaced bleakly.

"Yes, Sir Charles, I do, and now it is yours."

Sir Charles rocked back on his heels.

"Can you even do that?"

Owen pointed to the *Carte Blanche.*

"I believe it says there that I can."

"Perhaps," Sir Charles' eyes narrowed. "Why are you doing this? No one surrenders this kind of power willingly."

Owen gave an elegant shrug.

"With that kind of power comes a responsibility that I have neither sought out, nor desired. You've always said you were a reformer hampered by a lack of power. Well, Sir Charles, I suggest you reform while you can."

They were interrupted by a triumphant roar, as the Golden Dragon flew towards them, veering off at the last moment. They watched in silence as the magnificent being gently landed in the mouth of a cave high on the hill behind them.

"And now I believe you and your Chinese counterpart shall have to answer to an angry Dragon", Owen said dryly. "I do not envy you, if you cannot show him that you are on top of the plot."

"What plot," Sir Charles said crossly. "All I see is a mad woman murderess, and I was told something about a group of ships approaching the city while you were dueling. What did you do to MacAllister by the way? I've never seen a sleep spell work so well."

Owen sketched the outline of the plot briefly. Sir Charles regarded the information with an iron face.

"Not while I am Governor of this city," he said with iron determination.

Owen smiled at the Governor again.

"That's the spirit," he said encouragingly, "Now to deal with that Dragon."

Later Jinhao asked him about the duel.

"So what did you do to Mistress MacAllister?" The two of them sat around a glowing brazier in Owen's house. The weather had continued to be very chilly, causing even Owen to be grateful for the heat.

He pulled on his pipe staring into the glowing coals.

"I turned her life force back against her. She was pumping out such a lovely amount, throwing around big spells like that."

Jinhao looked at him uncertainly.

"I did not know that was possible."

Owen smiled wanly at her.

"It is perilously close to Necromancy, as far as Crown law is concerned. I trust you won't turn me in for it."

Jinhao gave her gentle smile,

"Of course not." She raised one patrician eyebrow, "That is, so long as you tell me what this plot was and how you figured it out."

Owen sighed.

"It all started with Partridge. Why should he hand such an important assignment to me, an avowed renegade? And why include such a powerful instrument as the carte blanche? I can follow his thought even now. 'Turn the young pup's head, and puff him up so that he does something stupid' is how I think it went." Owen blew out smoke.

"The only problem was that I could not figure out the British connection until the duel. Then it was very clear to me. Duke Caldwell, head of the delegation, had to be actually in favor of the Austrians taking over Hong Kong, which meant that the Order had to think that there was a way to not only avert the threat of World War, but bring someone like Caldwell to heel as well." Owen paused thoughtfully, before continuing.

"Doubtless Caldwell had some economic deal worked out with MacAllister for when she was head of Hastings House. That was the only motive that would explain his encouragement of the stupidity of the duel. He had no idea I am sure, as to the destruction the Austrians were planning."

"But Mistress McAlister was not the heir to the House..." Jinhao observed.

"Ah, caught that did you," Owen nodded approvingly. "That was one less reason to consider her a suspect at first.

The Austrians must have filled her head with talk of being given the title once they were in charge. Caldwell doubtless encouraged such thoughts with balderdash about royal patents and the like. No mind that it would have meant killing also Lady Hastings and her brother," Owen said.

"No self-respecting Englishman could possibly entertain such carnage," Owen stated. "Besides it would literally kill the goose and the golden eggs at the same time." Seeing Jinhao's puzzlement at the phrase, Owen quickly added some context. "It is a saying we have. I'll explain it someday."

Jinhao waved that aside.

"So how did you get the proof to give Sir Charles before he presented it to Lohan?"

"Oh, there isn't any proof, not really," Owen said breezily. "That simply must be the way it was."

Seeing Jinhao's incredulous look, he scowled.

"Wait until Mistress MacAllister comes to, or one of Caldwell's precious servants spend a night in gaol. Then you'll see. Gregg has already found clothing at MacAllister's that would make a good messenger disguise. Wait and see."

Chapter 21

Jinhao came downstairs just as the visitor arrived at the front door.

She had seen Sir Stephen Partridge from the upper windows and doubted very much that Owen would wish to see him. She also doubted that dear old Barton would be able to keep him out.

She considered, again, the merits of killing him. When Mistress MacAllister had come awake, her story matched what Owen had deduced all those months ago. While the now former Duke of Caldwell had paid for his part in the plot with public disgrace, Jinhao was certain that others such as Sir Stephen had escaped without repercussions.

Owen had convinced her that he was more trouble to go after than to leave alone, yet here he was walking right into her reach. She shook her head clear of the temptation as she opened the door.

Sir Stephen's eyes widened as she appeared.

The sign said 'Owen Strong-Magica Investigations and Inquiries' in both English and Mandarin.

"It is Owen's calling now," Jinhao said proudly. "He is gaining a name among English and Han alike, for being who one can go to when there is strange trouble in their lives, whether they be noble or commoner."

Sir Stephen Partridge sniffed.

"Well enough I suppose for a dilettante," he drawled. "Good-day to you Mistress Jinhao."

"And to you, Partridge," Jinhao returned. She watched in silence as the old man walked away. When she was sure he had gone, she turned to the front parlor. Entering noise-lessly, she watched the animated glow on Owen's face.

It looked so much better than the bored indifference he used to show. Jinhao knew the new look well.

That look on Owen's face meant that whatever the old woman was saying to him, Owen would take up her cause.

BOOK 3
STRONG JUSTICE

1885 A.M. (After Mithras)
Chapter 1

I am so glad that you can help, Owen. When I'd heard that you had moved to this corner of the world, I couldn't believe my good fortune." Owen smiled at this. James Findley had always had a strong sense of the dramatic, ever since they had been at Peakhurst Boarding school together. They were in Owens's front parlor sipping brandy and enjoying a warm fire. It seemed that it was unusually cold for this time of year in Hong Kong. The comforts of an aromatic brandy and a crackling fire had driven away the fingers of cold from the chilly fog outside.

"Yes," Owen said mildly around his snifter, "I am sorry, but I must have missed that before. How did you learn where I was?" he asked mildly.

"Oh we had your brother and Sandra over for dinner. He let it slip as it were."

James took a rather large swig of from his own snifter, and smiled sheepishly. "He didn't mean to, I'm sure. I wouldn't dream of invading your privacy except the circumstances are so dire."

It seemed that James's father had been indiscreet in money affairs. It wasn't that the British peerage wasn't normally indiscreet; it was that his father had the bad sense to give his personal note to cover the affair, which was very indiscreet by Britain Society rules. Now the note had been bought by an unscrupulous paper broker who demanded twice as much as the face value of the note, or he would expose the entire thing to Society at large, which would ruin the Findley name for at least a generation.

The paper merchant made Hong Kong his home, as did many of his kind. The laws were looser here. When his father had been stricken with a sudden illness, James had made his way to Owen's door.

"I've heard of this Liu Fong," Owen said. "Really, you can take this to the police. I know an inspector on the local constabulary who would help. Even in Hong Kong such acts as blackmail are illegal."

"But we can't," James cried, sitting upright. "The note might leak out no matter how discreet you say they are. It would be best simply to pay the man and be done with it."

"That is why I've come to you, Owen. I need someone to watch my back in this heathen country." He looked at Owen with sad brown eyes, which caused Owen to sigh.

"Don't let my roommate hear you call the Han 'heathen'. To them we're the heathen ones. Their culture is at least as old as ours you know."

"Ah," James looked around. "Is she your leman?"

"My lover you mean?" Owen chuckled, "No Jinhao is not that, she's well, she is herself. I fear that you won't be able to meet her though. She's away for a few days." James seemed to relax at hearing this.

"Ah," James said in response. "Then there is no reason for you not to accompany me tonight." Owen regarded his old chum in the flickering firelight. Being a sorcerer, Owen could have had the glow-globes in their overhead housings blazing, without worrying about the cost of recharging them. However, he preferred the softer light. He felt that it revealed character not readily visible otherwise. Those brown eyes, Owen thought to himself. He never could refuse them.

"I most certainly shall," Owen looked at the time-piece on the wall. "You say he wished to meet you at eleven?. That gives us plenty of time to have dinner. Mrs. Han is a splendid cook. You must stay for dinner and then we shall be fortified for when we go to recover your father's note."

"Really," James protested "I did not dream of imposing on you this much."

"Nonsense!" Owen said. He raised his snifter in a toast. "Play up school!"

"Play up school!" James replied. The two old friends laughed as their glasses touched with a clink.

~ ~ ~

Later when they had arrived at the address Findley supplied, Owen stopped him from climbing out of the enclosed coach. Holding the man's arm tightly, Owen looked James Findley in the face.

"Listen," Owen said gravely, "this may not go as you think it will." Findley's Adams apple bobbed.

"I am not sure what you mean," he said shakily.

"This is hardly the way business is done here, James," Owen explained. "You may believe that this will be a simple exchange. I assure you nothing is ever simple with these people, especially when they wish to meet in deserted areas at night."

An aether pistol suddenly appeared in Owen's hand, the clear charge tube at the rear of it glowing a baleful red in the shadows of the coach. Firing bursts of alchemical created elemental energy, aether pistols where very lethal and very illegal.

"Good Antlered Lord," Findlay exclaimed, looking at the pistol as if it were a snake.

"Violence, James," Owen said bleakly. "These people work on violence. You should remember that in the future." Owen extended the pistol to him. "I trust you still know how to shoot?" Reluctantly, Findley took it from him.

"Yes, but what about you?" He asked, hefting the weapon.

Owen held up his cane which faintly glowed the bright red of electrum, with a blue stone inset at the handle. The stone held a bright sheen. This was a sorcerer's focus, one that allowed Owen to direct the bound powers of the elemental tattoos on his body. The cane was far more formidable than any gun.

"I doubt that I will have any trouble," Owen said. His eyes searched his friends face. "Are you ready for this, James?"

Wordlessly James Findley nodded. They disembarked from the carriage and began walking, with Owen leading and James following. Owen looked out at the abandoned buildings that surrounded them, the fog already beginning to penetrate his wool cloak.

"I say old dear," Owen said sardonically to James. "This does not look like a legitimate business place to me, does it to you?"

"Well, I don't know what to say," James Findley stammered, "I'm sure this is the right address."

"Oh, I have no doubt of that," Owen turned to face him. "I said it wasn't legitimate business. Much like you are not, James. Legitimate that is." Findley startled at this.

"What do you mean by that Owen?" he questioned. "Why are you looking at me that way?"

"Oh you can drop the act now James," Owen said tiredly. "Did you think that I would let you lead me into being surrounded by them? Really, it is all so depressingly simple. You lead me into a building, we met the mysterious Liu Fong, and meanwhile I'm being targeted by snipers if he is smart, or simple thugs if he is not. They spring out to either kill me or capture me." Owen cocked his head to his old school chum. "Which is it James? Or do you even know?" Findley raised the aether pistol that Owen had given him, pointing it shakily at Owen.

"You always were too clever for your own good Owen," he said hoarsely. "They only wish to take you back to Britain. That is all I know. It was supposed to be as simple as you said, but now you've gone and mucked it up."

"Whatever hold they have on you James, I can help," Owen said gently. "It is still not too late." Findley laughed, a dead rattling sound.

"There really is a money note floating around, Owen. Only it doesn't belong to Father, but to me. They said that after they had ruined me they would see to Heather and the baby." Findley began crying. "They scare me Owen. All I have to do is give them you, and it all goes away." Owen sighed, leaning on his cane.

"If you follow through with this James," he said wearily, "it will never go away."

"Don't move," Findley said, holding the pistol more up-right. He raised his voice, "We're over here! He's gotten wise to us! Over here!

"Oh James." Owen shook his head. "Get down and hide!" he urged. "I can't protect you at the same time as I'm fighting them." Owen began to move towards the crates that were littered around.

"I will shoot, Owen!" James warned.

"No you won't, James," Owen replied sadly. "You really do not think that I would give a working weapon to some-one leading me into an ambush, do you? Now hide!" Owen dropped into the tangle of crates and vanished. Findley tried to pull the trigger only nothing happened. He tried again, and then tossed the pistol away.

"He's over here!" Findley yelled again. A big hand came down on his shoulders.

"Softly, Mr. Findley, softly," The voice belonged to a dapperly dressed European with slicked back black hair and a handlebar mustache. The hand belonged to a giant of a man who had seemed, to Findley, to be the speaker's henchman or something.

"We wouldn't want the Bobbies to come snooping around now, would we," The short man said rhetorically, while ab-sent-mindedly twirling a cane. He looked about lazily. "Now where did you say he went?"

Findley pointed to the tumble of crates. The cane-wielding man nodded and then silently gestured towards the crates. A number of shapes appeared out of the gloom like rats, each hunched over, and bearing long, wicked knives. Noiselessly they padded into the tumble of crates.

Owen crouched down awaiting them. Waterside toughs, he thought. More is the pity for them. The first one came around the corner, knife held out before him. Owen popped out the tip of his cane, briefly touching the man's chest, much as a fencer would score a hit. The man let out a short scream as the spot Owen had touched burst into flame and fell over dead. Outside the jungle of crates, the dapper European stalked back and forth listening to the cries of his thugs as they fell.

"This is untenable," The dapper man muttered, "Completely untenable." He turned to the giant man who was holding up James Findley like a rag-doll, his legs dangling. "And you're sure you didn't warn him Mr. Findley?" the air was cut by another death scream. Findley wiggled in the huge man's grasp.

"No Mr. Victor, No I swear," Findley gasped. "Owen Strong has always been too smart for his own good"! Another short scream rent the night, signaling the death of another one of the hired thugs.

"Completely untenable," the man known as Mr. Victor said again. "Do you not agree Mr. Percy?" The huge man grunted his agreement. "That is what comes of hiring out these days." The dapper man raised his voice. "Strong! Listen to me! My name is Victor, Mr. Victor, which is what

I shall be this night, have no doubts of it! I have your childhood friend here.

You have angered a number of very important people-with your meddling and poking about. They want you dead, and I intend to fulfill their desire. But there's no need for others to suffer from your stubbornness, like young Findley here. Throw down your cane and surrender! I promise your end will be quick!" Mr. Victor raised his cane, the electrum bands around it glowing a bright red, and pointed it slowly at James Findley.

"Otherwise, your Findley is dead first,"

"I am so sorry James,"Owen called out from the crates.

"Owen! Owen!" Findley cried, "You have to help me!"

"Oh do be quiet," Mr. Victor snarled, a bolt of lightning coming from the tip of his cane, aimed at Findley. It was intercepted by a lightning bolt from the crate jungle. Mr. Victor whirled, sending a sheet of fire towards where Owen hid.

"Hah! I have you now!" Victor cried out. The sheet of fire burst among the crates causing the stacked crates and everything in the path of the fire to combust. Several cries came from the mass of crates. It appeared that Mr. Victor didn't care if he killed his own henchmen or not. A vague man-like shape appeared in the flames, writhing in agony.

"Oh yes, you feel that do you?" Victor said savagely. As he slammed his cane into the ground, the shock wave of his strike rippled through the ground, tearing up the foundations, and exposing the waters underneath. Burning crates and figures began to fall into the dark fathoms below, much to Mr. Victor's surprise. The warehouse section they were standing on had been built out over the bay itself, it seemed, and his earth-slamming spell had disrupted the very decking below his quarry.

Owen struggled to keep his footing as the warehouse began collapsing beneath him. He had arcanely protected himself from Mr. Victors fire-spray with ease, only to be taken by surprise by the earth-slamming spell. A crate hit the back of his head, making him swoon. He felt himself falling as the darkness engulfed him.

"No!" Mr. Victor screamed in dismay, sending another bolt of lightning into the burning mess. The two villains and Findley watched as the wreckage sank into the black depths.

"Owen," sobbed James Findley, "Oh my Lord of the Woods! Owen!"

"Shut him up, Mr. Percy," Victor said watching the waters. The giant turned Findley's neck as easily as he would wring the neck of a chicken. There was a snap and James Findley became limp in his large hands.

"Toss him in there with his friend," he commanded. Mr. Victor continued to watch the water for a long time. When neither body floated up, he waited some more. Finally, he sighed and turned to the giant he had called Mr. Percy.

"It would have been nice to get the bonus of bringing in his head, but I do not feel like swimming tonight.There must be a powerful undertow beneath here." He stared at the water. "There is still something about this that feels odd. It was too easy." He shook his head. "We'll keep an eye on his house and that Chinese girlfriend of his for a few days. No one could have been able to survive that." He looked up from the dark waters of the hole in the wharf. He shook his head as if clearing it. "But something does not feel right about this. Luckily, we have the expenses purse." The giant shuffled his feet, wordlessly.

"I know you want to go, and so do I," Mr. Victor snarled. "I would love to be somewhere where the only thing they doesn't eat is rice." He raised his cane threateningly. "But we will do it anyway. Now move along!" The giant cowered in fright from his companion's threat, and began to move towards the road.

Owen desperately clung on to a spar on the underside of the wharf as the two talked above him. Though he had lost his cane and his awareness swam in and out, he retained enough sense to follow what the assassins had been saying. He silently cried for the death of James Finley as he felt his hands slip away from the rough wet wood. The water was cold and endless as it met his face.

~ ~ ~

Owen wasn't sure where he was, or how much time had gone by while he lingered in the dark. He only knew that he could breathe again and that he appeared to be on a hard, cold surface, alternately chilled and then burning, for what seemed like an eternity. In his hazy dream-like state his only clear thoughts where of an old man and a young girl, both Hannish, both of them standing over him. When the old man was present, he felt strange prickling at places on his body. Then he felt better, stronger it seemed. When the girl was present, she brought him delightfully cool water to drink and bathed his head when he was feeling way too warm. First by candlelight and then by bright sunlight he saw their faces.

As he didn't see either of the gateway gods that he had visited at his Initiation into the Greater Mysteries, he assumed that he wasn't in the land of the dead just yet, and he understood he still needed to be fighting. He began frantically feeling about for the focus of his sorcery, his electrum cane. Without it, the elemental binding tattoos on his body could not be keyed, leaving him, if not exactly powerless, than far less powerful. Hands gripped his hands to stop them from reaching for his focus, and a foul tasting liquid was forced down his throat. Dimly he heard a voice in Mandarin speaking,

"That should keep him," the voice said. "Remember, I need him alive. I will take that cane of his. He mustn't touch it."

The darkness swooped back over him in a wave and claimed him once again.

Chapter 2

Jinhao frowned. It wasn't like Owen to just vanish like this. It was true that she was not due back yet for a few days, but Owen had not mentioned anything that would take him away from the house. She turned back to Barton, Owen's clockwork man, a clankman, as the Europeans would call him. The Han preferred live servants, but she understood that automata such as Barton had been the fashion among the British for some time now. Owen called him family. Skeptical, Jinhao had found a valued friend in the mechanical butler, whose responses seemed to go far beyond the slotted cards that Owen placed within his chest from time to time. Still, she had a hard time viewing him as other than a wind-up toy.

"And you are sure he left no note, no hint of where he was going, or if he was going out with anyone?" she asked him again.

"No Mistress Jinhao. He left no note." The clankman visibly shook as his gears turned. "It is possible that he left with his friend from Britain." The butler's frame shook again.

Jinhao's head jerked up at this. "What 'friend from Britain'?"

"Master James Findley to see Owen Strong," the butler replied in the sing song that he used when reciting a conversation. "I do not have an appointment. Tell him it is Jimmy, an old friend from Britain."

"And did you see him go off with this Jimmy?"

"No Mistress Jinhao. Master Owen had me clear away the dishes after dinner and provide cigars from the humidor. I then retired for recharging."

"When was this, Barton?"

"The night before last night Mistress," Barton answered.

"Why haven't you mentioned this before?" Jinhao cried.

"You have not asked if he was going out with anyone before Mistress."

Jinhao wanted to scream. She had heard Owen tell her over and over that Barton was inhumanly literal but she had not really faced it before now.

"That means he's been gone for the better part of three days," she said. She herself had returned late last night only to find the place empty. Assuming that Owen was either carousing or on a case, Jinhao had gone to bed. Now it was nearly midnight again, and no sign of the dark-haired sorcerer.

That might still be the case, but Owen himself had insisted that they keep the other informed of their whereabouts. He pointed out that they were both engaged in dangerous businesses, and it might aid the one to know where to begin looking for the other. Except this time apparently, she thought to herself ruefully, which meant that Owen had thought he would be back that same night he had gone off with Jimmy, whoever he was. Jinhao nodded, coming to a decision. She quickly went up the stairs. Retuning in a concealing night cloak, she placed an envelope on the mantle. Turning to Barton she spoke.

"Command: this envelope is to be given into the hands of Inspector Gregg of the police, should he come inquiring about my or Owen's whereabouts. Otherwise it is not to be moved."

"Understood and logged, Mistress," the butler clanked out.

With that Jinhao ghosted through the front door. She awaited in the nearby bushes, to see if anyone was watching the house. Yes, she thought, there he is. She watched the same mustached man that she had seen earlier in the day. His cane marked him as a probable sorcerer, and his presence marked him as a probable enemy spy. There was no reason for a well-to-do man such as he appeared to be to be wondering the street for hours.

Very well, Jinhao decided, let him watch the house. She knew where he was, and could pick him off at any time. That is, if he was involved with Owen's disappearance. She had other ways to ascertain that. She snaked away, using the shadows to hide her until she came to the cross-street at the end of the road. Here all the rides for hire in the area would sit and rest. Here was also a small-time criminal called Jimmy the Nose. Though he was clearly of Hannish descent, he wore a threadbare European suit of dark burgundy to go with his European street name. The lower classes aped the Western ways slavishly, Jinhao thought to herself contemptuously.

Jimmy picked which cab was allowed to rest there as well who was given which fare. It made him a profitable income and kept order in the street. Thus were the customs in Hong Kong.

"Evening, Mistress Jinhao," Jimmy greeted her warmly enough. It was easy to see why he was called 'the nose', His nose jutted quite prominently from the center of his face. "Fare for one? I have just the right ride for you!"

"Perhaps in a moment, Jimmy." Jinhao discreetly held out a gold coin that Jimmy snatched from her deftly, before anyone could notice. "I want to ask a couple of questions first," Jinhao said. Jimmy gave her a slight bow.

"Of course Mistress, how can I help?" The little man asked with a slight whine.

"Did Master Owen Strong hire a ride about three nights ago?" Jinhao demanded.

"Ah well, I couldn't rightly say," Jimmy replied. "That would be meddling in a sorcerer's affairs. Nothing but trouble comes from that, even if you are his woman and all."

"I am not 'his woman' nor anything else," Jinhao allowed herself to loom over the street grafter. "And please tell your street bullies in the shadows over there to stop or I will tear their arms off, after I remove your head from your neck." Jimmy waved his men back and gulped.

"What do you want to know? Yeah, Lord Strong and some English Toff hired a ride about this time of night. I don't know where to. I sent them to old Hiram over there." Jimmy pointed to a man in a blue robe sitting in the driver's seat of a long hansom. The beast of burden appeared to be a giant man. Jinhao knew that the driver was a member of a strange Mid-east sect and the beast was really a magical construct called a 'golem'. Jinhao tossed Jimmy another coin. This one copper.

"Next time I ask, be more polite," she said. "That would have been a gold piece if you had."

Jinhao drifted across to look up at Hiram. She held up another large Imperial gold piece. He glanced down at her, his face twisted up into a grimace.

"Keep your money," the driver said to her shortly. "I will not take a female sorcerer abroad alone."

"I do not wish a ride, only information," Jinhao said levelly. Owen had always stressed how important it was to be polite to these strange people, that their pride was nearly as great as their power and their customs strange.

"Many people seek knowledge," the driver acknowledged. "What do you seek?"

"Three nights ago, do you remember a late fare, two men, one of whom carried an electrum cane?" The driver nodded quickly, up and down.

"Yes," his voice crackled like old paper. "Two British gentlemen if I am a judge. They wished to be taken to the old warehouse district down by the water." The driver shook his head. "I do not know of any businesses that still work out of there, let alone at that time of night. I fear they were up to no good."

"Exactly where did you let them out," Jinhao asked. The driver told her. She turned to go.

"There is no call to be chasing down the likes of them!" The driver called after her. "Card sharps and foreign dandies will only break your heart!"

Jinhao ignored him and went briskly down the street until she came to an alleyway that was not bathed in the brilliant light of one of the Mage globes hanging from the lamp posts that lined the street. She ducked down the alley and then stopped, awaiting pursuit.

It was a pity they did not live in one of the poorer sections in the city. The streets there were lit by gas or oil lamps and she could already have been scaling the building without being seen. When no pursuit was forthcoming, she hitched back her cloak and began scaling the wall beside her.

Chapter 3

The moon was only two days from full. Shining down from a clear sky, its misty light transformed the roof-tops into a fey world of bright silver areas and sharp-edged darkness. Chimney stacks stood like silent sentinels, their shadows offering protection from the revealing dazzle overhead. Jinhao flitted lightly from the dark shelter of one such sanctuary to another, her whole being alive in a way that it hadn't been since she had returned to Hong Kong.

This other world of the rooftops was called by some the thieves' highway and she could understand why. During the day, the city was thronged with loud clumsy people, includ-ing a surprisingly large number of Peelers. The night time roof-tops, by contrast, were a quiet dark land where one's business was one's own, especially if one was determined and sure-footed. She had encountered only a few other trav-elers during her explorations, easily hiding in concealment before they were aware of her. Jinhao had to admit some of them were almost as competent at stealth and concealment as she was. Almost. She doubted that there were any in the city who could match her in either skill.

Jinhao paused, crouching, before the gap that marked some alley or side street below. Someone had conveniently placed a board across the gap to ease passage, indicating that others passed this way frequently as well. She cast her spirit senses in a wide circle, searching for the betraying aura of another life nearby. Finding nothing, she pulled energy from her center, feeling it flow through her. Still crouching, she tensed her legs and then leaped across the gap, landing silently on the other side. She swiftly moved to the shadow of another pair of chimneys and paused again, senses awake and searching. Nothing.

She continued moving, spirit and body luxuriating in the effort and the quiet. She smiled as she recalled her training games as a child at the Imperial Academy for Adepts; during trips to Bombay, they played seek and stalk through the alleys. A 'kill' was managing to touch a teacher without being caught first, the reward for each 'kill' a coconut ice, a candy treat that she was still extremely fond of. She soon had many kills, surpassing her teachers in skill even before her bleeding began. Jinhao shivered from the cold of the deep night, pulling her gloves tighter. In truth, she missed those sultry nights and the innocence of those days.

Jinhao had grown up in Hong Kong. She found it cold at night now, even in what was called summer. One of Owens visitors, some professor from the University, had asserted that something was making the weather change, but what that something was, no one knew.

She had been told that now nearly two million souls called Hong Kong home; dirty, smelly, noisy people., The Europeans stank from eating too much meat and touching too little water. Jinhao found the atmosphere they created oppressive on her soul, which led her to seek the roofs at night. It was not that she was unfamiliar with large cities, far from it. She'd been to several in her travels.

She was most familiar with Shanghai and Beijing, the Imperial city, each of which claimed many more residents and were just as modern with Mage lights and clanking steam cars. But this place was as unlike the other cities of the East as an erotic dream was from a nightmare. She still wasn't sure rather to bless or curse the vision that had led her back to the mixed free port, where Grandfather's rule was absolute.

Jinhao had fled the bloody plans Grandfather had made for her soon after attaining her initiation as a young woman. While the parting was not what one could call amicable, Grandfather had let her go without placing the death mark upon her, in a rare show of mercy. Perhaps Grandfather thought that she would come home of her own accord if he waited. If so, Jinhao had vowed, he would have a very long wait indeed. For a time she had worked on her father's brother's merchant airship, learning the ways of being human, then, learning their ways.

When the Old Emperor died, the Dowager Empress had seized all power. For a time Jinhao did not remark on it. After all, the Imperial bureaucracy still ran, and if the Empress and her friends got rich for a few years, well, that was how it was. There was a new Emperor growing up in the Forbidden City, and things would change again. That too, was the way of things. Being raised by a Dragon gave one a certain perspective.

But the Empress did not relinquish power. Instead her grip became even more ruthless. Injustices sprang from the Throne like weeds, choking the life from the Kingdom. Even Jinhao was forced to realize that something needed to be done.

Grandfather had contacted her with the offer of a true alliance if she would consider becoming a concubine of the Boy Emperor. This she agreed to do, only to find that the Emperor was both powerless and innocent. He was kept in splendid isolation, and when Jinhao attempted to remove him from it, she ran into a trap set by the Dowager's lap-dog of a court sorcerer, Fan Zhou. Only the powers of her heritage had enabled her to escape his wrath. The Emperor would not come with her, to her regret.

While fleeing the Imperial Court, her Powers gave to her a vision that allying with a white-skinned sorcerer would save not only Hong Kong but the world. Her glimpses of the future came rarely, but she had learned to not ignore them.

To Jinhao's surprise, she met the Sorcerer from her dreams at a rest house near the Hong Kong border. By sheer fortune, he defeated a greater demon that the court sor-cerer had sent after her. The British sorcerer's name was Owen Strong. Even though he smelled of the Lotus drug that destroyed the mind and powers of Sorcerers over time, he still had more than enough power and wit to defeat the sending That it was impressive to her, she was reluctant to admit.

Since then, his powers of deduction as much as his powers arcane, had led her to believe that Owen Strong was indeed the man of her visions. Someone who would eventually be not only the symbol, but the truth of the good that the united peoples of Hong Kong could become. A fearless champion of every member the province. The start perhaps of an Empire neither British nor Han, but the best of both.

Jinhao turned to scramble up a sloping roof. She crouched in the shadow of the building's chimney and looked out over the city. The bright haze of the new electric streetlamps directly below her gave way to occasional grand clusters that marked the mansions of the wealthy. Beyond that, more lights winked on the ground as far her eye could see.

She turned back and looked up the hill towards the palace her Grandfather kept. It glowed with its own magical light against the moon and the night's stars. She sighed. It wasn't easy being the granddaughter of the Dragon of Hong Kong. There were expectations that needed to be kept. The balance between Easterner and Westerner was their family's obligation.

She grimaced.

Owen Strong was a large part of that responsibly for her. She admitted to herself that his wit and sense of justice was attractive, and made him easy to be around. She was sure though that her Vision was true, despite Grandfather's skepticism. She only hoped the British fool had gotten drunk and lost in a brothel somewhere with his friend, rather than murdered or worse. If pressed, Jinhao had to admit that she was fond of him in her way.

Jinhao paused at a rooftop's edge. She had reached the end of her sojourn. Here the buildings stopped, the road below meandering like a river through a canyon dividing the more residential buildings from the dockyards. She peered through the moonlit dazzle to see that the area was already crawling with searchers trying to be inconspicuous. Jinhao watched them move clumsily about, and decided to be patient. It would be no hardship, Adepts were trained to stalk patiently.

Gradually the figures gave up their search, walking unto the road where she could see them more clearly. The majority of figures wore some variant of the tunic and pajama pants common to the working classes. A few seemed to be crying.

Jinhao eeled her way silently down the side of the building and across the road. She paused in the shadows of a warehouse when she heard one of the searchers noisily walk towards her. Whoever they were, she thought, they had no training in being quiet.

As the lone figure passed her, she drew a dagger, springing towards their back. With a kick she knocked their legs out from under them as her arm came around their throat. A cry of surprise cut off when they felt the cold edge of the dagger at the side of their neck. They knelt very still.

"Now," Jinhao whispered in the dialect of Mandarin used by the working classes. "we shall have a nice quiet talk. I shall release your throat. Know that I will kill you should you attempt to shout or struggle to escape. I will kill you so quickly that your spirit will barely have time to leave your body." She eased the pressure of her arm across his throat. "Do you believe me?"

"Yes," The trembling man wet his lips. "Have mercy mighty one! I am only a fisherman from the harbor."

"Shh," Jinhao soothed him. "Quietly now. What is a fisherman of the harbor doing here?"

"My mother sent me to look for the body of my cousin, Mei Pen." The man's voice betrayed bitterness. "He was always loitering around the docks, playing the tough. Now he is dead, and my mother's family shall have to pay for his funeral."

"Then you found your cousin's body?"

The man began to shake his head, then stopped as he felt the dagger. "No, I have not. Nor did any of the others; it was likely dropped in the harbor when the *Quizi* Sorcerer broke the wharf decking."

Jinhao pressed the dagger so hard against his throat that it drew blood. "This other Sorcerer what do they say happened to him?"

The fisherman gasped, speaking in a rush, "They say that he died, Mighty One! Fell into the water and drowned after killing many of the men that were hired."

"This Sorcerer who hired your cousin, what was his name?" Jinhao demanded.

"Please, mighty one," the man trembled like a leaf. "I do not know his name! I swear it!"

Jinhao sighed. It was clear that she would get no more from the frightened man. Aiming the pommel of her dagger at a certain spot on the back of his head, she struck firmly. The fisherman fell over like a sack of grain, unconscious but unharmed. She disliked killing unnecessarily.

Leaving the man where he fell, Jinhao carefully moved about the warehouse complex. There had been a battle right enough. She followed the traces of sorcerous fire to gaze down into the dark maw where the wharf itself had been shattered. The black depths gave up none of their secrets, no matter how long she glared into them. The waters of the bay were cold and the currents were deep.

If there was a body within, chances were it was long gone out to sea. Her heart sank, then rose again. If there was no body, then Owen Strong might still be alive, but where? Where could he be?

Chapter 4

O wen came awake as he had been taught to do under trying circumstances, with no visible signs of being conscious, eyes still closed, breathing unchanged. His ears told him that there was only one other person in the room. His body told him that someone had put him into dry clothes of coarse cotton. They had tied him sitting upright to some sort of pillar, his hands bound behind him with hemp rope. He was not among friends then, he concluded.

Gradually he slitted his eyes open to see the small Han girl from his fever dreams sitting on a crate reading a book. Without looking up, she spoke.

"Good. You are awake at last." She put down the book and looked at him. "Are you thirsty?"

Owen opened his mouth to speak, only to find it dry as sand. He contented himself with nodding.

The girl smiled revealing full white teeth. She leaped down from the crate, picking up a wooden bucket and a long-handled ladle. The youngster scooped water up in the ladle and brought it to his lips.

Owen drank greedily, feeling the cool water cutting the dryness that fouled his mouth. When he had finished the first ladle he wet his lips with his tongue.

"You know," He said hopefully, "I could drink a lot easier if my hands were free."

The girls face crinkled up as if he had made a great joke.

"Oh no, Mister," The girl shook her head. "Mikey said that you would try to trick me into letting you loose. You wait until Mikey comes back with the rest."

"I see," Owen said. "Mikey must be very smart. Whom are the rest?" Her face lit up.

"Oh Mikey is the smartest! And the others are..." She closed her mouth, shaking her head. "Mikey said I wasn't to talk to you either. You just want to know how to hurt us like all the rich folk do. I am just to give you water and make sure you do not choke or anything." With that, she clambered back up onto the crate and picked up her book again.

Well, Owen thought sardonically, that went well. He tested his bonds to discover that there was no hope of loosening them. Whoever had tied the ropes knew what they were doing, his ankles were likewise bound. He had been placed on a soft mattress which kept him away from the cold of what must be an abandoned factory floor. There were plenty of those around the harbor district, remains of failed attempts to industrialize the city.

He wasn't uncomfortable now. Both his arms and his lower back would begin to ache from his posture over time, he knew from experience. He decided that he would wait it out for the moment, until 'Mikey and the others' returned at least. He shared a silent look with his young captor and settled to wait. Despite himself, he dozed off.

Owen came to again to find a strange couple standing next to his young guard. The woman was Western in features, with pale skin, blue eyes, and blonde hair carefully curled in the latest fashion. The man was Han, or some Eastern breed, with his black hair slicked back against his skull. Their clothing spoke of middle class prosperity that would not be out of place anywhere in the city. Owen blinked as the man spoke.

"You are Owen Strong," he said in English. Owen tried to straighten up. His arms and back had stiffened up in this position as he had feared they would.

"Perhaps I am Sir," Owen said calmly. "What if I am?" The man smiled like a shark, reaching behind him. He pulled forth Owens electrum cane with a flourish.

"Because I assume that Owen Strong would want this back."

Owen knew a moment of hope. He had been afraid that the cane was lost. As his magical focus, it enabled him to channel the elemental power bound in his tattoos into active manifestation.

"I am not sure if that is mine or not," Owen said. "Perhaps if you untie me and let me examine it I can tell you more." The man laughed.

"Oh, you are Strong," he said definitely. "Even down here, we have heard of the quizi nobleman poking his nose into others affairs with his magical red metal cane. But I know that you are helpless while we hold this." He twirled the cane. "The question is what will you do for it?"

"Mikey . . . I can call you Mikey can I not? I believe the question is, what do you want me to do for it?" Owen replied. Mikey glared at the younger girl sitting on the crate.

"I told you not to talk to him," Mikey growled.

"I did not, not really anyway," She said defensively. "He asked is all." The man turned towards Owen.

"Very well. Yes you may call me Mike. As to what I want." He pointed with the cane at the European woman at his side. "I want you to teach her your Western sorcery."

Of all the demands that Owen had expected to hear, that was not one of them. He looked from the Hannish thug to the Western young woman and back again.

"No," Owen replied, "it is simply not possible. I am no teacher, and you," he said looking at the woman, "how old are you?" He demanded looking at the woman beside 'Mikey'.

"I be twenty this Flower Day," the woman responded.

"She is at least ten years too old to begin training," Owen insisted. "I started at ten. Then there are the facilities with their special wardings." He looked around the abandoned factory house dismissively. "Which, trust me, you want to have in order to absorb any elemental mistakes." Mikey's face grew dark at Owens refusal.

"You mean you won't share your holli-polli tricks with those of the wrong class don't you? Think we're not good enough don't you?" He turned to the young girl sitting on the crate. "Mei, go get a candle," he ordered. She scampered down and was off though the door to the door behind them.

"It has nothing to do with *class*," Owen said with exasperation. "One of the best Air Sorceress I know started out as a Shepherd's daughter. This is not like teaching someone their ABC's! There is real danger in this!" Mei returned with a short candle, a metal bowl with a wick sticking up from it.

"Go ahead Mary," she said. "Show the poofter what you've got!" Mary took the candle, looking at Mikey for permission. He nodded.

Mary closed her eyes for a moment, frowning in concentration. The wick burst into flame to the delighted exclamations of little Wei. Mikey leaned on Owen's cane looking at him with a smug face.

"You see," he boasted. "She has the spark right enough."

"Mary," Owen said very slowly. "Do not open your eyes. Can you make the flame go out?"

"Well, I have never tried" she said in a dreamy voice. "Why would I want to when this feels so nice." Her hand came up, as if caressing it, and the flame danced higher in response.

"Mary," Owen said in measured tones. "I want you to listen to my voice." He wet his lips, guiding her through the opening trance, getting her to center her awareness to the point of her power located below her belly button in the center of her body, she swayed to his words. Mikey looked from one to the other of them, anger and suspicion knitting his brow.

"What are you doing?" He hissed at Owen.

"Do not interrupt," Owen hissed at him. "You will break her concentration!"

Mary gave a wordless exclamation as the flame shot up from the candle in sudden violence towards the ceiling. She began to throw the candle from her. Owen's calm voice stopped her.

"Mary," he said. "Do not throw the candle away. You are the master of the flame.You. Now, close your eyes again and breathe into your center. As you breathe out see the flame in your mind's eye becoming smaller." The tip of the flame began to ratchet lower with each one of Mary's breaths.

"That's very good Mary," Owen said softly, "very good. Now with this exhale send the flame away." As if a giant hand had snuffed it out, the flame vanished abruptly. Mary swooned and would have fallen to the hard floor save for Mikey scrambling to catch her in his arms. Mei leaped up from where she had been sitting on the crate, a large revolving air-pistol pointed straight at Owen's head.

"What did you do to her?" Mikey demanded. "She's never had this happen before!"

"Then you're bloody lucky," Owen ground out. "I did nothing to her. Look at the hem of her dress, there will be burn marks there, unless I am mistaken."

As Mikey eased her towards the floor Mary stirred, protesting that she could stand on her own. Mikey grabbed first the cuff on her dress's sleeve, then he bent to examine her hem. The whites of his eyes shone wide as he looked first at her then at Owen.

"There are burn marks on the cloth," He said shakily. "What witchcraft is this?"

"Her own," Owen replied wearily. Addressing the European woman he said quietly, "So Mary, strange bursts of fire appear around you? Clothes scorched, but you can't remember a flat iron applied to them?"

"Only in the last day or so," she replied meekly. Owen nodded, shifting his weight to make his bound arms more comfortable.

"Then it is still early days," he replied. "You are a fortunate young woman indeed." Turning to Mikey he said, "Mary has the gift of being a fire caller. She needs to learn how to manage her gift or it will consume her, and quite possibly you, in flames."

"I do not believe you," Mikey said angrily, his face a study in disbelief. "You westerners have many people that can call the fire, and they do not cause everything to burn down. You even hire them to start the street lamps, and they do not cause the street to burn down!"

"That is because they went to school," Owen shot back. "Where they learned the basic skills to be able to control their gift. We have an old saying, 'fire is the easiest to call, the hardest to control.' I am willing to bet that you do not teach that in your knock shop school!"

"Here now," Mei said in Mandarin. "Mary isn't like that! Nor is Mikey! You apologize for that!"

Mary laughed like a scarred bird. "I am you kind's refuse, Lord high and mighty! Mikey here," she laid a hand on his arm tenderly. "Mikey saved me from what you call the 'knock shop school'.

"He saved me too!" Mei said still holding her gun at Owen, "not to mention that he only wants Mary to learn so that she can!"

"Mei—that is enough," Mikey said more calmly than before. "We do not need to justify ourselves to his kind." He turned to Owen, "So, Owen Strong, will you teach her?"

"An untrained sorcerer is a danger to everyone, including themselves," Owen replied automatically with the old proverb. He looked absently at Mary. His mind had been working all along. Perhaps this was the answer to his problems too. He needed someplace to hide from 'Mr. Victor' if that was his real name. It was clear from what he'd over heard that Owen had offended the wrong people in power back home. They had sent this contract killer and his giant thug after Owen like predatory birds with cries of ill omens.

He could not return to home or even contact Jinhao, he decided. To place her in that sort of danger was not simply not done, not until he had dealt with these hired assassins at least. It was enough that Findley had been caught in their spiders' web. His death weighted on Owen heavily. Fine, he decided, perhaps he could made a refuge here. The girl clearly needed looking after. He looked up at Mary and spoke the old ritual words.

"Do you want to learn of these Mysteries, and in time, have the Greater Mysteries unfold for you? Do you promise to obey me in all things unquestioningly, from this moment onward?"

Mary looked at Mikey who nodded permission to her. Mary nodded at Owen in turn. "I do," she said solemnly.

"I cannot promise to teach her to be a full sorceress," Owen said to Mikey. "That is beyond my skill. But I can promise to teach her how to control her gift of fire calling."

"That will do for a start," the gang leader said.

"You also will have to follow my instructions if you want this hare-brained scheme to succeed" Owen continued. "I will require the return of my focus cane, and I want little Mei there to stop pointing that very big gun at me. I also need to be untied right now."

Mikey got a determined look on his face and advanced towards Owen, a wicked curved knife in one hand and Owen's cane in the other.

"I do not think it will be necessary to agree to all of that," he said to Owen grimly.

Chapter 5

Owen was given a surprising amount of freedom following the so-called negotiations with the street leader called Mike, although Owen would be surprised if that was his birth name, given those Hannish features. Owen had agreed to be the girl's teacher only because the arrangement gave him a place to hide while he recovered from the attack on the wharves.

That the man who called himself Mr. Victor had been a headhunter Owen had little doubt. Headhunters were a part of British society, Sorcerers who were really little more than hired killers. When deeds of Magia and Necromantic revenge had become part of your culture for hundreds of years, headhunters such as Mr. Victor would always arise, Owen reflected.

Headhunters were called that because of the vogue for British Nobles to hire Sorcerer-assassins who would cut off the head of their target, thus stopping the distressing tendency for victims of assassination to rise from the dead and seek out their killers. As most Nobles were also Sorcerers of some sort, this fashion kept down the number of revenants.

Even with Necromancy outlawed throughout the Empire, most Nobles were not above a little necromantic revenge. Headhunters were very expensive and very ruthless. Whomever Owen had upset must be reasonably wealthy, but that hardly narrowed the field of possible persons, let alone accounted for the organizations who would doubtless like his head. Eventually he would have to find Mr. Victors' employers, but first he would have to defeat the assassin himself.

Headhunters tended to follow certain habits and traditions, habits that Owen could exploit. Victor and his giant thug would doubtless be watching the house; one of those traditions was the destruction of the target's household. If that had truly been what Victor's employer had paid for, the Assassin would have used some other stratagem. Barton and the house should be relatively safe. Given that Jinhao would not be returning for a few days, and would thus be away from the danger, this opportunity seemed ready made for him to out-flank the headhunter.

Of course the fact that Mike still held his Electrum cane was a consideration, but not as great a hold over Owen as the street leader figured. He could always create another focus, although that would take a great deal of time as well as energy, and he would hate it. Owen had lost enough in this little adventure already.

He kept seeing James' face over and over again in the grips of that huge creature accompanying Victor. Owen fiercely clenched his hands together at the memory. He had never felt so helpless as he did when seeing James in danger, and then again when he heard his childhood friend call for his help. Victor was a powerful Sorcerer, Owen couldn't deny that. Most headhunters were. The man would face justice for James all the same, Owen vowed.

"Hey Mister, you alright?" asked the girl Mei who was behind him. Owen came to himself to find that he had stopped in the passageway down which he and the girl had been walking. Mei was the price of Owen's apparent freedom. The little girl with her big pneumatic pistol was his constant shadow as well as his guide.

"Yes," Owen said, "I am fine." He pointed towards the room ahead of them. "What room is that just ahead of us again?" Mei sighed in the weary manner that was the habit of children everywhere when confronted by clueless adults. Owen had to admit though, that she seemed sharper in wits than many adults he dealt with.

"That's the big eating hall, the re-fac-tory" she replied, stumbling over the English phrase. "You know, where we all eat and tell stories about the day."

"The refectory I presume you mean," Owen said simply. Mei gave an exaggerated shrug or grimace, Owen wasn't sure which, at his reply.

"Yeah," she agreed, that word. What is it with you British anyway? Why can't you just say *big eating hall*?"

"That would make things too simple," Owen explained. "We British have never shied away from the complex and the convoluted. In fact, we positively embrace it. Why call something one thing that everyone knows when you can call it six different things that only a few can understand?" Mei looked at him puzzled.

"You people are crazy," Mei pronounced. Owen nodded in agreement.

"Oh, absolutely," he said. He walked into the large hall, looking around. He was pleased to find it both clean and ordered, with long tables and benches that would not be have been out of place at his boarding school. To continue with the boarding school theme, he realized that he had only seen women and young girls wherever he went in to factory

"This is amazing," he said to Wei, "but where are any boys?" The girl looked up at him.

"Boys don't get left out by their families to die," she explained. "This is all Mike's doing. Some of us he takes in as small babies, others when they're older. The babies all live upstairs," she continued. "Once you're old enough though, you have to go out and nick things to keep the babies fed." She expanded her chest proudly. "I am the leader of the pick-pockets, because I'm the best."

"I am sure you are," Owen murmured while thinking. Abstractly, he knew about the custom of exposing infants, especially unwanted girls, but to his chagrin had never really thought about it, or about what happened to the abandoned. Suddenly the room swam in front of his eyes.

"Hey Mister," Mei called to him. Her voice sounded as if it came from down a well. Owen felt for the closest of the benches.

"I believe I shall just sit down for a moment," he remarked. The floor came up to meet him.

Chapter 6

When he came to, at least he wasn't tied up anymore. He opened his eyes to see his little guardian sitting on her packing crate. She tossed him a large bun.

"About time you woke up," Mei said to him. "Eat that and get ready to go out." Owen groggily bit into the bun to find it stuffed with curried vegetables that exploded with flavor in his mouth. He wet his lips.

"Any chance of a cup of tea?" He asked. Mei snorted at him.

"It's a working day," she said. "You should feel grateful for what we have."

"Working day?" Owen asked, hungrily eating the last of the stuffed bun. "What does that mean?"

The girl pulled herself off the crate, brandishing her rather large air pistol. Owen noticed the bulging gas chamber with some disappointment. If it had been a gunpowder weapon he might have been able to ignite the cartridges with his Fire talent, but it seemed that even among ruffians and street urchins that trick was too well known these days. Not, he reminded himself, that he wanted to.

"It means that Mikey wants you to come outside as we can't be bothered to watch over you anymore. Get up," Mei said grimly, training the weapon on Owen. Owen stood, considering whether to fight. At least he wasn't swooning anymore when he stood up. The strange old man they all called the Doctor had come, Owen vaguely remembered him holding Owens wrist while clucking his tongue, then sticking Owen with needles in various places. Owen had heard of this form of Hannish Medicine, though he had never experienced it before.

To his surprise, the needles didn't hurt, and he did feel quite better than he had. While he wasn't sure about it replacing a good old fashioned Western Healer laying on their hands, then giving him alchemical potions, he had to admit the man's ministrations seemed to work. Owen flexed his legs, regarding Mei and the distance between them.

The Western woman Mary came in through the double factory doors behind them at that moment. She was wearing what Owen judged to be a middle-class Western dress of lavender and sky blue complete with a feathered hat and large matching bag. A far cry from the grey pajama pants and tunic she normally wore. She stopped, taking in the sight of Owen and the little girl facing off.

"Wei!" Mary said in a tone kept for scolding children who were stealing sweets, "Where did you get that pistol? And why are you pointing it at Owen?" Mei tossed her head, black curls swirling. Owen noticed that the pistol remained rock steadily aimed at him.

"Ah, Mary," Mei whined, "I was just doing what Mikey said. He told me to scare the *Quizi* so that he wouldn't run off when we take him out." *Quizi* was slang for 'tricky foreign devil', a term Owen had often heard used in reference to Western Sorcerers. Mary frowned at this and strode over to Mei, hand outstretched.

"Give me that gun! You are not to refer to him as a tricky demon! He's my teacher! Am I a demon?" The little girl seemed to deflate under this scolding, and meekly handed Mary the pistol.

"Aw, no Mary," Mei protested. "You know that you're not!" She nodded in Owens direction. "But he's a rich magia user, and English, not to mention a guy!" Owen could not decide from this if Mei's main objection to him was his sex, his sorcery, or his birth. While he was still puzzling this out, Mike the gang leader came through the doors. He looked at Owen

"Good you are awake," he said crisply. He turned to Mei. "Get him up and ready to go out the door."

Mei looked between Mike and Mary. "Mary took my pistol," she said glumly. Mike whirled on Mary.

"What did you do that for?" He snapped. Mary frowned, the gun held loosely at her hip by the barrel.

"Mei was threatening Owen with it. That is no way to treat a house guest!" Mike answered her with a frown of his own.

"'House guest is he?" Mike looked at Owen. "You had better be worth it, *Quizi*," he said. Mary stamped her foot at this.

"He is no *Quizi*, he is my teacher!" she objected.

"Fine," Mike snapped. "Then you can be responsible for him today! That is, if I can trust you to shoot him for the safety of the gang!" Wordlessly, Mary aimed the pistol in Owens direction and pulled the trigger, while still staring at Mike. There was the whish of displaced air, followed by the thunk of a bullet hitting the wooden pillar behind him. Owen ducked down as sharp splinters flew around him.

"I can shoot him just fine," Mary retorted. "But you had better be willing to get me a new teacher!"

"You!" Mike whirled on Owen, who was still brushing off chips of wood from his shoulders. "This is all your fault! Just do as you're told and there should be no trouble! Wei," he ordered, "go round up your crew and get to the streets. Do the usual plays, I will meet you at noon." The girl nodded sharply, ringlets flying.

"Got it, Mike." She turned towards Owen. "Mind you do what Mary says, foreign devil!" With that admonishment, she swaggered out the double doors behind her.

"I would be happy to follow whatever directions you have," Owen said calmly. "Just what are we about? What is a *working day*?" Mike grinned at Owen savagely.

"We're running low on supplies," he explained. "So we're all going out stealing. I can't spare anyone to watch you here. Besides Doctor says that you should get out in the fresh air." He held up a warning finger. "Mind you if you try to run or tip off the constables to us, you'll be the first to die!"

"It would be to my advantage to not draw attention to myself I assure you," Owen said dryly. "I cannot be recognized." Mike narrowed his eyes at this.

"You are on the dodge from someone," he guessed. "The people who put you in the water." Owen shrugged.

"Perhaps," he replied. "I promise you that you also do not want to come to anyone's attention." He gestured to the clothes he was wearing, grey Hannish tunic and pajama pants, then towards Mikes suit. Like Mary he was wearing the epitome of middle-class Western apparel withdark charcoal pants, maroon embroidered vest and an ink-blue suit coat. "Should I not be dressed more as you are?" Owen asked. Mike squinted at Owen.

"Your clothes were torn up for scrap," the young ganger said. "They were too burned and soggy to save." He shook his head. "No I think that what you are wearing will do just fine. We'll get you a bamboo hat and no one will know that you are a foreigner. Mary here will keep you in line. Just do as she says."

"Well," Owen replied with a bow towards Mary, "Let us be about it by all means." Mary's face colored at him. She hid the handgun under an embroidered shawl that she wore over her bare shoulders. She glanced warily at Mike, then faced Owen with a determined set to her jaw.

"Just remember," she said fiercely. "I have this and know how to use it, so you just mind what I say." Owen raised his hands in a gesture of surrender.

"I promise, I shall be the epitome of obedience," he murmured. Mike pointed that he should go first, followed by Mary and then Mike himself. He walked forward without a backward glance. If they had intended to kill him they could have done so any time before this. Besides, it was clear that Mike truly needed a teacher for Mary, a fact that Owen still wasn't sure about in his own mind. Once through the double doors, he was greeted by a swarm of youngsters running about, all headed towards what he presumed was the doors to the outside. Owen looked around with interest as this was the first chance that he'd had to see the home of his erstwhile rescuers.

To his eye it appeared clear that the gang had been here for some time. He found himself in what appeared to be some sort of common room filled with benches, only guttering candles in mirrored holders vainly chasing away the gloom. Makeshift stairs ran up the walls to other rooms, the stairs all full of scampering youths in various modes of dress. Some in pants and tunics much like his own, others barefoot in smocks or shifts. The only common denominator again was that they appeared to Owen to be all female, most Hannish, although a few of the younger ones looked to be mixed blood of some sort.

Studded throughout the running stream were a few older women, dressed much as Mary was, in western dress, wearing stylish bustles and elegant hats. This mode of dress was very fashionable among the middle-classed Han, and Owen was surprised to see it here. The other thing that surprised him was the cleanliness that greeted him wherever he looked. While the ragamuffins might sport an artfully applied smudge of dirt on cheek or nose, their home was cleaner than any foundry had a right to be.

"There isn't any escape," Mike remarked from behind him, "You might as well stop looking for one, and march on out the doors there." Owen realized that he had stopped walking and turned his head. Mike and Mary looked the very picture of a respectable Hong Kong couple, he wondered what they were about. Doubtless, he would find out.

"Sorry," Owen said innocently. "I am simply not used to going out minus my cane. I do not suppose that I could have it?" Mike laughed, and shook his head.

"I don't think so," he said. "I've heard plenty of stories about what you Sorcerers can do with things like that. This way you stay powerless." Owen frowned at this statement. While it was true that he could not conjure the strongest manifestations of his powers, he could still do some small parlor tricks, which he was sure would catch them off guard. He could understand the natural reluctance Mike had to giving him a tool of escape. The fact was, he did not want to escape. Somewhere out there lay the assassin, Mr. Victor, as well as whoever had hired him. Returning home would have to wait until the situation had been dealt with. Fortunately, Jinhao was not due to return for a few days yet. That should give him enough time to sort things out.

"It is not that," Owen said to the gang leader. "You are correct in your surmise, I am hiding. The ones who are seeking me are a Western Sorcerer like myself, and a rather tall brute of a man who is accompanying him. Have you heard of anyone like that?" Mike frowned in thought.

"No, I can't say that I have," he answered slowly. "What does that have to do with your magic cane?" The heavy front doors were held open by a couple of small children. Owen stepped through quickly to find he was in a small alleyway. He followed the stream of young women while still talking to Mike, who walked behind him.

"Only that you are correct, in that it can be a powerful weapon in my hands," Owen confessed. "Should we meet these Assassins while about your business, I cannot protect you unless I can bring all my powers to bear." Mary frowned at this, while Mike laughed.

"Oh, I don't think that you will trick me that easily," he said. "I think that your precious cane will remain here." He flicked his fingers towards the doors. "Now go." Owen went.

Going outside turned into a walking excursion that re-
sulted in them emerging onto Main Street with its con-
stantly- moving sea of humanity. The vanguard of young
street urchins melted into the throngs and were soon lost.

"The young'uns are honing their pickpocket skills," Mike
explained cheerfully. "Mei is the leader of them. We'll meet
her at noon and see how the take is doing." He nodded as
the older western-dressed young women clustered around
them. "Meanwhile, we'll go shopping. Come along."

Owen held his tongue as the group of gaily dressed young
women sashayed down the street. They turned onto a narrow alleyway that Owen knew held shops that catered to the
city's upper class. At some unspoken signal from Mike the
women turned as one and entered a store, suddenly laughing and giggling as any group of modern young Hannish
women were wont to do. The doorman held open the door
for the group and bowed as they passed. He came upright
and blocked Owen's entrance with an upheld hand. Owen
placed the man's accent as having come from within the
sound of Bow Bells in London, which marked him as an
immigrant.

"Here now mate," the man said to Owen in his thick
voice. "This fine establishment is too rich for the likes of
you." Before Owen could speak, Mike turned back, addressing the doorman.

"Excuse me," he said to the cockney. "This man is with
me. Is there a problem?"

"Oh well, if he's with you," the man pulled back his arm and bowed towards Mike. "Sorry sir, it's just that he's not dressed proper, you see. But if you vouch for him I'm sure it must be alright. Mind you, watch him as you're responsible." Mike gave Owen a look that was at once smug and condescending as he addressed the doorman.

"Oh, I shall see to it that he stays out of trouble," he said to the man. Owen smile wanly back at them both while gritting his teeth.

Once inside Owen was taken by the décor of the establishment. It was as if London's Mayfair District had been transported to Hong Kong. The walls were of polychrome flecked gold against a royal purple back round, the lighting of very expensive magelight spilling from gilded sconces. A tasteful montage of portraits showing the royal family of Britain took pride of place on the wall. Everywhere was the glitter of gaudy bejeweled creations, ranging from tiny diamond covered bracelets to amethyst encrusted goblets. A florid Englishman in the same livery as the doorkeeper was trying in vain to keep track of the fluttering flock of well-dressed women that had descended on his glittering realm, chattering and picking up this or that glittery bauble.

Owen suddenly figured out why the gang had come to this establishment when he saw Mary quickly palm a necklace of emeralds and hide the string under her shawl. Apparently she wasn't quick enough as the store clerk must also have seen her. His head snapped to fix Mary with an unwavering gaze as he closed the distance separating them.

"See here Miss," the silver-haired man's horned moustaches bobbed as he addressed her in a low voice. "I must ask you to open your shawl please." Owen could see the dismay warring with indecision on Mary's face. Caught, should she pull the gun that she held to keep control of Owen? Sliding easily between the dismayed woman and the clerk, Owen faced those formidable moustaches, carefully placing one of the royal portraits behind him.

"Is there a problem here?" He asked carefully. Grateful for the intervention Mary gasped in feigned outrage.

"I am so glad you are here," she said. "He asked me to open my shawl!" Owen raised an eyebrow at this. The man's face turned a bright purple.

"Is this true?" Owen said to the clerk. The man took in Owen's peasant garb and sputtered.

"Who the devils are you?" he said. Owen smiled and inclined his head towards the portrait behind him.

"Who am I?" he repeated, gesturing again with his head. "Why I am no one." The store clerk turned a puzzled look up to the portrait of the royal prince Erick. His eyes widened in surprise and snapped back to Owen's face.

"You—your Highness" he whispered. Owen quickly held up a finger to his own mouth to quiet the man.

"I am incognito," Owen explained in his own whisper. "Do play along alright?" The man nodded dumbly. "Now what do you mean by asking my" here Owen paused significantly while taking Mary's free hand, "companion here about her shawl?" The man looked at Mary in a new light and shook his head violently.

"Oh, nothing," The man said hurriedly. "Nothing at all, My..." Owen held his finger again to his lips silencing the man.

"Remember, what I asked," Owen whispered. The older man's head bobbed up and down in agreement.

"Of course, uh, sir," The man smiled sickly at Owen and Mary. Owen gave him a broad smile back.

"That's the spirit," Owen said encouragingly. Turning his face towards Mary he said, "I believe that you should call the others dear. It is time we were heading back." Mary nodded, playing along.

"Of course, um, dear." She raised her voice and called out across the shop, "Time to go! Now!" She repeated this in Mandarin. Like a well-oiled machine the other women quickly and silently trooped out the front door. The others doubtlessly had been cleaning out the store while the lone clerk was preoccupied, Owen reflected wryly. Still he thought, that was no business of his. The clerk watched helplessly as the others melted out the doors, then he cleared his throat.

"Are they all..." He began ask as Owen cut him off verbally again.

"My companions?" Owen finished for him with a smile. "Yes, yes they are," The old clerk looked scandalized. It would be well, Owen had decided, to keep the clerk off balance until they were all away. He gave a slow dip of his eyelid at the man.

"Incognito, remember," he exhorted the old man in a good natured manner. "Not a word to anyone, eh?" The store clerk brought himself up stiffly and bowed the deep bow of an inferior to a superior.

"Of course, sir!" Owen nodded his approval at this. The man beamed the first smile that he had seen from him. Owen turned to face Mary.

"Come Mary," he said with a languid drawl, "let us take our leave of this fine establishment." With a shaky assent from Mary, the pair sashayed out the doors and down the alleyway to where Mike and the others waited, Mikes face a mask of concern. He frowned when both Owen and Mary burst out laughing.

"What is so funny?" he asked. "It looked like he was going to nick you both!" Mary shook her head at this, leaning into Owens shoulder, still laughing.

"This man is amazing," she said. "I thought that fat clerk had me nailed to rights. Somehow, Owen here made him bark like a dog and be all 'yes sir, no sir'" She looked at Owen "How did you do that?" Owen shrugged

. "I simply played on a chance resemblance I have to the royal prince Erick," he said. "A little suggestion and the clerk did the rest on his own." Mary looked at him quizzically.

"How close are you to the royal family?" she breathed.

"Oh, not close at all. Erick is my second cousin twice removed or something like that." He said carelessly. At the exclamations from the women around him he protested defensively. "Well, it really isn't close. I am something like sixtieth in line for the throne. My brother's son has a better claim than I do."

"Still," Mike said, with eyes like black pebbles, "You do have a claim." Owen raise an eyebrow at the gang leader.

"And does it matter to you if I do?" he asked. "It is not as if anyone is going to come looking for me, I assure you." Mike turned from him and looked around at the gathered gang members.

"Who made a nice nick at that last place?" he demanded of them. "Raise your hand." Everyone's hand came up. Mike nodded.

"Good," he declared. "You can all go back to the factory. We won't need to be going out again if I am any judge of the take." The young women let out a collective groan at this. Mike made a motion with both his arms as if shooing them all along.

"Go! Go!" he growled. "And go straight back mind you! No trying any schemes or lollygagging!" Mike turned to

Mary and Owen. "Not you two, I want you with me. It's time we met up with Mei and see how the young ones have done."

Chapter 7

Owen looked at Mary across the room. They were in the room where Owen had woken up captive. Mike, Owen still had a difficult time thinking of that as his name, had added two rough wood-hewn chairs to the factory room, otherwise it was the same. Filled with crates and the ticking on the floor for a bed. Owen knew better than to complain. He'd seen the cramped conditions that the girls slept in and figured that his status as teacher gave him the luxury of a private room, however humble the furnishings.

He had spent the earlier part of the evening under the watchful eyes of Mike and Mei who had taken back her large pistol. He was constructing wards around the room with his focus cane. The wards, those semi-intelligent guardians of the physical plane would, he hoped, contain any energies that Mary or he might generated and not endanger others.

"Well Mary," he said, sitting in one of the chairs. He motioned for Mary to sit in the other, "Now that you've had your fun out and about are you ready to get to serious work?" Mary sat in carefully in the other chair frowning at his words.

"Stealing is bloody hard work," she protested.

"Oh I know," Owen replied seriously. "I have stolen a fair bit in my day. Usually for far less honest reasons than what you took today. Tell me though," he cocked his head at her sideways, "why do you do it?"

"Why?" Mary looked at him agog. "Why?" She repeated with raising heat in her voice. "Because there isn't anyone will give the likes of us a crust off their table, and I like to eat. Because it's the only way to make sure that the youngers get to eat as well. If you've ever been around youngers then you know that they make an awful sound when they're hungry. Because the *Good People*," the scorn in her voice was unmistakable now, "decided that me and the rest of us was trash to be thrown out and so they did. Being too cowardly to just cleanly kill us as they is *Good People*. Why did you steal?" She asked him savagely.

"Oh, because people I trusted told me that it was the only way to save the lives of my fellow Britons." Owen shrugged. "I stole for Queen and country, for honor, and to be honest, because I could do so cleverly." He grinned broadly at her. "That last I must confess I only came to realize when I saw how dishonest the other reasons where. And yes, I have also stolen when I was hungry, believe it or not." He gave her a look that seemed to pierce her soul.

"But the reason I call this serious work is because from this moment onwards you need never steal again, unless you wish to do so. You have the power to make a different decision. That is what we truly shall do in this room. We shall work for you to find your power."

"Do you think that we can do that?" Mary asked in a whisper.

"The wise of many nations call those of us with a manifesting talent for Magia *the blessed*. Do you know why?"

"I can't see anything so blessed about worrying if I'm going to go up like a charcoal briquette like you say," Mary replied sourly.

Owen cupped his hands before him and a pillar of fire suddenly appeared in them. He looked at Mary through the flames.

"The flames cannot harm you if you decide that they cannot," he said calmly. "Do you want the flames to hurt you?" Mary instinctively shrank back from the flames. Owens face had been transformed by the flames into something from her childhood nightmares. She shook her head weakly in terror.

"No," she gasped out. The demon mask that had become Owens face snarled at her.

"I do not believe you," the mask rasped. "Do you want the flames to hurt you?"

"No!" she screamed, thrusting out her hands. Streamers of fire shot from them, engulfing Owens pillar with an explosion of fiery sparks. Owen went over backwards tumbling from his chair. He rolled to a standing position, quickly patting out the flames that licked at his tunic sleeves and pants. He was astonished at her raw power.

It had taken considerable energy and drawing on the powers of the wards to manifest the piddling flame he had. Mary had not only manifested a stronger flame, she had with no training projected it to overcome his own force. Owen judged that only the damping effects of the wards had prevented him from being seriously burned. *Horned One, he thought in admiration, what a sorceress she might become!*

Mary had leapt up as she looked at her fingers. The flames continued to run up and down them as if they had become living torches, refusing to go out no matter how hard she shook them.

"Well," Owen said to her dryly, "it appears that you have made your decision."

"Can you make them stop?" she pleaded franticly still shaking her hands desperately.

"No," Owen replied evenly. "But you can. First of all stop that silly hand waving. The flame isn't really hurting you is it?" Mary stopped waving her hands and held them before her. She watched the flames in a sort of horror as they wicked up her fingers.

"No," she said amazedly, "they aren't hurting me at all."

"Good," Owen nodded at this as if this was completely normal. The fact was that he had never even heard tell of a talent as strong as hers. He judged that once it was fully realized, she would be able to call such fire that it could immolate them both, wards or no. He saw no need to tell her that however.

"Now," he continued, "I want you to focus on your belly as I had you do last night, and breathe from there."

"Do I need to close my eyes?" Mary asked.

"No," Owen said. "Please leave them open. I want you to realize that there is no difference between what you do inside your mind and outside it. Now, are you right handed or left handed?"

"Ah, I use both of my hands for different stuff," she said forlornly. "Do you mean which do I use for the most things? I guess that would be my right hand." The flames on the fingers of her left hand suddenly went out.

"Oh," she exclaimed as she continued to look at her hands.

"Yes," Owen said. "That is very good. Now I want you to breathe from that point in your belly again, and feel yourself centered there. Your breath is the means to fuel your will, your will is the means by which the elements like fire manifest in the world though you. Do you understand?"

"Ah, not really," Mary confessed. Owen suppressed a sigh. Well theory would have to come later, he decided.

"That is all right," he said instead. "Just breathe from your center."

His Magia trained senses perceived the pooling of energies within the center of her aura. Damnation, he thought, auras were another thing he would have to educate her on. He could not assume that she knew anything. Perhaps he should ask her what she did know. Was that the right thing to do? He had not a clue, he was no teacher! Still, he did know Magia and sorcery in particular. When the energies had pooled enough in her center to be effective, he spoke to her again.

"Very good Mary," he said to her. "Now let the energy from your center reach up and move the flames from your little finger to your index finger."

"Which one is that?" she asked in confusion.

"Your pointing finger," he said exasperatedly.

The flame on her index finger grew higher. Mary let out a little sound of wonder. Under Owens careful guidance gradually all the flame went out save the one on her first finger that now towered above her head.

"That is very good Mary," Owen repeated. "Now, look at me," he ordered. Mary did. "Now do you master the flame or does the flame master you?"

"I master the flame!" She shouted in exultation.

Owen bowed to her. "Very well. If you would, please dismiss it."

The flame went out abruptly, leaving Mary swaying triumphantly. She smiled at him even as Owen was afraid that she might collapse. He pointed behind her.

"Please sit down," he ordered. Mary fell into the rough wood chair, looking up at him perplexedly.

"Why do I feel as if I've just run the length of the city?" She asked.

"Because your body has used as much energy as if you had," Owen explained. "Manifesting any elemental energy is a tiring business. Still, did you feel the fire respond to your will?"

Mary nodded. "Yes! It was as if suddenly I knew it and it knew what I wanted." She bit her lower lip. "Does that sound daft?" Owen smiled

"Not at all. You have just taken your first step into a much broader world." He sat down again across from her. "Running is not a bad example," he continued. "Now that you know how to run, it is simply a matter of the hard work of flexing the muscles, so to speak, until it becomes second nature."

"How do I do that?" she asked, eagerly leaning forward in her chair. Owen's smile tightened at this.

"By getting up, centering and calling fire again," he said shortly. Mary groaned.

"Oh, please not!" she protested. "I don't think I can stand."

"Yes you can," Owen said implacably. "You had better at any rate. Who is the master, you or the fire?" Mary shuffled to her feet, a look of stubborn determination on her face.

"I am," she said in a steely voice.

"Good for you," Owen approved. "Now show me," he said challengingly.

He kept her at drill until both of them were covered in sweat and exhausted. Giving her a series of exercises to practice, with the extorted promise to work with them daily, he finally bid her go to her own bed. He watched her as the double doors closed behind her.

She was a first rate student, he thought. Her talent deserved better, she deserved better, than his clumsy hands. Owen shook his head again at the strangeness of fortune. If Mr. Victor had not surprised him with that Earth blast, he wouldn't be here now aiding Mary.

That he had only gotten to her before her talent caused tragedy, he was certain. He sighed. Now he must remain until he was satisfied that she was in control. Then there was the matter of the settling with Mr. Victor and his grotesque lackey. Still, he missed Jinhao and wondered how she was fairing with her sister.

Chapter 8

Jinhao paused on the rooftop above the illegal gambling den, watching until the activity died away in the hours just before dawn. After her talk with the fisherman, she had gone back towards Owen's house intent on talking to the man who seemed to be watching it. Unfortunately, the dapper little man seemed skilled in avoiding any place where she could successfully ambush him.

After changing places with his giant partner in surveillance, he started walking, forgoing the cabs at the end of the hill. He kept to the main streets, avoiding being close enough to buildings to enable her to drop down on him from above. She could not risk an open fight with him. To do so invited the intervention of the city's constabulary, who may see her as an Imperial Adept, and a very illegal one at that. The Adepts were men and women who were able to perform feats of outstanding martial prowess; they were exclusively under exclusive orders from the Han throne. Jinhao was, to put it charitably, absent without leave from the Imperial city and likely there was an *arrest immediately* notice out on her.

While Grandfather would never allow her to be transported north in chains, she preferred to depend on herself to deal with the problems of life. She had listened to Grandfather before, and all of her current troubles with the Throne came from that. She was reminded of the old saying, 'never make an agreement with a dragon, for they are subtle and have no thought to the years'.

She agreed with Grandfather that there needed to be an alliance between British and Han but she preferred her own way of reaching that goal, a way that did not involve waiting for centuries. One reason was that she did not think the Han Empire could wait centuries. She had seen the effects of the unlicensed traders selling their opium, the fat mandarins squeezing their farmers to produce more tea on more land for the foreign trade, while the farmer's children went hungry. No, the Han people needed a hero, and what better hero to have than an English sorcerer-lord who would help them regardless of caste or color. She frowned. That is, she amended in her thoughts, if the fool hasn't gone and gotten himself killed.

She watched in frustration the back of the shifty foreigner who could answer her questions, a sentiment that turned into puzzlement as he entered a place that was known to her as a low-rent gambling dive. What attraction could such a place possibly have to a rich foreigner? A girl? Perhaps he simply liked to feel he was slumming? No matter, she decided, he was now somewhere she could corner him.

Swinging across the narrow gap separating the two roofs, Jinhao paused long enough to pull black gauze over her face. She lowered herself down the outside of the den, and through an open window. She floated down the hallway, her feet making no noise on the old floorboards, following the echoes of a familiar voice. Jinhao paused at the corner of the hallway, as the voice came closer.

When the first bodyguard came around the corner, she dropped him with a blow to the throat, quickly stepping around the corner. She saw a little rat-faced man dressed in shabby silks that attempted to mimic a mandarin's robes. His eyes grew wide and he gestured frantically to the two guards behind him.

"Put down your swords, you fools," he hissed in Cantonese so thick you could pour it with a spoon. "Do you want her to kill me as well as your stupid asses?" The little man bowed almost to the floor. "Mighty lady! How may poor Wing serve you?"

"Where is the Englishman with the cane?" Jinhao demanded in the same language.

"Mighty Lady, I am not sure who you mean," the rat-faced Wing protested with shifty-eyes.

"Do not try my patience Wing," Jinhao drew one of her swords. "There is no profit for you here . . . only pain."

"Ahh, the Englishman," Wing exclaimed. "He sought another way out of the building and took it." He pointed at one of the guards. "Take her to the back entrance".

"You had best be true with me Wing," Jinhao turned to follow the guard down a flight of stairs. She stopped and turned back. "Wing," she called out. "spread the word that none are to give that man aid of any kind upon pain of my displeasure."

"It shall be as you say, Mighty Lady," Wing replied with a shaky bow.

When they had gone, the remaining guard, who was an old companion of Wing and could be so familiar, looked at Wing in puzzlement.

"Why did you give the quizi to her, Master? He gave us only pure profit. You called her by the title of Mighty Lady. Who is she?"

"Who is she?" Wang echoed the words tonelessly. "She is a shadow who was before your time. I was but a young man when last she appeared to my old mentor. I have prayed that the day of her return would never come. Take my counsel and forget everything that has happened here tonight. Who is she?" Wang repeated. "She has no name, except one . . . she is the *Claw of Lohan*."

Chapter 9

Jinhao followed the silent bodyguard down the stairs. They quickly passed an open doorway from which the heavy scents of opium and tobacco billowed, followed by the desperate clack of Mah-Jong tiles. Going down yet another flight of stairs, the still unspeaking guard opened a hidden door in the cellar. He wordlessly pointed.

"Where does this come out," she asked, looking at the dim passageway with skepticism.

"Not far," her guide could speak after all, she thought. "Two streets over. The hidden doorway opens out into an alley."

She nodded in acknowledgment. Drawing one sword she began to carefully make her way down the corridor. Fortunately it was dimly light by small crystal chunks of Magelight that has been affixed to the ceiling at intervals. Coming to a stairway that went up, she sheathed her sword to free her hands, and began to climb up them. The door latch took only a moment to work. Jinhao found herself standing in an alleyway. A wall of fire suddenly roared towards her from the right. Only her Qi powered reflexes saved her. Dropping flat, she felt the heat pass over her.

Springing up again, she threw a handful of iron spikes towards the figure standing with an upraised cane at the mouth of the alley. She followed that by running up the side of the building towards the sorcerer, drawing her blades as she ran. A vortex of wind came whirling down the canyon of the alley, tossing her spikes harmlessly about while knocking her violently back down to the ground.

Crouching there in surprise Jinhao considered the man she had been following with narrowed eyes. He was at least as powerful as Owen in combat sorceries, she judged. She gripped the hilts of her swords tighter, readying her next move.

"I have no quarrel with you woman," he cried out. "I only need to be sure that I killed your boyfriend, the Englishman. There is no profit in us tangling. Let me get my proof and leave. There is nothing you can do for him now."

She was about to give him her answer to that with the edges of her blades when the police whistle sounded behind him in the street. It was quickly answered by others, and a deep male voice sounded to his attackers left.

"Here now, sir! There is to be no unlicensed Magia workings in this neighborhood!"

Snarling, the sorcerer pointed his cane towards the voice. A thin jet of flame shot from its tip, followed by a cry of pain. Turning back towards Jinhao, he spat out, "Keep away from me!" He spun off down the street at a run, the whistles growing louder as the policeman's body was discovered by a fellow officer.

Jinhao took to the shadows, quickly climbing up the side of the alleyway to the rooftops. It would not do for her to be found near the burnt corpse. Besides, there was Owen's murderer to follow. After a time of casting about, she had to admit that she had lost his trail. All the police milling about like angry bees did not help. Dejected, she followed the rooftop highway back to the mouth of the alley, where a small crowd had gathered. Even at this time of night, the misfortune of others was a strong attractor.

From her vantage point overhead, she watched as a police van pulled up, discharging a small knot of officious looking men in suits. The fat one must be the police Sorcerer that Owen had told her about, another with a doctor's bag must be a coroner. After a few minutes, the two of them began some sorcery over the body, while a tired looking man with a notebook and pencil began talking to everyone.

Jinhao knew that the two men were not only preserving the body, but making sure that it could not be re-animated by a sorcerer of ill-intent. She had never really understood the British taboo against death until Owen had explained to her that a powerful enough sorcerer could re-animate the corpse of your dearest one and send it as a raving beast to attack. She shuddered at the thought.

The tired man with the notebook must be a detective she decided, even though he bore no resemblance to Inspector Gregg, Owen's ally among the police. Should she seek out Gregg to help her find Owen's murderer she wondered? No, the sorcerer that had ambushed her had not been sure himself that he had killed Owen, which meant her duty was still to find Owen if he was alive. But how? As she absently scanned the growing crowd, a slow smile came to her when she saw the inevitable street urchins. It must be a sign from the Gods. Very well, she would call on *Him,* the one who the street urchins treated with reverence. Quickly, Jinhao removed her sword harness, pulling out her night cloak.

The girl startled when the shadowy figure made the Dragon sign to her for their place against the corner. Glancing around to be sure that no one was watching her, the little girl slid over towards the figure. When the shadows resolved into a woman in a cloak, she was doubly surprised. Jinhao smiled at her surprise, holding out the small message tube.

"This must reach *Him* tonight," Jinhao whispered, "Can you do this?"

The girl nodded wordlessly. Being a member of the *Eyes* meant not only extra food and the occasional coin to make life bearable; it also meant total obedience to whoever gave her the sign. While she had received the sign from a few strange people, there was something intimidating about this woman that required silence, as well as obedience.

"Good," Jinhao said. A silver coin appeared outstretched between her fingers. The girl made the coin vanish and scampered off down the street. Jinhao watching her as she went.

The Eyes were the inspiration of the former intelligence chief of Lohan, Dragon ruler of Hong Kong. Though the man was now dead, the urchins still served as the wily old Dragons' eyes and ears throughout the city as they were able to go most anywhere and report on what they had seen. They also made superb couriers who no one would suspect of carrying vital messages.

Jinhao sighed. Whether she wished to or not she would have to deal with Grandfather if she wished to know if Owen was still alive, and if so, to find out where Owen was.

Chapter 10

Jinhao picked her way carefully over the vegetation that threated to cover the trail completely. Built to the Dragon Lohan's express design and covering what was formerly Cantonment Hill, Dragon Park as the place was known, was a two mile spot of green in the center of the city. It not only served as one of the Dragon's favorite mediation places, it did double-duty as a place where unofficial meetings could take place. Lohan's house at the top of the hill held too many prying eyes for Jinhao's peace of mind.

She had not gone back to the house that she had shared with Owen Strong that night, but stayed in one of the small safe places she had made for herself years ago throughout the city. When the fall of darkness came again, she knew that Grandfather would be waiting for her.

~ ~ ~

Pausing at the end of the trail she looked thoughtfully at the clearing lit with mage lights in paper lanterns. The Old Dragon sat on one of the stone benches in his human guise. She had to admit he was imposing in his chosen form. He wore the seeming of a hale but older man, with magnificent white mustashes that came to sharply groomed points near his chest. He was dressed in layers of green and gold silk that shimmered in the light.

"You may come out Granddaughter. We are quite alone," he announced without looking at her.

"Thank you for meeting with me Grandfather," Jinhao replied, stepping into the clearing. She refused to be surprised. He was trying already to push her off balance with his tricks of perception, but she would not be moved.

"Thank you for your message, Granddaughter. It is always a joy to hear from one's children. One of the few joys of old age. Please sit." Lohan pointed to the place on the ground where some servant had set a large cushion. Jinhao walked towards the cushion, stopping to stand above it. If she sat, Lohan would be higher than her thus dominating the conversation.

"I thank you Grandfather,' she replied with a bow, remaining standing. "I trust that you are in good health and good fortune."

"Bah," the dragon waved a hand as if shooing away flies. "The British Governor and the Imperial Satrap are at each other's throats again, but that is hardly new. I could wish for the old days when I could safely send their severed heads back to the thrones they claimed to serve, but those days are gone. Now it would only lead to a messy war."

"But you are not here to talk about that," he said. His eyes narrowed as looked up at her. "You are as stubborn as your sister and will give me a crooked neck standing like that you know. Why are you here?"

"Forgive me Grandfather, but I have pulled a muscle and must not sit on the ground," Jinhao replied regretfully. It was not true, and she knew that he knew it was not, but politeness counted almost as much as truth with the Han.

"As to why I am here, I come as a humble supplicant. I fear that my companion, Owen Strong, has run afoul of evil." She proceeded to tell him the circumstances of Owen's mysterious disappearance and the foreign sorcerer in the alley.

The old man listened gravely then shook his head, "And what would you have of me? You have placed yourself on a strange path with this worthless Britisher."

Jinhao straightened her back.

"The people of Hong Kong need a champion, Grandfather. One who will not care about their wealth or status, one who will walk into the darkness for them. You have spent too long upon that hilltop of yours. When was the last time you even came within touching distance of one of the street classes?"

"And you believe that this man Strong is that person?" Jinhao could see the red flames dance in the old man's eyes, and feared that she had gone too far. Still she knew it would be worse if she backed down now.

"Yes," she said baldly. "The age where the people's heroes are semi-divine has come to an end. I believe what will unite the British and Han people of this city is a hero that both people can see themselves in. And this will bring the two closer together as you have worked for all these years."

"Hrumph," the old man made a dismissive sound. "I remain unconvinced. Again Granddaughter I ask, what would you have me do about your situation?"

"I know that you can sense every emanation of what the British call Magia throughout the city. I am sure that Owen Strong gives forth a powerful emanation. I simply wish to know if he is alive and where he may be."

"You know not what you ask," the old man replied. "You should be able to do this small thing yourself if you would quit being so stubborn."

"I thank you, Grandfather," she bowed shortly to him, "but I am not ready for such a commitment."

"Hrumph," the old man said again. He squeezed his eyes closed. Jinhao waited patiently and quietly. Finally he opened his eyes again. "Your Sorcerer is alive and in the dockside area."

She let out a breath that she did not know she was holding in. He was alive, she thought in relief.

"Where is he," she asked. "The *dockside area* is quite a large place. Can you not be more specific?"

"No, I cannot," he snapped at her. She saw the flames in his eyes again. After a moment, they vanished as the old man shrugged in his robes. "Perhaps I can tell more upon meditation, should I choose to waste my time," he allowed.

"That would be a great aid to me," she replied sincerely. She bowed more deeply to him.

"Have you considered that this Britisher may simply not wish you to find him?" The dragon asked pointedly.

"I have," Jinhao replied stiffly. "I have reason to believe that is not the case."

"There is no harm in caring for a mortal," he said, squinting at her is if he could divine the truth of her replies. "I found caring for your Grandmother most satisfying."

"It is not like that with Owen Strong," she said swiftly. "I simply believe that he is the man we most wish to encourage. It would be a waste of my time for him to die now." She turned her head to one side regarding him. "You have never spoken of Grandmother before."

"Nor shall I now," he replied briskly. "You now owe me a debt. Do you acknowledge it freely?"

319

Jinhao hesitated. To acknowledge that she owed a debt to the Dragon was a chancy proposition. She had worked hard to be free of the Dragon's sphere of power.

"I shall not serve you as I once did," she declared.

"Nor would I ask that you do," the dragon replied with a strange smile. "Still, you have acknowledged the debt. I shall call upon you sometime in the future. See that you remember it." He waved a hand. "Now you may go."

She startled at the abrupt dismissal, until she recalled that this was Lohan's way. She bowed the bow of child to elder.

"Grandfather," she murmured. Then turned away to thread her way back though the wilderness to the city that surrounded the park. The old man, who was anything but a man, remained behind.

Chapter 11

Y ou did not practice your lessons last night!" Owen Strong looked at the girl and sighed. "How do you ever expect to succeed at this if you do not do them?"

"But it's only been two days!" Mary protested. "So I didn't do the stupid exercises last night! It shouldn't matter that much!"

"You think not?" Owen twirled his cane. "Do you really believe that you are ready to face the energies your blood can call forth? That you can control them? Make them do your bidding?"

"I managed just fine without you and your stupid exercises before!" Mary cried. Between her clenched fists a glow and the flicker of firelight began to grow.

"Then look to your hands, girl" Owen snapped.

Mary held up her hands. Her face was a study in shock as the flames pooled in her palms. She screamed and tried to fling the flames off her hands. Fire dripped off them in globules. Owen quickly called on his own affinity for the water element through his tattoo and channeled it down his electrum cane, dousing the flames.

"No, no," he cried. "Center yourself, Mary! Breathe from the center point of your belly, breathe!" The girl did so, the flames in her hands gradually dimming back to flickers, then stopping as if blown out by some wind. Mary stood up straight, eyes closed, hands at her side.

"That is the way of it Mary," Owen crooned at her softly, almost hypnotically, watching her very closely. "Breathe in, and as you breathe out see the fire run down into the earth, harmless and inert. You are the master of the fire, the fire is not the master of you!"

The girl had both power and the will to harness it, Owen had to admit. She belonged in a school with a Master of the Elements to aid her in learning true sorcery, not in an abandoned warehouse learning a fire caller's tricks. Still, he knew that if he had not come along Mary might well now be dead, the Fire turning inwards and burning her alive. He promised himself that he would see her to a true school. In the meantime, it wouldn't do to let up on her . . . she could still harm herself or those around her.

"That's right, Mary," Owen directed in the same soothing voice, "and now you can open your eyes and still be centered." The young woman opened her eyes.

"But I didn't do anything," she cried. The flames licked up around her head like a halo. She bit her lower lip and concentrated. The flames dropped away harmlessly.

"Still think that you can 'manage just fine'," he asked sardonically. "Your power will not let you be lazy on this you know. It will manifest whether you wish it or not. I warned you of this," he said gravely.

"Am I to understand that being a Sorcerer means that you hold all five elements in your body? How do you ever, manage?" she asked, with a quiver in her voice.

"You learn," Owen replied. He shrugged, "Control becomes second-nature to you with time and practice. I do not even think on it these days. It is much like the muscles you use to walk, or to pick something up with. The muscles are always there, but you are not constantly running." He pulled back the sleeves of his right arm. Mary gasped at the line of scar tissue that ran ruler straight down it. "I began as a fire caller. This is the result of not practicing my lessons. *You* must learn."

"But you told me that you needed your Focus," she nodded towards his cane, "to make the elemental energies manifest. How can I do that without one?"

"Most simple talents do not require that one undergo Sorcery training to master them. Your connection to the Source of All is limited, as is the power that you can manifest, whereas mine is not." Owen smiled at her. "It would not do for me to immolate my cab driver just because he drove recklessly, no matter how angry I get at him."

"Then the Focuses and the Tattoos and all that are just mental tricks?" she asked.

"No," Owen shook his head vehemently. "They are real tools that enable Sorcerers to wield the unthinkable power of the elements without harm. You are not surprised when a train driver wears thick gloves and goggles to protect his hands and eyes, are you?" Mary shook her head mutely. Owen nodded.

"Well, the same thing is true of Sorcerers," he said. Your gift, and it is a gift never doubt that, is simply the birthright that we all share. It does not require the specialized technique of the Sorcerer to use. Very few people have the Gifts to that degree." And those that do usually belong to one of the Noble families, he thought to himself. That Mary was some by-blow of the branch of a great tree, he had no trouble believing.

He was under the impression that Mary had been abandoned as an infant as had the rest of Mike's little gang, left to die on the streets. That the Han still practiced such cruelty towards their own children was not really surprising to Owen. That solid Englishmen had taken the practice up made him quite literally see red. He kept his outrage to himself. Such would *butter no parsnips* as his nurse used to say. He gestured towards the makeshift chairs of over-turned buckets that served as his sitting parlor.

"But enough of that," he said, flicking the cuffs of his black peasant tunic, his cane upright between his knees. "Now recite for me the Five Elements of Sorcery."

"Earth, Air, Fire, Water, Spirit," she chanted promptly.

"Very good," Owen said. "Now what are the properties of each Element?"

"Fire, that's my element," Mary said shyly, "is the easiest called and the hardest to control. It warms us from the sun and the fire in the earth. Water is its opposite." As Mary droned on Owen tried to look attentive. He had learned these things in common school when he was seven.

When Mike came to get them for the communal supper, Mary skipped ahead while Owen hung back to walk with Mike. When Owen had learned that Mike took in the girls abandoned to death as infants or very young girls, his attitude towards the young man had shifted somewhat. Granted, he was teaching them how to steal, but at least he was teaching them how to steal well and survive. Still they did not end up in some crib used for some person's foul lust, a practice that Owen knew occurred often enough in Hong Kong. This was a source of relief to Owen as he needed a refuge to hide out in, and he had worked hard to cultivate his captors towards that end.

In the same way, Mike's attitude towards Owen had shifted. Once Owen had convinced him that he really intended to stay and cause no trouble, Mike had given him back his cane, furnishing Owen with another set of clothes, the tunic, coat, and loose pants that everyone seemed to wear. He even began calling him *Sha Tui* which Owen understood to be a sort of nick name meaning 'tall man'. Although Owen barely stood five foot eight inches in height, compared to the rest of them he was indeed a 'tall man.' That Mike had some ulterior motive Owen had no doubt, that was the way the game was played. Still when his purpose was revealed, it was a bit of a shock.

"So, tell me Sha," Mike said looking up at Owen, "Can she be ready to fight with the fire in two days?" Mike mimed throwing a firebolt.

"Fight?" Owen repeated blankly. He nearly stumbled. "No one ever mentioned anything about fighting! Perhaps in two months, she might be able to light a candle and not set the building on fire," Owen pronounced. "But fight with fire?" Owen shook his head firmly, "No, absolutely not!" Mike's face turned cold upon hearing this

"Do not give me that, Foreign Devil," he hissed. "If she can't fight then all your fancy learning is useless to me!"

"It is not useless to her," Owen shot back. "You cannot expect Mary to develop skills overnight, these things take time!" Owen gave him a sideways glance. "And do not give me that Quizi manure!"

They had been talking in the slang ridden dialect of what passed for Mandarin among the lower classes. Owen switched to English as his vocabuary failed him. "Why do you need her to fight with fire? Thinking of expanding your territory?" Owen guessed slyly.

"No!" Mike waved his hands, then lowered his voice as they neared the dining hall. His walk slowed to a stop. "There is another gang. Jimmy the Horse's gang. They are expanding their territory. Jimmy has a, what you call fire caller. Evil brat. We will go to a meeting, supposed to work it out. Jimmy will use him then. Kill people and take our territory." Mike shrugged. "I do not suppose that you upper crust types would understand." Owen also stopped moving, and leaned on his cane as he addressed the ganger.

"Let me see if I have this right," Owen said. "An ambitious rival wants to expand into your territory. You suspect that he will kill your representatives at a peace summit using forbidden magic to do so." Mike nodded solemnly. Owen smiled at him dryly.

"That is positively refreshing in its simplicity," Owen said. "You should see some of the plots we have to deal with among the Noble Houses back home." He frowned, then looked down at the smaller man. "Mary still cannot hope to hold her own, let alone be an effective fighter by that time." Mike pulled himself up regally.

"Then you had better see to it that she is!" He strode into the mess hall to many smiles and cries of greeting. Owen had to allow that the affection that the women and girls showered on him was clearly given freely. He gestured at Owen to be seated at his right.

The woman everyone called Guan placed a fresh roast chicken in front of them. Owen had been pleasantly surprised at not only the western style tables and chairs, but at the quality of the food as well. Owen suspected that there was more to Mike than met the eye. In fact, he was certain of it. He was just unsure how to use the knowledge to the best advantage. Jinhao would no doubt call that his British snobbery, but Owen was certain that Mike was not street-raised despite what Mike might claim.

"There is only one thing for it then," Owen said to Mike as he took his seat. "I shall have to go as a counter to any Magian threat." Mike narrowed his eyes at him suspiciously.

"Why would you do that? We are only street scum to you. And what happened to that 'I am in hiding' idea? Why risk your life for us?" At that moment, little Mei, the girl with the big gun who had first tended Owen, came dancing into the hall.

"Oh," she burbled seeing the feast laid out before them. "Guan got us a chicken!!"

For a time everyone ate in companionable silence. In addition to the roast chicken, there was plenty of vegetables and rice served in wooden bowls that matched the drinking bowls that everyone held. The drink in question was clean water garnished with some citrus fruit that Owen could not recognize, there was no alcohol, not even rice wine. He had to admit that his recovery was going much faster due to the simple diet.

After dinner when the bowls and eating implements were cleared away, the leaders of the various groups stood at the front of the room and reported on the activities of the day, especially the loot they had stolen. Little Mei, gave a humorous report of the swarm of small girl urchins who pickpocketed the rich crowds at the markets that had everyone laughing. Even Owen chuckled.

"What will happen to her, if Jimmy the Horse wins?" Owen asked Mike quietly while Mei carried on. He looked around at the girls laughing, and if not care-free than at least free of care for the moment. Mike puffed out his chest.

"I would not let that happen," the gang leader said. Owen nodded solemnly at this.

"Spoken like a true leader," Owen replied. "To answer your question, I am going for Mei and the other girls' sake. You may not be the best refuge they could have, but you are a refuge."

Mike frowned, as if turning over what Owen had said. His English was good, but there were still places for misunderstanding. Finally Mike nodded as if understanding that it was a compliment.

"No, Jimmy would be bad for us all," Mike confirmed. "You can go," he said after a long pause. His eyes narrowed again as he looked at Owen. "But I am still in charge—still the boss."

"Oh, absolutely," Owen replied breezily. "I would not dream of interfering with your authority." He hefted his cane. "As for hiding, I can paint this I suppose, and no one will be the wiser." Mike looked at the cane and then at Owen.

"I believe we can do better than that," the gang leader said with a smile.

.

Chapter 12

Jinhao turned the corner making sure that she was not being followed. In her persona of 'Lady Jinhao' she had to be more circumspect than if she appeared as the Claw. Her inclinations to simply ransack the dockside areas would not do under the circumstances.

She knew two things. One, that the mysterious *quizi* sorcerer thought that he had killed Owen, but appeared not to be sure; two, that Owen was most certainly alive. Lohan was never wrong about such things, and for Jinhao to raise a hue and cry now might lead this Mr. Victor straight to Owen. What irked her most was that Owen had not seen fit to get a message to her.

Jinhao shrugged mentally. She would forgive him as he had no way of knowing that she had returned from her trip early. The Emperor's Concubine, was safe now. It had taken much less time than she had planned for that to be true.

Still, if it turned out that Owen was attempting some sort of protective gesture, she would kick him herself.

The dockyards district was full of sailors and merchants from every corner of the globe. Jinhao threaded her way through the throng, passing giant laborers from the ice fields to the far North, their bright golden hair and pale skin marking them, as did their height. She passed small dark porters with copper-skin and ink black hair from the Americas. Jinhao paused as a litter bearing a fat courtier, resplendent in her silks, pushed its way through the crowd going the other direction.

Not only was Hong Kong a trans-shipment point serving the routes from Asia to Europe, it also was the only port that allowed Europeans to trade with the Kingdom of Han, which the foreigners called China. The city was jointly ruled by the British Empire and the Han Imperium. This was only allowed by the Imperium because the Dragon Lohan ruled over the coast where the city was placed. If you said that the Dragon forced the Han throne to accept the arrangement, you would perhaps be more accurate. That is, if Jinhao knew the Dragon at all. She turned down a relatively quiet alleyway, risking a quick glance over her shoulder to see if her paid informant was still following.

Behind her came the marketplace storyteller. Besides making a living telling tales in the streets, the unsavory man also made coin telling those who wished it news of the underworld of the docks. She steeled herself to face the smell of rancid oils and opium that clung to him like a mist as he leaned towards her.

"I hear that you seek knowledge of the under-docks," he said in the deep voice of a trained speaker.

"The Sage says that to seek knowledge is the best of all pursuits," Jinhao temporized. "I am interested in only certain types of knowledge, however."

"Ah, then you have inquired in the right quarter," he said hopping from foot to foot. "I possess only the most discerning of information."

"I shall be the judge of that," she said, holding up a small silk purse. The man's eyes widened. The purse alone would be the equivalent of a days' take for him. His hand reached for it. Jinhao quickly snatched it back.

"After I hear the knowledge, I shall judge if it is worthy," Jinhao held the purse just out of his grasp.

"What is it that the Noble Lady wishes to hear?" he rasped.

"Tell me of *Quizi* Sorcerers that have recently appeared on the docks." She demanded. The storytellers head bobbed up and down in agreement.

"The Noble Lady wishes to hear of the short man named Victor and his tall mountain of a henchman," the storyteller said with a shake of his head. "They are very bad joss," he pronounced. "They have the ill-eye of the Dragon upon them it is said."

"Have any other *Quizi* appeared lately?" She demanded.

"There have been no other foreign devil sorcerers dockside lately," he replied mournfully at Jinhao's frown. She held the purse before him again. "There is the Englishman named Thomas but he has been at Jasmine's more than a year."

"No, I am not interested in Thomas," Jinhao affected a bored tone in her voice. "They would have appeared in the last week or news of them would have."

"There have been no appearances of the foreign devils that recently," he said. "Nor has there been talk of such down here."

"Are you certain?" the purse jingled.

"Yes," he said. Then his face brightened. "Perhaps the noble lady seeks knowledge of those who practice the foreign devil magic."

"Perhaps," Jinhao replied. "But I grow impatient. What do you know?"

"There are many who seek the illicit power that the Devil Magic makes," he said hurriedly. "The latest I have heard of is Mike's gang down in Factory Street just this last week. They tell of an old relative who has appeared to aid Mike in his fight against Jimmy the Horse. He carries the walking stick of the Devil Magic."

"I see," Jinhao murmured, "and how does this old relative appear?"

"I have not seen him myself," the storyteller allowed. "But he has long whiskers and is quite tall, though stooped with age, or so they say."

Jinhao frowned. It could be Owen, the whiskers and the stoop were easy enough to fake. But why would Owen ally himself with a street gang?

"Tell me more about Mike's gang," she ordered.

"There is not much to tell," the storyteller with a dismissive wave of his hands. "The gang is all women and girls save for Mike. They say that Mike rescues the cast-offs and has them stealing up in the posh parts of the city."

"Why would such need someone familiar with the Devil Magic?" Jinhao wondered aloud.

"Oh, that is easy to tell," the storyteller said eagerly. "Mike is running up against Jimmy the Horse. Jimmy wants Mike's territory. It so happens that Jimmy has a young quizi who can make the fire magic to burn his enemies to death," the storyteller shrugged. "You know the old saying, bring Devil Magic to fight Devil Magic."

"And where might Mike's gang be found?" Jinhao asked.

The storyteller grinned, miming a motion of counting coins on his hand. Jinhao repressed a very un-lady like response, and instead opened the silk pouch and tossed a small coin towards him. The coin vanished in a flash of gold.

"More when you tell me more," she said shortly. "And you had best make sure there is not something you forget."

335

Bowing, the storyteller gave her directions which she noted. She made purse disappear with a flicker of her fingers, and left the alleyway as quickly as she could. By the time the storyteller looked up, Jinhao had vanished into the crowd.

Chapter 13

Upon hearing the address of the gang, Jinhao retired to a different bolt hole, to wait for dark. This particular one was located beneath the cellar of a dockside wine shop. She play-acted the part of the rich lady who was obviously very fond of the shop's wares, disguising herself with a careful walk and a veiled face. Such sights, Jinhao knew, had become all too common during the reign of the Dowager Empress as more women and men sought to ease their suffering with too much wine. The refuge itself could only be entered by a cleverly hidden door that was concealed among the wine barrels. Jinhao paid the owner a sizable sum to simply forget that the room existed.

She pulled back the veil with a sigh of relief as the door closed behind her. Moving by feel, she found the crystal-like Mage light in its alcove, and pressed the sigil that cause it to fill the room with light. She looked around, well satisfied with what she saw.

The room was small, barely wider than the cot-like bed that took up most of it. She didn't need more. Various compartments along the walls held a variety of tools, weapons, clothing and so on. She had created this and other hiding places when things had been more turbulent in her life. Shucking the heavy silk outer robes, she reclined on the cot, grateful for her foresight.

Jinhao calculated that she might as well wait for the aid of nightfall before breaching the gang's base. There were three possibilities she decided, either Owen was alive and she would rescue him, he was not there, in which case she continued her search, or the gang had killed him already. In the latter case, there would be many fewer gang members she vowed, far fewer. Given these conditions, approaching at night was the best option for her to take. She settled down on the bed preparing to nap.

Her internal clock woke her some time later. She knew the sun had gone down. After eating and attending to various other needs, she opened up a storage space hidden in the wall. Here was a full set of all the weapons that an Imperial Adept might use, as well as a set of black clothing. Carefully she dressed, further entering the special state of mind with each article she donned that would enable her to call upon the Qi powers of the Adept. She spared a moment to silently give thanks to her teachers, now dead, who had given her such control and power.

Finishing, she moved like a ghost out of the room and back into the wine cellar. Jinhao chose to take advantage of an unused coal chute to reach the outside unseen. There, she quickly climbed up to the thieves' highway. The night was clear and warm. Jinhao traveled the distance to the gang's home quickly and without incident, exulting one again in the freedom of the rooftops.

Jinhao stopped at a building across from the old factory where the gang was supposed to hide. Jinhao had to give them credit for if she did not know better, she would never have given the building another look. The sentries were well hidden and no hint of light or scent of cooking fire escaped the dark building. There was also no sign of Owen. She unslung a coil of rope from around her waist, preparing to cross and enter the factory from above.

Stalking through the building, she discovered two unusual facts. One was that the inhabitants appeared to be all females. Jinhao spied no males whatsoever. The women she did discover were all young, and as near as she could tell were in charge of the gang. There did not seem to be a single one of them here that did not want to be. The second fact was that there were far fewer of them present than the number of rooms and possessions would indicate. Where was the rest of the gang? And more importantly, where was Owen? She heard the soft creak of a floorboard and spun around. She found herself facing a small girl with a large air pistol.

"No more sudden moves," the girl said in clear Mandarin, "I do know how to shoot and will." Jinhao measured the distance between them, calculating that she could easily disarm the waif before she fired. She allowed her body to appear to relax, holding up her hands.

"You have the advantage over me," Jinhao said, speaking through the black gauze mask.

"Mike was right to worry about Jimmy sending someone like you to queer whatever deal they cut at the meeting." The little girl hefted the pistol. "I will not allow that."

"Wait," Jinhao held up a hand. "What if I tell you that I know not who this 'Jimmy' is, nor do I answer to him?"

"Then what are you doing here?" the girl asked suspiciously. Jinhao noted with silent approval that the girl's aim never wavered. Jinhao decided that she would win the girl over. She lowered her face mask.

"I am searching for a man," she explained, "a British Sorcerer named Owen Strong. Have you heard of him?" Her young ambusher's eyes widened.

"You're a woman," she gasped.

Jinhao decided that the moment of indecision would be enough. Moving at the speed only an Adept can, she disarmed the girl, throwing her against the wall, ending with the girl's own pistol held under her chin.

"I asked," Jinhao said carefully, "If you had heard of him." Her ambusher glared at Jinhao.

"What could you possibly want with Sha-Tui anyway?" The young girl spat out. "I will tell you nothing! Kill me if you wish!" Jinhao smiled.

"Long legs?" she repeated at her captive. "I suppose you could call him that. So he is here." Jinhao released the girl, tossing her gun back to her carelessly. "You can show me where he is."

The girl deftly caught the gun, looked from it to Jinhao, then lowered it, as if realizing how useless it was. Stubbornly, she shook her head.

"No?" Jinhao echoed sadly. "Then I shall have to find him myself."

"Wait!" The girl exclaimed. "He is not here! He has gone with Mike and the others to meet with Jimmy the Horse! He had to go, as he hasn't been Mary's tutor long enough."

"He went willingly?" Jinhao asked. The girl nodded. "He will return?' She nodded again. "He is being someone's tutor?" She nodded again. Jinhao regarded her. "What is your name?'

"Everyone calls me Mei," the girl answered. She frowned at Jinhao. "The guest should declare her name first!"

"Guest am I?" Jinhao said bemusedly. The girl nodded even more definitely.

"You must be a guest of Sha-Tui's," Mei explained seriously. "That way you never needed to overcome the head sentinel of the base."

"Ah," Jinhao said. "And that sentinel would be you?"

"Of course!" Mei looked down at the gun in her hand. "You really promise that you are not here to harm Shu-Ti?"

Jinhao placed her hand over her chest. "I promise that I do not intend him harm"

"Alright," The gun disappeared behind Mei's back. She looked up at Jinhao. "What is your name? "

"You may call me Jinhao," she said solemnly. Jinhao held out her hand Western style. Mei gravely accepted it.

"There should be refreshments for the guest," Mei offered. "We can find them downstairs, where we can wait for Mike and Sha-Tui to return."

Jinhao smiled faintly. "I accept the hospitality of the house, and am honored. Lead on Head Sentinel Mei."

Chapter 14

Owen hobbled forward across the floor of the restaurant. A wig, dark glasses and glued-on thick whiskers hid a multitude of his European sins. The restaurant that was the meeting place for the two gangs was run by a very oily-appearing old woman named Zhang, He wondered how she felt about two gangs of unruly and deadly street urchins taking over her restaurant. That they were deadly was clear from the way that the members of the two gangs had faced off against one another, faces grim, holding on to their makeshift weapons. Mike swaggered forward, placing a hand on a hip.

"So, it is good that you want to talk rather than fight," Mike said. "You know who I am! I am Mike!" He folded his arms and waited with them crossed. A young man in a silk variant of the lower class's tunic and wide pants stood forward. He had a scar that ran in a straight line down the side of his face from just below his right eye to his thin cruel lips.

"I only agreed not to fight so that not too many of my troops would suffer from broken nails or sprained toes," he boasted. The youth cast an exaggerated glance over Mike's line of gangers. The look changed upon seeing Owen but he recovered quickly. "I thought that I might as well treat you and your . . . gang," his lip curled up into a sneer as he said it, "to some good food for a change. I am Jimmy the Horse!" He made a grab at his crotch. "Some of you will soon know why!" He ignored the way the women of Mike's line murmured angrily, holding their weapons tighter. Jimmy pointed at Owen. "Who's the greybeard?"

"Oh that is simply my uncle's cousin's brother," Mike replied easily. "We all call him Sha-Tui. Mike raised his hands as if in a shrug. "I said I would look after him. Family. What are you going to do?"

"Long legs eh? Huh," Jimmy the Horse folded his arms in front of his chest. "I wouldn't have thought you knew who your own mother was much less whatever you call him." Jimmy shook his head. "I don't like it. I don't like it at all."

Owen stepped forward. He had to deflect this kind of talk before it wound up with Mike's side into doing something foolish. Mike's people held anything that could hit as a weapon, from an old rusted rake to a board with nails in it, and they were ready to use them. Jimmy's line of warriors on the other hand all held long knives, short swords and spiked maces, all burnished bright. Owen wondered as he spoke how profitable Jimmy's street business must be to allow them that sort of kit. He did remember to stoop.

344

"I am but an old man," Owen rasped out. "Please, let there be no fighting on my account!" He looked at Jimmy directly. "Besides I hear there is food. We should eat, should we not?"

"We should," Jimmy the Horse declared deciding to give in on the point of Owen's presence. He patted Mike on the back hard enough to leave a bruise, Owen was sure. Mike looked as if he was being offered a mangy rat to eat for a moment and then put on a brave face.

"Let us eat together," he said to his people. "We may as well." The gang members looked dubious for a moment until the old woman, Zhang, opened the doors to the banquet room beyond the front hall. The aromas that came from the room were enough to convince a horde of starving women and men to stream towards the laden tables that lay within. Owen, Mike, and Mary came at a more dignified pace behind them, accompanied by Jimmy and a young man who looked half-Han and half-Westerner to Owens eyes.

"This is my personal retainer, Huang," Jimmy said by way of introduction. The young man looked at them all with slight distain and in a curl of his lip. After a moment's awkward silence they all continued walking into the banquet room. Owen had taken an instant dislike to Huang. He was one of those pretty boys who knew he was, and besides, Owen was willing to bet he was Jimmy's Fire caller.

Once they were all seated with Jimmy at the head of the table, Mike, Mary and Owen in that order sat down the left side, with Huang and some of Jimmy's bully boys to the right. After a short speech which could have been taken as insulting to Mike by Jimmy, the food and wine began to flow.

Owen was pleased to see how Mike dealt with Jimmy's barbed comments so adroitly. That Jimmy was trying to goad Mike was clear, but Mike refused to rise to the bait. They all continued eating and drinking, Owen watched his own wine bowl closely so as to not accidentally over-indulge. He noticed Mike was doing the same thing and made a mental note to praise him later. At that moment, Mary startled, looking at Huang across from her.

"Mind where you place your feet sir," she said in careful Mandarin.

"What," Huang said with a smirk, "I don't know what you mean."

"Very well," Mary said with a sigh. She resumed eating, her gaze focused on her plate.

"I said," Huang's voice rose louder over the noise of the feasters. "that I don't know what you mean, Bitch!' I think that you should apologize!"

In the hush that followed this pronouncement all eyes turned towards Mary. She blinked, looking down at her plate, utterly silent. Jimmy the Horse who had been watching everything carefully, picked up his wine bowl.

"You should learn to keep your woman in line better," he said to Mike, drinking a large draught. He held out his bowl wordlessly to have it refilled, his eyes intent on his rival gang leader.

"She is not my woman," Mike replied quietly. "Her name is Mary, and she belongs to no one. Perhaps it is you who should keep better control of your baboons,"

"No one calls me a monkey!" Huang cried. He pushed his chair away from the table as if to rise up. Mike looked at him as if he were a barking dog, then calmly turned to Jimmy the Horse.

"I have no idea what he is going on about," Mike protested innocently. "I was referring to your pets. You do keep pet baboons do you not?" Jimmy guffawed loudly, gesturing for Huang to stand down.

"Yes, I do," Jimmy admitted, still chuckling, "which means either your spies or your information sources are very good! I must say Mike that you keep your cool admirably, and have your people well-disciplined also." He stroked his chin with a finger thoughtfully. "Perhaps we should do business together. I suspect fighting you would hold little profit for either of us."

At that moment the tablecloth between Mary and Huang suddenly smoldered, then burst into flames without warning. Huang leapt to his feet shouting,

"She is attacking us," he screamed. His hand whipped back, then forward to send a stream of fire towards Mary. Owen reacted by springing to his feet, cane pointed. He first stopped Huang's stream of fire, then quenched the table blaze, by calling upon his water tattoo.

"He did it!" Huang drew a long knife from his belt, pointing it at Owen. "He's a Sorcerer!!"

Loyal fighters from both sides scrambled to their feet with various shouts, grabbing their weapons. Only the width of the table kept them from coming instantly to blows. Owen raised his cane, a blindingly bright flash of light accompanied by a loud boom came from the cane tip. Everyone froze in place.

"Calm down," Owen shouted. "There has clearly been a misunderstanding!" He gathered Mary to him with one hand, his cane held up in a cautionary way in the other. "We and the rest of Mike's group shall retire peacefully. We shall resume this in the morning when our heads are all clear of the wine!" He looked towards Mike and Jimmy the Hand. Mike had his sword out aimed at his rival gang leader. Jimmy held a rather large bore air pistol aimed at Owen's face. A very large bore, Owen observed.

"You are no old man," Jimmy accused. "Nor are you harmless."

"Sorry about that," Owen said. "We wanted to make sure that your tame fire caller there," he nodded towards Huang. "would not start anything. Looks like he did anyway,"

"What does that mean?" Jimmy asked suspiciously.

"You should ask him," Owen said blandly with a nod towards Huang.

"I never did nothing!" Huang protested.

"Mike, I do believe that we should leave." Owen looked at Mike.

"It will depend on him," Mike said. The gang leader kept his sword aimed at Jimmy's throat, while Jimmy the Horse kept his gun aimed at Owen. Jimmy's eyes shifted from side to side weighing by some sort of gang leader calculus, Owen thought. Finally he spoke.

"Alright," Jimmy said. "You can leave," He gestured with his pistol. "We meet here tomorrow," he said to Mike. "Bring the Sorcerer with you."

"I will bring or not bring who I like," Mike snarled.

"Mike," Owen interrupted, "Not now." He started backing towards the door, one arm still around Mary. If she manifested her fire now, it would not be pleasant. Owen hoped that his aura was dampening her power sufficiently. Mike and the others of their group slowly followed, all of them walking slowly backwards. The tension was thick enough to cut with a proverbial knife. Owen only hope it would not be in anyone's back.

How wonderful, Owen thought. All it would take is one of us to stumble and there will be a bloodbath. Jimmy's boys would jump all over us. While confident that he could stop a number of them, Owen could not stop all of them, he knew. Someone would fight and likely die. However, no one stumbled. He did not breathe easy until they reached the outdoors. The girls crowded around Owen, Mary and Mike, hefting their makeshift weapons. Mike's gaze took them all in. Mike nodded after doing a silent count.

"All right," Mike said firmly. "Gou, Jin, scout ahead for traps. Everyone else stay together. We are going home." His eye rested on Owen and Mary. "You, I will talk to when we get there," He pronounced coldly.

The walk back was a nightmare of twisted alleys, the tension radiating from the others as they waited for Jimmy's band to ambush them. Mary walked beside Owen dejectedly. Finally she responded to his inquiries as to how she was.

"It is all my fault," she whispered gloomily.

"What? How do you see that," Owen turned his attention from scanning the nearby rooftops to the young woman beside him.

"If my blessing as you call it, had not gotten away from me, we might be eating dessert at Jimmy's restaurant, and making peace with him," she snarled.

"Do not fancy yourself," Owen said dryly. "First of all, Jimmy was trying his best to provoke a fight. Do you honestly think that that oaf Huang would do anything without Jimmy's say so? Second, did it really feel to you that you lost control?"

"Well," she said hesitantly, "that was what was confusing. It did not feel as if I had lost control."

'Exactly," Owen said. "Keep in mind that you were not the only fire caller at that table"

They had reached the old factory that served as home to the gang safely. The look outs waved Mike and the others inside. As they reached the threshold Mary grabbed Owen's arm.

"Then I am not at fault? That is such a relief, thank you!"

Owen places his hand over Mary's in a gesture of reassurance, whatever he was going to say however was interrupted by Mike stopping dead in front of them.

"Who the hell are you?" Mike demanded. Owen peered around his shoulder to see who he was talking to. He saw Jinhao in her black Adept clothes, sword scabbards hung over the back of the western style chairs at the mess table. Across from her sat Mei. Both of them were bending their elbows with drinking bowls, and appeared to have become fast friends.

"Oh hello Jinhao," Owen said calmly.

Chapter 15

Well, now I can see why I haven't heard from you. Mary is indeed a fine figure of a woman. Hardly seems like your sort, but that is as may be." Jinhao looked at Owen with an arched eyebrow. After Mike had been appeased about Jinhao's appearance, the two had stolen to off to Owen's room to talk.

"It is not like that at all," retorted a flustered Owen. "I am Mary's teacher." Jinhao smiled at that.

"Oh, I am certain that you are a most excellent teacher," Jinhao said blandly.

"Now see here Jinhao," Owen proclaimed, "It is no laughing matter! Mary is an untrained Fire caller, and therefore a danger to herself and others." Owen rapped his cane on the factory floor. "Besides, there is the very real danger that there will be a gang war that Mikes' lot will lose on the morrow. That means that your little drinking friend there, as well as everyone in this building will be either dead or in the grip of a sadist named 'Jimmy the Horse'. Not to mention that I seem to have picked up a European sorcerer assassin and his brute of a giant pet." Owen told her of

Findley and the encounter at the dock with Mr. Victor and Mr. Percy.

"Ah yes, I believe that I have met the gentleman although not his pet as you call him." Jinhao said.

"What," Owen exclaimed. "How did that come about?" Jinhao relayed all that had befallen her since she went looking for Owen.

"He seems to believe that you are dead, but still seems to be looking for your body," Jinhao concluded. Owen nodded thoughtfully at that.

"Yes," he muttered around a frown. "He is probably looking to take my head back as proof of his success. Very traditional and very expensive. The custom started as a way to be sure that the target could not be re-animated against the hirer you know. That indicates very deep pockets indeed. Now, who among the old peerage could I have pissed off that much I wonder?"

"Wait," Jinhao said curiously. "You mean that among your people even after you kill an enemy, that enemy may still attack you on behalf of another enemy who uses Sorcery?"

"Necromancy actually. It requires someone who has mastered the element of Spirit. They then have to be willing to subvert that element. It usually ends badly for the operator with them using up their own life force. Ironic really when most Necromancers are searching for eternal life in the body," Owen explained. "That is why there are so few Necromancers left. We rather frown on that sort of thing in

Britain nowadays. Our run in with Renton, shows how few and far between they have become. His activities were not even recognized as such. Still, the custom persists."

"I do not like your people at all sometimes," Jinhao said.

"Neither do I," Owen replied. He looked at Jinhao with a pained look on his face. "Speaking of which, why do these urchins insist on using the most prosaic English names that they can find, rather than what I am certain are perfectly fine Han names?"

"Because they sound exotic and fashionable," She shrugged with indifference. "They appear to be names of power and strength." She looked at him. "Surely you are not comparing the fashions of Han street thugs to raising the dead."

"I am simply pointing out that every people have distasteful customs," Owen replied wryly. He frowned. "No, it appears that this Victor shall have to give up the name of his employer, which means that we shall have to capture him alive."

"Difficult when he wants to behead you," Jinhao observed.

"Yes, there is that," Owen allowed. "But it cannot be helped. If I kill him first, then his employer simply sends another assassin. One that I might not catch in time."

"Let me help," Jinhao said.

"You already have," Owen replied. "Truly Jinhao, I wish that you would go be safe somewhere. A Sorcerous assassin can be a very deadly thing. "

"I knew it!" The Adept accused. "You are hiding out here out of some noble but misbegotten sense that I need protecting!"

"Well, not as such you know," Owen protested. "I honestly thought that you would still be dealing with that business with your sister. It is just that you are no Sorcerer. I am sure that the old life-debt thing that you keep quoting does not apply to hired Magian-killers"

"Owen," Jinhao looked at him with great patience. "It does apply. When will you recognize that we are stronger together than apart?" Seeing the beginnings of protest on his face she pressed on. "When we looked into the case of the missing fishermen, who killed the beast?"

"You did," Owen said.

"And when we were investigating the case of the curious clockworks man who found the key?" Jinhao asked.

"You did," Owen answered lamely.

"Speaking of Renton, who killed him when his re-animated monsters were attacking us?"

"You again," Owen said with a sigh. "See here Jinhao, you have made your point. No need to belabor it." Owen looked down at the ground for a long time. Finally, he raised his head, grinning at her ruefully. "Besides I really did miss you, you know."

"And I you," she said softly. "But no more toughing it out alone, do you hear?"

"Right," Owen agreed with something of his usual cheer. "I should have known that turning that Demon that was trying to kill you was a mistake," he quipped, referring to their first meeting at an inn outside of Hong Kong.

"I did know that it was a mistake," Jinhao said with a bland face. "but I decided to let you rescue me anyway." She held out her hand. "I believe that one usually shakes hands when agreeing on a partnership."

"Quite," Owen responded cheerily. "To us!" He took her hand in his own. Jinhao nodded firmly as she squeezed it back.

"Now that that is done," she said shortly. "What is our next move to catch this Victor?" Owen shook his head.

"We have to first save the gang from this oncoming war," he asserted.

"Why?' Jinhao asked bluntly. "They nursed you back to health with their own advantage in mind. Why help them?"

"Because if we do not," Owen said seriously, "All of them will either be slaughtered or pressed into prostitute cribs."

"Why not simply kill this Jimmy the Horse, and be done with them then?"

"Have I mentioned that I have missed you?" Owen smiled at her. "Your approach is delightfully direct and refreshing. I am afraid that in this instance though, it will not serve. Another gang will come along when we are not about. If we can get these two groups to work together they should be able to hold off any other group that wishes to cause them trouble. Besides," he said forcefully, "it is not right that these women have no prospects of bettering themselves simply because they were tossed aside at birth."

"Why Owen," Jinhao remarked. "You may become a re-former after all!"

"Hush, evil wench!" Owen replied sternly. "I am in danger of no such thing," He looked up at the ceiling while stroking his chin with free hand. He looked back down at Jinhao. "I simply hate to see waste. Besides it is an interesting problem for the mind to get the two sides to come together in peace."

"Oh, I see," Jinhao said evenly. "It is purely an intellectual exercise then."

"Quite," Owen said. "I am glad you understand."

Jinhao refrained speaking more on the subject. She couldn't help but reflect though that her Grandfather would never have shown such concern for a group of non-caste women outlaws.

"Well I suppose that we should see about getting some sleep then," she said, attempting to be practical. Discovering that Owen was alive and well brought a lightness to her heart that she would never admit to the Englishman. She could barely admit it to herself. She glanced over at the blankets crumpled in a pile on the hard floor. "I see that they provide only the finest of sleeping accommodations," she remarked.

"It is a bit rough," Owen allowed. "I could say that you get used to it, but that would not be true." He moved towards the door. "I will see about getting some more blankets, shall I?"

"This shall work quite nicely for me I think." Jinhao placed her sword harness against the pillar. She began rearranging the blankets to her satisfaction. She looked up at him, "Do you really intend for us to stay with these people and avert their petty dispute?"

"Yes," Owen replied seriously. "I do. With their aid after that, we may perhaps come up with a plan to capture friend Victor."

Jinhao settled herself against the pillar with a blanket for a pillow between it and her. She smiled at him. "Well then I wish you luck in finding more blankets!"

Owen looked back at her crossly and went out the door. He returned shortly with two of the girls carrying large bundles of blankets and pillows. Owen thanked them both and began arranging the additional blankets to his own satisfaction. Then he then laid down, placing his cane within easy reach. Owen settled a pillow against his own pillar and smiled. With a wave of his hand the oil lamp that had been providing them with illumination went out.

"It seems that they managed to find some pillows as well," he observed innocently in the darkness.

"They look nice," Jinhao allowed from her nest of blankets.

"Of course, I would never dream of disturbing your no-doubt comfortable arrangement," He vowed to her.

"Oh, of course," Jinhao replied. "I shall simply lie here and dream of feather beds." After a pause, Owen spoke again.

"Jinhao," He said softly.

"Yes?" She responded. One word came back to her from the darkness.

"Catch."

She brought up one arm and caught a pillow that came towards her. She placed it between her head and the pillar. She smiled into the friendly dark.

"Jinhao," Owens voice came from the darkness.

"Good night, Owen," she said sleepily. Best to stop him before he becomes uncomfortably sentimental, she thought.

"Ah, good night, Jinhao," came the reply.

~ ~ ~

Jinhao came awake quickly when the door was kicked in. Rolling off to the right of the pillar that served as her pillow, she was up on one knee with her throwing spikes at the ready before the splinters of the door hit the floor. Fortunately for their intruder Owen was also quick. He used his trick of heating an opponent's weapon to disarm a raging Mike. Jinhao held her hand.

"Mike," Owen exclaimed. "What the Horned One are you about?" He stood there cane in one hand.

"Where is she," Mike snarled, "What have you done with Mary?" He was bent over holding his gun hand in agony, an air pistol at his feet.

"Mary?" Owen echoed. "What makes you think I have done anything with Mary?"

"She is not in her room," Mike came upright glaring at Owen. "If you have seduced her, you will pay for it, *Quizi* Sorcerer or no!"

"I have done no such thing," Owen protested. He reached for his trousers, cane still held on Mike like a gun. "She should know better than to go out walking or some such nonsense. We must find her!"

At that moment, little Mei who stood as the leader of the look outs appeared in the doorway. "Mike," she said to him grimly. "A messenger from Jimmy the Hand has come. You will want to speak with him."

"Put him in the mess room," Mike ordered. "Mary is missing and we must find her."

"It's about Mary that he has come," Mei said unhappily. "You will wish to see him," she repeated.

"What?" Mike said. "What can he know about Mary?"

"He claims that Jimmy the Horse is holding Mary for killing someone named Huang,"

Chapter 16

Jimmy the Horse had clearly pulled out all the stops to greet his gang rival. The street approach to the restaurant where they had met the night before was lined with very visibly armed and angry members of Jimmy's gang. Owen doubted that there was much intention on Jimmy's part to let them leave alive after the meeting. Not that they had much choice about agreeing to it. The messenger had been quite clear that Jimmy intended to kill Mary out of hand in retribution for killing the young man Huang if they didn't attend.

Owen cast a covert glance up to the rooftop line. Jinhao was still unknown to Jimmy, and was their ace in the hole so to speak. He chided himself silently for looking up. If he could see her, she wouldn't be Jinhao. Owen refocused on the restaurant entrance, the double red doors flanked by scowling sword-wielding youths. Wordlessly they pulled open the doors just far enough to allow Mike and Owen to slip inside. The other members of Mikes gang that had followed them were barred from entering, their grumbles silenced by a single sharp word from Mike. The women stood fingering their makeshift maces and butchers knives with bloody intent but otherwise remained quiet.

As Owens eyes adjusted first to the gloom of the reception area, he quickly grabbed Mike by the elbow.

"Show no reaction," Owen breathed into the gang leaders' ear. "Stay right here and do not move."

The gloom was suddenly pierced by the ignition of twin torches. The sudden light showed Jimmy wearing a Western suit of dark red, air pistol holstered at his waist. Behind him was Mary, tied to a pillar with ropes, a crude gag about her mouth.

"So," Jimmy snarled, "You had the guts to come after all." He gestured behind him. "I guess that your pet assassin must mean something to you after all. I thought that you would refuse after the way you sent a woman to do your killing for you."

"I do not know what you are talking about," Mike said levelly. "Mary is no killer, nor did I send her here. Last I knew we were going to meet today to discuss peace."

"Peace, eh?" Jimmy grunted. "Then why send your Fire doxy here to kill me? I'm sure that Huang must have caught her creeping in here, which must have led to her frying him."

"Nonsense," Owen rapped out. "That is as likely as my being able to sprout wings and fly!" One of Jimmy's henchmen pulled a pistol, swaggering towards Owen while waving the gun in his face.

"Shut your trap old man," he growled. "That innocent act does not make it here!"

"Jo, wait," Jimmy ordered. He looked at Owen. "Go on."

"I believe that we should hear from Mary what happened." Owen nodded at the bound woman.

"Ain't nothing she can tell," Jo snapped. "We all heard Huang screaming for his life in the banquet room. By the time we made it downstairs, he was dead. Burnt live. She was standing over him." Mary struggled with her bounds, trying to speak. Owen appealed to Jimmy.

"If you really want justice for Huang," he said. "You should allow Mary to speak." Jimmy frowned at this. Finally he nodded.

"All right," he said. "Jo did the right thing though so as that she couldn't use her voice to bewitch anyone. Boys, be ready to shoot either her or the Britisher."

Owen grimaced at Jimmy's rank superstition. Despite it being the 1800's People still thought that somehow using one's voice was important in using *magia* that gave someone control over another, a superstition that was not true. Still, folk legend dies hard. Owen approached Mary carefully and slowly as the boys had drawn pistols from somewhere, all of them pointed at Mary, Mike or himself.

Freed from the crude gag, which was nothing more than a piece of cloth shoved in her mouth, Mary whimpered, trying to speak around a dry mouth. Owen carefully patted her face, speaking in soothing tones as he might to a distressed dove.

"There Mary," he intoned, "It shall be alright. Mike and I are here." Raising his voice, he spoke to the room in general. "May we have a glass of water here please?" At Jimmy the Horse's nod, one of the boy put up his weapon and fetched some water in a wooden bowl. Mike seized it and muscled Owen aside to press it to her lips. After gulping thirstily for a few moments, she shook her head to indicate that she'd had enough. Owen pushed back against Mike so that Mary was looking at him again.

"Better?" Mary nodded wordlessly. "Good. Now can you tell us what happened?" She nodded again and wet her lips to speak.

"I am so, so sorry Mike, Owen. I know that I shouldn't have but when the note came I couldn't say no to it!"

"Shh," Mike hushed, "there is no need for apologies."

"What Mike says is true Mary," Owen said gently, but in a voice that said he would not be turned away from his course. "Start at the beginning and tell us everything in order. Leave nothing out, no matter how insignificant it may seem. Can you do that?" The bound woman nodded once and began speaking.

"So I wandered outside to get some air before bed," she began. "I know I am not supposed to, but after all that gone on, I still knew that somehow I was the reason that the talks were in trouble. Despite your kind words, and the words of Mike I knew it. My mind was awhirl about what I was to do, so I thought that some air would be just the thing." She looked down shamefaced.

"I had heard some of the other girls talk about how to sneak out quietly so that the look outs did not catch you so I did that," she went on.

"Once I was outside, a boy came up to me out of the shadows. He nearly scared me into screaming for the look outs. In fact, I had opened my mouth to do this that when what he whispered silenced me.

"'Are you Mistress Mary?'" he asked. 'Yes,' I said. He held out an envelope. 'This is for you,' he says. 'I am to wait.' And he stood there in the shadows as I opened the strange message. It was written in simple Mandarin."

"'I know what you are,' the note said," as she continued. "'Come alone to the restaurant where we met before. Together, you and I can avert a war. Tell the bearer of this note, yes'" She tilted her head. "Might I have some more water?" She asked. Mike held the bowl forward. After she had drunk, she continued.

"I looked up at the boy in the shadows and said yes. He came forward with a grin and spoke, 'Huang said you would say that. You are to follow me.' We went by a winding route through the alleyways which left me completely lost. Finally we came to a window at what I assumed was the back of the restaurant.

'You climb in here', the boy said'. Why, I asked him. 'Because we do not want to alert the guard. Jimmy would have a fit.' He said." At this Jimmy the Horse made a rude noise and muttered something that sounded to Owen like 'Damned right,' but otherwise held his peace. Mary continued.

"With his help, I made it through the window, with some difficulty. I found myself in a dark room that seemed to be some sort of storage place. It was filled with large sacks filled with rice and there was the smell of different spices so thick as to be overpowering in such a small space. There was, however, no one to meet me."

"I turned back to look out the window only to find my guide had vanished. Determined not to panic, I saw light outlining what was a door at the other end of the room. As quietly as I could I made my way across the room to it. Upon opening it, I found myself in a brightly lit corridor. It was then that I heard the screams. The inhuman, ghastly screams."

"I ran down the corridor and opening the door at the other end of it, I found myself in the banquet room that we had been in earlier. There was a horrible smell as if someone had burned meat. Then I saw the-the body." Mary's voice took on a quiver as she continued.

"The next thing I knew I was surrounded by angry men with guns who were yelling that I had killed him." She looked at Owen pleading in her eyes. "I did not kill him! I certainly did not mean to! Tell me I cannot do that!"

Owen petted her face, soothing tones in his voice. "No I doubt very much that you did Mary." He tugged at the ropes binding her. "Can we at least free her," he asked Jimmy, "She has told us that she had nothing to do with Huang's death."

"No," Jimmy replied. He eyed Owen shrewdly, "Owen did she say? I knew you were no 'old relative'! You are that Britisher, Owen Strong, the sorcerer who is meddling in other people's business."

"Guilty as charged," he admitted. Owen stood up straight, one hand pulling off the graying moustaches. He pretended not to notice the shifting of the youngsters' aim to himself. Jimmy nodded as if pleased with himself.

"I keep hearing how you solve mysteries that other people have." He gestured with his pistol into the air. "Well, if she did not kill Huang, then who did? Seems to me that is what you have to find out." He looked smug as he talked. "Meantime I already got me a witchy killer to hand who I do believe murdered Huang. It will take a lot of proving to convince me otherwise."

"You cannot mean this!" Mike exploded. "I can fight you!"

Jimmy's face took on a hard look at hearing this. "You can try," he said in a dangerous voice that belied his obvious youth. He pointed his pistol at Mary's head. "The first casualty will be the doxy."

"There is no need of that," Owen said wearily. "I can investigate the boy's death." He held up a hand. "But I will not promise that I can find the killer. You need to release Mary."

Jimmy shook his head, pistol not moving from Mary's head. "No, you need to find the killer if it is not her, and convince me of their guilt."

"That may be rather difficult as you seem to have your mind resolved on this matter already." Owen observed dryly. The youth named Jo stirred at this.

"Jimmy always judges fair," he growled, pointing his gun at Owen. "You just want the witchy whore to not get killed."

"Well of course I do not wish to see her killed," Owen agreed amicably. "I will say though, that if you do not get that pop gun out of my face, I will make you eat it."

"Jo!" Jimmy snapped. "Put it in a basket." He gestured towards Owen. "You—mister fancy talking, you have until sundown on Fourth Star Day to bring me Huang's killer—if it really is someone else." Jimmy looked around at his followers. 'That seem fair?"

At that moment, Jinhao chose to make her entrance. To the consternation of Jimmy and his bodyguards, she dropped onto the floor of the reception area, a masked figure in black with short swords harnessed over her back. To Owens surprise, Jimmy the Horse choked up, and dropped to the floor, his forehead touching it, his pistol laid at his side. He ordered his guards to do likewise. Soon Owen was left standing in bemusement along with Mike while the blood-thirsty gangers all kept bowing like waves of the ocean. Owen noticed that Jinhao did not seem surprised at this treatment, but took it in stride as seemingly her due. He caught Jimmy mutter something about the 'Claw' but had no idea what he was referring to. Jinhao, masked, strode towards the bowing young man, standing over him, her hands on her hips.

"Release the woman to me," she ordered Jimmy. "I will guarantee that justice will be done your fallen man." Jimmy remained facing the floor.

"I saw you many years ago when you visited my fore-brother, the one who led us in those days. With respect I must ask, is this the guarantee of the Dragon?"

"You dare to question me?" Jinhao responded archly. "Do you believe that the Dragon has time for the likes of you?"

Jimmy looked up at her defiantly. "He does if your words are true, and if you value the life of this woman. Otherwise, it has been many years since any have seen the Dragon's Claw, and I will not be moved for less."

Owen imagined that he could see Jinhao sigh, although she kept her attention fixed on the kneeling gang leader. He decided that as he had not a clue what was going on, his wisest course was to say nothing.

"Very well," Jinhao allowed. "Release the girl, allow the Englishman to question who he wishes and go where he wishes to find the murderer. The Dragon will sit in judgment."

"In two days," Jimmy pressed, "no more. And the witch woman must stay here until the day comes." Jinhao hesitated, then nodded.

"Very well, agreed," She said. Jimmy slowly rose to his feet, looking at Jinhao.

"Agreed," he answered. "Untie the witch," he ordered.

Mary fell into Mikes' waiting arms sobbing. Owen watched the touching scene for a few moments, then slid up to Jinhao. Jimmy was just getting to his feet, his minions still on their knees.

"What have you done," Owen asked Jinhao sotto voce.

"Gained you two days to find the killer," Jinhao replied in the same low tones. She continued to look at Jimmy impassively behind her mask. Owen sighed.

"And how is it that the sadistic delinquent listens to you as if you are royalty?" he asked mildly.

"It is a legacy from a former time," she replied shortly. "You needed the woman alive clearly. I simply made that possible. What shall we do now?"

"I suppose we should look at the banquet room and hopefully the body," Owen said."That is if it hasn't been disturbed yet."

"No it hasn't," Jimmy said quietly. He glanced over at Mike and Mary with a look of pure hatred. "I wanted Mike to see just what his killer had done."

"Well, let us be about it then," Owen said, cheerily looking around at the occupants of the room. He spied the older woman who had been present last night hovering near the doorway and looking even more anxious than she had if that were possible. Owen walked over to where she stood.

"Hello," Owen said to her with a smile. "And how are you?" The woman looked at the floor, saying nothing.

Jimmy spoke up from where he stood. "That is the owner of the restaurant. She is of no consequence." Owen turned where he stood to regard Jimmy.

"Then I believe that being the owner of this place makes her of much consequence," Owen said. He looked back to the restaurant owner. "It is all right," he said, "No harm shall come to you. What is your name?" The woman looked up at him like a frightened deer. She scampered across the floor to stand behind Jimmy the Horse, who glared at Owen. Owen looked across at Jinhao who only shrugged wordlessly. Owen returned the gesture ruefully. He looked over at Mike and Mary.

"Mike will you be a dear and bring Mary along," Owen asked in a breezy tone.

"Is that really necessary," Mike asked him in cold tones.

"Oh, I believe that I really must insist," Owen replied in the same cheery manner. He looked at Mary, his voice changing to a gentler tone. "You can bear this can you not? I would not ask if it were not important." Mary nodded silently, still clutching Mike close.

"Very well," Owen said. He looked at Jimmy and his henchman Jo, "Lead on please."

~ ~ ~

Jinhao had never seen the banquet room before. It was a large well-appointed room with a large statue of Fu-Shoji in one corner to bring luck and harmony to the dinners. The smells of the room told her a tale of pain and death however. Her gaze came to rest on what appeared to be a forlorn pile of burnt offerings on the floor near the head seat of the long banquet table. Jimmy the Horse stood over it.

"There," Jimmy said in a hoarse voice, hands clenching into fists, then unclenching them. "There," he repeated. "Now you see what that Witch has done." Owen came up beside him.

"I am sorry for your loss." Owen said quietly. Jimmy spun on him as if stung.

"Huang was a good soldier," Jimmy said gruffly.

"Of course," Owen murmured soothingly. He wondered why the gang leader seemed so touchy about feeling bad about the death of a trusted lieutenant, then dismissed the thought. How could he possibly know anything about these strange waifs of the streets? Owen gestured behind them.

"Would you mind standing back so that I can examine him please?" Jimmy nodded jerkily, and stepped back. Owen knelt beside the corpse, looking at the burnt remains intensely. Then clicking his tongue in thought he glanced down the length of the room. He raised his cane, passing it over the body which became covered in a faint violet haze. Jimmy started towards him, only to be stopped by a masked Jinhao quickly stepping in front of him.

"What are you doing to him?" Jimmy demanded. Owen replied without looking up, his face a study in concentration.

"Every Magia emanation leaves its mark," Owen explained absently. "I am currently attempting to follow this one back to its source. Would you mind standing back?" he repeated. The violet haze drifted up like smoke in a strong breeze. Jinhao pushed the gang leader back, his eyes showing their whites in amazement as the haze moved almost lazily down the length of the hall. It came to stop in front of Mary who was still holding onto Mike, both of their faces showing amazement and fear.

"I told you that the witch killed him!" John exclaimed excitedly. He pulled his pistol hastily aiming it at her.

"Would everyone please calm down," Owen said. "Mike, Mary would you please step to the left." The hostile gangers paused, their weapons out, confused. Mike pulled an equally confused Mary to the left of where they stood. The violet haze drifted past them both and stopped at the wall. Owen gave a small sound of triumph. Carefully, he stood up, walking the length of the banquet room to stand facing the far wall. He tapped the wall with a fist.

"I say, there appears to be something of a hidden doorway here," He said drily. The older woman stirred at word of Owen's discovery. "Jinhao," he said lazily, "do not let our hostess leave. It seems to be no surprise to her." Jimmy the Horse stepped between a fearsome and masked Jinhao and the old proprietor of the restaurant.

"Leave her alone," he said. "She has nothing to do with this!"

"Indeed," Owen purred from his place by the wall, "And how do you know this?"

"Because she is my mother! Her name is Zhang. Zhang Woo." Jimmy awkwardly placed an arm around her. The woman looked surprised at his action, then gave in and leaned into her son's embrace. Owen continued to face the wall.

"I see, that is very touching," he replied in a sharp tone. "I assume that you know about this hidden doorway as well."

"It is an old servant's way," Jimmy replied. "It leads to the kitchen."

"Yes, yes," Owen said testily. "How do you open it, man?"

"Oh, that." Jimmy walked over to the statue of the Buddha. With his back to the room so that no one could see what he was doing, he worked. Eventually there was a click and a section of wall swung inward. The violet haze raced into the dark of the revealed passageway like a hound chasing its quarry. Owen peered after it.

"I believe that we will need some torches here," He called out.

Once some open bowls with wicks and oil in them were brought forth, a strange procession made its way down the narrow corridor illuminated by the smoky light of the bowls. The violet haze stretched out to a pencil thinness before them. Eventually the haze came to stop over a slumped body.

"Hello," said Owen. He knelt at the body's side. "Help me turn it over," He ordered Jimmy. The ganger knelt beside Owen and the two of them turned the body over revealing a tall man of European features dressed in what for in this district would be considered fine clothes. A pistol underneath him was covered in Owen's violet haze. He picked up the weapon carefully.

"Well Jimmy," Owen said easily. He held it out the pistol to the ganger. "Here is the murderer of your man."

"What is it?" Jimmy breathed, not reaching out to touch it.

"We call it an 'aether gun', Owen explained. "They are made by alchemists. Very expensive, and very, very deadly." He pointed to the clear tube on the end of it. "This holds what they call an alchemical fluid. Although this one is empty, I would wager that it held a fire fluid. The weapon is capable of shooting fire, or some other elemental energy the same as a sorcerer can with his power, instead of bullets like your air pistols." Jimmy looked at the weapon in Owen's hand as if it were a venomous snake.

"I have heard of such things," He said hoarsely. "Western abominations."

"I can but agree with you," Owen said. Jinhao had ghost-ed up beside them, kneeling to examine the body.

"This one is still alive," she said calmly.

Chapter 17

They carried the mysterious stranger up the stairs. Upon examining him, it was discovered that he had suffered a blow to the head that had rendered him unconscious. Despite this, he had been tied to a chair while Jinhao ministered to his head wound. The man muttered as she worked.

"What is that he is saying?" Mike asked. Owen stood by the doorway watching Jinhao at work.

"It is Germanic," Owen replied. At Mike's blank look, Owen amplified his statement. "That is the language used by most of the Austrian Empire." Mike nodded.

"I have heard of them," he said, looking at the bound man. "They tried to invade the city last summer." Owen who along with Jinhao had stopped said invasion merely nodded in agreement.

"Yes," Owen said gravely, "They are definitely bad eggs."

"What is he doing here?" Mike wondered aloud.

"Perhaps we may ask him when he regains consciousness," Jinhao said drily, as she tossed a bloody rag into a basin. She carefully wrapped his head in a makeshift bandage.

"Then he will recover," Owen asked. Jinhao raised her hands palms up in reply.

"It is always uncertain with head wounds," she said. "However I see no reason why he should not."

"There is no need for that," Jimmy the Horse said grimly. "He killed Huang with his devil-science gun, this is clear." Jimmy turned towards Mike who still held Mary close to him. He bowed at the rival gang leader.

"It seems that I may owe you and the woman an apology," he said briefly. Mike retuned the bow.

"It is very kind of you to say so," Mike replied with equal brevity.

"Of course," Jimmy said stiffly, "We will have to question the culprit before I am completely satisfied."

Mike bowed again. "Of course," he agreed calmly. While the two of them were talking, Owen had slid over to the tied-up captive. He pulled back the man's shirt-sleeve to reveal the tattoo of a skull on his arm.

"Tokenkoff," Owen hissed in surprise.

"What's that?" Mike asked Owen.

"Deaths-Head," Owen translated. "Our friend here is an agent of the Austrian Secret Service. A rather elite agent come to that," Owen mused. "Does anyone recognize him?" At the chorus of no's Owen turned back to the unconscious man

"*Waken Sie*," he murmured. The man moaned and opened his eyes.

"*Ja*," he said groggily. His head snapped back and his eyes narrowed in suspicion as he realized that he was tied to the chair. "*Was ist loss?*" he exclaimed angrily.

"Sorry old man," Owen said in English. "But we have you red-handed. It will go much easier on you if you cooperate. You do speak English do you not? It would make it easier for our friends here if you speak either that or Mandarin."

"I can speak both," the bound man replied coldly in English. "Tell me why I should," he finished in what Owen thought was horrible Mandarin. Enough of the meaning got through that Jimmy sprang at him with a roundhouse blow to the head that rocked the man back. Jinhao sprang in front of Jimmy, grabbing him in what appeared to be a painful hold

"Because you talking is the only thing keeping you alive," Jimmy yelled. "Because nobody kills one of my boys and gets away with it!"

Owen stood up between Jimmy and the captive. He addressed Jimmy earnestly.

"Listen," he said to the gang leader. "We still do not know why Huang was killed. If we do not find the answer to that, then he died in vain, do you understand?" Jimmy stopped moving in Jinhao's grip.

"Yeah, I get that," Jimmy said "Why do you think that he's still alive?" Owen looked at the bound man over his shoulder.

"I think that you should talk," he said to the Austrian agent in his native language. "I do not know if I can hold him otherwise."

"Hey," Jimmy said angrily. "No talking in that funny jabber. Speak English! His Hannish is awful." Owen nodded an acknowledgment, turning back to the seated man.

"You heard our host," Owen said evenly. "We have recovered your aether pistol, and linked it conclusively to the murder of the boy called Huang. What we want to know is why." The man began to laugh darkly.

"Und if I tell you," he said in a thick Austrian accent, "you will simply kill me the quicker." He shook his head. "No, I am ready to go to Her sweet embrace now thank you." He closed his eyes, then closed his lips resolutely.

Owen caught Mike's eye and nodded his head towards Jimmy and then the door. The ganger caught Owen's message and turned towards the other gang leader.

"Come now Jimmy, let us go outside and leave the professionals to do what they do best," he said in Mandarin while moving with Mary towards the door.

"How do we know that he is on the level?" Jimmy demanded, pointing to Owen.

"Because I say so," Jinhao snapped, her voice oddly muffled by the black gauze mask she still wore. "and I speak with the voice of the Dragon." Jimmy held up his hands towards her in placation.

"All right," Jimmy said hastily, "all right. I do not intend to anger the Dragon." He followed Mike and Mary quickly out the door. Owen pulled up another western style chair, settling himself next to the prisoner. He reached into the deep pockets of his tunic, producing a cigarette case. He extracted two cigarettes, holding one up to the Austrian's face.

"Want one?" Owen asked. "Now that the children are gone, we can relax like reasonable adults." The Austrian laughed low.

"You are more a fool than I take you for Britisher, if you think those are anything but murderous rats rather than children. But yes, I would like one, out of your courtesy please." He licked his lips as Owen lit one of the cigarettes, holding it up to the Austrian's lips. He inhaled gratefully then Owen took it away from him.

"Is that why you killed Huang," Owen asked casually. The Austrian laughed again.

"I haff not killed anyone," he said ruefully.

"See here," Owen said calmly, "I have seen your tattoo so everyone now knows that you are an agent of the Austrian secret police, but why would you be sulking around here? I do not understand it," he continued, "And I assure you that you want me to understand it. I may be the only thing standing between you and dying open-faced to the world. I doubt that your Goddess would approve of that." The Austrian laughed again.

"Then you do not know as much as you might think," he returned smugly. "The Grand Bishop herself blesses each member of the Chosen who must go out into the world of sinners. My place is already assured."

"Ah," Owen nodded. "Then it is as I conjectured, you are a member of the Tolken-knoff."

"I did not say that," the secret police officer quickly interjected.

"You did not have to," Owen returned with a touch of his own smugness. "If you were simply a refugee, you would not be a member of the Church of Her Divine Radiance. If you were an ordinary member, I doubt that you would be receiving dispensations from the Grand Bishop." The bound man bared his teeth at Owen. "Nor would you bear that rather distinctive mark," Owen added, tapping the man casually on the forearm.

"We shall enjoy sending you to the eternal fire," the Austrian snarled. "The Goddess shall not be denied, nor shall we stop until the whole world bows before Her Radiance!"

"Yes, yes," Owen said wearily. "I shall suffer from not having been turned by the lunatic ravings of a dead Mideastern prophetess, whose teachings are no doubt twisted from the original by the Church anyway. I would think that you would want to claim credit for killing an infidel, no matter how young." Owen took a deep pull on his own cigarette, letting the other one fall to the ground. The secret policeman's eyes followed its trail down to floor forlornly.

"As I have already stated, I have killed no one," he said to Owen in a haughty tone of voice.

"Of course not," Owen replied, sarcasm dripping from his voice. "You were just for a pleasant walk with the murder weapon in a secret hallway near the victim." At this point Jinhao spoke up. The good person/bad person interrogation technique was one that they had practiced before.

"Now do not be so hard on him," she said sympathetically. "No doubt he stumbled in the hallway, fell down, and hit his head." The bound man looked offended at this.

"I did not stumble!" He snapped. "I was hit over the head!" Owen looked at Jinhao, then at the man.

"I am sure that you were Hans," Owen said voice still dripping sarcasm. "Did you by chance see who did it?"

"No!" the agent said vehemently. "And my name is Deter, not Hans!"

"So you are saying that you were hit over the head and your pistol used without your knowledge?" Jinhao asked.

"Yes!" Deter exclaimed excitedly. "That must have been what happened!"

"And will you tell us why you were in the corridor of the restaurant?" Jinhao pressed. Deter turned away his head away from the pair of them.

"I have said too much already," Deter closed his mouth with a snap.

"Oh I do not think that you have said nearly enough." Owen returned. "You want to consider that we are your only friends in all this. There is a bloodthirsty gang leader outside who wants nothing more than to kill you slowly and painfully. Frankly, I am still inclined to allow him to, Deter. You are going to have to give us something more to go on than mysterious assailants. You think on that." Owen motioned with a nod of his head for Jinhao to accompany him out the door. Once outside the room, they were accosted by an anxious Jimmy who stood waiting with Mike and Mary.

"Well?" the gang leader demanded eagerly. Owen held up a hand.

"Do not kill him yet, Jimmy," Owen said tiredly. "Let Jinhao and I talk for a moment first." Jimmy gestured angrily for them to move down to the far end of the hallway. Once out of hearing, Owen turned to Jinhao.

"Well," he began, "What do you think of our secret agent of the Austrian Republic?" Jinhao frowned in thought.

"Strange as his story seems, he has the ring of truth to his voice," she said. "You have had more dealings with his countrymen though, what do you believe?"

Owen winced as he thought on her question.

"Unfortunately, I believe him too," he whispered back. "No assassin has such a stupid capture story as he does. Still, he was up to something, I would give a lot to know what." They both turned at the sound of someone on the stairs. It was Jimmy's mother come up the stairs with towels and fresh water. Head bowed, she made her way towards the door which held their captive.

"Here now," Owen called out to her. "What do you think that you are doing?" The woman scampered behind Jimmy the Horse, peering out at Owen. She spoke some dialect strange to Owens ears as she looked around Jimmy at him.

"She says that she was only going to clean his wounds," Jimmy explained. "What is the big deal? You won't let her take care of him. I would think that you would be glad to have her look after the scum. Did you get him to confess?"

"No," Owen said. "Nor do we think that he is your killer." Jimmy split on the floor before Owen.

"Come now!" He exclaimed. "First the girl didn't do it. Then you find a strange abomination of science that you say did the killing, but that the wielder of it didn't kill Huang either? Then who did?"

"Someone else," Owen said simply.

Chapter 18

Fair Lady Weaves Shuttle flowed into Stork Spreads Wings. Jinhao gracefully moved from one position to another in the courtyard, concentrating on the movement of Qi through her body, aware yet unaware of the gathering crowd of street urchins that were watching her move through her morning routine as she slipped deeper into the fighting trance of the Adept.

All Adepts practice such disciples to keep themselves at the peak of their powers and to keep the body and mind attuned as one. While many of the forms had a fighting application, some were purely meditative. Jinhao felt the need of such clarity at the moment so she had chosen one of the more meditative groupings.

When Owen had convinced the gang leaders to call off the fruitless interrogation of their Austrian captive, the night had ended on a very unsatisfactory note for everyone. Deter was still a prisoner, Owen's Mary was still under suspicion, and while the murder weapon had been found due to Owen's arts, neither Jinhao nor Owenbelieved that Deter had committed the deed.

With Lohan due to make an appearance by the next day, it was vital that they unmask the real killer before then, unless they simply wanted to make an unwitting mockery of the Dragon's appearance. She winced inside at the thought. Lohan would not be very understanding, she mused, that is if he even bothered to come at her request at all.

It had been decades since Lohan had moved among the people of the city. Without a culprit ready to hand for a show trial, it could be disastrous. If he did come, most likely he would convene his Court, hear the story so far, and without a villain decide to execute everyone including her. She knew that her relationship with Lohan would give her no safety when it concerned a matter of *Mianmu*, that quality of dignity Westerners mistakenly called *face*.

She allowed such thoughts to move through her as the Qi moved through her body, without attachment, hoping that her spirit would coalescence them into some sort of answer. As she came to the absolute stillness found at the end of the form, she was disappointed that no answer had come to her dilemma. She felt the calm that a good workout gave, but not the peace of vanquishing her enemies. The young urchin girl from Mike's female gang came scampering up to her, a towel held up in her outstretched hands. Jinhao took the offering from her with a smile.

"Thank you Mei" she said taking the towel. Mei's eyes shone at her.

"I have never seen anything so beautiful," the girl breathed. "Can you teach me how to do that?" Jinhao paused at the girls question, towel raised to wipe her face. Her first impulse was to refuse her, but then she thought better of it. It was true that only someone with a sponsor would be able to enter the Temple for the training. While Jinhao currently had only the standing of an outlaw in the Imperial Temple, who knew what the fates might bring?

"Perhaps," she temporized, handing the girl back the towel. "Why do you want to learn it?" Mei smiled at her, a look in her eyes that made Jinhao uncomfortable. Her eyes shone with a look akin to worship towards the older woman.

"Because you look so graceful doing it, and," she made her hands into fists, "you can fight anyone at all, and that means that you are not afraid of anything!" If only that were true Jinhao thought ruefully. Still, the noble heart that the girl had was deserving of some encouragement.

"I tell you what," Jinhao said. "Why don't you join me for Form in the mornings, and that way you can see what it is really like. If you work hard, you might get to the Imperial Temple." Mei made a rude sound with her lips.

"Me at the Imperial Temple?" She shook her head, ringlets flying. "I'm not holy or anything." Jinhao laughed.

"Do you think I am?" Jinhao asked. Mei frowned at that. Her face scrunched up as she worked through the question.

"No, not really," Mei said hesitantly. "You drink wine and hang around with foreign devil sorcerers."

"Well, Owen is not really much of a devil I must say," Jinhao said laughing. "Although I did see that his feet are clawed like a birds,' she whispered to the young girl. Mei gasped.

"No they are not!" The girl protested.

"Have you ever seen Owen without his shoes?" Jinhao asked her.

At that moment, Owen came out of the restaurant, walking towards them. Mei got a very determined look on her face and raced up towards him. Owen smiled down at her and opened his mouth to speak. Before he could say anything however, Mei stomped down hard on his foot. Owen exclaimed in surprise at this treatment, hopping about on the un-abused one. Mei whirled to face Jinhao.

"He does not," she proclaimed. Then with a guilty look at Owen, she sped off into the restaurant.

"'He does not' what?" Owen asked in surprise at Jinhao. The Adept held up her hands in negation.

"Children," Jinhao said simply. "who can understand them?"

"Well, you have that right," Owen said grumpily. He limped over to where she stood. "I was wondering if you had any brilliant insights occur to you overnight as to who our killer may be."

"No," she replied, shaking her head miserably. "I assume from the question that you have not either."

"Not a clue," he said cheerfully. "I fail to see how anyone else could have committed the deed save friend Deter, yet, I feel certain that Deter did not commit it."

"Where does that leave us?" Jinhao asked.

"Well," Owen replied while rubbing his chin thoughtfully, "That means that we shall have to do it the hard way by questioning everyone, and deducing who it is from that. Certainly from my brief exposure to the boy I am sure that he had many a person who wanted him dead. I know I did!"

"Fortunately we still have a day before Lohan's arrival," Jinhao said. "It would not do to have no one that Lohan could publicly judge and condemn." She looked at Owen meaningfully. "It would be very bad in fact."

"How bad exactly?" Owen asked in curiosity. "And while we are on the subject of the Dragon, how is it that you 'speak with the Dragon's voice'?"

"That is old history of what I once was," Jinhao replied with a wave of her hand in dismissal. "What we must focus on now is finding the correct killer. It will be a matter of Mianmu for the Dragon if we cannot present the culprit to him when he arrives. If we cannot," she concluded looking at Owen, "he may condemn us in the killer's place."

"I see. A matter of *face*" Owen translated with a raised eyebrow. "Well, I am glad then that we have that extra day."

"That is if he comes at all," Jinhao added. "He has not left either his caves or his gardens for many years." Owen was about to ask something else when one of Jimmy's boys came running into the courtyard shouting.

"The soldiers are coming!" he cried. "The soldiers are coming!" Then he ran out again. Distantly came the sound of drums. Owen looked at Jinhao.

"That cannot be what I think it is," Owen said to her disbelievingly.

"I fear that we shall not have that extra day," Jinhao said sadly. "Lohan comes!"

~ ~ ~

Owen and Jinhao went to the front entrance of the restaurant as did many of the gang members. The main difference was that Owen and Jinhao did not come bearing weapons in their hands as the gangers did. The drum beats grew louder as the boys and girls murmured uneasily among themselves, their hands grasping hilts more tightly. Jinhao looked at the massed gang members and shook her head.

"There will be trouble if the gangs are not reassured, and quickly," she remarked to Owen. At that point an out of breath Mike appeared with a flushed Mary. They were followed by a disheveled Jimmy the Horse.

"What is all this about soldiers?" Mike snapped at Jinhao. "You never said anything about soldiers! You said only that the Dragon would come to judge the murderer!"

"And do you think that the Dragon would come without escort or without his counselors? What do you think is meant by 'court', except the Dragon and his court?" Jinhao snapped back at him. Mike blinked at this.

"Then they are not here to kill us all?" he asked. "Why are they a day early?"

"If you would ask the Dragon for judgment then he comes when he pleases," Jinhao answered. She threw up her hands. "As for if he intends to kill you all, if someone does not calm these children down, I am sure that there will be a massacre!" Mike nodded grimly at this and stepped to the front of the seething group.

"Calm down," He said holding up a hand. "Calm down! This is the Dragon Lohan coming to us to render his judgment in the death of Huang! Stand easy! The Dragon is coming to *us*!"

Owen saw the mass of gangers slowly relax at this. The idea that someone as powerful as the Dragon would come at the request of their leaders was not lost on them. It was an enormous giving of *Mianmu* to both Mike and Jimmy and so to each of them by reflection. Still they were wary of such a thing as they should be, in Owen's opinion.

The drummers came into view on the street, a line of them beating in unison followed by two lines of uniformed figures bearing arms. Owen saw the mistake that the lookout had made. These were not soldiers of either the British Queen or the Hannish Throne, but Hong Kong police constables in dress uniforms of midnight blue, their brass buttons gleaming. Still, their air carbines were as deadly as those of any soldiers, and Owen had no doubt that they were as proficient in their use.

The double line of constables were followed by a garish assortment of Hannish and British personages. The Hannish in bright silk robes and the British in dress coats and top hats as brightly colored as the Hannish. Behind them all came a curtained bier bore by four large blond Northmen. The bier was carefully lowered to the ground. The drums came to an abrupt halt. The courtiers bowed like wheat stalks before a wind.

"Come quickly," Jinhao murmured to Owen as she sprang forward. The British Sorcerer sprinted to her side, then executed a formal court bow as the curtains parted and a familiar old man stepped from within.

Owen contained his surprise as he recognized the old man with the long white whiskers. He was the same old man that Owen had chatted to at Government House during the Austrian invasion affair last summer. Owen had simply taken him for some government dignitary, never dreaming that he was talking to Lohan himself! He glanced up to see that the old man had recognized him.

"Owen Strong," Lohan said gravely. "You have not come to my home as I invited you."

"Great Lohan," Owen said, resuming his bow. "I regret that circumstances have prevented me from such pleasurable activities." The old man's face broke into a brief smile.

"You are at least well spoken," Lohan remarked. The Dragon turned to Jinhao beside him. "So Grand daughter, I have come as you asked. Now, I assume that you have this murderer in hand that I might convene the court together to give public judgment in this matter."

"Mighty Lohan," Jinhao said. "The matter has proved to be very difficult."

"Difficult?" The Dragon repeated. Owen thought that saw a glint of red fire in the old man's eyes for a moment. "Difficult in what manner?"

"Perhaps we might do better to go inside," Owen suggested.

Chapter 19

Of course it wasn't as simple as the three of them walking off somewhere to talk. There were the very delicate introductions of both Mike and Jimmy to be made to Lohan, as well as introductions to the owner of the restaurant they were entering. The poor woman was practically beside herself between showing her obeisance to the Dragon by prostrating herself flat on the floor and the need to bustle about readying a suitable place for them all to talk inside. Finally Lohan took pity on her and informed her that she need not perform a full obeisance herself every time she entered his presence.

Then there was the matter of what to do with the police constables and courtiers who had made up the procession. Owen was pleasantly surprised to find that his old friend in the police, Inspector Gregg, was in charge of them. They exchanged words in the courtyard while the Dragon went inside.

"So I see that you have made Chief Inspector, Gregg." Owen remarked, gesturing towards the dress uniform the man was clearly uncomfortable wearing

"Deputy Inspector, thanks to that bit of with the Duke of Chu's niece." He growled, finger seeking to make looser the tight collar of his dress uniform. "It just means more paperwork and more dress circuses like this one." He give Owen a gimlet eye. "I should have known that you had a hand in this, Milord. So what is the situation? We heard talk of a murder, which as this is my district, didn't sit well with the higher ups when I had to confess that I knew damn all about it!"

"Yes, well there has been a murder," Owen confessed. "I fear, however, that the culprit is not in hand."

"That could be very bad Milord." The policeman acknowledged. "This was put about as an afternoon's lark among the court." He looked as if he had bitten into a sour lemon. "Something about the Dragon dispensing the High Justice among the lower classes." He sniffed, looking around. "Seems to me the lowest classes is more like it. I know the court was looking forward to seeing some simple thing with maybe an execution before they went back up the Hill to their perfumed pansies. If you don't have the guilty party to hand, there's little that I can do to help you I'm afraid."

"Well," Owen said, "We do have an Austrian spy in plain clothes. But I doubt that he committed the crime"

"The devil you say," Gregg exclaimed. "That should keep your neck from the block at any rate." Gregg shook his head. Mei came bounding up, interrupting them.

"Jinhao says that the Dragon is settled inside, and that both Mike and Jimmy are there. You should come at once she says, before things get too out of hand."

"Right then," Owen said to the small messenger. "Thank you Wei." He turned back to Gregg. "Are you coming Gregg?"

"I had best see to these," Gregg encompassed both the courtiers and his fellow police who were milling about in the street. "Gods help me if someone gets their pocket picked. I'll be along."

Owen went inside to the banquet room where Huang had been killed. There he found the table had been removed and the Dragon was sitting on a throne-like chair that had appeared from somewhere. Both Mike and Jimmy had paced off, facing each other before the Dragon who did not look amused at either of them. Lohan was blowing on a tea cup when Owen entered. He looked at Owen over the tea cup. Jinhao stood behind the chair in the position of trusted bodyguard, a placement not lost on the British aristocrat. She looked at him in silent warning.

"So, Lord Owen of Strong," the Dragon said by way of greeting. "These fine—gentlemen—were just telling me about the murder of some street thug and that I am to punish the murderer. Unfortunately, according to them, there is no murderer caught or so they tell me you say to them.

What do you say to me?" Owen bowed deeply at this before he replied.

"Mighty Lohan," he said carefully. "The culprit of the crime for which you are here is here upon these premises. I believe that you will find that convening your court would be most advantageous to you, that all may learn your wisdom." The Dragon leaned forward in the chair, cup held delicately between his fingers.

"Indeed, Lord Owen," the Dragon-seeming of an old man gave him a smile of approval, which held no reassurance. It reminded Owen of the grin of a shark just before feeding. "Will you tell me who you have taken for this crime? Was it the Austrian spy?"

"Mighty Lohan," Owen replied still bowing, "given that a foreign national is involved, might one suggest that this case could be a great showcase for the modern thinking that imbues your court of justice." The Dragon frowned at this.

"What do you mean?" Lohan asked Owen sharply. "If I have to call that stupid Austrian ambassador, it will make the whole affair only more tedious." The Dragon sighed. "That woman is such a bore under normal circumstances."

"Well, that is one thing that unfortunately you should consider doing," Owen allowed. "Treaties and all that." He pushed on. "No, what I was referring to was your fervent embrace of modern Western criminal justice procedures." The Dragon leaned back in his chair at hearing this.

"And what exactly are these *modern procedures?*" he asked archly.

"Instead of having a confession in hand at the time of the court convening," Owen explained. "The court impartially hears all the evidence and then makes a wise and just decision." Owen was uneasy as Lohan smiled again his shark smile.

"Ah yes," he said briskly. "Two people, called I believe a prosecute and a defender, present all the facts before me and I then decide who is guilty. Splendid idea, it will be a spectacular hit with the court." He waved a hand. "You shall be the prosecute, and the Austrian spy shall be the defended."

"Ahem," Owen said clearing his throat. "I am reasonably certain that the Austrian is not the murderer Mighty Lohan."

"Well he is certainly guilty of being a spy in my city!" The Dragon asserted.

"That is true," Owen allowed, "but while he may have been that, as well as furnished the murder weapon, I rather doubt that he pulled the trigger."

"A detail only, I am sure," Lohan replied. "The penalty is the same for both crimes, and I can only have him beheaded once. Besides, if someone else performed the murder then you shall have to bring them out before the Court. I believe that is what a prosecute does."

"Prosecutor," Owen corrected him faintly. "The role is called the prosecutor, and I am hardly the right person for the role," he protested.

"Nonsense," The Dragon asserted. "I have decided it. You will do greatly, I have every confidence. You are present, and I still want to do this today." He looked down at Owen and sighed. "I shall have to call upon the Austrian Ambassador I can see."

"I fear so," Owen replied steadily. He had hoped to simply delay the Dragon from convening the court to witness his judgment, thus saving face all around. Now he found himself having to find the real killer before the court instead.

"What about us Your Lordship?" Jimmy the Hand asked in Hannish. "I want to be assured of justice for Huang!"

"What about you?" Lohan sniffed. "I am not here to assure you of anything! You should feel grateful that I shall not have you hauled off to the vagrant's gaol! No, you shall both watch the proceedings of the court. Should you fail to show proper respect, my displeasure will be great, I assure you!" At that moment, Inspector Gregg entered the room behind them along with a trickle of courtiers. Lohan, on seeing the Inspector, called out to him.

"Inspector," the Dragon commanded. "Find me a messenger. I need to send a message to the Austrian Embassy."

Chapter 20

Owen stood outside in the courtyard staring up at the sky. It was a beautiful day without a cloud in sight, far too beautiful a day to die on, he thought resignedly. He supposed that he could attempt to steal away, perhaps secretly pass across the border or stowaway on a British ship. Anything else would be too dangerous. If he did, however, he would have to leave Jinhao behind, which wasn't an answer that was acceptable to him, no not in the least. And of course, any attempt to steal away by the both of them would only double their chances of being caught. At that moment, Jinhao came up behind him, deliberately making enough noise that he knew it was her without having to turn around.

"Hello, Jinhao," He greeted her wearily.

"Do you truly know who killed the boy Huang?" she asked softly.

"I haven't the faintest clue," Owen confessed to her. "Nor,it appears, shall we have time to find out, not with this Court business convening in just a few hours at most."

"Perhaps we could escape beyond Lohan's reach," she ventured. "We could make our way to my sister, she would take us in."

"And become jolly pirates, singing 'yo ho ho and a bottle of grog'?" Owen answered this with a wry grin and a shake of his head. "No, I don't think that would fit either of us. Besides I was just thinking on this very subject. Not only would we have to escape the watchful eyes of the constables," he nodded at the uniformed pair with their rifles across the courtyard. One of them actually nodded back. Friendly sorts, Owen thought, far too trusting for their jobs. "Which on the face of it would not be too difficult." He whirled to face her.

"But we would also have to plan on leaving behind Barton, not to mention the redoubtable Mrs. Chin the cook." He shook his head violently. "No that would simply be intolerable."

"Then what shall we do?" She asked forlornly. Owen threw up his hands.

"Stall for time," he said desperately. "I want you to question everyone you can in both gangs, perhaps someone saw something."

"Why can we not simply let Lohan kill the Austrian spy?" she asked. "You know that Deter would gladly kill you if he could."

"Actually, I know no such thing," Owen answered. "He, at least, is a professional, however inept. Even if he were so inclined, that would mean that Huang's killer would escape justice. I will not allow such a thing."

"Why?" Jinhao asked.

"Because it would not be," Owen took a deep breath before continuing, *orderly*." He stomped his cane hard against the flagstones of the courtyard for emphasis. Multi-colored sparks flew upwards from the contact. "I will not have some upstart non-professional thinking that they can kill someone on my watch and get away with it!"

"You mean to say that you will risk both our deaths for the sake of your sense of order?" Jinhao said incredulously.

"Well," Owen had the good grace to look sheepish. "Yes," he allowed. He turned away from her. "As I said, question as many of the youngsters as you can. Someone must have seen something."

"What if it was a professional?" She asked. He turned back to her.

"What makes you say that?" Owen asked eagerly, "Something that you have only now remarked on?"

"Nothing of the sort," Jinhao replied. "Only if it was a professional, she would be long gone by now."

"Oh, and I thought that you might have something there," Owen said dejectedly. "You simply cannot be correct you know. Because if you are, we are well and truly hacked." He turned away again.

"Where are you going?" She asked to his back.

"To see a man about a horse," Owen said without turning. "All this green tea is an abomination to my stomach."

Unlike the upper classes, the gangs rarely bothered with commodes or chamber-pots. A southern wall of the courtyard seemed to work fine for most of them. Owen stood next to one of Jimmy the Horse's gang lads and unlaced his breeches. The lad next to him let out a sigh.

"Now there's a good thing," he said. "Not like when you're out on lookout and have to wait." The two of them finished their business and turned to go.

"Say," the ganger said with a sideways look, "Aren't you that Magi of Mike's gang?"

"I am a Sorcerer it is true," Owen allowed. The gang member looked unimpressed.

"I heard that you are going to find the killer of Huang," the young man said.

"That is true," Owen said.

"That shouldn't be too hard, not that anyone except Jimmy will miss him," The ganger said. "I heard that it was that sauerkraut eater."

"You heard incorrectly then," Owen said. "It was not him."

"How do you know that?" The ganger asked. "It was his fancy fire weapon I heard."

"Yes it was," Owen allowed. "However consider this please. You have just shot someone down in cold blood. You then hit yourself over the head so that when the secret passage where you are hiding is discovered you will be captured and accused of the crime. Not very likely," Owen shook his head. "No," he continued, "someone else had to be present."

"Also," Owen said, "consider that you have caught the culprit after his dastardly deed and knocked him out. Why do you not sound the alarm and get aid?" Owen shook his head. "No the only logical answer is that the killer found the Austrian in the passage way, knocked him out, and then killed Huang with the Austrian's fire pistol, leaving him to take the blame for the murder."

"Say that's a pretty smart answer," the ganger said rubbing his chin in thought. "I hadn't looked at it like that. Seems kind of obvious when you put it that way. So who did kill old Huang?" Owen refrained from pointing out that a nineteen year old male was hardly old, but imagined that it depended on your point of view. The speaker might have been that *old* himself, it was difficult to tell. Instead Owen decided to press on as long as the ganger was feeling so talkative.

"That's what I intend to find out," Owen replied. "What were you doing that night?"

"You don't think I had anything to do with it, do you?" The ganger asked clearly startled by the question. "I mean, I didn't like Huang or nothing, but I would hardly kill him!"

"No, no," Owen soothed, "Nothing of the sort. I simply am looking to find anything that you might have seen or heard that would help me find the killer. You never know, anything might be helpful. For example," he asked casually, "Why did you not like Huang?"

"I was hardly alone in that," the young man snorted. "Huang was always after the other guys if you know what I mean. Didn't matter if they liked him back or not. He'd just sneer at them and pick on somebody else, no matter what the rest of us thought. Jimmy though, wouldn't listen when we tried to tell him about Huang, Guess he liked having a firestarter in the gang, and wouldn't listen to nothing bad about him." The ganger looked down at the ground as he finished.

"I see," said Owen slowly. "Did Huang force his...attentions on the rest of you?"

"Nah, nothing like that," The ganger said scornfully. "He'd have gotten a knife in the ribs some night no matter what Jimmy thought." He leaned in towards Owen and lowered his voice conspiratorially, "He just liked to tease the rest of us, really mean like. Nobody liked how Huang was always hanging on Jimmy neither. Jimmy seemed to like it though, encouraged him even. The other guys just figured that Huang had a likin' of Jimmy, but I knew better."

"Very little gets by you, I perceive," Owen remarked.

"That's true," he said with pride, "You asked what I was doin' that night. I was a lookout. Like I am most nights. Everybody in the gang knows I got sharp eyes."

"A lookout." Owen echoed. "Then you are just the man I wish to talk with." Owen leaned towards him on his cane, matching the ganger's conspiratorial tone. "Did you notice anything unusual that night? Anything no matter how small might be useful." The ganger rubbed his face again in thought.

"No," he said slowly. "That was the night that we had all eaten something bad at the restaurant." He patted his stomach. "All the lookouts had to take extra-long breaks if you know what I mean."

"That must have made it difficult to keep a close eye on things," Owen said.

"Nah, Jo directed us so that we all had over-lapping areas. He's smart like that." The ganger proudly pulled out a whistle he had hung around his neck. "It was Jimmy came up with the idea of using whistles to all talk to each other over distances. That's why he's the Boss."

"So Jo directs all the lookouts?" Owen asked.

"Yeah, he's been doing it for some time now."

"Did you know that Mary was coming to see Huang?" The gangers nodded enthusiastically.

"I was facing where she came in," he explained. "Jo whistled that we was to let her through. You want my opinion she is the one that you want for the killing. I never seen anyone so guilty sneaking before." Owen tensed upon hearing this.

"You are sure that Jo whistled that you were to let her through?" The ganger nodded again.

"Sure I'm sure. There isn't any way she would get through otherwise," he declared. "Nobody gets through us."

"Well, the Austrian did," Owen pointed out. The ganger's face drooped at this.

"Yeah, well that is true." He said with a sigh.

"Did you know about the hidden passageways in the restaurant?" Owen asked.

"Most of us old timers with Jimmy's crew knew about the passageways in the restaurant. The building was supposed to be the headquarters of some rebel group back in the day. Place is full of them. That's why we use it. I think only Jimmy knows all of them being as he grew up here." The ganger explained. Owen smiled at him.

"Thank you. You have been more help than you might know. I am sorry, what was your name?"

"My name is Gung," The ganger replied looking at the ground, suddenly shy again. Owen spied a particularly rotund individual in silk court robes mincing his way towards them.

"My thanks again Gung," Owen said. "I see that a court gentleman is coming our way. Unless he has some business with you, I believe that he likely wants to talk to me."

"Talk to me?" Gung squeaked "Uh no, I don't think so!" With that Gung sprang off in the opposite direction to the portly official.

The rotund official came up to Owen, his eyes following Gung as he sprinted away. The officials face looked as if it had swallowed a frog. He stopped short in front of Owen and bowed as deeply as his stomach would allow. When he came up again, his face still borne the same expression.

"I am Hu-San Fong," he announced. "I am, I was that is, the Court Prosecutor. Our Illustrious Lohan has informed me that I am now the defender of the Austrian man Deter, and that you are the prosecutor in today's Court. How do you intend to proceed?" Owen rendered a bow back to him and spoke as he came upright, his cane resting in front of him.

"I intend to use the proceedings to uncover the truth." Owen replied. Hu-San Fong shot his magnificent green silk cuffs before stroking his equally magnificent black mustaches theatrically.

"An interesting choice of strategies," the courtier purred. "Of course, my client is innocent of the murder."

"Of course," Owen agreed amicably. Hu-San stopped his stroking, his bushy eyebrows shooting skyward in surprise.

"You agree?" he asked incredulously.

"Well, yes." Owen said. "Of course, he's still guilty of being an Austrian spy in Hong Kong. I understand that Lohan still intends that he receive the death penalty." Hu-San motioned with his hands as if to wave Owens words away.

"That is no concern of mine," he said easily. "If he is not found guilty of the murder I have done my job."

"I see," Owen said. "Then you do not care if your client is killed or not?"

"Why should I?" Hu-San asked. "He must be guilty of something, else he would not stand accused, is that not so? I shall plea his innocence of the murder based on the ancient rule that there is no confession by him to that effect."

"Meaning that your torturers have not had a chance to question him you mean," Owen said.

"Say what you will," Hu-San said smugly. "The old ways always work the best. All I must do is convince Lohan that he did not kill the urchin." He smiled at Owen. "It sounds as if you will help me with this. You have the much more difficult task, if I may say so."

"Are you saying that I cannot count on your help in uncovering the murderer?" Owen asked the court official. Su-Han shook his head sadly.

"Why would you expect my aid?" He said as if to a child. "I stand to gain nothing by aiding you."

"Only the knowledge that you are aiding the side of justice," Owen retorted mildly. Hu-San tilted his head to one side and stared at Owen.

"What strange ideas you have Westerner," he said.

"Think on it," Owen said dryly. "You may find that what the Sage said about the law applies here, 'better an honest pebble than a diamond'," Hu-San'sface turned a dark color.

"You would dare to lecture me about the words of the great Sage? I have spent twenty years studying his words!"

"Perhaps you should spend less time studying him and more time thinking on what his words mean," Owen remarked. Whatever Hu-San was going to say was cut off by a constable in her bright uniform striding into the courtyard.

"All hear! All hear!" she cried out in High Mandarin. "Let those with the business before the Court of the High Lord of Hong Kong gather near! Let those of the Court gather to attend the High Lord!"

She deliberately did not look at Owen and Hu-San as she spoke, instead aiming her voice at the walls of the courtyard. She turned and walked out of the door leading into the street outside. They could her repeat the cry.

"Well, I believe that is for us," Owen said to his adversary. He bowed the way towards the dining room. "Shall we go?"

"I shall win," Hu-San warned him

"So shall I," Owen replied with a tight smile.

Chapter 21

Owen saw that the dining room where the ill-fated dinner between the gangs, not to mention where Huang had met his fate, had been transformed into an opulent room filled with hanging silk drapes and fragrant incense and candles. There was even a pair of expensive-looking mage lights framing the now raised seat where Lohan sat to hold Court. In addition to the lights, a brace of constables stood with their deadly air-rifles at port behind the human-form Dragon.

The courtiers were lounging about the walls of the room with some seated and others standing, all attempting to affect an air of polite boredom. Owen saw Deputy-Inspector Gregg talking nervously to a man in a western style suit. Mike stood in one corner with Mary, and with him stood Jimmy with a pair of cronies. A uniformed constable with a mountain of gold braid on his shoulders bowed towards both Owen and Hu-San.

"Lord Owen Strong, Lord Hu-San Fong," he greeted them both. "I am charged with insuring the protocol of the Court today. My name is Bailey. The accused will be brought out shortly." Bailey gestured as he spoke, "Lord Owen, as Prosecutor would you stand to Our Mighty Lord's right, and Lord Hu-San if you would stand to the left, I will call the Court to order." Owen stood where Bailey had indicated as Jinhao entered the room, gliding up next to him. He bent to hear what she had to say.

"It appears that our deceased Fire starter had a particular liking for the other boys," she murmured to him.

"I know," Owen murmured back. Was Lohan giving them a stern eye?

"Did you also know that he had a particular passion for Jimmy the Horse and that rumor has it that his Mother, the restaurant keeper, did not approve?" Owen shot her a glance at this news.

'No, I did not," he whispered. Out of the corner of his eye he caught the Dragon stirring on his makeshift throne, glaring at them.

"Thank you Jinhao," Owen whispered. "I think that I had best attend the Dragon now."

"Lord Owen." Lohan suddenly spoke in a deep grumble. It sounded like a thousand boulders crashing together. "We shall be tolerant as this is your first time in these proceedings. Be warned however that Our patience is not inexhaustible." Owen and Jinhao stopped talking and looked up attentively. The Dragon gestured at the failing Bailey. "Get on with it!" He snapped.

"Hear all! Hear all" Bailey proclaimed in flawless Mandarin. "Let all who have business with this Court draw near to witness the mercy of Lohan, Lord of Hong Kong!" He repeated the same in English. A pair of Constables brought in the Austrian Deter, his hands bound in manacles in front of him. He gave Owen a hang dog look, standing in the place where the constables had prodded him towards with their rifles.

As Bailey stopped speaking, the Dragon stirred on his great chair, staring down at Owen. Owen thought he detected a red glint in the Dragon's eyes, which could not bode well for them.

"Lord Owen," Lohan spoke in that same gravelly voice. "You have volunteered to show us this modern Western way of justice. How shall you proceed?"

"Mighty Lohan!" Hu-San raised his voice theatrically. "As Defender of the Accused, I must protest! There is no confession as is proscribed in the Illustrious Code of Law. Therefore the Accused is innocent of this crime, and should be released!" The Dragon looked at Owen.

"Well, Lord Owen?" Lohan inquired. "How do you respond to this?"

"It is true Mighty Lohan that the Accused, the Austrian Deter, had not confessed to the murder of the boy Huang. A boy who was horribly killed right where you are sitting,

I believe." Owen said calmly. The Dragon startled in his chair at this, and Owen was certain that he saw the red glow gleam more strongly in the depths of the Dragons eyes.

"None the less," Owen continued, "I feel that it is my duty to point out that the confession my illustrious opponent refers to," here he bowed towards Hu-San who bowed back. "Is usually obtained by torture of the accused. A method that is suspect at best."

"It is allowed under the Illustrious Code of Law!" Hu-San protested. "As such its lack should be allowed as proof of innocence. This has been true for five hundred years!"

"Be that as it may," Owen shot back. "The whole point of modern jurisprudence is to gauge the truth, the innocence or guilt of the accused, by means of fact and cross-examination. I must agree that there is not enough fact to condemn the Austrian, Deter, of Huang's murder. There is only enough, I should point out, that he may be an accomplice to the crime as well as the spy of a foreign power."

"I must object!" Hu-San cried. "Neither of these are the crimes we are here for! Nor has the Lord Owen offered any of his much vaunted proof!"

"The proof is that Deter is an Austrian, who by his own admission to me, belongs to the Church of Her Light and is abroad without a face mask," Owen answered. "It is well known that only those who serve the Austrian government as spies are allowed such leeway. Second, he was in possession of an alchemical fire pistol which was the murder weapon that did kill the youth Huang."

"The reasons are sufficient to continue," The Dragon allowed in his gravelly voice Hu-San's shoulders slumped in defeat. Owen had to admire the voice trick. He had heard Lohan speak before and wondered how the Dragon managed to go from dulcet tones to such a menacing grumbling, leaving the hearer with the impression that they very likely would be eaten. He was certain it was some application of Magia. It certainly cut down on arguments, Owen reflected.

There was a commotion at the door, which had Bailey, the Court protocol person scrambling to deal with it. Bailey turned somewhat forlornly towards the center of the room and began to speak,.

"Mighty Lohan..." Bailey began, only to be shouldered aside by a menacing figure in a black uniform with a billed cap, a face-covering cloth mask hanging down from the cap. The soldier gave way in turn to a slender figure wearing gold robes and a head-hugging cowl. The suggestion of a smiling face was stitched in glittering gems across the covering of where a face would be.

"Mighty Lohan," the figure said in a carrying soprano tone, "please forgive the interruption. I came as quickly as possible when I received your note."

"Madame Ambassador," Lohan replied in his grumbling voice. "Your entrance leaves much to be desired in terms of respect." The gold figure bowed, smooth as oil.

"When I heard that a fellow Austrian may be in peril, I came with all due haste. Surely you will forgive me if I sidestep protocol for the safety of one of my people." The cloth of gold covering searched about the room, finally settling on Deter.

"Ah, there he is, the poor lamb!" the Ambassador slid forward towards the fettered Austrian. Her passage was blocked by the rifle-bearing constables. The black clad soldier stepped in front of the Ambassador, hand clamped on a holstered pistol at his waist. The menace radiated by the faceless figure was palpable even at a distance. The Ambassador turned towards Lohan.

"Chains?" The Ambassador inquired. "Why is he in chains? What is the charge?"

"Do you admit then that this is one of your fellow countrymen?" the Dragon asked softly. The Ambassador recoiled as if bitten. Owen could tell she was looking at Deter askance, even through the cowl and face covering.

"I have not had a chance to speak to him," she answered. "How would I know? Is that what he claims?"

"He does not need to *claim*… that he is what he is," Owen said. "That he is an Austrian of the Church of Her Radiance is beyond dispute, and his tradecraft is horrible. He revealed himself to our entire party with his first words. That members of the Church only are allowed to show their faces if they are spies for the Austrian Church, excuse me, the Austrian Government, is well known. You still maintain the fiction that you have a separate government? It does make the unwarranted invasions and pogroms deniable does it not?" Owen asked archly. "Furthermore, he was caught with an alchemical fire weapon. While unfortunately common, the possession of such a device is a crime in Hong Kong. Do you still wish to claim him as one of yours, Ambassador?" The cowled figure had stood stock still during Owen's speech. The black-clad soldier turned towards Owen, hand still on his weapon.

"You vill address Her Radiance as *Your Radiance* infidel dog," he warned in his thick voice. "And you vill wait for leave to speak from Her Radiance." Owen turned towards the Dragon at this.

"Mighty Lohan, are we to tolerate threats during Court proceedings? Owen asked guilelessly.

"Mighty Lohan," the Austrian Ambassador demanded. "Who is this *person*?" She snarled.

The Dragon gave a rumble deep in his chest that might have been a laugh. He looked down at the Ambassador for a long moment before replying.

"I notice that you do not deny what he says Ambassador," Lohan observed wryly. "As to who he is, he is the appointed Court Special Prosecutor named Lord Owen of Strong late of the British Empire. Also, he is correct, this is an official Court function." There was no mistaking the red glow in Lohan's eyes now.

"MY Court, Ambassador!" The Dragon snarled. "Now, as is required by international treaty I have informed you that we may have one of your country's citizens in custody. Do you wish to acknowledge him?" The Ambassador took a step back.

"Not at this time," she said weakly. "Although the Austrian government reserves the right to view the proceedings."

"Then find a place against the wall, Ambassador, along with the other members of the Court," Lohan ordered heavily. She quickly complied, dragging her guard with her. "And Ambassador," the Dragon continued, "one more threat from your lackey, and he will be next to feel my displeasure. My patience has neared its limit." The Dragon turned towards Owen.

"Well My Lord Owen, how will you proceed?" He demanded. Before Owen could speak he held up a hand. "And do not say it requires that you mock the Ambassadors to my Court. What I found humorous once I may not again," he warned. Owen bowed towards the Dragon.

"Mighty Lohan," he said. "I thank you for your forbearance." He twisted his head towards where the Austrian Ambassador had claimed space along a wall, "And I ask forgiveness of the Austrian Ambassador if I answered her question too fully." At this, some of the Court twittered. Little love was lost between the Austrians and the citizens of Hong Kong after last summer's attempt at an invasion by the Austrian Navy. An attempt that had been blamed on 'rogue naval elements' by the Austrian government. An excuse accepted by the other Great Powers to avert an even more horrendous world war. Lohan frowned at Owen, who continued quickly.

"I believe that I can render these proceedings quickly to both to your satisfaction and to the cause of justice," Owen said with a smile. "May I call a few people to testify?" Lohan made a show of considering this even though he must know this was how it was done, Owen thought.

"I see no difficulty in this do you Lord Hu-San?" Lohan asked the Defense Councilor. Hu-San also made a great show of considering this, stroking his magnificent mustaches.

"No, Mighty Lohan," he said at last. "Although I also wish the right to question these people should it seem warranted." The Dragon turned his head back to Owen.

"Acceptable to you Lord Owen?" Lohan asked.

"Very acceptable. I even encourage it, Mighty Lohan," Owen responded.

"Very well," the Dragon said. "Call whom you will." The Dragon effected a bored tone which would fool no one who noticed the agitated light smoldering beneath his eyelids.

"Thank you Mighty Lohan," Owen replied with a bow towards the makeshift throne. "For my first witness," Owen pronounced, "I wish to call the man known as Jimmy the Horse."

The sounds of the murmuring voices of the Court rose like an angry sea.

Chapter 22

Lohan nodded to his acting master of Protocol, the constable Bailey, who turned at Lohan's signal back to face the room. His voice rang out across the room cutting through the murmurs of the Court.

"Jimmy the Horse draw nigh! You are called to bear witness before the Court of the Mighty Lohan, Lord of Hong Kong. Jimmy the Horse draw nigh!" Bailey cried out. The gang leader stepped forward at this, a dazed look upon his face. He looked between Owen and Bailey.

"I am Jimmy the Horse," he said to both of them, "What do you want?"

"You must stand there," Hu-San pointed with a scowl to a spot in front of the Dragon midway between Owen and himself. Jimmy moved to comply. "Stand there and do not move!" The former Court Prosecutor said. Hu-San bowed wordlessly with a smile first to Lohan and then to Owen.

"Thank you my Lord Hu-San," Owen said dryly. The constable Bailey quickly moved to stand in front of Jimmy.

"Do you swear by the Gods that you hold dear, that all that you shall speak here shall only be the truth, knowing that you are bound by the Question to answer so?" He asked the ganger. Jimmy visibly swallowed at this. 'Bound by the Question,' meant that any Court official that didn't like his answers could have him tortured until he gave answers that they did like.

"Yeah," he replied stoutly, glaring at Owen over Bailey's shoulder. "I got nothing to hide." Bailey moved smoothly aside leaving the ganger facing Owen.

Owen stepped towards Jimmy with a smile, his cane tapping the ground as he walked.

"I am sure that you do not have anything to hide, Master Jimmy," Owen said. "I simply wish to ask you some questions about the victim and the night of his death in particular. Is that agreeable to you?" he finished. Jimmy the Horse visibly relaxed, shaking loose his shoulders and arms at hearing this.

"Sure," he said. A rumbling growl came from the direction of the Dragon. Jimmy risked a glance in that direction before turning back. "I mean, ah, yes Lord Owen."

"Good," Owen said. "Did you see Haung the night he was killed?"

"Sure," Jimmy said. "You saw him that night too."

"Yes I did," Owen allowed. "Did you see him after I had left?"

"Yeah," the ganger said with crossed arms. "I talked to him after you left with Mike and his girls. I wanted to know who had started with all the fire making. I was sure it was that doxy of Mike's."

"And was Huang able to tell you who had started with all the fire-making?" Owen asked. "Was it Mary?" The ganger hung his head, and looked at the floor.

"No," he said in a small voice. "Huang admitted it was him that started it."

"I see," said Owen mildly. "So at an important meeting of yours, Huang disrupted it by using his fire talent. Perhaps he was seeking to take control away from you? That must have made you very angry."

"Well sure," Jimmy said. "I was figuring Huang would try something like that. But that don't mean I killed him!"

"No of course not. Did that conversation happen here in this room?" Owen smiled at him.

"Yes," Jimmy said in puzzlement at the change of questioning. "Afterwards I went up to my room here in the restaurant."

"Did anyone see you go upstairs?" Owen asked.

"Sure," Jimmy said. "a bunch of the guys were still out in the hallway and saw me go up. I went to sleep, and was woken up by Jo, who told me that Huang had been killed."

"Was this the same Jo who headed the lookout guards that night?" Owen asked.

"Well, yeah," Jimmy said scornfully. "Jo has been with me almost as long as Huang had been. Few others can wake me up." Owen nodded at this.

"I have no more questions for this person," Owen suddenly announced. Hu-San glided forward.

"Mighty Lohan," He said. "I have a few questions if I might be permitted." The Dragon nodded testily.

"Yes," Lohan allowed, "But make them brief." Hu-San bowed and then turned towards Jimmy.

"Jimmy the Horse is such an interesting name," Su-Han began silkily. "Surely that is not the name that your mother gave you."

"Well no," Jimmy said, "That one was boring."

"'Jimmy' is short for the western name 'James' is it not?" Hu-San asked. "And what does Horse mean?" Jimmy laughed, pulling up his sleeve and shoving up his arm rampant like a penis. The Court twittered.

"What do you think it means?" The boy answered with a leer.

"Precisely," Hu-San responded unruffled. "Yet, you bear with pride a false name. Why is that? Is it not to conceal your criminal activities?"

"I don't know what you're talking about," Jimmy replied easily.

"Do you not?" Hu-San said. "I remind you that you are under the question." He paused significantly before continuing. "Your mother must be very ashamed of you," he continued.

"She is right here," Jimmy retorted. "Why don't you ask her?" He pointed towards where Zhang the old woman who owned the restaurant stood.

"Mighty Lohan," Owen interjected. "I fail to see what Hu-San is attempting with this questioning." The Dragon looked at Hu-San.

"I must agree," the Dragon grumbled. "What are you seeking to prove Lord Hu-San?"

"Simply that this person," Su-Han sniffed, "Is nothing more than a common born criminal, whose word is not to be trusted."

"I had no more questions for this witness," Owen pointed out.

"Then let us move this along," Lohan ordered. "Does that meet with your approval Lord Hu-San?" The Dragon asked dangerously. Hu-San bowed deeply, knowing when to bend.

"As you wish Mighty Lohan," the court official said unctuously.

"Do you have any other people that you wish to call as witness on in this matter, Lord Owen?" Lohan asked him.

"Yes, Mighty Lohan," Owen said. "I wish to call Madame Zhang."

After Bailey's calling and swearing in, the old restaurant owner stood trembling between Owen and Hu-San while the Dragon looked down at her. She twisted the long hem of her black robe nervously in her hands.

"Now, Madame Zhang," Owen began easily. "Is it not true that Jimmy the Horse is your son?"

"Yes," she said proudly. "He truly is a fine man, no matter what some may say," she said with a pointed glance at Hu-San. "He takes care of his friends and seeks to help them."

"I am sure of that," Owen said. "It must have been hard raising him while taking care of this huge restaurant,"

"Oh, it was not that hard," Zhang said with a smile. "When I inherited this place from my uncle. Jimmy, as he likes to be called, has always helped me out where he can."

"Ah, so it was your uncle's place before it was yours?" Owen asked.

"Oh yes," Zhang said, "We have barely kept it going since he passed on, but we try."

"And how long have you know our Austrian friend Deter over there?" Owen asked. Zhang's voice hesitated.

"I am not sure what you mean," she quivered.

"All this," Owen said with a wave of his hand, "used to be the headquarters for a dissident group. That is the reason for all these passageways is it not?"

"I do not know about that," Zhang said faintly.

"Was that the time that Deter showed up and offered to help you save your son, when you took possession of this building?" Owen asked gently. Zhang looked up at Lohan, then back to Owen with her lips tight. Owen gave her a sympathetic look. "It really will not do to pretend any longer Madame."

"Yes," she said finally.

"I am sure that you did not know who Deter worked for when he approached you," Owen said sympathetically. "What did he tell you Madame?"

"That some of my son's associates were not wholesome fellows," Madame Zhang spat out. "He offered to remove my son from the life that he had."

"How did he propose that he would do that?" Owen asked. Madame Zhang shrugged violently.

"He never said," she snapped angrily. "Only that if I showed him where the tunnels where and introduced him to some of the other boys, that my little Wong would be saved." She glared at Deter. "But that never seemed to come true."

"I see," said Owen. "And was Huang, the murdered youth, one of the ones that you introduced Deter to?"

"Yes," she admitted. "Although, again, nothing ever seemed to happen until the other night! When Deter roasted that foul perversion alive!" The Court burst into a babble of noise at this revelation.

"I object!" screamed Hu-San. The Austrian Ambassador seemed to leap from the wall to his side, adding her voice of objection over the roar of the courtiers. Bailey struggled in vain to restore order. A mighty voice exploded from the throne where Lohan was seated.

"ENOUGH! BE SILENT!"

In the strained silence that followed, Owen could see people attempt to work their mouths, only to clutch their throats in growing dismay. Somehow Lohan had actually silenced the entire room. A feat of sorcery that Owen had never even heard of before, let alone seen. It was very impressive. Most of the room fell to their knees before the Dragon Lord of Hong Kong, silently abasing themselves. Owen remained standing. Lohan continued in a deep rumbling growl that penetrated ones bones.

"Your voices will return momentarily, more is the pity," the Dargon said remorselessly. "There shall be a short intermission to allow everyone to gather their decorum about them." The Dragon stirred on the throne. "And I will have decorum my Ladies and Lords! This is MY Court! Now go!"

Everyone slowly cleared the room, the crowd spilling out into the inner courtyard. Jinhao appeared at Owen's side.

"So much for our thinking that Deter did not kill Huang," she remarked.

"Do you really think so?" Owen asked her with a raised eyebrow.

"How else would you interpret her statement?" Jinhao asked in astonishment.

"Watch and see," Owen replied merrily. "At least now I know who killed Huang. I even have a plan to reveal him!"

"What plan?" Jinhao asked looking at him closely.

Before Owen could answer a westerner wearing the black and maroon colors of the British crown came up to them. His black cutaway coat was as neatly tailored as if he had just come from London itself. A small round hat perched on his head.

"Lord Owen," he said with a nod. He bowed perfunctorily towards Jinhao. Straightening up, his hands moved in an intricate pattern. Owen sighed at the recognition signal.

"I have no time for Order monkey business," Owen said to the man curtly.

"My Lord!" The newcomer replied in shocked rebuke, darting a glance at Jinhao. He was further disconcerted when Jinhao bared her teeth at him in distaste.

"Oh it is alright," Owen assured him. "Jinhao is very familiar with the Obsidian Order. What does our dear Uncle Stephen want now?" The man gobbled for several moments as he took this in. The Obsidian Order was the powerful and secret intelligence order of the British Empire, and as such, preferred to work in the darkness of obscurity. Sir Stephen Partridge was one of the senior adepts of the Order.

Owen had been a secret agent of the Order before he left it in disillusionment. Uncle Stephen was Owens' nickname for Sir Stephen Partridge, the head of the Orders overseas operations, and Owen's former mentor. Owen's use of his irreverent nickname clearly shocked the young dandy. The un-named man gathered his dignity about him and stood straight. His eyes darted left and right before he spoke.

"This word comes from Sir Stephen himself," the man said in a low voice. "You must find the Austrian innocent of the murder of the Chinese boy. Such a thing could only exacerbate international tensions."

"Regardless if he's innocent or not eh?" Owen said dryly. "Good thing that I had already figured out that he was innocent then. Anything else?"

"Yes," the man said furtively, "Your own safety is directly in danger from assassins. Sir Stephen does not know who or when only that you should take heed. He is attempting to discover more."

"That warning comes about a week too late," Owen replied. "Tell Partridge that a westerner sorcerer named Mr. Victor is hunting me. He has the air of a mercenary and a slight Belgian accent to his vowels. See if that helps him in his inquiries." Owen exclaimed as the man took out a note pad and stylus. "Do not write that down! Memorize it! Victor. Mercenary Sorcerer. Belgian! By the Dark Woods, what degree are you?" The man swallowed hard, putting away his writing implements.

"I am a first degree, Worshipful Lord," he stammered. "This is my first assignment."

"I thought as much." Owen said with a sigh. "And do not call me that. I am not a Worshipful anything. "Can you remember what I have told you?" The man nodded his head.

"I think so," he replied uncertainly.

"See that you do," Owen said. He refrained from rolling his eyes at the man's response. "Now go," he ordered. "Tell Uncle Stephen that I have the matter of the Austrian well in hand. And do not forget," he admonished holding up his hand. A single finger went up at each word. "Victor. Sorcerer. Mercenary. Belgian."

~ ~ ~

The messenger nodded his head jerkily, and hurried off. Owen and Jinhao watched him weave his way clumsily through the courtiers.

"Well that is one way to be remembered," Owen remarked drolly, watching as the man ran head long into a fat Court mandarin. After a moments hurried bowing, the young Westerner scampered off.

"Not like when we were staring out at all, oh grey beard," Jinhao said with a brief laugh.

"We were never that young," Owen replied sourly. He turned towards her. "Now listen, here is what I want you to do." He outlined his plan. Jinhao grinned when he finished.

"Lohan, will be impressed, and possibly very upset with you," she remarked.

"Let him," Owen replied with a shrug. "So long as he doesn't set me on fire or eat me, I think I shall endure."

"Dragons do not really eat people," Jinhao said carefully.

"And someday you will have to tell me how you know that, and how you are acquainted with Lohan for that matter." Owen said with a quizzical tilt to his head.

"No, I do not have to," Jinhao replied, grinning at him. They both turned as the constable Bailey's voice called to all to return to the Court. Owen straightened up.

"That is our cue," he said. "Off you go then." Jinhao nodded.

"I shall await your signal." She replied.

Chapter 23

Owen took his place before the Dragon and waited for the other Courtiers to settle. Baileys' calls for order were finally obeyed and the room grew silent. Su-Han stepped slightly forward.

"I have a few questions for the witness, Mighty Lohan," Lohan looked to Owen.

"Do you have any objection, Lord Owen?" the Dragon asked.

"None, Mighty Lohan." Owen said. Hu-San looked at Madame Zhang craftily.

"Madame," he asked. "Did you see my defendant shoot the boy Deter?" Zhang shot upright at this question, clearly reluctant to answer it.

"I remind you that you are under the shadow of the question," Hu-San said mildly at her reluctance. Finally she spoke.

"No I did not see him burn the boy down," she admitted. "But I know that he had promised to see my Wang, my Jimmy that is, safe."

"And Huang was not safe for your son to be around? By all accounts they were the best of friends." Su-Han remarked incredulously. Madame Zhang curled her lip at him.

"No, he was not," she paused, looking down as if uncertain how to proceed. "I do not know the polite words for it," she went on finally, rising her head. "Huang was a lover of men" she finished using the course term for a homosexual male. Hu-San expressed shock, which Owen was certain must be faked.

"Truly," he breathed. "I shall spare you having to recount how you know such a thing to be true," he said sympathetically. "Still," he continued, "many a young man has a special male friend. Such a relationship is neither against the law or shameful in the eyes of the Sage, Confucius."

"It is if the *special friend* is both a witch and a white-face!" The old woman spat out.

"Which is why you killed Huang is it not, Madame Zhang?" Hu-San asked triumphantly. "You knew about Deter, you must have known about his witch-weapon, and so you killed Huang with it, and then blamed Deter for your foul murder, knowing that he would accept the blame rather than betray you as a traitor-agent of a foreign power!"

He finished with a rhetorical flourish, smiling in victory at Owen as the room exploded yet again in exclamations. Owen saw that Jimmy the Horse was shouting his objections. He was held back by the gang member Jo and another ganger. Madame Zhang stood mute, shaking her head in negation.

Bailey called the room to order yet again. Everyone waited, scarcely breathing, to hear what the Dragon would say to these revelations. Lohan cast his gaze on Owen.

"Lord Owen," the Dragon rumbled. "What have you to say to this?"

"Mighty Lohan," Owen bowed to him. "While I applaud Lord Hu-San for his imagination, I must point out that he is completely wrong. With your permission I wish to give a small demonstration that will reveal the true killer of the boy Huang." Lohan looked to Su-Han.

"My Lord have you any objection to this?" he asked. Su-Han bowed graciously towards Owen.

"'Better a diamond with a flaw, than a pebble without meaning,' so the Sage tells us on matters of the law," Su-Han quoted smoothly. "I have no objections."

"Very well Lord Owen," Lohan said, "You may proceed."

"Thank you Mighty Lohan," Owen said with bow. He began to pace around the cleared space in the center of the room, swinging his cane as he talked.

"Let us go back to that night, the night of the murder. The fire caller Huang sends a message to the other fire caller in Mike's gang, Mary. Why?" Owen asked rhetorically. "This question becomes all important. Why send for your rival in a rival gang in the middle of the night? The explanation becomes very clear when you answer this question. You send for them because you wish to subvert them to your cause. How can you do that?" Owen paused to look at Deter.

"You can do that," he said, "Because an agent of a mighty political power promises you the moon and stars. He promises you that you can rule not only the gang you belong to, but also the gang of your rivals if you convince the other fire caller to join with you. So that you never become aware that your every move is being directed by a foreign power."

"What was the plan Deter?" Owen asked the Austrian agent, "To lure the unwanted urchins into spying for you? Perhaps to use the power of a fire caller to perform an assassination or two?"

"Do not answer that!" Hu-San directed Deter. He moved to stand between Owen and his charge.

"The Austrians hold that those who can wield the western sorcery are fit only for burning as they violate their code of holiness. They themselves proclaim this publicly! " Hu-San protested. Owen smiled a predatory smile at this.

"Yes they do, do they not?" He asked rhetorically. "Which is something that Deter could have counted on us assuming, that dealing with a sorcery wielder no matter how simple their talent was something a good follower of the Church would not do. Thus he could preserve his mission even after being caught." Owen stopped and leaned on his cane as he spoke.

"Deter was kind enough to brag that he had a special dispensation from his Bishop," Owen continued. "This got me wondering, what else could he have a dispensation for? Perhaps setting up an asset that can be as useful as a street gang for terror and sorcerous assassination would be worth a little soul uncleanliness. Wouldn't you agree Ambassador?" He turned to address the last towards the Austrian Ambassador. Rather than reply, the cowled figure started moving towards the exit.

"I believe that you should wait until Lord Owen is finished Ambassador," Lohan ordered from his elevated chair. "It would be a pity if you were to leave just as things were becoming interesting." A pair of constables crossed their air rifles barring the exit. The Austrian Ambassador bowed towards Lohan, her bodyguard glowering at the exits guards.

"You will forgive me Mighty Lohan," her sweet voice came from under the cowl. "I have recalled that urgent business awaits me at the Embassy. I do not have the time to listen to the ranting of madmen."

"None the less," the Dragon insisted. "I require you to await Our pleasure in this matter." The Ambassador bowed again, gesturing to her soldier to stand easy. Owen turned back towards the Dragon.

"If I might continue Mighty Lohan?" he requested of the Dragon.

"Please do Lord Owen," Lohan replied. "I am eager to hear what you have to say."

"Thank you Mighty Lohan," Owen said. He smiled again at the Ambassador. "I wonder if the esteemed Ambassador would still characterize my dissertation as the 'ranting of a madman' when I assert that Deter did not kill the boy Huang!" Again Bailey had to call the room to silence at this pronouncement. Owen waited before continuing.

"Make no mistake, My Ladies and My Lords," Owen began pacing the center of the room again. "Deter came prepared for murder. Why else carry an Aether pistol to meet with your contact? But the intended target was not Huang, but Jimmy the Horse. If you killed the beloved gang leader, what better way than to do so by fire? If you are lucky than no one is the wiser. If not," he looked over at Mary, discreetly holding Mikes hand, "then you can blame the enemy gang's fire caller. Bu there was one thing that neither Huang nor Dieter counted on." Owen raised his cane and pointed it at Lohan. Owen's voice rose over the murmurings of the Court.

"Think of that night," He pressed on. "Huang is sitting exactly where you are now, Mighty Lohan. If you are Deter, you want to have control of your contact's attempt at subversion, so you hide in the hidden passageway, where you can hear every sound." At this, a loud thumping came from the wall behind the courtiers causing them to jump away from it.

"While you hide there, you are ambushed by one who takes you unawares, rending you unconscious." Another loud thump comes from the wall. "He takes your weapon and then bursts out, pistol blazing!" The wall parts and Jinhao stands in the suddenly revealed opening in the wall. She mimed aiming a handgun at Lohan. The Dragon leapt to his feet roaring in surprise at the swiftness of the attack.

"But who would do this?" Lohan demands. Owen lowered his cane.

"The only person who could know everything," Owen explained. "The one who knows all the comings and goings that night, the leader of the lookouts in Jimmy's gang that night. I call to witness the gang member known as Jo," he pronounced. Jo attempted to bolt for the door upon hearing this, only to find Deputy Inspector Gregg and a constable conveniently placed to restrain him. Jo yelled as they struggle to bring him to the center of the room.

"I did it for you Jimmy!" he screamed. "I knew they were going to kill you and I burned down that bugger Huang first, that's all! I did it to protect you Jimmy!" The boy stopped screaming as they reached the center of the room. Owen looked at him, then at the Dragon.

"I submit, Mighty Lohan," Owen said tiredly, "that his outburst constitutes a confession. Thus are the ancient laws of the Han fulfilled, as well as what I hope will become the more modern proceedings of criminal justice." He bowed as the room exploded in noise.

Chapter 24

Owen inhaled his cigarette with satisfaction as he stood outside in the cool of the courtyard. The shadows were just becoming long as the summer day spun to its ending. The Court of Lohan, Lord of Hong Kong was slowly dispersing back to the richer parts of the city, secure in the knowledge that the Dragon still dispensed justice to all regardless of class or standing.

After the sentence of Lohan was carried out, and Jo was beheaded in the very courtyard where they now stood, the Dragon had called Owen to come closer. Staring at him without speaking, Lohan had then said something that Owen was still puzzling over.

"She may be right," the Dragon had grumbled. "We shall meet again Owen Strong." Leaving Owen with no explanation of who *she* was, or what she was *right* about naturally. One did not cross-examine a Dragon, not if you wished to remain breathing. Now Owen stood in the courtyard with Jinhao, Mike and Mary.

"What will happen to us now?" Mike asked. It was Jinhao who answered him, before Owen had a chance to speak.

"I suspect that you will find that the Dragon has taken a special interest in you," Jinhao said. Deputy Inspector Gregg strode up to them while she was speaking. Mary flinched away at the sight of his uniform while Mike placed a hand on her shoulder in comfort. He gazed at the policeman with cold eyes.

"Are you the one they call Mike, leader of what's called Mike's Gang?" the Inspector demanded. Gregg's face radiated extreme displeasure as if he hated what he was saying.

"Yes," Mike replied evenly. "I am he."

Gregg reached into a pouch on his uniform belt, pulling out a small scroll bound in red ribbon. He extended it towards the gang leader as if Mike were a large rat that Gregg was afraid would bite him.

"This is a city wide safe-conduct." Gregg explained. "The Dragon said you were to have this. If any city police give you difficulty show them this." Mike took it with wonder in his face.

"Thank you," he said shakily.

"Don't thank me," Gregg said shortly. "If I had my way you would all go to the lock-up." He dipped his hat towards Mary. "Begging your pardon, of course, milady." He turned towards Owen. "Good bit of business that with the Court, My Lord. What will happen to that Austrian dog do you suppose?" Owen exhaled a cloud of smoke, his eyes distant.

"Oh, I imagine that he will be traded for someone or something from the Austrians," Owen replied in a lazy voice. "Such arrangements are done all the time. It would not do for Deter to come to a public trial for espionage you know." Gregg shook his head.

"I suppose so, My Lord," the policeman said. "Still, it seems that he gets away with it."

"Do not imagine that the Austrians accept failure gladly, Gregg." Owen said with a wintry smile. "I do not doubt that his masters will vent the full force of their displeasure on him."

"As you say, My Lord," Gregg allowed. "I must go now to direct the bloody convoy that will wind its way back up the Hill." The Inspector gave a heavy sigh and moved off. Mike looked down at the residing back of the Inspector and then down at the scroll in his hands. He held it up before Mary.

"Do you realize what this means?" he said to her excitedly.

"It means that the Dragon wishes you to assume a new role." Jinhao interjected quietly. "At another time and place I shall tell you of the Eyes."

Owen looked sideways at Jinhao. Was it Jinhao that Lohan had referred to when he had said 'she may be right', Owen wondered? He knew very little about his companion when it came right down to it. Certainly she had some kind of connection to the Dragon that he was unaware of, another mystery to be solved.

"You have kept your word to Jimmy regarding the Dragon's justice," Mike said. "But you did not tell him that it would result in the Pinchers taking him away. Is this more of the same?" He said looking at her defiantly. Jinhao gave a twist of her shoulders.

"Jimmy never asked," she retorted. "As for you, I remind you of the old saying: 'Dragons are subtle and powerful. Beware of any dealings with them'." She met Mike's gaze.

"In this I remind you that I speak as the Dragon's Voice, not as my own." She looked at him ruefully. "In this, we will both have little freedom."

"Alright," Mike allowed. "I shall listen to what you have to say about these Eyes you speak of."

"At least it shall mean that we don't have to worry about being pinched ourselves," Mary said to him. "Be grateful."

"You need not worry about that," Owen said. "Due to western influences, there are no provisions anymore for holding females in the city gaol, a grievous oversight in my opinion."

"Well, yeah," Mary said, "But that only applies to us girls." She squeezed Mike's arm. "That's no comfort to Mike here." Owen finished his cigarette, grinding it out with his foot.

"Oh I would not be too sure of that," Owen said off-handedly. "Mostly you should be afraid of some disgruntled father or brother claiming Mike as one of theirs, I imagine." Mike stiffened visibly.

"How long have you known?" Mike asked him softly.

"Almost since the beginning actually, when I read your aura," Owen explained. "Auras have three components you see. One part that reflects your mind, which is decidedly male in aspect. One part that reflects your body which is decidedly female in aspect. Unfortunately the city's law still only recognizes the latter." Mary looked at Mike wide-eyed.

"You mean, you are like me?" Mary hesitated, unsure how to continue.

"Yes," Mike said to her, refusing to meet her eyes. "I was born female, does that matter to you?"

"Well, yeah," Mary said exasperatedly. "I've been wondering why I feel the way I do about you," she abruptly stopped talking, pulled Mikes face towards her, and then kissed Mike firmly on the mouth. After a startled moment, Mike returned the kiss heartily. When they stopped, they turned to find Owen and Jinhao still facing them.

"However can we ever thank you?" Mary asked huskily. Mike nodded agreement his fingers entwining with Mary's.

"Whatever we can do, just ask," The gang leader vowed. Owen smiled at them both.

"I was hoping that you would say something like that. How would you like to help confound a Sorcerer-Assassin?"

He asked. "I will not lie to you, it will be dangerous." Mike and Mary looked at each other and shrugged their shoulders.

"Tell us more," Mary demanded.

"We will need Mei I think," Jinhao mused.

"Mei?" Owen turned towards Jinhao. "Isn't she a bit young for this?"

"She dealt with you handily enough it seems," Jinhao pointed out. "Wait until you hear my plan."

"Very well," he conceded. "Mei it is." He gripped his cane in both hands. "What plan is this?"

They all listened carefully as Jinhao began speaking.

Chapter 25

Mei looked up at the Westerner called Mr. Victor with a blank face. He was just another pasty-faced man who wore funny clothes and smelled bad. She knew that he was supposed to be some sort of scary Sorcerer/ Assassin type, but so far she was unimpressed, even if he did carry one of those fancy canes that Sorcerers used. Even that was unimpressive, looking like an old wooden stick with the red magic metal set in bands around it. Owens had been much more impressive, being made entirely out of the glowing red metal, which she knew was very expensive and powerful.

Mr. Victor had believed her easily enough when she had said that she was *peaching* on Mike to get rid of Owen Strong, just as Owen had said he would. Westerners apparently had no sense of honor, near as she could tell. Of course, there were some like Owen who clearly had spent long enough around civilized people like Jinhao that the concept must have rubbed off. The smelly sorcerer had even followed her eagerly down to the factory district with his pet ape, the giant man he'd called Mr. Percy. Mei didn't like him, he reminded her too much of the big trolls that she'd heard tell of in the stories, all mean and tricksy-like. She forced herself to pay attention as Mr. Victor jabbered at her again in trade-Mandarin, which he didn't speak nearly as well as she spoke English.

"So, they've made an old factory their home have they?" the man asked, hovering over her. "And there is a back entrance you say?" Mei nodded and pointed again, then spoke in slow English. Once she sent them down this alley, which she had been told was full of traps, she was to circle around to the front door, her part done.

"Yes. Go down that alley, turn right, follow it until you come to back-door. No one watch now. All sleeping or out stealing." She stuck out her palm. "Give me money."

In response, Victor grabbed her arm roughly, holding up the cane towards her face. A blue flame spouted from it's tip. Mei felt the heat of it and whimpered.

"Oh, I don't think so my little pretty," the man breathed. "I think that you will lead us to this back-door first, and make sure that there are no traps. Else I will burn off your beautiful little face. Do you understand that?" He shook her arm Mei nodded silently.

"Very good," The man said as the flame went out like a candle, "You first." Mr. Victor turned to his hulking partner.

"Come along, Mr. Percy," He ordered. The giant grunted in response, pulling a huge air pistol from inside his suit, Still gripping her arm tightly, he thrust Mei out before him as the three of them started down the alley. They carefully walked its length, Mei scarcely breathing as she waited for them to trigger some horrible deadly explosion. They came to the door without incident, which left her both puzzled and dismayed. Mr. Victor shoved her up towards the back door, keeping himself well back from it. He pointed the end of his cane at her like a gun.

"Not quite what you were thinking, eh?" he said to her. "Now open the door. Im willing to bet that they've set it up as some sort of mouse trap and you are going to spring it." Mei looked at him and then at the door hesitantly.

"Open it!" Victor snarled, his cane tip never wavering.

Taking a deep breath, she touched the doorknob. Nothing. She turned it. Nothing. As the door opened just wide enough for her to slip through she paused. Nothing.

Quickly tuning back towards Mr. Victor she made a rude gesture, sticking out her tongue at him, then dived through the opening, closing the door behind her. His cry of rage cut off by the door shutting. She squinted in the gloom of the factory.

"Mei, quickly over here!" Mary's voice cried out from the crates stacked along one wall. She ran towards Mary just as a blow shuddered against the back door. On the second blow the door came crashing back on its hinges. The hulking shape of the giant named Percy strode in, his gun searching in the gloom. Like a giant spider Jinhao dropped on him from above, her short swords gleaming in the light of the open doorway.

With a speed that was amazing for someone of such size, Percy brought his arms up to catch her slashing blades, throwing her into the side wall with great force. As Jinhao scrabbled to regain her footing, the giant silently raised his pistol. There was a crack of displaced air. The giant staggered, his pistol dropping from his lifeless fingers as he looked down incredulously at a hole that had appeared in the white of his shirt. He looked at the blood pouring from it then fell face down on the floor with a crash.

Mary came out of the shadows holding Mei's pistol towards the roof. As she swaggered forward she smiled at Jinhao who shouted a warning at her.

"Get back," the Adept shouted, just as a wind like a typhoon burst from the open doorway. Mary was flung backwards by the blast into the shadows, her weapon flying from her fingers. Jinhao struggling to remain upright, turned to see the sorcerer, Victor, enter the room, his cane raised before him like an avenging spirit. Then, Jinhao watched as an amazing thing happened.

As his foot touched down inside the factory, a circle of light filled with strange lines sprang up on the floor. Victor's body was thrown into the air as if a strong wind came from the circle. He hung there suspended and howling, his cane rolling across the floor away from the circle. Owen sauntered out from the shadows, twirling his cane easily, to stand in front of the assassin.

"You really are very predictable you know," he drawled towards the suspended man. "It is a failing for someone in your line of work that can be fatal, as you'll soon find out."

"What. Did. You. Do?" Victor bit out each word as if in great pain. He hung in mid-air above the glowing circle, his hair moving as if in an invisible breeze.

"After our last encounter, I surmised that you would be reluctant to attack using an Earth spell again," Owen glanced around the factory. "Untidy things that they are, they might have brought down the whole building around our ears, and you would still have no head to fulfill your contract with. When Jinhao told me how you attacked her almost instinctively with what sounded like an Air spell. I cast a rune that would only work on someone who had opened themselves up to element of Air. The rune would be undetectable, as all it does is reflect back that element which you called forth. I presume that Air is the Element you were born channeling?" Victor screamed again. Owen clicked his tongue.

"Dear me," he remarked with poisoned honey tones, "it does sound as if you are in some pain. Are you?"

"I. Think. Hip. Is. Broken." The Assassin ground out. "Down."

"You want me to place you down?" Owen asked innocently. Victor moaned. "Yes I can see where that would be an uncomfortable position to be in with a broken hip." Owen moved so that his legs were wide apart, his hands firmly on his cane, which he put in front of him as if waiting. When he finally spoke, it was in a voice like steel. "First though, you will tell me who hired you to kill me." Victor's body shuddered in what might have been a laugh.

"You. Don't. Know." Victor gasped out with a grin. "Enemy. Powerful. Not stop with me. Kill. You. Dirty."

"I am sure." Owen returned dryly. He hefted his cane, aiming the tip at the assassin. "Give me a name and I will put you out of your misery." Owen felt Jinhao ghost up beside him.

"Owen," she said calmly. "You do not want to do this. You are no killer of the helpless."

"Jinhao," He returned coldly, still looking at the floating man, "while I value you we have not known each other that long. I must point out that you have no idea what I am or what I have done. A death for him would scarcely begin to pay for the death of a man like James."

"Yes," she conceded, "that is true. Still who you have been is not who you need to be now. Do you truly wish the others to see killing as the answer?" Owen saw Mary, Mike, and Mei out of the corner of his eye. He hesitated to cast the Fire spear he held ready. His attention was caught again by Victor's outburst.

"The Black Rose!" Victor shouted out.

"What?" Owen repeated, "What did you say?" The headhunter grunted out each word in pain.

"Black Rose! Is. Name. Of. Employer. Now. Kill. Me!" He gasped.

"Who hired you is called Black Rose?" Owen pressed. "Is that a person or a group?"

"Yes!" Victor all but screamed. "Now kill me!" The assassin fainted away, hanging limply. Owen looked to his side to see Mei staring at him with wide eyes. With a muttered curse Owen gestured violently with both arms. The glowing circle vanished, the unconscious Assassin fell to the floor like a sack of wet clothes. Owen turned to the little gang member.

"Mei," he said calmly. "Would you be kind enough to go to the local police station and bring back Inspector Gregg please?"

~ ~ ~

Inspector Gregg closed his notebook, then looked at Owen and Jinhao carefully before he spoke.

"Well Milord," the tired policeman said, "it is a good thing that you were able to subdue such a rascal. He is a famous Assassin you know. I just received a notice to look for him if he showed up in Hong Kong."

"Really, Inspector?" Owen replied incredulously. "I can't imagine him being that dangerous. I was able to stop him rather easily."

"And it was just luck that the big Northman that was his companion was shot by someone as well," Gregg returned. "Of course, it's a pity that you didn't see who that was."

"Yes it was," Owen said. "We are thinking that it must have been some sort of gang member. The villains must have run afoul of them somehow." Gregg nodded.

"Typical of their kind I suppose. The Sorcerer seems to have survived, and perhaps he'll talk before we hang him." The all watched as a group of uniformed officers picked up Victor on a palette, carrying him out the door. Gregg looked around the factory floor.

"Speaking of gangs, where did that little girl run off to?"

"Oh, I'm sure she's gone to spend the silver piece I gave her," Owen remarked. "Lucky for her that she came along."

"Yes," Gregg responded, "Lucky. I had best return to the station." He began to turn away then stopped and turned back to face the pair. "I understand that the Dragon and the Court look upon you both pretty favorably after the other day," he said seriously. "Still, I would not have too much luck if I were you."

"Do not concern yourself, Inspector," Owen said reassuringly. "We intent to go back home and enjoy a bottle of wine. I happen to have a lovely Vinland '23." He turned to look at Jinhao. "Does that not sound suitable to you?" Jinhao nodded.

"Owen is attempting to teach me his Western wines," she said to the Inspector. "I am a most dedicated student." The police Inspector smiled at this and tipped his hat towards them.

"Well, I wish you a happy experience Milady." He nodded to Owen, "Milord."

Mike and Mary came out of the shadows after the police had left. Mei trailed along behind them

"Thank you for not tell him about our part in things," Mike said to them. Owen raised an eyebrow in greeting.

"You are welcome," the British Sorcerer replied. "I thought that including you all would simply confuse matters. Besides," he continued, "While Gregg is a good sort, I am sure that he would arrest you simply for coming to his attention so soon after that business at the Court." Mike nodded agreement.

"You are likely right," he responded heavily to Owen. "What will you do now?" Owen shrugged.

"I expect pretty much what we told the Inspector," Owen said. "We shall return home and consume an outrageously expensive wine." He cocked his head at them. "Would you like to accompany us?" Mike sneered at his offer.

"I doubt that we would fit very well in your fancy house," the ganger said. "I suppose that you should just go and enjoy it, forgetting all about the likes of us. We know how to avoid our betters."

"Nonsense," Owen responded firmly. "I am inviting my comrades-in-arms to enjoy a victory drink with me."

"Besides," Jinhao continued. "You still have to hear what I have to offer you from the Dragon. He was impressed with you." She smiled at Mike and Mary, "Being the Dragon's Eyes and Ears will not be easy I can promise you. But his service will leave you all very well to do. No more will you have to steal to live." Finally, Mike nodded agreement.

"All right, I will hear what you have to say," he said.

"Capital!" Owen exclaimed. He extended an arm to Jinhao, who gracefully accepted it. "Now, let us be off." He turned to Jinhao.

"While we are on the subject," he said, as they moved towards the door, "what is all this *Dragon's Claw* business?" Jinhao sniffed.

"While I value you," she recited, "We have not known each other that long." Owen grunted at this.

"You are not going to tell me are you?" he asked forlornly. She just tilted her head andwith a secretive smile turned and sashayed out of the building, without answering.

"I didn't think so," he muttered, following her into the night.

Books by Raven Bond

STEAMPUNK MAGICA

Strong Adept

Strong Magic

Strong Justice

Strong Mystery (Books 1-3) Collection

STEAMPUNK SECRET WAR

The Wind Dancer

Alien Devices*

*Coming soon

AUTHORS NOTE

Thank you for reading Strong Mystery. If you enjoyed it, I very much hope you will review it to help other readers find this world and the stories. If you read the digital version, it is lending-enabled so please share it with a friend.

My other Steampunk series 'The Secret War' is also available from Impish Press.

You can read more about what I'm up to, what I am writing, and life as it is lived at my author blog.

http://ravenbond.com